Loving Monsters

Loving Monsters

James Hamilton-Paterson

Granta Books
London

Granta Publications, 2/3 Hanover Yard, London N1 8BE

First published in Great Britain by Granta Books 2001

A CIP catalogue record for this book
is available from the British Library.

3 5 7 9 10 8 6 4 2

ISBN 1 86207 425 9

Typeset by M Rules

Printed and bound in Great Britain by Mackays of Chatham plc

Acknowledgements

I am grateful to Artemis Cooper for generously supplying me with a copy of her *Cairo in the War 1939–1945*, which is required reading for anyone interested in the period. It greatly supplemented my own memories of a later era besides affording much entertainment.

Sonja and Hannes Hintermeier aided me by finding the titles of August Moll-Ziemcke's two books, to say nothing of prompting me to spell his name correctly.

Monica Arellano Ongpin was informative and ribald about conservative local practices in Tuscan cuisine, as well as being a generously supportive presence.

Many friends and acquaintances in the *Comune* of Castiglion Fiorentino were patient and helpful with my enquiries. The Mayor, Prof. Giuseppe Alpini, and Arnaldo Valdarnini were particularly enlightening about their town's history. I owe them all sincere thanks. I am equally happy to acknowledge the help of Dr Tahir Safti of Alexandria and various well-disposed staff members of London's Public Record Office.

For nineteen years of friendship, hospitality and forbearance with my endless questions I owe most of all to Marilena, Sergio and Juri Mazzini. Now, since Jayjay's death, I have also become indebted to Claudio Tronchesini as well as to his daughter Marcella Larghi and her family for their memories of him. Dario Larghi's anecdotes have been especially diverting.

Margaret and Andrew Hewson and (as usual) Neil Belton helped considerably to improve my text, while an incisive reading by Dr Charles Swann of Keele University was crucial to the final shape of this book.

Miranda and Stephan Feuchtwang. For years.

Everyone has loved and been loved for a while. We lie about this and pretend it was otherwise. We want some other love than the one we had, some other history. But we have loved and been loved.

Harold Brodkey

RAYMOND
JERNINGHAM JEBB
N. 3·7·1918
M. 3·5·1998

1

The figure in the hospital cot was shrunken and yellowed but still recognisably Jayjay. Being slightly deaf he perhaps had not heard me come into the room. He lay staring up at the ceiling, not blankly but slightly frowning at it as though trying to puzzle out a way in which it might be turned to his advantage. It was this typical expression which made him so readily identifiable even though he was not speaking, not moving, and had acquired in the last weeks something of the look of a dinosaur chick. A brilliant bar of Tuscan sunlight fell through the window beside the bed and across his wrist, which bore a white plastic tag. Swallows were jinking across the endless blue of the sky outside while below them Arezzo's traffic followed not dissimilar paths, weaving and whizzing and sending faint contentious sounds into the room. At length the jaundiced eyes swivelled towards me.

'Come to witness my demise, have you?'

'Actually, I was hoping to avoid that bit,' I said. 'I always think these things are handled so much better by professionals.'

'True. If I were an ancient Egyptian I should already have hired people to wail dementedly in the corridor. I have reduced Dr Farulli to a state of abject honesty. He told me this morning there was little hope.'

'Did you want any?'

'Not really. I asked him what sort of hope was on offer to a man of eighty in my condition. My eighty-first birthday, for instance? He threatened me with nuns. That's their ultimate weapon, you know, for not making the right kind of death. The cry goes up: "Send in the nuns!" and softly in the distance, but growing ever louder, the tramp of stout boots can be heard approaching your room. What have you brought me that's nice?'

'This,' I said, sitting on the edge of the bed, opening my brief-case and handing him a 20 × 30 colour print. He examined it with eyes that still needed no spectacles.

'Cheap,' he said at length.

'It's what you said you were prepared to pay, Jayjay. Not that you *have* paid.'

'I had naturally assumed, James – as any normal person might in the circumstances – that you would have felt obliged to match my sum in a discreet sort of way. However, you are not normal and chose to be literal. Well, no doubt it'll do. How much was it?'

'Three hundred and forty thousand *lire*.'

'God almighty. I should have thought it could be cast in bronze for half that. This is your rock-bottom basic headstone. What is it, cement?'

'He said it was marble from Michelangelo's own quarry at Carrara.'

'Travertine, I expect. I should be thankful it isn't plaster of Paris. Still, don't think I'm ungrateful.'

'What would you prefer, Jayjay? A headstone in Eltham? One of those mottled pinkish things that look like slabs of compressed meat? And you lying beneath half a hundredweight of green glass chips within earshot of Rochester Way? Here, at least you will be reposing rather exclusively beneath the walls of Sir John

Hawkwood's castle in Montecchio, clearly marked by this elegant tablet so that generations of pilgrims will have no difficulty finding you.'

'Of course, the pilgrims,' Jayjay croaked delightedly. 'I can see them now. Earnest young students lost for a contemplative hour in the ivy-bowered hush of the *camposanto*, drawing from my lively shades the inspiration to finish their theses –' He squinted more closely at the photograph. 'They've left out the bloody hyphen.'

'No, they haven't. You don't have one. I know you think I've skimped on time and trouble, not to mention cash. In fact I made the effort to ask the consulate in Florence and they checked with London – Somerset House or whatever privatised registry it has become. You are Raymond Jerningham Jebb, not Jerningham-Jebb, and it was pretty decent of me to suppress the Ray, all things considered.'

But Jayjay had let his attention wander. There were voices in the corridor outside and a mild crash as if someone had banged a doorway with a metal trolley full of surgical instruments. A door closed. At length he picked up the photograph again.

'Discreet of you to have left the year of my death blank,' he observed. 'It shows uncommon delicacy. You didn't even risk putting "19—" as they sometimes do, confident that there's no hope the person is going to make it to the twenty-first century. There isn't, of course, a cat in hell's chance that I shall ever see 1999 as you, I and Dr Farulli know perfectly well.'

'There are such things as miracle remissions,' I began cautiously, but he only made a contemptuous sound. 'Anyway, the *marmista* says he will fill the date in as and when, at no extra cost. That, of course, is the moment when I shall have him add a choice inscription. It looks awfully bare at present. I'm toying with *Musicae sono murmurant colles*. I always think a nice bit of Latin adds tone.'

He might have been eighty but there was nothing wrong with Jayjay's brain. He fixed me with a stern eye in which the *arcus senilis* was scarcely yet visible. 'If you put "The hills are alive with the sound of music" on my tombstone I warn you I shall return to haunt you. One way or another, James, I shall contrive revenge.'

He fell silent again, frowning upwards as if pondering retribution, but when he next spoke his voice was more surprised than anything.

'I've been noticing something funny,' he said. 'You see those cracks in the ceiling? I'm damned if they're not a street map of Eltham. At least, the area around Beechill Road. A bit crude, but that's Gourock Road across there, joining Westmount Road which runs down to the top end of the High Street. Just before it gets there, on the left where that stain is, see? That used to be a green-grocer's called Starr & Britt. Then around the corner by all those fly specks is where the bus from Welling stopped – the 228 or the 241? I can't remember. Single-decker, anyway.'

'All stops to Memory Lane.' I thought it required a wistful imagination to discern any sort of map in the network of cracks overhead.

'You're so heartless, James. Can't you see how extraordinary this is? Here I am, lying on my deathbed in Arezzo right beneath a street map of my birthplace a thousand miles away in southeast London. It's too punctual for words. How can one not believe in fate?'

From the window embrasure outside came a sharp burst of wings and a strident cheeping. Two tiny feathers, no more than fragments of down, drifted in through the opening and began sliding down the sunbeam, very slowly, turning and glittering like phytoplankton streaming towards an illimitable ocean floor.

'I shall be forgotten utterly,' the man in the bed said suddenly.

'You're not going to give way to self-pity at a time like this?' I asked in alarm.

'No. It was just the sudden realisation. When you, too, come to find yourself in this unenviable position, James, in however many years' time, you will discover that even if your whole life appears to have been a dream from start to finish certain things achieve an insistent sort of clarity.' He raised an arm whose skin had clearly been designed to fit someone larger a long time ago and examined the bony wrist with the name tag. 'Iebb Iernigam,' he read. 'Apparently that's me. That it should have come to this.'

'If you become maudlin I shall leave.'

A long silence fell, intensified by the background sounds of swallows and traffic going about their business in the bright sunshine outside. A timeless inertia congealed in the room, redolent of moated granges. I thought Jayjay had fallen asleep. Then he opened a saurian eye and said, 'No, you won't leave. Not yet. You still want to know what's in my will.'

I didn't deign to respond and the eye closed again. This time he really did doze off. The sun's ray slid across a corner of the crumpling plastic bag of glucose and saline mixture that was seeping into his arm. From chance prisms in the brilliantly illuminated liquid tiny rainbows were struck. More footsteps approached in the corridor. The door opened softly and a nurse appeared, half hidden behind an immense bouquet of flowers swathed in cellophane. Even I, who had chosen them and dictated the note, was impressed and a little horrified. Now they were no longer in the flower shop they looked less like an expression of cheerful good wishes than a tribute fit to be laid on a cenotaph by a head of state. Still, it was too late now. I got to my feet, put a finger to my lips and took the bouquet from the nurse with a smile of thanks. She smiled back, glanced at the sleeping patient and tiptoed out again. The cellophane was the soft kind that didn't crackle and I carefully peeled enough of it back to divest the flowers of their funereal aspect. At least he would be able to smell their freshness. They were the first things Jayjay saw from inches away when he opened his eyes. Maybe in his confused state he thought he had already died. He gave a great gasp.

'No! Take them away! Away!'

'Don't be silly, Jayjay. They're beautiful. Smell how fresh they are.' I thrust the bouquet under his nose. 'And look, here's a note. Don't you want to know who sent them? Just now you were moaning about being forgotten and it's perfectly obvious someone

has remembered you. I'll open the card, shall I?' Glancing sidelong, I noticed his eyes had filled with tears. I slid the card from its
little white envelope, observing my handiwork with some pride. I
had made the florist copy a message of which she understood not
a word. Her uncertain Italian penmanship looked convincingly as
though she had taken it down from an overseas phone call.

'Good Lord, Jayjay!' I cried. 'You'll never guess who they're
from.'

'No!' he croaked.

'They're from the Queen Mother. "Sent at the express wishes
of HM the Queen Mother with her heartfelt prayers for Mr Jebb's
swift recovery." It's signed "Reginald Wilcock, Deputy Steward
and Page of the Presence". How about that, Jayjay?'

A scrawny hand reached out for the card. Tears had run back
into his white sideboards. 'It's absolutely her style,' he wheezed,
'even if Reggie did have to remind her. A little tight, the Bowes-
Lyons, they all are. Always were, even back in their Hertfordshire
days. It's not *such* a big bunch to have ordered from England, is it?
Well, bless the old girl for the thought. After all, we did have
some good times.'

He was overtaken by an alarming paroxysm of coughs that
shook his bed and splintered the rainbows in the drip. I rang the
bell and waited for the nurse to take over. When she bustled in I
gave Jayjay a reassuring pat on the hand and got up to go outside.
It was clearly a moment for professional expertise and I was
merely in the way. Besides, it was time for a *caffè* at the bar in the
hospital grounds. I looked back from the doorway. His clawlike
hand was clutching an empty plastic drinking cup which lurched
up and down in rhythm with his coughing. 'Fill it,' I thought I
heard him gasp querulously. 'Oh, *fill it!*' I smiled as I sauntered
down the corridor. It was a recognisable piece of the Jayjay impe-
riousness that occasionally broke through his normal charm. After
half an hour I went back in to take my leave of him and found a
full-scale medical drama in his room. Before I was shooed out
again I had a glimpse of oxygen cylinders, the bedclothes flung

back to expose Jayjay's naked upper half, a defibrillator on a trolley. Still needing to retrieve the briefcase I had left by his bed I wandered off to wait on a bench in the sun. When eventually I returned he was dead. It was 11.40 in the morning of May 3rd, 1998. A grave Dr Farulli told me how inexpressibly distressed he was. Signor Jebb had taken a syncope brought on by acute respiratory crisis and there was nothing they had been able to do. The cancer, of course, had undermined all his resistance. One could never tell what, exactly, might kill a patient as ill as Signor Jebb. All the same, one had been surprised to find the Signor's lungs so badly obstructed with mucus today when yesterday his breathing had been excellent. Was he in a very emotional state? Had he perhaps been allergic to something? To flowers, even?

It is not easy for a biographer to accept that he might have been instrumental in bringing about the death of his subject. The ex-Monsignor and seventies guru Ivan Illich once told me that all biographies in some sense involve an act of murder, although he may have read that somewhere. Nevertheless, this was altogether too literal. That my own little act of deception, innocently intended to cheer a well-connected old man on his bed of sickness, may have been so lethal was shocking. It was of no comfort that the death certificate duly gave natural causes deriving from advanced metastasising carcinoma as the reason for Jayjay's death. It was not criminal charges I feared but my own conscience. Some months passed before I could once more bring myself to open my notes of Jerningham Jebb's life. Even now I wonder if this book is not as much an act of private expiation as a labour of genuine affection. It is of course possible that such motives never can be completely separated.

2

'Congratulations!' chirped a promotional leaflet in Italian from the bottom of my supermarket trolley where it had been callously abandoned by a previous shopper. 'Your name has been exhaustively selected for a highly personal offer.' I was reflecting on this concept of mass exclusivity when a distinguished-looking man leaned respectfully across my trolley and said in English, 'You must excuse me. I have been wanting to speak to you for some time.' My spirits lifted briefly before falling again. Evidently I stood out as much as he did, reaching up for a bottle of imported Gordon's. Castiglion Fiorentino is a smallish town and this a smallish Co-op; scarcely an international social nexus even in summer when the Tuscany groupies arrive from Munich and London. He was a dapper figure in the old-fashioned *milor* style: white espadrilles, pale linen trousers, dark-blue lightweight jacket with a silk handkerchief pushed military-style into one cuff. I now realised I had seen him before, maybe even several times. It seemed likely that at some point in the recent past I had stood aside to wave him through the till ahead of me with the ill-tempered gallantry one reserves for people carrying a few things awkwardly in their arms.

'You must be the writer, surely?' he said. 'Even in a place as small as this one likes to be certain. Biding my time. You must excuse my breaking into your thoughts. I could see you reaching that ratty point of indecision in the *spumante* section. "Am I going to blow nearly eight thousand lire on the Riccadonna, or will the Gancia *Grand Reale* do quite as well? After all, it's only fizz at the end of a large meal and who's going to notice the difference?"' He carefully placed the bottle of gin in his own trolley and smiled easily at the shelf.

'You've been here before,' I said.

'In every sense. It's precisely these trivial dilemmas that go on repeating themselves. All one's instincts are to go for the *brut*, of course, which costs more but drinks better. Then one remembers that the ladies, although they may be impressed by the price you've paid, would much prefer the *dolce*. It's cheaper, too. So: does one go for expense, palatability and social cachet, or does one opt for the cheap and cheerful which most people here secretly prefer? A very worldly little puzzle. One always solves it in the same way' (he glanced down at the cheap bottle of *Gran Spumante Valdesino* in my own trolley) 'but it can leave one slightly disgruntled.'

Although I had finished my own shopping and could have gone straight to the checkout I found myself waiting beside him in the delicatessen section while he bought cheese, salami and olives.

'I might have a proposition to put to you,' he said, sampling an olive the woman behind the counter had given him to try. 'Of a professional nature.' He tucked the stone discreetly into his breast pocket. 'Although I'm sure you have a lot of work on at the moment.'

I thought of my approaching deadline, of the pile of manuscript lying stalled at about the halfway mark. 'Scribblers are always in the market for propositions.'

'Quite. By the way, my name's Jerningham Jebb. You might as well call me Jayjay right away. You will eventually, in any case.'

In this way I was invited to tea. In due course I followed his car a few hundred metres up the Valle di Chio to a farmhouse among olive terraces. If you craned your neck you could just see Sir John Hawkwood's (or Giovanni Acuto's) castle at Montecchio standing on its little hump in the distance. Il Ghibli turned out to be a charming house, though I would hardly have expected otherwise. A pergola, a terrace, lots of greenery in terracotta pots, thick doors and slabby refectory tables, twisted ironwork, chestnut beams and *mezzane*. Standard vernacular stuff. Mr Jebb (or was it Mr Jerningham-Jebb?) began to rattle about in the kitchen. I followed him through the house at a more inquisitive pace. Nosy, actually, nosiness being the best-polished weapon in a writer's armoury. I already had him tagged as a bachelor who had a local woman in twice a week to do the housework. Stone flags gleaming with a burnished patina like dirty ice; dust-free bookshelves, a scrolltop desk with – but what's *that*? House of Lords Library letterhead peeping out, sandwiched at a slant between two books that look as though they're currently being read. Is he still safely putting kettles on? Yes. A quick nudge so the top book slides over enough to reveal the text of the letter.

Saturday p.m.

Dear Jayjay,

Of course, this note would be quite impossible had you not confided in me the other day.

Proctoscopy is not something one wishes to dwell on. So please accept my gratitude for your concern and kind wishes.

Yours ever, Margaret

And that, if I was not mistaken, was the Baroness's own handwriting. I nudged the book back to where it had been and joined my host in the kitchen.

'Lovely place,' I remarked.

'Yes,' he said with a swift gaze up from the teapot as if disappointed by such a conventional remark. 'I suppose it is, really. Not bad, at any rate.'

Could he have seen me reading his correspondence? No, I was quite sure of myself. He was just being politely disenchanted with the old shack. The syndrome was common enough in these parts: Britons feeling they ought to be slightly embarrassed at being caught with a house in Tuscany, having heard it all before. I took the tray out to the terrace and he followed with the pot. We sat and watched the swallows flash and swerve among the olive trees, busy with such flying ants as had not shed their wings around the holes in the ground from which they had emerged that day. I fell to banal and silent reflection about ephemera, about the gift of wings that either fell off as soon as the insect hatched or else bore their owner straight up to the swift beaks sieving the air overhead.

'I'm embarrassed to say this, James,' he murmured, 'but you're probably going to write my life. I know how presumptuous it sounds – and vain, and so on – but I really do think that's what you will end up doing. I've had rather an *exotic* life, actually, and I don't believe you'll be bored. I've read enough of your books to have an idea what might appeal to you. I may be wrong. I'll pay you, of course.'

'Vanity publishing?'

'Oh no. That's why I chose you. You will produce something a publisher will pay for in the normal way. I'm just sweetening the deal.'

'Just at the moment –'

'– you've a lot of work on? Surely. Of course you have. But there's no rush. Not yet,' he added, watching the birds with cup and saucer held against his chest.

'You certainly seem to have decided.'

'Not at all. How could I? It all depends on you. If you mean I seem very sure of myself, I am. It's a characteristic that has enabled me to live my peculiar life.'

'"Exotic" was the word you used.'

'Peculiar, exotic, erotic. Not run-of-the-mill, perhaps.'

My host drifted off into a reverie, the forgotten cup sagging in his hand and slopping tea into the saucer. I did not draw his attention to this. Something about him reminded me uncomfortably of myself: the private, slightly abstracted manner of a person accustomed to living on his own, neither needing nor welcoming an outsider's well-meant attempts to smarten up his habits. He would tell me in his own good time what his life had been and why he called it peculiar. An ex-diplomat, I wondered? The area around Cortona, a neighbouring hill town a few kilometres from here down the Perugia road, was stiff with retired diplomats of sundry nationalities. Maybe after years of grim postings interspersed with fallow periods back home in an administrative capital like Brussels, Bonn, London or Grottawa (as a Canadian diplomatic friend calls it) there was something restful and civilised about Etruscan hill towns. The entire landscape was reassuring. Its terraced hillsides, cypresses, umbrella pines, olives and vines posed a calm counter-argument to the panicky eco-disaster discourse of the times. Here was a landscape that had been completely moulded by the hand of man for the last three thousand years, and far from being ruined was in its way a work of art. Indeed, one saw daily and at every turn scenes that could have formed the background of any Renaissance painting. It was a visible reminder that human activity could, if it chose, produce startlingly graceful vistas for the eye's beguiling, even as the mind knew they had been fertilised with uncounted gallons of blood. An urbane feast for the eyes of old diplomats in retreat from the punishing world of *Realpolitik*, in that case. A fine omelette of a landscape from which the passage of so much time had erased all memory of broken eggs.

A visit to my host's downstairs lavatory more or less clinched my guess for me. Propped on a shelf with just the right degree of offhandedness, partly hidden behind a stack of hand towels, was a signed portrait of Henry Kissinger. Who but a diplomat would have such a thing? Unless, of course, it was the celebrated surgeon Mr Jerningham Jebb sitting out there on the terrace drinking tea: the one man who had proved capable of bringing Henry relief from his embarrassing ailment. Yet he did not feel to me like a medic. I should need to browse his bookshelves for additional clues. No time for that now; but there was a pile of books by the lavatory for defecational reading, mainly the preposterous stuff that ensures a smile before beginning the day. Here was 'a bold and fearless indictment of Prussianism' published in 1918 by Robert Blatchford and entitled *General von Sneak*. Here also a book by the astrologer Leonardo Blake, dated 1939 and called, with some assurance, *Hitler's Last Year of Power*. There was a signed copy of *One Hour of Justice* by Cecil Alport, described on the dust jacket as 'a sharp denunciation by a British doctor of the present treatment of the Egyptian peasant' and dedicated to 'the twin gods of Decency and Justice'. There was even a copy of Elise Pumpelly Cabot's splendid *Arizona and Other Poems*, signed in biro by Peggy Guggenheim. 'Into the giant saguaro brave birds have bored their way to safety.'

'Did you size the joint up?' he asked as I resumed my seat.

'If you mean did I poke and pry, then the answer is no. Still, one can tell a lot about a person from his lavatory. For a start, it's reassuring when it doesn't flush blue. And then, of course, few people have portraits of Henry Kissinger tucked away in their smallest room.'

'Oh, you spotted him, did you? Yes, poor old Henry. Without wishing to be disdainful, because I grew quite fond of him in a limited way, his picture is hardly the sort of thing one can keep out in the open, is it? I've always found that the great and the good function as a cultural giveaway. The British don't much care for having such things on display. It strikes us as immodest. Not only that, but celebrities are generally so two-dimensional – "famous for being famous" as the fellow said – and it would be awful to think a visitor might suppose one was in any way serious about them. Have you ever been in houses where grand pianos are used as display cabinets? Massed ranks of signed photographs in silver frames? One behind the other, like toast in a rack. The home-owner teeing off with the President; guffawing with a starlet; being urged by a Kennedy not to forget Aspen in eighty-nine; caught at a table overlooking Lake Tahoe with Frank Sinatra and assorted mafiosi. *I am whom I'm known by.* That sort of thing.'

'You seem quite interested in fame.'

'Oh, I am. Yes, very. It's a fascinating thing. I'm always intrigued by what people want from their lives, how they use this little seventy-year flicker of daylight in the middle of aeons of nothingness. Nearly eighty, now, in my case. How best to spend rationed time. What to be. Yes, very interesting. The *only* inter-esting thing, one might almost say. The amazing lengths to which people will go in the foredoomed quest to put their thumbprint on eternity. Don't you feel the same?'

'Perhaps more from the opposite tack of those who refuse to compete in the first place. No sooner are you born than they start threatening you with what will happen when you die. You know – Judgement Day, wall-to-wall cherubim, science-fiction fauna with too many wings. Faced with the whole baroque Book of

Revelations scenario, what does mortal man do? He sits inside, jerking off to porno videos or watching re-runs of *The Muppet Show*. I like that: it shows chutzpah. If I were the Creator, the defiant bleak wilfulness of the human race would send me slinking back to the cosmic drawing board to reconsider whether the deal I was offering wasn't in fact quite intolerable. My heart goes out to people who opt to live in a world of TV soaps and mail-order catalogues.'

'Unseduced by the sirens of fame?'

'Precisely. It shows an instinctive grasp of the true nature of the deal. The gift of time comes from an Indian giver.'

My host put down his cup. 'Many years ago you worried about being thought cynical?'

'I'm an admirer of Lily Tomlin. "No matter how cynical you get, it's not cynical enough."'

'I think you and I will probably get on. We may even turn out to be surprisingly alike in some ways. Given that we all have to construct ourselves from scratch, you seem to have done it on paper while I chose to do it by inventive living. There isn't much difference.'

This had been an entirely unforeseen meeting and I was becoming conscious of the deep-frozen seafood *frittura mista* steadily defrosting in the Co-op carrier bag in my car. Past experience suggested I would already have to scrub the floor mat with bleach to neutralise the raw octopus juice which invariably seeped through the welds in the bag. Otherwise it would brew up in the Mediterranean heat into a reek of corruption that would yet again bring to mind a journey I had once made across Manila in a hearse with broken air-conditioning when we were trapped for six hours in a series of traffic jams.

'You must excuse me, Jayjay,' I said. 'This has been a most intriguing meeting and there are a million things I want to ask you. Clearly we're going to meet again.'

'Of course we are. It has been very good of you to give me your time. A total stranger, just out of the blue like that.'

He led me courteously through the house. I found his well-filled bookshelves reassuring, especially the healthy mixture of older volumes and brighter modern paperbacks. These last ranged from (snatched glance) Aldo Busi and Primo Levi in Italian to James Ellroy in Southern Californian. Plus half a yard of Patrick O'Brian, which somehow sat comfortably with my preconceptions of my host. My eyes also fell on a strange object that lay like an ornament on a bookshelf. A battered piece of metal about the size of a child's sock, it was nevertheless brightly polished and obviously silver. That anything so flattened and creased should be carefully preserved suggested it was a curio.

'There's a story behind that,' he said, observing my curiosity. 'Now, then, your writer's imagination to the fore: guess what it is. Or was.'

'As a matter of fact I recognised it at once. It's one of the king-sized silver-foil toothpaste tubes specially made for John Jacob Astor. This one must have been recovered from the wreck of the *Titanic*, having been crushed by the extreme pressure on the seabed. How did you get it, if you don't mind my asking? Surely not from Bob Ballard? He would die rather than remove anything from that ship.'

'Oh, bravo! Most inventive for the spur of the moment.' He flashed me an amused glance in which there was – what, exactly? Thoughtfulness? Complicity, perhaps? 'The truth is, however, even stranger than your fiction. In 1847, when Lady Amelia Dance set off on her courageous mission to inspect Janissary prisons, she took with her two silver dildos modelled from Disraeli's cock. It was well known that her marriage offered her few satisfactions. Indeed, she famously wrote that "Poor Dance would be well engulph'd by a candle-snuffer", which made things pretty clear. I have her *Diary* here, by the way. So she put herself in the hands of Arcangelo Viotti. Viotti was an immigrant silversmith from Cremona who had set up in Cheapside and quickly earned a reputation for such skill and discretion that he became patronised by society. You can imagine the sort of thing. Some feckless blood would pop a priceless heirloom to settle his gambling debts at Oxford and urgently need a first-rate copy to fool his family until he could buy back the original. Viotti would do it and keep silent. So Lady Amelia went to him and explained her requirement and Viotti arranged to have an impression taken from Disraeli during a poker session in Grosvenor Square. Don't ask me how: it's one of those historical mysteries one likes to speculate on in the bath. He made two identical objects in sterling silver to her design. They were hollow and the bottom part – what she called "the orbs and follicles" – was threaded and formed a stopper. Several days after leaving London on her journey – I think she had got as far as Karlsruhe, I'd have to check – she confided to her diary the discovery that there were "ever more refinements of phantasie" to be had from filling one with iced hock and the other with hot soup "such as will long retain and most readily transmit its chearful glow". In fact, she had just made the same discovery about soup that Gladstone did some years later, that it keeps hot appreciably longer than mere water. I'm sure you've heard that splendid old BBC Archive recording of Gladstone's manservant remembering that the old statesman used to fill his hot-water bottle with soup for exactly that reason? Anyway, long story short, poor Lady Amelia was eventually captured by the Cadi of Smyrna, mistaken for a nobleman's son, and had a most unfortunate end. Her baggage, of course, was ransacked and the dildos vanished. However, one of them came to light when it appeared at Christie's so-called "black auction" in 1972, the famous occasion when Napoleon's phallus also came under the hammer. It is now one of the reserved items in the Gilbert Collection and bona fide scholars can examine it if they make a special request. Its companion is here.' Jayjay picked up the battered piece of metal and handed it to me.

'Pardon my scepticism, but how do you know?'

'The hallmark. It's identical to the one in the Gilbert Collection. Both have Viotti's monogram.'

'And why does it look as though it had been sat on by an elephant?'

'Ah, that we shall never know. I acquired it in Vienna. I like to think some outraged Customs official there had confiscated it from a collector as obscene and laid it on the rails as the Orient Express pulled out, but one shouldn't embroider historical facts to suit one's own fantasies.'

I kept a thoughtful silence until we reached the car.

'You have me at a complete disadvantage, Jayjay. You do at least know who I am, whereas I haven't the remotest idea who you are, what you've done, why there are signed portraits of Henry Kissinger in the house. Never mind flattened dildos.' I managed not to add *to say nothing of notes from Margaret Thatcher*. 'Not a clue. You shouldn't be either surprised or insulted, though. People think of me as a recluse. They are always amazed by what I don't know. So you might at least help me decide why I should want to become your biographer. I've got you down as a retired dip., incidentally, but I don't suppose you are.'

He was watching me with a mischievous smile. 'I assure you, you have nothing to apologise for, and I everything. It was most discourteous. I should have made it clear from the start. There is no earthly reason why you should have heard of me. I told you quite truthfully that I consider fame to be fascinating but it is also true that I myself have always shunned it. You might say I rely on quiet recognition at most. What I am, you see, is a professional impostor.'

For long afterwards I could not shake the idea that our meeting had not been fortuitous but carefully engineered. Surely Il Ghibli had been most artfully set-dressed, the hook so discreetly baited that even the least greedy and most discerning of fishes (for like everybody, I fancied myself as such) would have taken a cautious nibble? But then I would promptly reject this as pure vanity. Why should anyone go to such elaborate trouble to put a straight-forward business proposition to a mere writer? The following week I would be de-convinced anew. I would argue that he must have arranged the whole thing, having long before ascertained my weekly habit of shopping in the Co-op on that day and at that time. Not only had he baited the hook but he had fully intended me to appreciate it. For some as yet unknown reason it was not just any old writer this professional impostor wanted, but me.

Inevitably, I ran into him again before I could make up my mind. This time it was in the Co-op car park. He had just replaced his trolley in the steel shelter where its fellows were nested and was clearly miles away, standing paused by his car door, though he might have been contemplating the word *fica* someone had spray-painted in black on the shelter years ago.

'I'm still thinking,' I told him.

'Think on,' said Jayjay sunnily. 'There's no real hurry. Only bear in mind I shan't be giving you my *entire* life. Nothing so conventional. I shall only be telling you the interesting bits. I don't know if you agree with me but in my opinion all the really important stuff happens quite early on. The first thirty years of one's life are lived; the remainder is dreamed. I'm convinced we have an inbuilt sense of time that gives undue weight to our youthful years, the reason being that for nearly all mankind's exis-tence a life span probably averaged forty years, which is very much what you still see in the harshest societies today. After that the clock's increasingly bamboozled and accelerates as though search-ing out its end, which is why the older one becomes the more time seems to speed up. You yourself have already noticed this, of course. Indeed, I remember at our very first meeting you said that the gift of time comes from an Indian giver. So you ought to bear in mind that I'm not one of those people who find old age a matter of increasing and rather wonderful serenity. You will find – or you *would* find if you decided we had a deal – that I shall be skewing my life very much in favour of its first half. The second half has really been little more than a series of increasingly flavourless recapitulations, although the great conspiracy requires that I claim to be having the time of my life. Which of course I am, as you can see, shopping at the Co-op in Castiglion Fiorentino and wondering why a graffiti artist would bother to spray a word like that over there when people obviously don't even care enough to scrub it off. It must be very disheartening to a rebel adolescent to have aroused so little reaction.'

'It wasn't an adolescent who did it,' I said. 'It was actually the manager himself, trying to turn his own clock back. One night years ago he drove up in his BMW at two a.m. and sprayed the word. Then, finding he just felt tired and silly instead of young, he let himself into the back of the Co-op and hanged himself in the staff lavatory. *Fica* is his epitaph, and we shall never know whether it was a mere expletive or an invocation. Now I'd better go and do my shopping. I gather they have a special offer on the Elixir of Life this week. I trust you've bought a bottle?'

'Certainly I have,' said Jayjay. 'Only for some obscure marketing reason they've disguised it to look like Gordon's gin.' He nodded to a bottle visible in a basket on the back seat of his car. 'Anyway, James, I do hope you make up your mind soon. It really might just cheat my own clock if I were to re-live little bits of the past.'

'If ever I did agree, I ought to warn you that I would stop if you began to bore me.'

'So I would expect. Just as I would sack you if I saw you weren't up to it.'

All this certainly added a gram or two to the balance in favour of working with him; but what with one thing and another, including the work I already had in hand, I came to no conclusion. Thus did the weeks go by, leaving me in apparent indecision. But it turned out to be only apparent.

3

Raymond Jerningham Jebb was born at 58 Beechill Road, Eltham on July 3rd 1918. Since most of his next eighteen years were spent in or around the London postal district of SE9 he qualifies as a genuine child of the suburbs. What is more, far from presenting the remainder of his life as a flight from the restricting horrors of petit-bourgeois gentility, he often spoke of the place, as well as of the inter-war period, with a degree of nostalgia. A biographer labels this Exhibit A.

He was, he said, the only child of Harold Jerningham Jebb and Olive Sargent, about whose ancestry he was not very forthcoming. I don't think he was particularly interested. Piecing it together, it appeared Harold's own father was originally from Shropshire (there are some Jerningham graves in Ludlow) and had been brought when still a child to Herne Hill where his family had bought a poultry farm beside the Effra. Jayjay spoke of geese, a lucrative trade especially in the Christmas season. Harold was born there on the precise day in May 1885 that John Ruskin, a few hundred yards further up the hill, finished the dedicatory preface to *Praeterita*. Despite the spread of the railways that Ruskin so deplored this area of Kent was still remarkably countrified, for all that it would soon qualify as south London. Jayjay's father remembered being driven in his own father's donkey-cart through the lanes of Dulwich, Peckham and Lewisham and often beyond Bromley as far afield as Widmore, in those days a remote Kentish village. These were delivery rounds, and the boy Harold would scramble out at each of the high-street poulterers, lugging geese that weighed almost as much as he did, their beaks and feet tied with a loop of bass and their wings pinioned. Harold had also recalled the new streets even then being laid out across fields of buttercups. The heaps of London bricks waited on each plot, the blond skeletons of roofs stretched their bright pine trusses in perspectives a hundred yards long waiting for the tilers with pads of sacking on their knees to cover them up. This was the work of men like Cameron Corbett, who built estates over large parts of Eltham and Hither Green and became the first Lord Rowallan on the strength of it.

Somewhere around the turn of the twentieth century the goose farm beside the Effra was bought and it, too, quickly disappeared beneath brick and asphalt just as the river itself was destined to vanish. Harold's father did well out of the sale of his land and thereafter the family moved briefly to Tulse Hill before fetching up near Well Hall station at the foot of Eltham's modest hill. Well Hall itself was an eighteenth-century house built on the remains of a Tudor manor and here at the age of fifteen Harold became an all-purpose knives, boots and jobbing boy. If Jayjay were to be believed he also became the clandestine lover of Well Hall's tenant, Edith Nesbit. E. Nesbit had moved to the Hall in 1899 and stayed until 1922, a good deal longer than Harold's association with her household. He had certainly left her employ, and supposedly also her bed, well before 1906 when she published the book that made her famous, *The Railway Children*. By then Jayjay's father had become apprenticed as a ship's broker and settled into the career that was to sustain him and his family for the rest of his working life. Why that line of business, particularly? Maybe he was responding to a force of nature that in one way or another still influenced the life of every Londoner of the time. The buttercups, orchards and paddocks of Herne Hill and the rest of suburbia might be fast disappearing, but the River Thames was at the full flood of its vitality. From Eltham's eminence there were views northwards (fog permitting) towards Woolwich and Greenwich. The Royal Dockyard was not three miles away. Just across the river lay Silvertown and the great commercial hub of the docklands. The port and its shipping were London's heart as well as the Empire's.

When his son was born in 1918 Harold was already thirty-three and had been married seven months. The Great War put normal life into abeyance where it had not stopped it altogether. Harold was lucky. His knowledge of ships, their cargoes and insurance had earned him a desk in a crowded Admiralty office instead of a posting to France. It was while he was there that he

met Olive, who was working in the Censorship. AWSCD* was the department whose job was similar to that of the civilian censorship: checking the letters of RN personnel for inadvertent breaches of security as well as for signs of a more intentional espionage.

– I will tell you about my mother – said Jayjay early on – in the hopes that I shan't have to refer to her again. When they met it seems she was by no means a beauty though apparently very jolly. By the time I can remember her she was anything but jolly, having lost a favourite brother in the last week of the war and then falling

* Admiralty War Staff, Censorship Division.

victim to a terminal attack of religion. This was a particularly crippling strain where any sense of irony was concerned: Methodist or Wesleyan or Congregationalist, I forget which. Really, I've blotted it out completely and it would take a hypnotist to recover the memory. Somewhere I must know the answer perfectly well. The house was full of tracts and she was always going to church meetings. You never met such dreary people as her friends. They had in common a worthy dowdiness, or possibly a dowdy worthiness. Not unkind to me as a child, certainly, but the sort who would practically faint with horror if ever someone offered them a glass of sherry.

– At the time when my father and Olive met in the Admiralty, though, she was still allegedly good fun and quite bouncy. She was also fearsomely bright. I later heard this from a couple of people who had known her in the Censorship and they said my mother had the best brain of anyone they had ever met, male or female. That must mean something. In those days women weren't as a rule given the credit for having the intelligence to come in out of the rain, not unless a gallant gentleman with an umbrella assisted them. So what happened to her in those ten years or so after the war? I really don't know. I'm afraid she went considerably batty. Marriage to my father, I suppose. Plus her health was not up to much. But she went on being bright in a strictly formal sense even as Jesus rotted away the rest of her intellect. I remember she carried all our household accounts in her head. I never once saw her use pencil and paper to add up bills. She also whizzed through the crossword in my father's *Daily Telegraph*. Anyway, let's not dwell on my mother. She really had nothing to do with my life other than in a limited biological sense. –

At these words (Exhibit B) the biographer sits back and taps his teeth with the end of his pen, sensing that it will be useless to challenge head-on a statement that cannot possibly be true. The tone of voice in which it is delivered, one of throwaway finality, suggests clearly that any further probing will be met with truculence.

To catch this monkey one will need to go very softly indeed, behind Jayjay's back if necessary. Since when was it assumed that anyone wanting their life written will necessarily tell the whole truth? Or even any of it?

– One can hardly have grown up this century without having absorbed some of that Freudian over-determination – he said on another occasion. – You know, when things people *don't* want to talk about take on heavy significance. But why mightn't it be that the most important things in a person's life sometimes really are the ones that seem the most significant? Now in my father's case there was a side of him that I think did have a lasting effect on me, whereas I could never say that about my mother. Except, of course, that I'm a devout atheist and stupid with figures. I'll get to my father's influence shortly.

– There's no doubt that, seen through our neighbours' eyes, my father would have appeared completely conventional, quite unexceptional. The Pooter par excellence, the nine-to-five man incarnate. Every morning, rain or shine, off to work in the City. Dark suit, bowler hat, overcoat, brolly and briefcase. A short walk to Well Hall: left into Balcaskie Road, down to Glenlea, left again and you're practically at the station. Up to Charing Cross on the eight-seventeen. Strap-hang the District or Circle line to Monument, another short walk up Leadenhall Street. He worked in the new Lloyds building. New then, I mean; I think they built it on the site of the old East India House in the late twenties. Once there he must have been just one of a vast army of underwriters sitting at desks all day, probably in their shirtsleeves and wearing cuff protectors. Over the years he became quite senior, but essentially he remained an underwriter. Then in the evening the reverse journey back to Eltham. A picture of regularity. Much later, of course, that sort of working life became the butt of endless jokes about wage-slavery and unimaginative, drab existence. Still, I would bet that nowadays an awful lot of men would cheerfully put up with it if given the chance. People like routine, you know. They need it. At the end of a long life I am convinced that security is number three on the human list of basic essentials, right up there after food and shelter. That's where politicians go so wrong talking about people needing to adjust to not having a job for life, to working with six-month or one-year contracts, to moving house all the time. It goes against human instinct. We need our continuities, we ache for places. So I think many people would rejoice if told that, all else being equal, they would still be doing the same work in ten, even twenty years, gradually moving up the ladder of seniority, bringing home a little more money and taking slightly longer holidays.

– So if I describe my father as an archetypal nine-to-five man I'm certainly not mocking him. The twenties and thirties were hardly a stable period, what with post-war prostration and the mass unemployment of those who came back. Then the Wall

Street crash, the Slump, the hunger marches. To be in a skilled and essential line of business like my father's was a godsend for a man with family responsibilities. As long as there was trade there were merchant vessels; and as long as there were valuable cargoes shuttling about the world on the high seas my father would be in employment. Not true of goose farmers, after all. –

Maybe it was partly this aspect of his father, that of the hard-working small burgher with aspirations, to which Jayjay was referring as having had consequences for himself. Harold Jebb's own schooling, such as it was, had stopped when he was four-teen, a year before he allegedly entered night school at Well Hall under the tutelage of that ardent socialist, E. Nesbit. Harold's eventual redemption through his apprenticeship at Lloyds evidently left him determined his son should have a better chance. Accordingly the shipping broker stretched his modest though reliable income in order to send his only son to Eltham College.

Eltham College was, and still is, an independent school with a reputation for solid academic standards. It was founded in the 1840s for the sons of missionaries who were usually sent home for their secondary schooling from India and Africa and China. Typically, such children boarded or were farmed out to relatives or church families in the locality, living out of steamer trunks in spare bedrooms, exiled from their parents by thousands of miles of ocean. English literature of the period is full of the cries of children who grew up articulate enough to describe the desolation these banishments could entail. Kipling and Saki were both examples of the type. This was no direct part of Jayjay's own experience, of course. By his own account his suburbia was benign and support-ive. Yet from time to time a certain melancholy would tiptoe in behind his descriptions of childhood Eltham and just stand there, like a summoned employee respectfully waiting for his boss to get off the telephone before he can speak. Later, having myself become familiar with the area in the course of my researches, I can say that anybody might visit one of those semi-detached houses in streets named after Scottish glens, all of them built to much the same pat-tern as Jayjay's birthplace in Beechill Road, and sense how it might have been for a child uprooted from his family overseas. Each landing halfway up the stairs has a sash window and, unless it has been modernised, each window has ornamental borders of stained glass. The exact patterns and colours may vary in detail from house to house, from street to street, depending on the whims and sup-plies of the original builders. It is possible to stand on the landing halfway up the staircase and, at the head-height of a child, look through a panel of coloured glass and completely transform the world outside. By slightly moving one's head the back garden plunges through acrid green to desert ochre, from ultramarine to hellish red. It is the Saki trick, turning a suburban garden into an exotic world, somewhere else, *anywhere* else: a cool, undersea land of mysterious longing or a vengeful inferno as the doomed planet falls into the sun. To visit these houses is still now and then to be fleetingly possessed by the clamorous ghosts of children who once stood, chin on forearm at the narrow sill, staring out for hours, temporarily transforming their world by means of tinted glass, mesmerised by unformed thoughts which, as soon as they turned away, slipped from their minds even as the mist of their breath vanished from the pane.

When Jayjay first went to Eltham College in 1930 he just failed to overlap with a boy seven years his senior who was to become a writer and an artist: Mervyn Peake. The future inventor of Gormenghast was born in China and sent back to Eltham to school and a suburban adolescence. It seems plausible that this experience crystallised into Gormenghast itself: less an extravagant gothick castle than a metaphor for a world fossilised by the conventional, the elderly and the stiflingly dull. Perhaps it is too easy to see how Peake's internal image of Gormenghast might have been built up stone by stone in Eltham on medieval foundations laid in China, the Castle's bleak flagged corridors and loveless characters proliferating in his exile's mind. Yet the wrench of being sent half across the world was real enough; and one begins to glimpse how the stolid, conventional community in south London Jayjay so often described must actually have been stranded through with nervelike threads leading straight to the roughest corners of the world and nurturing powerful, even violent fantasies. Kent's lost Arcady might lie shallowly beneath tarmac and crazy paving, which was how Jayjay presented it, but a potential for subversiveness had always undermined this early commuterland. Great angers, despairs and yearnings were confided to awful wallpapers in small bedrooms dotted about an outwardly placid and respectable community. The same everywhere, no doubt. One must always suspect the placid.

Eltham College's records show that Mervyn Peake left in 1929, the year before Jayjay entered. As to Jayjay's own career there, the school's annals do little but note that he left at the end of the

summer term of 1936. He himself was not at first forthcoming about his schooldays, although he did cite going on the Eltham College Travel Club's trip to Andorra in 1934 which he remembered as being led by a Mr McIver. I very easily found McIver's name in the Staff lists and for some reason this corroborative detail gave me a confidence in Jayjay's account that the mere dates of his entry and departure somehow had not. Why? What was there to distrust? He even looked out a little booklet done in faded violet ink on a duplicating machine that commemorated the trip. It was almost as though he wished to reassure me of the authenticity of his past self, which it did until I began wondering why he should ever have kept such a trivial relic.

In fact he often turned out to be surprisingly good at producing obscure pieces of documentation. I remember a lengthy session one morning during which he reminisced fairly uninterestingly

about some Vietnam peace talks of the nineteen-sixties and various conversations he had had with President Thieu of South Vietnam, General Ky, Henry Kissinger and the US Ambassador of the time. Towards the end Jayjay remarked that Ky had been little more than an airborne cowboy and fancied himself as a jock in a fighter plane's cockpit when he flew with the Tiger Squadron out of Bien Hoa. A proper warrior like Biggles, on the other hand, would doubtless have settled the Vietnam war in a week, given only his three trusty henchmen and some stout British biplanes.
– You remember Biggles? W. E. Johns's heroic air ace? Have I mentioned that I met him? Johns, I mean. –

It was at this point, surfeited with Kissingers and Johnsons and Ho Chi Minhs, that I accused Jayjay of name-dropping. He promptly excused himself, left the room, and after only a brief delay returned with a faded autograph book which he tossed into my lap. Typical of its period, which was the thirties, it was a four-by-three-inch booklet with *Autographs* stamped at a slant in gold script on the cover. Alternating pale pink, blue and green pages were covered with signatures, short messages with exclamation marks and hasty sketches.

– We all had one of those at school. I don't know why. It seemed important. Find the picture of a biplane. –

I leafed through until I came to a neat pencil sketch of a First World War aircraft falling out of the sun on an unsuspecting Hun, guns blazing. It was signed, but not dated, 'W. E. Johns, with best wishes'. I take it all back, I said.

– I never claimed I *knew* him. He was my boyhood hero. He visited the school one day. I suppose he was talking about his experiences in France, inspirational stuff for boys with the idea of drumming up recruits for the RAF. It would have been about 1933 or 1934: it's a pity he didn't date it. Like plenty of others who'd fought in the war Johns was watching Hitler's rise to power and Germany's re-arming with dismay. He used to bombard the Air Ministry with warning letters. Like Baden-Powell, the gist of his message was 'Be prepared'. –

There was something touching in seeing Johns's little drawing and signature in Jayjay's book. I myself would have killed for it when I was twelve, Biggles having been a hero of my own back in my pre-teens in the early fifties. By then, of course, Hitler's Luftwaffe had long since made the fatal error of coming up against this legendary British pilot and had been obliged to retire in disarray, its hands raised en masse. I had been a Biggles fan at the age of twelve, but hardly at fifteen and still less past the age of fifty. Biographers are vulgarians at heart, of course, always sniffing around casual asides and reminiscences for the significant, for the childhood enthusiasm that can be press-ganged into foreshadowing the adult character trait and thus *explain* things. (This over-valuing of explanation, of dreary old cause and effect, is immensely tedious but made necessary by the narrative convention into which most readers, as well as subjects, expect a biography to fit.) So I, too, had gone away to sniff at Johns's life, provoked by Jayjay's hoarded autograph book and enthusiasm in order to discover something about this portly old pilot that might justify the nostalgia of a septuagenarian. At the time, I failed.

– I really admired Johns. At school that day I definitely wanted to become him. He was large and assured and a great raconteur. He made us boys think there wasn't anything we couldn't do provided we had the nerve. –

At the time the ex-pilot signed Jayjay's autograph book he was the editor of a flying magazine, a scholarly columnist in gardening magazines and a regular contributor to the *Boy's Own Paper*, as well as a churner-out of innumerable stories and novels, adult as well as juvenile. He lived in a whirl of energy on the move from one journal's office to another, dashing off passionate editorials, lightning stories and flaming letters to Whitehall about the Nazi menace and the unprepared state of Britain's Air Force. The authorities found him dangerously radical because *Popular Flying* had a large and lively circulation and his editorials were widely read. All this threw some moderately interesting light on an author about whose life I myself had hardly speculated while reading him. Still, I couldn't quite see why Jayjay had been so taken. Then he added a titbit which I filed away in case it had a bearing on this old man on the sofa opposite who was leafing through his school autograph book with an unreadable half-smile.

– Did you know Johns had a secret love? Soon after he returned from the First World War his marriage collapsed and he began a lifelong affair with a lady named Doris. Because his wife was a vicar's daughter he hadn't quite liked to talk about an official separation and by the time he was a famous children's writer in the thirties and forties his publishers absolutely refused to allow him to divorce and marry Doris. They said that the creator of Biggles, that paragon of British virtue, couldn't possibly acknowledge in public that he was divorced. So Johns was obliged to go on living in sin. When he died in 1968 he and Doris had been cohabiting, technically unmarried, for over forty years.

– How could anyone fail to be taken by the idea of this peculiar man? Here is Biggles, a hero whose daredevil flying and brilliant tactics made him an ace in the skies over France. Yet his creator's own flying must have brought aid and comfort to the Kaiser, while the morality of the times obliged him to live a lie. That's the good thing about writing, isn't it? On paper you can always go back and do things properly. Is that what I'm doing, do you think? –

I am not at all sure yet what to think but am beginning to brace myself to hear the career of a man of action rather than of one who has indulged in a lifetime of Proustian reflectiveness in heavily curtained rooms. Who would mention a boyhood hero in such detail unless he thought the matter relevant? Have I made a silly mistake in taking on this literary chore? And at what point will I realise that I'm merely compounding the mistake?

In those early days of listening to Jayjay's diffuse reminiscences I was, like any other biographer feeling his way, still unsure about what was strictly germane and what digression. In general I use a tape-recorder sparingly. I am not fond of the machine. It encourages an interviewer not to listen but to drift off in daydreams of his own, knowing it can all be replayed later. So it can, at the cost of a further tranche of time, but the tensions and nuances are generally lost for ever. Still, a tape-machine is an essential backup for the political stuff I occasionally write. I am not about to leave myself unprotected from the casual displeasure of ex-dictators and assorted monsters who cannot believe their words in print were those they actually spoke. But Jayjay's memoirs are a different matter. He is not going to have me mugged or arrested in some steamy Asian capital. With him I can simply respect the laws of libel as well as those that govern truthfulness. When interviewing real people like him I prefer to rely on speedwritten notes, which have the advantage of retaining the spontaneity of one's immediate judgements as to what is relevant and what merely padding. Perhaps because sheer chance arranged that I was working on ex-dictators and Jayjay simultaneously, I used both a tape-recorder and speedwritten notes haphazardly with him for many months. This was to make for curious and sometimes unsettling variations in his narrative voice but I'm not displeased with the effect since it does preserve the flavour of the man's own ambiguity, as though in his confessions he were for ever skirting around a secret.

Indeed, the impression I had from the start was that despite his having been keen enough to 'tell his story' he was by no means certain what that story was until he began to speak. Far from dictating a version that was already clear in his head he would start our morning sessions as unsure as I where his reminiscences might lead. I quickly passed beyond any suspicion that he was making things up as he went along. From first to last I thought Jayjay truthful, whatever that means. But there was always the sense of a person who contained assorted versions of himself, and entirely different flavours of that person could be obtained depending on what one chose to put in or leave out. On successive Tuscan mornings I would drive to Il Ghibli along the appalling track from my house on the hillside, down through patches of early sunlight slanting between the tangled branches of scrub oaks, curiously excited and half apprehensive as though in the course of the next few hours I might learn something dangerous about myself.

Eventually I did, of course. But that was not for over a year, by which time another spring's Red Admirals were rising before the nose of my truck with their characteristic floating flight. These scraps of life, vivid scarlet-on-inky-velvet as they balanced on thermals, mixed themselves in with what I heard and became associated with the whole experience of that period. Now when I think of Jayjay the butterflies cross over his name and face.

4

He takes me out on the terrace and says this is all a dream, *this* being a cold, overcast Tuscan morning in early March. Offstage are the insistent, repetitive sounds of a tractor ploughing narrow fields of olives, at each short turn borne on the wind as clankings and revvings. In the valley light grey smoke careers upwards from several brisk bonfires of olive prunings. Another agricultural year getting under way. Immemorial as you could wish, he remarks, as seen in two thousand years' of art from tomb paintings onwards, though minus the tractors, of course. Really happening really now, but a dream for all that.

What is not a dream, then?

– Nothing. Oh, Eltham, maybe. Unlike the present, seventy-five years ago doesn't feel like a dream. It's with me awake, asleep, just as with anyone my age. M. R. James's ghost story 'A View from a Hill' had a pair of binoculars filled with liquid distilled from a corpse and through this refractive ichor one could see the past. I think our eyeballs still contain the very fluid through which we saw the world seventy years ago. Aqueous humour? Vitreous?

It is not to be found by dissection. No matter where I look I see only a thin illusion of the present. Only when we reach an age do we realise how long it is since we experienced the uncontaminated present. Somebody once tried to sell me a Zennish subspecies of Buddhism and the only thing I remember now is his insistence on the importance of living in the absolute present, whatever that might be. According to this fellow, who I only let through the door because I was intrigued by the colour of his great woolly socks, the unenlightened are constantly held back by the past, which is irrelevant and illusory. But how else does one learn anything except through memory? How else grow into the person one is? I'm afraid I remain as doggedly unenlightened as that day I gave the chap sixpence for the bus fare to return to his presumably nonexistent home. After all, it's not that I so love the past I can't bring myself to leave it. It simply gave me all the bearings by which I know I'm me. What I like is not Eltham but the depth Eltham now gives an otherwise superficial life. Things acquire their own patina. The most the present can do is stick to me briefly like clingfilm until the static wears off. It's irritating and I can see through it. –

I suppose he *is* calling the shots so I will indulge him his fanciful images and wait patiently, even though it is cold out here on the terrace. Luckily he is *caffèdipendente*, like me, and hates to be separated for too long from his espresso machine.

– If you went back there now you would find whole streets of houses remarkably unchanged. What has changed is their use. Even quite small semi-detached houses have been subdivided and sold off piecemeal or let to students, immigrants, transients. Or else a pair of houses has been knocked together and turned into a des. res. for the upwardly mobile, the front gardens paved over for parking space. In the twenties and thirties the air was more one of stability and permanence. Another difference is that it used to be quieter and more spacious. The streets were twice as wide, not simply because I was small then but because almost no-one owned a car. Nowadays in London cars are parked on both sides of residential roads which effectively narrows them by ten or twelve feet. The mere fact of their presence shows the house-holders' mobility, their unrootedness. In those days we could play in the street, always provided our parents didn't forbid it as being what they called dirty or common. We boys used to go whizzing around in soapboxes on wheels: completely home-made, of course, like everything else. The best ones were steerable and used the wheels off old prams. Most of them lacked rubber tyres. I can still hear the sound the rims made going over the cracks between paving stones. You could be out there all morning and hardly see a motor vehicle. There were a lot of horse-drawn carts about still. Delivery services. Milkmen. Sweeps. Rag-and-bone men. Ah, rag-and-bone men. I must have M. R. James's liquid in my ears, too, because that's another sound I can hear. The streets being so empty and quiet they had much more echo to them. Sometimes at night here in Tuscany I can hear the rag-and-bone man who came through our streets in Eltham. He must have died at least half a century ago but I can hear him as clearly as if he were drawn up outside. 'Ra'n *boon*,' he went. 'Ra'n *boon*.' You could hear him streets away, that echoing *boon* the most melancholy cry imaginable, him and his horse clip-clopping slowly away, fainter and fainter into silence. I think he lived with the Gypsies over Blackfen way. Even my nose has been M. R. Jamesed because I can smell his horse, that comforting scent of hot oats and ammonia. We would run out to scratch its face and look in the nosebag and marvel at how well polished the man kept all the tack, especially the blinkers. Glossy black rec-tangles. Well of course that's why they said we mustn't play in the street because it was dirty. It wasn't oil they meant but horse shit. Heaps of steaming nuggets until the sweeper came along with his handcart and broom, or else we would collect it ourselves for the garden.

– Oh the garden. That was it, you see. Still Kent as much as London SE9. Only thirty years earlier it had been copses and fields and orchards. Just up the road Eltham Park was still pretty much unreconstructed countryside with a few municipal tokens. A drinking fountain. A shelter. Some railings. Things like that. The park-keeper's house. That park-keeper was fearsome to us. He'd probably only been demobbed and out of uniform ten years and might well have flown with W. E. Johns in the Royal Flying Corps, but he seemed ancient. He went about in leather gaiters like a nineteenth-century gamekeeper and often patrolled on horseback. We boys lived in mortal dread of him. We'd go up to Shepherdleas Wood for conkers. At the right season you could find mushrooms there: horse mushrooms and parasols, mainly. If you wanted blewits the place to go was Shooters Hill. But whatever we went to the park for, we used never to come back without sticks for kindling. There was a grate in every room. The cleaning-out and laying, the black-leading, the hauling and emptying. Imagine the labour of it. Plus the front doorstep to be scrubbed daily and whitened. And the letterbox, knocker and bell-push polished with Bluebell or Brasso. There was real pride in suburban home ownership. Who nowadays would polish the flap of their letterbox? By the end of the thirties the legend on our flap saying 'Letters' had been rubbed away until it was barely legible, like the inscription on a medieval brass.

– Coal fires with gas pokers to light them. Cooking was by gas, of course. If you wanted hot water in the bathroom you lit the geyser, which came on when you opened the hot tap. As the gas ignited it made a great *wumph!* and rattled the windows. Off the kitchen was the scullery, a step down from lino to red quarry tiles. My mother did the laundry there. She had a mangle through which she wound the sheets. They came out hard and curved in a solid mass: 'mangled', I suppose. Outside lavatory, freezing cold, with a cast-iron cistern.

– Now I think about it, coal was everything. Before each front doorstep was the round iron cover of the coal hole. The coalman called regularly, a big dray with two Suffolk Punches pulling it because the load was heavy and came uphill from the depot at Well Hall. When I was about ten or twelve the firm bought an

Albion lorry instead with a sunburst on its radiator. Coal's another
thing I can still smell. Hundredweight sacks, often with rope handles. They gave off this wonderful tarry reek, as did the lorry and
the coalmen. You could smell them from the end of the street.
The men were black with dust. They wore leather jerkins and
filthy caps with the stuffing coming out. Their eyes and teeth
were very white in the middle of all the dirt and their arms were
sinewy from all the hauling, although I now realise the men were
often thin and quite probably undernourished. I remember big
blue veins amid the filth on the insides of their arms. They would
flip the lid off the coal hole and come up the path bent under
these great weights. Then in one movement they would stoop
and jerk the sack over their heads so it fell mouth downwards
over the hole. That's partly why they wore caps, although all
working men wore caps in those days. You could hear the coal
crashing down the chute into the cellar. Twenty trips to the ton.
Then they would sweep up around the hole, drop the lid back into
place and hand over a grimy delivery note. Tradesmen always carried a pencil behind one ear. You wouldn't open the cellar door for
an hour or two until the dust had settled. What with coal deliver-
ies and ash pans and the sweep, soot and coal dust were
everywhere. Hence all the cleaning and polishing.

– Since coal was everything in those days London smelt quite
different. So did the entire urban landscape of Britain, come to
that. Motor traffic was growing all the time, of course, and petrol
and oil smelt cruder then. I suppose everything came from lower
down the fractionating column, less refined. Coal, gas, creosote,
tar. Even the green Southern Railways' electric trains smelt of
phenol, I imagine because their various condensers and resistors
and transformers were coated with phenolic resins for insulation.
When hot they gave off this clean, medicinal smell. I associated it
with doctors' surgeries, probably because carbolic was still being
used as an antiseptic. Tar fractions were in the air everywhere,
which of course was exactly the problem and the reason for those
famous Dickensian fogs which persisted in London until the

Clean Air Act began to take effect in the late fifties. When I said my father never missed a day's work it wasn't strictly true. I was thinking of illness but I'd forgotten the fogs. I don't know if you remember how bad they could be? So thick and yellow you couldn't see from one lamp-post to the next? People could get hopelessly lost within twenty yards of their own front gates. A big fog might last for a week, a fortnight, even longer. When it was like that the trains often couldn't run at all because the signals weren't visible. My father would stay at home and fret, but only after he had tried every means of getting to the office short of walking up to the City. Occasionally he had to sleep at the office because he couldn't get home.

– Fog days were exciting if you were a kid. A real pea-souper was as thrilling as a heavy snowfall because it changed the world overnight. You woke to undersea gloom and deathly quiet. Like snow it muffled sounds and there was anyway less traffic to make a noise. People moved slowly through the streets with torches. Moisture condensed out on every cold surface. Everything ran damp and tasted acrid. It would, of course. Droplets of sulphuric or nitric acid which killed people off like mad and ate away brick-work. But there was nothing the matter with my lungs and I loved the disruption, the way things loomed and looked. The pave-ments and kerbstones became greasy. I liked the irony that it took a really thick fog to make certain things visible. The privet hedges and hydrangeas in front gardens were suddenly festooned with spiders' webs which you could now see because each strand was covered in tiny grey beads. They were always there, of course, but normally you never noticed them. The smell of the fog was really just an intensification of the smell of any winter's dusk at tea-time when everyone was lighting fires at once and sending up a million London chimneys the scent of pine kindling and the cool tarry yellow smell of cheap coal. It faded a bit after an hour as the grates warmed up and combustion became more efficient. For me, that smell went with the mournful sound of ships' foghorns and hooters coming up from the Port of London.

– Do I make it sound harsh and industrial? Too much in the lee of satanic mills? Maybe I haven't done justice to the gardens, then. As I said, they were where you saw the county of Kent fighting back against bricks and asphalt, and people took great pride in them. A lot of the gardens both front and back had mature trees in them, often big old plums and pears left from the orchards that had been built over when my father was delivering geese as a boy. Even so, Eltham was already full of exotica, especially those sub-urban staples like hydrangeas, laburnams, buddleias and monkey-puzzle trees. Not one of them native to Britain. As for domestic animals, quite a few people kept chickens. That, as well as the tradesmen's horses, was why you could go on finding corn chandlers in high streets like those of Eltham and Sidcup until well after the Second World War. The one in Sidcup just by the Black Horse Inn was owned by a man called Patullo Higgs, I remember. Gypsy name, I should think. Another of those Blackfen families, no doubt, who sent their women from door to door with wax flowers and lucky white heather. We kept chickens, sometimes rabbits, even the odd goose for old times' sake. That's why there were often farmyard smells mixed in with all the coal and gas fumes and one could hear cocks crowing in the morning above the groaning noise the trams made going up the hill from Well Hall.

– A lot of insect life, too. I began collecting moths as a boy and took thirty-six different species from our own back garden. Old Lady, Red and Yellow Underwing, Cinnabar, Silver Y. A few hawk moths, mainly Lime and Privet from all those hedges, little hummingbirds that fancied the flowers in people's rockeries, Small Elephants which liked honeysuckle and rhododendrons. And once, great day, a rather sad and battered Death's Head, probably from a potato patch or beehive in an allotment up the road. Plenty of butterflies from all the buddleias, though never (and how I hoped and yearned) a Camberwell Beauty. A transient, alas, a migrant. Hopelessly rare. Those rockeries, by the way, often contained few genuine rocks. Instead there were lumps of fused slag which you could get from the gasworks down in Greenwich. They were odd colours: firebrick orange, black, hectic purple; full of bubbles and craters like lava. If you smashed them with a coal hammer you could smell gas. Ash paths in back gardens. Of course. What else to do with clinkers from the kitchen boiler? Fascinating, that juxtaposition of the rural with the industrial. After all, half the residents of these newish suburbs had come from the country. The irony of today's London is that it has long since left off being an industrial city, yet despite all those garden centres and that modish environmental concern nobody has a clue about rural things. In those days in Eltham back gardens you'd see a row of runner beans next to a cinder path. Rhubarb leaves frothing from the tops of tall old chimney pots set in the earth. A compost heap of horse dung rotting nicely in a frame made of the old lead gaspipes they dragged out from under the floors when they wired the house for electricity. They left the pipes in the walls, of course. Too big a job. So you had these little stubs pushing up behind the wallpaper where the gas mantles had been capped off . . . I'm surely boring you? –

Perhaps, Jayjay (I feel and then suggest out loud as the tractors of Tuscany clank and blare on and on in the distant background), perhaps you ought to be writing this yourself, you seem to be remembering it all so vividly. Buy yourself a tape-recorder, like me. Maybe what you need at the end of this tumult of reminiscence is an editor, not a biographer. No, he says emphatically, while managing to suggest both wistfulness and contempt. Me write? God, no. Though no doubt I have the required sensibility. (Oh no doubt, I remark bitterly to myself. In another moment he's going to tell me that the only thing keeping him from being a latter-day Shakespeare – or Mozart, come to that – is a rueful lack of self-discipline plus too many other interesting things to do. Really, Parnassus is pretty much like Everest these days: open to practically any Tom, Dick or Harriet who can be bothered to take a week off, make the effort and afford the gear.) The sensibility (he repeats) but not, I fear, the application. Though (this comes out more graciously) it no doubt takes a certain gift as well? One wonders. (Goodness, one does. Mean old faggot, if that is what he is. What *is* he? Why did I agree to this? What am I doing here, meteless and moneless on Tuscan hills? Or rather, cold and coffeeless?) Town gas was very formative in my young life, he is improbably saying.

 – There was of course the lamplighter episode. I must have been about five. I was fascinated by this man who went around the streets of the neighbourhood with a long pole, lighting up the lamps as it got dark. No doubt you'll be able to check this, but I vaguely remember the lamps had little pilot lights that were always burning so perhaps they came on when he nudged a tap on with the tip of his pole. I do remember the lamp-posts had an arm sticking out at the top, a bracket to prop a ladder against. This lamplighter had a pouch of tools on his belt. I think I fell in love with him. One does at five. One day he suggested I feel the front of his trousers to guess what he had inside. I had the image of a large piece of wood and connected it somehow with the pole he used for lighting: an extension, maybe, or a spare part. Why he would have kept it inside his trousers is not a question a five-year-old asks in a world where everything is so new and marvellous that no single thing is more rational than any other. Things just *are*. I believe I quite often felt his bit of wood. –

 You don't think (I enquire in my role as fact-checker and tester of likelihoods) that someone among the good burghers of Beechill Road might have noticed and said something?

 – Oh no. It was lighting-up time, getting dark. Besides, in winter he wore a long coat that smelt tremendously of gas. And linseed oil, too, since he carried a ball of putty in one pocket, presumably to repair leaks. Lots of things smelt like that in those days. Even coal cellars smelt of gas and putty because that's where the meter was. The other thing about coal gas was that it could be used to help you escape the army. I remember after the National

Service Act of 1947 plenty of young conscripts tried to dodge
being called up and they used the same tricks some people had
used during the war to avoid active service. When you were called
up the first thing was to report for a medical. If you wanted to fall
at this early hurdle you could try telling the MO you couldn't wait
to be enlisted and get among all those gorgeous young male
bodies. Claiming to be queer wasn't guaranteed to work and
besides it could lead to official records and all kinds of unpleas-
antness. A less stressful gambit was to drink a pint of milk through
which you'd let coal gas bubble for an hour or so. It tasted
unspeakable but it did give you several very convincing symp-
toms which included palpitations, lead-coloured lips and tongue,
foul breath, dilated pupils. Just about everything an army doctor
least wanted to see except hammer toes and syphilis. Quite simply,
you were temporarily poisoned. Some people did actually die of it,
I gather. Hardly the way to win the approval of a man like Captain
W. E. Johns, in any case. –

Mercifully we break here for a long-overdue fix of caffeine. For a
while we sit in comparative silence, his presumably reflective and
mine more convalescent after his unbroken onslaught of memories. The bonfires of olive branches mark the progress of pruners
moving about the hillside with billhooks and chainsaws, carving
surplus wood from the trees. I have already heard Jayjay on the
subject of Tuscan rural life, couched in terms of a Horatian *eheu
fugaces* (how contagious his style is!). Not that he isn't accurate and
even evocative in his descriptions of harvesting olives in late
October and November, about how days are lost when rain clouds
droop low over the hillsides like mist and the beaded nets waiting
beneath the trees become like the cobwebs of Eltham made visible by fog. He is good, too, on olive-picking as a neighbourly
activity when friends come to do their stint, balancing on home-
made ladders among the swaying branches, their gossip
interwoven with cheery obscenities and inventive blasphemy. He
notes that these days the friends are mostly middle-aged or older

and behind this festive ritual, as behind so many others in the agricultural calendar, there is the undisguised apprehension that what has gone on for a thousand years is not guaranteed to last indefinitely.

It is here that Jayjay and I part company in that I lack his strong nostalgia and his sense that change necessarily means irreparable loss and degeneration. He is rueful that the sons and daughters of Tuscan hill farmers have increasingly little interest in such laborious ways of spending their lives. They prefer driving delivery vans or working in a supermarket. Boys with little formal education are happier to work on a garage forecourt and to feel part of the glittery stream of life that daily washes through. Not for them the uncanny quiet of the hills, tapping ancient knowledge for a hard living, labouring alone in the woods and the groves . . . Jesus Christ, Jayjay (I say), are you *surprised*? The Eltham of your childhood was no Eden, either. Why would people today bother growing their own runner beans when they can buy deep-frozen bags of them at the supermarket for a fraction of what they would have spent in cash, time and effort to grow the damn things themselves? The same goes for olive oil. I, too, have heard these local Tuscans grousing in their kitchens. Is it not a kind of treason, they say, the way the certainties of millennia are being overturned in a single generation? One worked in order to leave carefully tended fields of vines and olives for one's children, even in the days when one didn't own the land, to be passed on in turn to theirs; and so the generations went by. But now, *Ddio boia*, on the edge of the twenty-first century, we own the land and the bad old feudal days of *mezzadria* are safely dead and it's no longer clear what it means to be a small farmer, a *coltivatore diretto*. It's not even clear, my friends, what it means to be a father these days, with disobedient children who have too much money and who do exactly what they want . . . Golly, how they do go on, and so does Jayjay in similar vein until I tell him this is a boring and hackneyed threnody. It's just that people don't like change unless it's obviously going to make them rich. End of story. (I admit I take issue with him at least partly to conceal my own unease about the same thing. It's bleakly comforting to demolish one's own position when someone else is too fervently holding it.)

Jayjay and I drink our coffee without speaking. I am conscious that the sounds of ploughing fill the silence left by his passionate reminiscences. As a fellow resident of these parts he is as susceptible as I to having certain trains of thought started by seasonal activities. At length the grandson of a goose-farmer who made a living beside the vanished Effra says:

– My father. My father. I became sidetracked. I was describing him as the typical nine-to-five man. But there was another side to him, one I never remember him showing at home, and that's the bit I probably inherited from him. I only ever saw it on the rare occasions he took me to the Port of London. He truly loved ships and shipping. For him it was never just a matter of office work and ledgers. He knew hundreds of ships by name and not merely British ones, either, although in those days the British merchant fleet probably made up a good half of the world's tonnage. With his Lloyds pass he could go all over the docks and I would trot along beside him, absolutely transfixed. In those days ships were still romantic, even the cargo vessels. They were the complete opposite of these modern container hulks laden with anonymous steel boxes. Container ships aren't worthy of the name, in my view; they're little better than oceangoing lorries. But the London docks in the thirties were something to see, believe me. Every kind of merchandise from all parts of the Empire being lifted out of holds and swung into heaps on the quays. The smells, especially in summer: those are what I remember best.

– Those East End thoroughfares like East India Dock Road were full of commercial stores and warehouses and godowns. If a shipper had queried a consignment's condition my father might go in person and inspect it. There could be huge sums of money involved. I have an image, no doubt compounded of several different occasions, which has come to feel like a specific memory. I was in a godown stacked to the rafters with tea and coffee and spices. No, that's wrong for a start: no coffee merchant would store his sacks in the same warehouse with spices because the flavours would contaminate each other. But anyway. It was hot in there and the spices only added to the warmth. There were crates and barrels and boxes and jute sacks piled up in cliffs with only narrow passageways between them. I was dwarfed, a twelve-year-old. And on every side were these millions of mysterious berries and leaves, buds and pods, beans and seeds, all giving up their scents at once. My father said something about the smell of tropic suns. I could feel myself becoming drowsier and drowsier, anaesthetised almost. At the same time I was excited. All this produce came from a world completely hidden from me, full of unknown people eating strange foods and living unimaginable lives. I wondered what boys my own age did in those far-off lands. Were they, too, saving up for a bicycle? But there was something else as well, something unconnected with imaginary people doing imagined things. It was altogether vaguer, more powerful. It started what I think was a deep restlessness in me. Something akin to longing? That's maybe it, muddled up as it was with schoolboy ideas of roaming the world's seas on endless adventures. Then the oddness of going back outside the warehouse again and finding the air suddenly chilly and smelling of coal gas and river. And although the London bustle was familiar enough it no longer seemed the same London of an hour earlier. You know what I mean. A dream can do it sometimes and make an entire day feel unreal. Yes, I knew the clatter and grind of those steel-tyred barrows over polished cobbles, the splodges of horse dung, the sad hootings and blarings of the river traffic in the background. All these were the London I'd known from infancy. But now I was in a different world. I'm not sure that I ever completely found my way back again.

– I think my father shared something of these feelings, which is why he never did become Mr Pooter. We neither of us ever talked about it directly, not beyond expressing enthusiasm for the docks in general. But I would see the way he watched a ship as it berthed, the tugs taking the strain and grey Thames water being wrung out of rope hawsers in a fine mist. The cranes would groan at the hatch covers and the seagulls wheel. Hatches being lifted that had last closed on the sun in Rangoon or Surabaya or Bombay. I think he was secretly as moved as I was by the ships and warehouses and the smells of distant places. By the *poetry* of them (Jayjay says unexpectedly). I can't think of a less absurd way to put it (he adds, abstracted and quite pink with recall). Stand on any dockside with water at your feet and tell me you don't secretly believe that real life is going on somewhere over the horizon. Especially if you're twelve. –

Jayjay admits that an obvious next move would have been a cadetship in the merchant navy. Well over sixty years later he can remember discussing it with his father though not what his father's attitude was. This is odd since my image of Harold Jebb is of a man with quite firm opinions even though they went with a character not that of a disciplinarian. Maybe he knew too much about the reality rather than the romance (Jayjay hazards), and discouraged his son with accurate descriptions of what apprenticeship could entail?

– John Masefield's *Dauber* ought to have made any sea-struck adolescent think twice about a sailor's life, especially if he were cursed with any kind of sensibility. The boy in the poem was an artist, of course, while I had no artistic talents whatever. Still, I remember studying the poem at school and thinking things must have changed since those days under sail when boys were sent up aloft in all weathers. And then there was all the fuss about James Hanley's *Boy*, which was banned when it came out. Maybe I'd left Eltham College by then?* Not that my father would have read it, or anyone at school, come to that. It was far too near the knuckle:

---

* He hadn't. *Boy* was first issued in 1931 in a limited edition and then republished properly in 1934. This was the widely noticed edition that was withdrawn after police action.

savage and scandalous and gaff-blowing. Much more harrowing and outraging than anything D. H. Lawrence ever wrote, in my view. That court case about *Lady Chatterley's Lover* in 1960 was really about the triviality of being able to print the words fuck and cunt. Lawrence's aristocrat-and-gamekeeper business was just a vulgar and titillating fantasy. But *Boy* was much more radical because it was stark social realism, not fantasy at all. It was about how thousands of British working-class children had actually lived and sometimes died in twentieth-century Britain. Anyway, I never did join the merchant navy.

– Still, I felt myself tugged outwards even then. I was a centrifugal boy, you might say, but content to wait because I was sure that before long my life was destined to push me out to the rim, to the strange and the distant. For one thing, nearly all my schoolfriends at Eltham College had been born abroad. Maybe I picked them because of that. Their real homes were far overseas and not just in the Empire, either: the dreaded Gospel knew no bounds. I listened to them talk about their *amah*s and servants, their *syces* and *punkah-wallah*s, about snakes in their bungalows and jackals in the garden and the hooded crows that pecked out the eyes of sleeping babies; about the bandits who periodically came down from the hills and looted their homes; about corrupt local police chiefs secretly in league with the bandits, and local militias who could be trusted on parade only with wooden rifles. All this became mixed into the exotic smells that had so fascinated me in Docklands. In my imagination I must have built up a land that lay in wait for me. It didn't exist but it was vivid all the same. Tropical, full of dense greenery with flashes of brilliant plumage and hung with extraordinary fruit. Lawless, too; or at least its cultural norms stood on their heads all the hallowed precepts of British society. I was fascinated by the idea of a cultural difference that was radical yet still perfectly viable on its own terms. What my friends unwittingly convinced me was that the British, Christian way was not the only possible kind of life for something as grandly diverse as the human race.

– This was my first important piece of knowledge, in some ways the essence of my time in Eltham. The last sixty years have proved its truth to the hilt. –

In these early stages of working with Jayjay I knew that part of the disgruntlement which occasionally settled on me like dust as I drove home was due to a sense of being dragged backwards to my own English childhood. There were only twenty-three years between us, and social change in those days had lacked the headlong quality of today's world. Consequently, much that he described in London in the twenties and thirties was still unchanged in the forties and fifties. Some of his reminiscences evoked details of my own childhood scenery, churning up muddy relics I had been content to leave as indistinguishable lumps beneath the general silt of the past. It was not so much that they were unhappy memories, more that I felt I'd succeeded in deposing that early period of my life in favour of things that interested the person I now am. I had no desire to go back to the buried past. This had nothing to do with the wisdom of monks in woolly socks but entirely with a boring past having been superseded by a stimulating present. Jayjay's wrenching me into the thirties was doubly irritating because when we'd first met my thoughts were on the political realities of modern Southeast Asia and I resented being distracted. Why then had I agreed to his flattering insistence that only I could write his story? Was it the automatic response of the self-employed writer who daren't turn down work, no matter how inappropriate? Or was it the prompting of a more insidious inclination? Only time would tell: itself a platitude likely to make anybody glum.

5

The landscape that lay immediately in wait for the eighteen-year-old Jayjay was very different from his Douanier Rousseau imaginings. In the summer of 1936 he boarded the Orient Line's vessel *Orontes* with a ticket to Suez in his pocket. 'The first big ship I was ever on,' he recalled. 'I can remember more about her and that voyage than I can about most of my other travels. Twin screws, two yellow funnels, 19,970 tons, launched in 1929. We touched at Toulon, Naples and Port Said. After Suez she went on to Colombo and Australia. I travelled steerage.'

He babbles on, full of details about turbine engines and the behaviour of the variously dissolute and reprobate travelling companions with whom he shared his cabin, while I try to remember where I have heard the name *Orontes* before. (It comes to me much later. It was the name of the troopship that brought the invalid Dr Watson back from India and eventually into the companionship of Sherlock Holmes.) For the present I want to know why Jayjay had gone, what he was going to do.

– My father was getting fed up with me. He kept calling me a dreamer. Perfectly true, I was. But according to him it was self-improvement I ought to have been dreaming of. After School Cert. he wanted me to go on to university and a profession: doctor, lawyer, teacher, whatever. I'm afraid there was a vulgar streak in him. He must have been nurturing some fantasy about the Jerningham Jebbs going from goose-herding to Harley Street in a mere two generations. Maybe that's unfair. I suppose it isn't vulgar to wish one's family to better itself. What else was suburbia about? For his father's generation of folk who had clawed their way up from smallholdings along the Effra, Eltham was a broad ledge on a precipitous cliff where one could catch one's breath and consolidate. It was sunny and secure. And if the cliff-face above disappeared abruptly into daunting mists, the downward view was wonderfully clear, revealing just how far one had come and just how unthinkable it would be to slip back. Hence all that anxious rhetoric about backsliders. But my father's generation saw it differently. By then they looked on the place as temporary. For them it was the view down that was misty and unreal while the peaks overhead sparkled enticingly. Where else to go but up? –

But you were not one of those either.

– No. I was as bored with the mountain as I am by this metaphor. For me the only way from this ledge was *outward*. Far horizons. The blue empyrean. Follow the heart, though heed the head's directions. All that. But heavens, the propaganda one had to hold out against! One of those frightful hymns we had to sing at school had a verse which went something like:

> *Not for ever by still waters*
> *Would we idly rest and stay;*
> *But would smite the living fountains*
> *From the rocks along our way.*

A pretty clear statement of the Protestant work ethic, even if it does sound as though it's recruiting hydrologists for the Third World. Excelsior! Onward and upward! I didn't fancy a life smiting rocks so I said goodbye to Beechill Road and went off to Suez. My father had leaned on someone in Anderson & Green, the Orient Line's owners, to give me an office job. Something to do with coaling. He thought I would go, find Suez a hell-hole, and after salutary bouts of homesickness and malaria come back with my tail between my legs, my lust for dreaming satisfied and eager to settle down to a sensible career. –

Leaning back in his chair Jayjay smiles with a sad shake of his head as though he can see his father's figure superimposed on the Valle di Chio and acknowledge without rancour the man's blameless misjudgement of a son he never understood. Smoke tumbles upwards from a bonfire of last year's brambles Claudio has lit down by the *orto*. Long-dead fathers and their long-dead wishes dissolve into a cloudless blue sky. From within the house come faint domestic sounds as Marcella goes about her cleaning, which presumably includes polishing Lady Amelia's dildo. On a spring morning towards the end of his life this man is gazing outwards from his terrace with an expression more private and excluding than his frank manner implies, but this is to be expected in the presence of a comparative stranger and with so long a stretch of time sending up its inner wafts. As I glance covertly at him a fleeting facial resemblance reminds me of that famously ambiguous photograph by Islay Lyons of Norman Douglas at the age of eighty staring (maybe seeingly, maybe not) at a bust of himself aged ten. The bust is in the foreground and, as the cynosure, it would seem to dominate the picture. Yet it is the marble boy's older self we look at as he appears to contemplate his former likeness from behind a grandfather's disguise. His expression is unreadable, meaning we can read into it any from a swift list of possible interpretations, beginning with melancholy and passing through mischief. (Is that a knowing smile hovering in the great nose's shadow? Wry amusement that, given the impossible chance, he would cheerfully have bedded his earlier self with full legal rights over his own flesh and blood?) Or finally, is he even looking at the child at all? Those

eyes could long have skidded off the bust's left shoulder and the
downward gaze be fixed reflectively on the unseeable vanishing
point of eighty years. Nothing is clear except the strikingness of
the composition with its two different yet identical subjects, both
allotropes of the same elemental person. That and the chasm it
shares with the viewer.

And now Jayjay is gazing at the sky with an amiably frozen
expression which might be that of an old rogue peering down
wells of his former iniquities or else evidence of a sudden minor
stroke. Today the biographer feels belligerent. He wants clarity.
He has the urge to toss all manner of fig leaves and olive branches
into the flames.

No, why did you *really* go to Suez? Was it for sex?

– That's your entire month's vulgarity allowance used up. –

Merely taking your cue, Jayjay. You were the one who told me
at our very first meeting that you had had rather an erotic life.

– Very well, then. No, I told you: my father threw me out. –

For not being in sympathy with the Protestant work ethic? His
son of eighteen? I don't believe that. Or else you've deliberately
misled me about your father, whom I take to have been a mild
man with a badly repressed streak of romanticism. Very English,
in fact.

– Well, all right, perhaps it was a bit more complicated.
Certainly his Englishness extended to the matter of Protestantism.
Like many decent Englishmen he fully endorsed the Christian
ethic and had not the slightest interest in Christ. I never remember him showing the least sign of spirituality or churchgoing, not
even as an occasional act of solidarity with his wife. I think he was
both baffled and embarrassed by her sudden conversion to that
bustling low-churchery. All those hymns and prayers and tracts
and meetings and exhortations and generally spreading the
Gospel: they jarred on his retiring sense of the proper. So no, he
might never have been clear in his own mind about a pilgrim's
upward progress, but he did feel to his fingertips the idea of a
person's self-betterment. Where I was concerned he was not

unreasonably put out that all his hard work and self-sacrifice at Lloyds in order to give me a decent education was being repaid by a son who showed little interest in study and even less in 'playing the game': that numinous British concept which, if you had to have it explained to you, meant that you weren't properly British.

– Fact is, I'd got into what they called bad company at school and very soon I myself became the bad company about which other boys were warned. There was a lad there named Michael who was a year older than me and to whom I was extremely attracted. It was partly because he was a rebel, but then most boys of seventeen have a streak of that. In Michael's case, though, it was backed up by real ideological fervour. He used to go to political meetings at weekends instead of playing rugger. Imagine cutting a school sport in order to listen to Harry Pollitt, who by then was Secretary of the British Communist Party, haranguing the faithful in some draughty hall. Mind you, there always was a small element of radicalism in the school, but it was of a politically unthreatening kind. Some of those missionary households still had strong working-class connections and a certain brand of socialism went very happily with evangelism. For instance I remember our kitchen dresser always had saucers full of Co-op tokens on it. They were the equivalent of today's box-top discount credits, only made of tin. They were the size of coins and came in various shapes and denominations: penny, threepence, sixpence, that sort of thing. Our local co-operative was the Royal Arsenal Co-operative Society and my mother was a loyal RACS shopper. Those bits of tin represented her dividends as a shareholder. Joint ownership, social equality, the community. So if you're thinking of Eltham and Eltham College as just being stuffy and reactionary, I've misled you. They certainly had that element in abundance, but they also contained a small degree of old-fashioned working-class radicalism which I suppose had roots going back to the eighteenth-century peasant movements. Did you ever read Mark Rutherford's *The Revolution in Tanner's Lane*? Very much that sort of milieu.

– So Michael's political enthusiasm might not have been as *outré* then as it now sounds. Of course you could have gone into many a house in Beechill Road and found nothing in the way of improving literature other than a *Hymns A & M*, a *Bradshaw's* railway guide and a *Whitaker's Almanack*. But plenty of other houses had considerable fireside libraries which often included those yellow-jacketed books Gollancz published with the serious-minded autodidact in mind, or Penguin Specials by people like the Duchess of Atholl. *Women and Politics* was one of hers, I remember. So were *Conscription of a People* and *Main Facts of the Indian Problem*. Heavens, how the titles come back! When I was under Michael's spell I devoured them and dozens like them. *Germany puts the Clock Back, Mussolini's Roman Empire* . . . Funny how one so easily recalls such long-ago books when you would think they'd have been almost immediately swamped by the very events they were warning us about. But there they were, part of my coming-of-age and as much of their period as Captain W. E. Johns who, though scarcely a socialist, was busily campaigning for re-arma-ment with premonitions every bit as dire as theirs. They were restless times both politically and intellectually and all those socialist ideas unquestionably contributed to Churchill's post-war defeat and Attlee's Labour government in the next decade.

– The thing about Michael at school was that he was dashing and dangerous. Typically, boys like that were steered on to the games field to become captains of rugger and go on to play for their teaching hospitals if they were medical students. We had a lot of eventual medics at Eltham. Michael was neither so conventional nor amenable. In fact he was downright intractable, which was most of his attraction for me. He used to mock his teachers as fossils. He had a running battle with a geography master who was a real old imperialist. I suppose even in the thirties it was possible still to believe in the Empire if you had been born in the last century, and it must have been made all the easier if your job involved teaching boys born overseas from a map of the world where so much was coloured pink. Michael, of course, supported nationalist leaders like Gandhi. Being younger I was unfortunately never in the same class so I can't give an eyewitness account of the morning he reduced one of the teachers to tears: of rage, of helplessness, presumably. But it was around the school like lightning and Michael was flung out. Or rather, his guardian was asked to remove him; his parents were Bible-thumping in Tanganyika Territory. I saw him once or twice afterwards at political meetings but he had already wrought his magical damage in me and I think I no longer needed him. Once he had gone, everything at school slumped back into dreary normality. It was as if the communal scapegoat, carefully heaped with all sorts of dirty linen and driven forth into the wilderness, had left the place restored to a state of prelapsarian grace. Absolute balls, of course, but I expect ninety-eight per cent of the boys readily agreed that he had just been a troublemaker. I was among the two per cent who admired his having made trouble by showing that the world could be described in versions other than the received one.

After Michael left the school I was thought to have inherited something of his rebellious mantle and that was why my father was so anxious to get me off to Suez where life was stern and earnest and uncontaminated by polemic. Under Michael's influence I used to make loud lefty political noises, especially at home, because I knew it irritated my father. Dad promptly got his own back by arranging to send me out of harm's way for a short, sharp shock. He thought a few months of life in the raw would bring me to my senses and convince me how much there was to be gained by settling down to study for a serious profession in England. Poor man, he misunderstood me completely, not least by taking my adolescent polemics seriously. I might have sounded in public like a junior Red but I was not about to lay my life down for the proletariat. I certainly had no intention of going anywhere near Spain. I suppose you could say that was my first public role as an impostor. –

Not a firebrand, then, this urbane man's adolescent self, but a disciple, a seducee. Something is not quite right, there are still gaps to be filled. My question about sex *had* been vulgar, of course: a blundering attempt to jolt him into confession. It was crass, and I now blushed for his brief reptilian glare. This was a beady old sophisticate who could well afford to appear stuffy if he chose. Still, all that being said, the fact is that nobody dreams of a private landscape, whether jungled or ideological, without something erotic hovering nearby, bouncing ominously in the thermals. Let it go for the moment. Sooner or later it will alight as it always does: that persistent scavenger of ideals that pecks out visionaries' eyes and tears away their flesh to expose the bone.

Meanwhile the *Orontes* has picked up a pilot in Port Said, has passed through the Canal to Ismailiya, down through the Bitter Lakes and the lagoons of Old Suez to Port Taufiq where she docks. Across a stretch of cluttered water Suez town is a jumble of white and ochre buildings seen as through a lattice, so dense are the masts and rigging of intervening vessels. From over the water drift blares and cries and the mechanical howling of cranes, while the air smells of rotten water, ammonia and dried leather mixed in with something dark and spicy. Port Taufiq is clearly more modern than Suez town across the harbour to which it is connected by a causeway with a railway, so it is presumably the industrial suburb created by the Canal. Several black pyramids of coal dominate it, coal Jayjay cannot yet identify as Yorks washed steam mix. Yet anyone approaching Suez port from the south might be more impressed by the dominance of oil, since clusters of immense petroleum tanks are what first take the eye. On that seaward side of the *Orontes*' bows a bay opens out with a red lighthouse standing on an islet in the middle. To either side the roads are dotted with moored shipping. Of this a black tramp steamer, a mile or two off at most, must represent the outer limit of the port's wiry activities. On the right are the red cliffs of Gebel Ataqa, beyond which the Gulf opens out between dwindling grey-blue hills to a landscape empty as far as the eye can reach. The ultramarine water vanishes into a yellow haze of airborne sand somewhere beyond the distant point of Ras el Adabiya. Nothing breaks its glittering monotony except the white sails of a couple of *feluccas*. There is a sense of being at the twentieth century's outermost fringe: that immediately past the harbour's sullen rainbows of floating oil lie the Gulf's aquamarine waters and a Biblical world of Sinai and camels and nomads' tents.

The eighteen-year-old from Eltham, the first-time traveller, worries that his trunk will disappear among the brown press of porters and stevedores elbowing and burrowing and shouting their way up through the disembarking passengers, or else that it might be left in the hold and carried on to Ceylon. But then he is seized with excitement, by the vibrant novelty of the heat and smells and vertical light, by the mysterious allure of that sand-coloured horizon. Pale-faced, he at last has a foothold in that world of spices he once evoked from tantalising scents in a warehouse. Cool, grey, faraway London. He feels a sudden affection for this ship as a link with home, his magic carpet, its very substance transfigured into salty paintwork too hot to touch, her crew now wearing tropical gear. When he disembarks he will be alone and adrift. His eyes fill with tears of excitement and the thrill of endless possibility makes his stomach tingle. A more fearful part of him urges that it is still not too late to remain safely aboard, see Colombo, catch a home-bound sister ship and within a matter of weeks watch the gloomy gantries of Tilbury once again harden out of estuarine mist.

He is met by Richards, a close-barbered youngster with a small moustache, veteran airs and tanned extremities, as revealed when the linen sleeve rides up with his proffered hand to expose a forearm nearly as pale as Jayjay's own. A perfunctory flash of white teeth somewhere beneath the shadow of his hat.

'A & G sent me,' he allows through the moustache, as though in a private rage that he of all people should have been detailed to meet a junior clerk off one of the company's liners. He has a slight Birmingham accent. 'Good trip, no doubt. She's quite a comfortable old tub,' and raises a seasoned traveller's eyebrow at the black wall of the ship's side.

'Hardly old. Nineteen twenty-nine.'

This is not deferentially said, and it is obvious from this moment that these two strangers are not about to embark on one of those deathless friendships.

'You're in the Caramanli,' says Richards shortly. 'If you don't like it you can no doubt transfer to the Bachet or the Bel-Air. At your expense, of course. Hardly worth it since they're all much of a muchness but some people like to give themselves airs. You'll get your own accommodation in the Anglo-Egyptian Bank building after three months if you stay the course. Juniors come and go. They get homesick' – a contemptuous flash – 'or just plain sick, so we've found it's pointless putting them into Company digs right away.'

Richards has already commandeered a taxi to take them over to Suez. As its dented radiator noses through the dockside throngs a not very crestfallen Jayjay tries to make amends.

'How long have you been here?'

'Three years this April.'

'Heavens, I should think you must be about ready to move on,' says Jayjay ingenuously, looking happily around him. 'It surely can't do much for a chap's career to be stuck in a place like this for any length of time.'

'Port Taufiq,' says Richards in a heavy I'll-have-you-know tone and leaning back cautiously in the appalling Chevrolet, 'is an extremely important posting, as you will shortly discover. In fact, it's pretty damned odd that you don't already know, or mightn't have guessed if you'd bothered to give it a bit of thought. Only practically every ship that passes through the Canal coals up here, that's all.' An immense pair of camel buttocks fills the glassless frame of the car's windscreen. A stick thwacks heavily into them, producing no discernible effect other than a puff of dust.

'But what about Aden? And anyway, I thought coal was a thing of the past. Surely it's all oil-burners nowadays, like the *Orontes*?' Another thwack.

'Look, Jebb, I'll tell you frankly and it's for your own good. It would be a big mistake to make a poor start here. We're a small community and I don't mind telling you we set quite a store by first impressions.' The camel at last moves aside, the taxi churns down a street pocked with khaki puddles of donkey stale and stops. 'Quite a store' (as he pays the driver with a careful disbursement of piastres and milliemes and signals imperiously to a listless *boab* to come and unstrap Jayjay's trunk from the grid at the back). 'You'll find we're pretty easy-going here but we're not much for cockiness, if you get my drift.'

The Caramanli is at rest on the border between lodging-house and hotel, neither rising nor sinking. Gentility is served by a man in a fez asleep behind a concierge's desk, an ormolu clock without hands, two fake Directoire chairs and a copper vase containing a single dusty ostrich feather. Richards goes into full old-hand mode.

'Misa'l<u>ch</u>ir, ya rais. Fih hagze 'alasanu,' indicating Jayjay.

'Good afternoon to you too, good sir,' replies the elderly Turk in English, stretching politely and blinking. 'The gentleman's name, if you please? Was the reservation made in person or by the telephone?'

'I daresay you can manage to find your room without my help,' says Richards to Jayjay when this farce has run its course and the *boab* again shoulders the trunk with a loud sigh and begins the Sisyphean trudge up a flight of marble stairs that promise to revert to plain cement as soon as they are out of sight past the first turn. 'We start work at seven in the morning, which does *not* mean ten past. Everyone knows where the shipping offices are. Watch out for pickpockets. Try not to catch the clap before tomorrow.'

He strides out and is instantly swallowed in the blare of light beyond the Caramanli's chipped portals.

'Ignore him, I should,' an amused voice says at Jayjay's elbow. 'Richards is a complete twerp, I'm afraid. Nothing to be done about it, although I gather there was once a plan to black his bollocks and sell him to the Arabians as a slave. One deduces from the steamer trunk and the home counties tan that you've just arrived? Oh, sorry, my name's Milo.'

'Jerningham Jebb, but most people call me Jayjay.' This Milo was a small, raffish-looking fellow in his late twenties with a frozen eye. 'Are you with the Company, too?'

'Which company would that be?'

'Oh, well, Anderson & Green. The Orient Line, you know.'

'Certainly not. What a dreadful thought. Don't tell me you work for them?'

'That's what I came to Suez for. Why, what's wrong with them?'

'Nothing, I shouldn't think. Not *qua* company. But the work'll get you down. Within a month you'll start to like Richards. Within a year you'll have *become* Richards.'

'No fear!'

'On the contrary, it's a dead cert. Still, there are plenty of other fates on offer here, though none as bad. Do you drink?'

'Not that often,' said Jayjay guardedly, thinking of a naughty glass of sweet sherry at Christmas and a couple of beers Michael had once bought him which he had much disliked.

'I should keep it that way. It doesn't agree with this climate, believe me. You'll shortly be running into a cove named Hammond at your office. Take note of same. Are you a ladies' man?'

'Well, er . . .'

'Put it this way: would you *like* to be a ladies' man? Sorry, none of my business and all that. Over the mark. I was only going to suggest you stick to Europeans, not that that's much guarantee these days. There isn't a taste Suez doesn't cater for, and what with boredom and no longer being under Aunt Edna's eye one can go awfully wild for a week and then spend the next thirty years watching bits drop off the old bod. Blighted prospects and so forth. Forgive the sermon, just thought I'd mention it. And now the good wishes, the extended hand of friendship and the adieu. I've no doubt we shall bump into one another from time to time.

One does in this place.' And with that Milo also vanished into the glare of late afternoon.

As Milo had predicted the work turned out to be grim indeed. It soon dawned on Jayjay that an exotic location was inadequate disguise for a job he would not for a moment have contemplated doing in London, not even at the very edge of penury. It was only on reflection that he realised it was essentially the same sort of work his father had been doing uncomplainingly for almost the last twenty years. He shared a large office with six Egyptian clerks and a fat boy named Simpkins from Tottenham whose stomach was in a state of constant rebellion even as his mind dwelt wistfully on plates of his mother's toad-in-the-hole which, he asserted, would have had him right in a jiffy. Since to his dismay Jayjay found himself also sharing rooms with Simpkins in the Caramanli there seemed no refuge from his compatriot's intestinal tract. In the clerks' pool three fly-specked fans turned listlessly on stalks up in the high ceiling. Below them, none the cooler, Anderson & Green's junior employees sat at desks tallying ledgers. In the maritime world 'coaling', as Jayjay had perfectly well known on first meeting Richards, was an old-fashioned term that had long since been extended to include fuel oil. These days it was interchangeable with 'bunkering'. He now found he was assigned duties that related exclusively to oil. He was supposed to enter the incoming supplies from the Anglo-Iranian oilfields at Abadan and tally those figures with the reserve tonnages held in Port Taufiq's storage tanks as recorded by the tankmaster down at the terminal. Or something of the kind. After a year of this, and in the absence of any cock-ups on his part, he might with luck be allowed to graduate upstairs to an office with a single fan to do some invoicing. He found it was of no comfort to reflect that Rimbaud had once worked as a bookkeeper for a coffee and leather-goods merchant in Djibouti, some hundreds of miles away down at the other end of the Red Sea.

Within a week Jayjay had uncovered the great conspiracy of office work and found that it was usually possible to clear a day's worth in well under an hour, given average intelligence and an urgent wish to get it out of the way. An employee's skill therefore lay in dissembling in the most convincing manner so as always to appear hard at work when some shirtsleeved senior looked in. In this case the senior was the man Hammond whom Milo had mentioned. Having never encountered a hard-core alcoholic before, Jayjay took a while to match this amiable man's appearance and behaviour with the gossip that surrounded him. According to office wisdom 'Pusser' Hammond was steadily and unregretfully drinking himself to death with bottles of whisky slipped him by the grateful pursers of passing liners in return for waiving certain paperwork and formalities. An ex-ship's purser himself, Hammond was at ease with his life in the manner of men who have found a level that feels both acceptable and predestined, leaving them without the least ambition to better it in any way. He had been in Suez since the end of the Great War and in due course fully expected to wind up in a corner of the Christian cemetery. The prospect bothered him not one jot. Indeed, it amused him to think of the baking soil slowly leaching the last molecules of Johnny Walker from his marrow-bones. In the meantime he was content to live with a Greek lady and four hairy children in a flat above the greengrocer's shop her family owned. At the grandparents' insistence the children were brought up to be Orthodox. The girls were demure and stayed at home practically in purdah; the boys were dark and serious and could be seen trotting daily to the English school, satchelled and well combed. None of them in the least resembled Hammond physically. In due course Jayjay learned that Hammond never quarrelled, never raised his voice and seldom neglected his scant duties whether in the home or at work. He was relaxed and vaguely effectual in a land scarcely noted for brisk efficiency, and in this town his comparative honesty in financial matters made him positively outstanding.

It was 'Pusser' Hammond who enabled Jayjay to slip away from the office on strictly unnecessary errands to the port or the terminal. 'Figures in books one thing, bottoms on water quite another,' he would observe. Jayjay would even volunteer to act as a messenger, by this menial expedient contriving to visit the yellow-painted Egyptian Health Office building in the little bay by the entrance to the Canal as well as assorted government and private offices in Rue Colmar, Suez's main commercial street. Before long he had acquired a grasp of the town's geography as well as a small degree of street wisdom. This amounted to a bare degree of familiarity with typical fares and prices, together with a smattering of pidgin Arabic; yet it was already more than his queasy roommate Simpkins had managed in almost a year.

Was Jayjay homesick? Not perhaps in the usual sense of a constant awareness of being in the wrong place, of that interior hollowing which renders an entire landscape no more than a blank sheet on which are projected the fond pinings of the inner eye. But a feeling of missing familiar things would sometimes break through without warning while he was doing something that required no thought, such as cleaning his teeth in the Caramanli's cavernous bathroom, a place of cracked tiles, ornate taps lacking handles and dark corners full of the sweetish breath of cockroaches. Suddenly this no longer felt like a rewarding adventure. He would long for the sound of trams on Well Hall Road, for the smell of Eltham in a winter's dusk. How he yearned just for a moment to swap Suez's hot reek of donkey urine and fuel oil for the cool incense of smoky fires being lit in suburban grates! To exchange the bedlam beyond the Caramanli's windows for the musical tinkle of pine kindling being laid in a hearth; to trade the sky's desert glare for the blossoming glow behind a sheet of newspaper held taut across a fireplace to make it draw! It was the vividness of the details that made them poignant: being able to summon the exact smell of hot newsprint as the fire behind it began to scorch the paper, knowing to an instant the right moment to take it away before it burst into flames between one's hands, hearing the paper crackle with dryness as it was refolded. Thus could one sit on a seatless lavatory in Suez and meticulously perform an unrelated task two thousand miles away. It was painful and peculiar. Maybe this was not the massive ache Saki's Unbearable Bassington had felt as he watched children romp at sunset on an African hillside, but for a moment Jayjay thought he knew how exile might feel. He wondered if it would have been the same if instead of being a day-boy at Eltham College he had been a boarder, accustomed to long separations from home. And he marvelled that this was what some of his overseas friends must have been feeling, cut off from their families for years at a time, even though, because they were Britons in England, one had never thought that they might be homesick. But he soon discovered that being truly homesick only lasts as long as there is nothing better to be. Being interested and diverted works wonders. There was too much too new about Suez for him to feel seriously bereft.

One morning Jayjay accompanies Hammond to the docks to meet the *Otranto*, which has just arrived from England on the Australia run. 'Pusser's' good-natured equanimity (or drunken indifference) has maybe responded to his newest apprentice's evident boredom with the office. They take a gharry, sitting up beneath a decrepit hood like a patched bellows. The horse's hide is shiny black leather stretched over protruding croup bones. Only when they have crossed the harbour and are in Port Taufiq does the traffic – always anarchic – become immovable, with barrows and hand-carts filling the spaces between higgledy-piggledy vehicles. The driver's whip cracks over his nag's bones more out of ritual than to effect progress. It is the same gesture that makes the drivers of motor vehicles lean on their klaxons: something one does when one is stationary. It is directed at nobody, a brainless declaration of one's immovable presence. Quite unbidden there comes into Jayjay's mind a habit of his father's which he has always disliked without knowing why, a habit shared by several of his schoolfriends' fathers. This is to stand with his back to a fireplace with his hands in his trouser pockets, loudly jingling his small change and slightly rocking back and forth on his heels as he does so.

'Figures in books one thing, bottoms on water quite another,' Hammond is saying. He is clearly oblivious to the surrounding chaos as he is to the omnipresent flies that cluster on lips and around eyes. He digs in a pocket and hands Jayjay an Orient Line badge to wear on the lapel of his lightweight cotton jacket. 'Your usual Port pass won't let you aboard.' A lorry so overloaded with some kind of fodder that it looks like a haystack has broken down. As they grind slowly past the knot of gesticulating men Jayjay sees that a rear wheel has collapsed. The vehicle is so antique the wheel's spokes are wood. Eventually they bounce over the sour mat of compacted vegetation that lies at the Port's entrance.

It is only a six-hour layover for the *Otranto* and few ongoing passengers without brief and urgent business in Suez have troubled to disembark. Jayjay assumes the stewards have already gone around as they had on the *Orontes*, telling all who would listen that Suez was a 'hell-hole' and recounting with relish stories of previous voyages when unwary passengers or greenhorn crewmen went ashore only to be robbed blind or found unconscious with their pockets cut out. 'The British are here in Egypt to run the Canal for the Egyptians (like clockwork of course) but the Egyptians are supposed to run everything else and as you'd expect it's a corrupt shambles. If you get robbed don't blame me, and don't go near a policeman is my advice. They're the worst of the lot. I could tell you a few tales, make your hair curl . . .' (A deck-hand on the *Orontes* had been obligingly graphic.) Now, seeing a British liner from the perspective of a denizen of the port everyone aboard has been warned against, Jayjay is aware of its defensive condition. The single, canvas-sided gangway deployed is surrounded at both ends by junior officers in white duck uniforms keeping a wary eye on all comings and goings. Those who were disembarking have long since done so. Now the ship lies, taking on various provisions as well as fifteen hundred tons of fuel oil, moored to the dockside as though with wary reluctance. Jayjay notices that the immense hawsers fore and aft all wear large metal cones like megaphones to prevent rats, mice and all manner of other vermin from invading the ship.

After greetings and handshakings at the top of the gangway 'Pusser' goes off to pay his respects to the Captain and no doubt enjoy convivial tots in the cabins of various officers and old friends. 'Make yourself known to the Chief,' he says in parting. 'He'll show you bunkering from his end.' So Jayjay wanders aft, being directed down through ever less carpeted and hotter regions, from stairs to companion-ladders, from doors to water-tight hatches dogged open with immense wing-nuts, from passageways to perforated metal catwalks. At last he gazes down into a sweltering cavern in which the liner's twin turbines bulk three storeys high. In a soundproof booth at one end of the engine room he finds the Chief Engineer watching dials and introduces himself. Seeing that Jayjay is new to all this the Chief explains the finer points of bunkering, most of which seem to concern distrib-uting the fuel between various tanks. 'The way she lies to this pier, bowsering's to starboard so it's all coming into 5 and 6.' He points to the quivering needles of two dials. 'But fifteen hundred ton would trim us by the stern, see, and we can't have that. Our paying guests would be complaining the bleeding water in the swimming-pool isn't level. Apart from matters of draught here in port. She draws enough as it is. So we pump some of it forrard to 4 here' – an oil-black fingernail prods at a diagram – 'and on up to 2 here . . .'

The explanations make Jayjay drowsy, or else it is the heat in the engine room combined with the heavy reek of oil and the noise. Although the main engines are shut down there are several lesser motors clattering away for the various generators supplying the ship's electricity, keeping fans churning the stifling air in dark-ened cabins and maintaining subzero temperatures in the walk-in meat lockers and food refrigerators. The Chief's control booth may be comparatively soundproof but for someone unused to it the level of noise is trying. It dawns on Jayjay that although he is standing in the bowels of a liner with Port Taufiq's rancid waters less than fifteen feet below his shoe soles he might as well be in a Birmingham factory for all the nautical romance. As soon as he can he leaves the Chief to his dial-gazing and blunders back up in the direction of those carpeted zones where occasional portholes give glimpses of daylight.

Somewhere along the way he becomes aware of being followed and glimpses a red-haired figure darting ever closer. Mildly alarmed but curious he waits for the man to come up to him in an otherwise empty passageway.

'Milo?' says the stranger softly, glancing again over his shoulder.

'I'm afraid not,' says Jayjay, and then without a thought adds, 'But of course I know who you mean. Chap with the rum eye.'

'He sent you instead?'

'Exactly.' (To this day Jayjay remembers using this word, recognising that it sealed his new career as an impostor. What made him say it he cannot tell. It was an impulse faster than thought, accompanied by an exciting sensation of boats being burned, of years of principled raising being reneged on in a jiffy. The only token remnant of having been brought up to tell the truth was in finding it easier to say 'exactly' rather than the more outright version of the same lie, 'yes').

'Come 'ere then, quick.'

The stranger, whom Jayjay was to discover was a Second Mate, leads the way to a cramped and smelly locker without a porthole. A 40-watt bulb reveals clothing lying in dark puddles on the floor. To Jayjay's surprise the man swiftly treads off his own shoes, gropes inside them and comes out with a pair of cork insoles which he thrusts towards his startled visitor.

'That'll be twenty quid,' he says. 'You tell Milo he'll get the usual after the Colombo leg.'

'Twenty quid?' exclaims Jayjay, astounded. 'For . . . for *those*, you mean? You don't imagine I've got twenty quid?'

Very alert, the man peers at him for a moment in the gloom.

'You bastard,' he says bitterly. 'He never sent you, did he? Well, you bloody get out of here. And you can bet that by the time you've told your guv'nor and they've sent the uniforms down they'll have had a wasted journey. These will have disappeared.' He makes a gesture both insolent and menacing in Jayjay's face with the insoles. 'And you can tell them not to bother trying it on again with me.'

'I don't know what you're talking about,' says Jayjay truthfully and quickly leaves. Regaining the lower deck and mid-morning's searing light he leans for a while over the port rail trying to make sense of what has happened. His heart is beating faster than the climb justifies. Gradually he becomes aware of some crude bum-boats of bleached wood bobbing at the foot of the forty-foot cliff that is the *Otranto*'s side. Barefoot traders in tattered robes balance expertly as they shout up to a group of male passengers whom Jayjay instantly recognises as steerage class. One of them, a man in a white panama with a jauntily lurid hatband, is lowering a tiny wicker basket on a string. When it reaches the boats several brown arms stretch up simultaneously towards it before one grabs hold and reaches inside. Having made sure it contains what he expected, the Arab substitutes what looks like a white envelope which is duly hauled up. The knot of men crowd around the panama before some remarks and laughter can be heard. Again the basket descends.

For the umpteenth time since leaving England Jayjay has the sensation of having briefly intersected with an utterly different world, one he knows nothing about and which is obviously not entirely above board. At the same time he wants very much to know what it is and how it works, to learn whether it can offer him advantage or pleasure. Despite the shade of the promenade deck immediately overhead the sun is scalding, and he is young, and an expectant seagull glides past only feet away with its beady head cocked in his direction and an evilly knowing look in its eye. It was no doubt born here and is a lot more clued up about the world than Jayjay. He turns as though his mind were made up, although in fact it is still in turmoil over a pair of cork insoles. Twenty *pounds*? Five weeks' salary?

On the return drive to Anderson & Green's flyblown office he is careful not to hand back the Orient Line lapel badge that Hammond lent him. The 'Pusser', now well lubricated by ship-board hospitality, has obviously clean forgotten about it.

6

For some time my uneasiness over this project of Jayjay's biography had been growing. At out first meeting he had clearly said he would pay me to write the book – I seemed to recall something about 'sweeteners', which I took to imply regularity of payment if not great largesse. The uneasiness was partly self-recrimination for my own unprofessional behaviour. I was after all a full-time writer with an agent, a publisher and an editor. I already had a commission to write the account of a deep-sea treasure hunt in mid-Atlantic from which I had not long returned. Meanwhile, a contract was being drawn up in London for a book about Southeast Asian politics which would probably jell around the issue of dictatorships. In theory the next two or three years were already spoken for.

A further uncertainty could be summed up as an insistent *Why me?* Why had Jayjay singled me out to write his story? The reasons he had given were plausible enough, yet my doubts persisted. He claimed that he had read my books, had decided that I was 'on the same wavelength' as him and could give a sympathetic account. When I asked him which particular book he was thinking of he singled out the stuff I had already written about Southeast Asia. This surprised me but he threw little light on it other than to say that he liked the books' exotic aspects and my refusal to condemn. According to him I had a quite un-British approach in that I did not see things exclusively from the perspective of my own culture and avoided making moral judgements about behaviour that would normally have been roundly denounced. From what he said it was obvious he knew the books well and this was not just some blarney he had thought up on the spur of the moment. I never went further into this since I am residually British enough to be embarrassed at having to talk about my own work. I also distrust praise.

Sometimes when I thought about Jayjay's having chosen me I told myself it was surely no mystery. Sheer convenience explained everything. I lived nearby and was a professional writer of the correct nationality, age and background. Why look any further for reasons? He was getting older, probably a little lonely and, no matter how well acclimatised to life in Italy, felt the need for some belated contact with his own cradle culture. I didn't think this project of his was a mere pretext for company, exactly, but I did suspect this factor played a part. Well, all right, provided his story was worth it. Yet at other times I found even this commonsensical theory unsatisfactory. What really had he seen in those books of mine he claimed to have liked? No piffle about fine style and adroit characterisation; what he chose to mention was a refusal to condemn. For the first time I began to wonder if there were not some disreputable secret in Jayjay's life for which he was slowly softening me up, all the while cautiously testing me for signs of impending disapproval.

In any case none of this changed the immediate necessity to put our relationship on a more professional footing, especially as regards money. I had plenty of other work to do at present and more than enough calls on my remaining time not to be able insouciantly to write off entire mornings down at Il Ghibli. My 'private life' (as theatrical folk artlessly call a *vita sexualis* they make sure is public gossip from Hampstead to Hollywood) was its usual undemonstrative self, running at a gentle tick-over. From time to time I would drive a visitor back down to Castiglion Fiorentino station and change the sheets with that mixture of relief and regret which is the hallmark of the failed hermit. 'Very *young*,' I would tell myself reprovingly for a day or two afterwards as though I knew I ought to have outgrown the juvenile and instead be deriving deep satisfaction from the marriage of true minds. Mainly, though, their going enabled me to get back to those pressing hillside tasks that never end: keeping the feedpipe from the spring in the forest free of silt, laying in logs for the winter, adjusting the Toyota's clutch (thanks be to Haynes' manuals!), extending the irrigation system to include the baby apricot trees. Or else the seasonal pleasures like collecting new chestnuts, making sloe gin and picking wild rosehips for the jelly that tastes to me of childhood, an example of food for free much promoted during the war as being rich in vitamin C at a time when oranges and lemons were virtually unobtainable. And at all seasons there were the bees to consider.

It is a half-truth that, except at certain critical moments, bees can pretty much be left to their own devices for most of the year. The other half of the truth is that they need a constant eye kept on their welfare and for signs of disease. An affectionate ear, too, should regularly be pressed against a hive. Much can be deduced from the sound made by an industrious community of forty thousand individuals who together constitute five solid kilos of insect life. One is alert for the raised, agitated note that means they are uneasy about something potentially disastrous such as the failure or even complete absence of their queen. Like any social animal, bees need order and hierarchy before they can function properly. In fact anything approaching democracy makes them radically unhappy and their society falls apart. Somehow the older I get the less this surprises me but let's not pursue *that*. Jejune philosophising aside, there are always frames to be re-wired, wax to be recovered and similar maintenance tasks one put off doing last year.

So as I say, at the moment when Jayjay had insinuated himself so charmingly into my life I lacked neither work nor play. And from the start, despite his blithe hint of remuneration and my own supposed professionalism, our precise relationship remained unclear. I was definitely intrigued by him, there was no question of that. I did not seriously begrudge a single minute spent in his company. But as time went by I increasingly found myself driving back up the track saying, 'Yes, but what am I actually *doing*? Is this old gentleman a new acquaintance, a future friend or a job of work? These regular visits to his house, all this attentive note-taking: are they a disguised act of charity or part of a business deal?' I resolved to have it out with him. By now I was assuming from impressions I had already formed that he was more likely to be a canny rogue about money than one of those people who are genuinely pained at the mention of anything financial. Besides, I was beginning to feel guilty about keeping the whole thing from my agent. He also stood to benefit from this deal, assuming it *was* a deal. Well before it ever reached the stage of a typescript in search of a publisher both he and my editor would have to know.

It was typical of Jayjay to have out-thought me. I realised at once that I should have known he would. The very morning I rang Il Ghibli's bell and Marcella (who happened to be dusting by the front door) let me in, he greeted me by handing me an envelope with its flap discreetly tucked in.

'Long overdue, James,' he said apologetically. 'I see from my records that this will be your ninth visit and some of our sessions have dragged on for as much as six hours. Dragged on for you, I mean. For someone in his anecdotage I can assure you the time has passed in a flash. But it's eating into your life. You will find in there a thousand pounds. Well, it's rather to the north of three million *lire* and you must tell me if you prefer to be paid in Guatemalan quetzals or something to suit your no doubt arcane and shrewd offshore banking habits.'

So nonplussed was I by misplaced surprise and chastened that the man I'd thought of as an old rogue had in fact been keeping scrupulous accounts, I came over all British and heard myself blurting things like 'Heavens, Jayjay, I'd completely forgotten . . . Surely far too much . . .?' and then (even more British), 'Well, if you're *quite* sure?'

'We both fell into the trap our countrymen often fall into. But nice chaps and well brought up as we both are, we are also too old to get tangled up over money. I said I would make it worth your while to hear about my life, and I know you heard me say it. Quite simple. We now have to discuss whether a thousand pounds is enough for what you've already undergone.'

So we did indeed thrash the whole thing out. To relate the details would be wearisome as well as compromising from the taxation point of view. The important thing for me was that my trust and liking for the old boy went up several significant notches. Matters involving cash are very revealing of character, of course, which is exactly why we surround them with such comedies of manners. People like Jayjay who, unprompted, acknowledge debts and pay on the spot lead one instinctively to believe they will conduct their other affairs in a similarly principled fashion. We expand towards them, we feel easy and confident. What a contrast with others we have known and liked, often for years, who one day do something that can no longer be overlooked and we find ourselves totting up (and how readily the list comes to mind!) the previous occasions when they have reached for their wallets just too late in a restaurant, or said once too often that oh dear, they can't pay you back right now because they seem to have nothing smaller on them than this five-hundred-thousand note. *Tight* (one hears oneself saying bitterly, feeling diminished by so trivial a resentment). Just plain goddamn *tight*.

Jayjay and I flourished under our new dispensation so that I felt less like a salaried amanuensis and more like a paid companion. To my surprise I found his story did not interfere with my

other writing commitments. It seemed to inhabit a too well
defined world of its own. Our sessions were often at irregular
intervals. For several weeks at a stretch I stayed on my hillside,
concentrating on my notes of recent experiences in the Atlantic.
These had been scribbled on the deck of a ship towing sonar
scanning equipment and in the cramped capsule of a Russian
submersible as it groped its way five kilometres down in a light-
less universe of dunes and pillow lava. Concurrently, I was
reading tendentious and often barely literate journalists' prose
about Asian dictators. When I could no longer bear it I went
down to see Jayjay for the sheer relief of urbane conversation and
a world apart. The candid warmth of his welcome assuaged any
worries that I might not have been fulfilling my part in our
unwritten bargain. Within half an hour I was back once more in
the fossil sunlight of pre-war Suez.

– How naïve I was! – Jayjay reflected, safely on the far side of sixty
years. – I could have done you a chunk of *A Shropshire Lad* into
passable Latin verse, or a *Times* leader into French, or even at a
pinch have got the valencies right for a simple chemical reaction.
I could have told you about the Repeal of the Corn Laws and the
chief exports of Glasgow. I even had a hazy idea where one might
find silly mid-off on a cricket field. But I couldn't recognise good
Greek hashish when it was waved under my nose. You see at once
the drawbacks of a public-school education? No 'street smarts', as
the Americans call it.
  – Luckily I had Milo to introduce me to Suez. He really was
quite disreputable. He'd been thrown out of Haileybury for
screwing his housemaster's wife, got turned down by the Army on
account of his eye, and sort of drifted. By the time I met him he'd
got a finger in half the rackets in Suez. We'd met in the hall of the
Caramanli on that first afternoon because he had a studio upstairs.
The hotel was never able to fill the top floor so Milo had per-
suaded the manager to rent him a couple of rooms up there, one
of which he'd turned into a dark room. He was doing a lot of

printing for the dirty picture trade. As predicted, we kept on bumping into one another. By the time I knew my job was a washout Milo came as a life-saver. He was breezy, scurrilous and kind. He proved to be as much an antidote to my virtuous upbringing as Michael had been at school, while nobody ever mistook Milo for a socialist. He was soon introducing me to various cafés and dives in the non-European quarters of town. Endless mint tea and sweet sludgy coffee. Everyone watching everyone else over the mouthpiece of a hubble-bubble. He knew fat men in fezzes and characters who looked like brigands you'd expect to see roaring down a Turkish mountainside, their chests crossed with bandoliers and waving long muzzle-loaders. For all that he was so British in obvious ways he somehow managed to blend in with these people. He looked completely unlike them, of course, but not out of place all the same. It took me a while to twig that some of them were his bosses, in the sense that it was they who were actually running the rackets. He was just scratching a living from the edges of pornography, drugs, prostitution and the black market. The brigand types turned out to be Greeks rather than Turks. It was the Greeks who ran Suez in those days although we British imagined we did. The Brits ran the Canal but it was the Greeks who worked out how to carve the fat off it.

– One night Milo introduced me to a tough old Arab with only half a foot who had sailed for years with Henry de Monfreid. De Monfreid? He was an astonishing French adventurer with an American father who couldn't bear bourgeois life in Paris at the turn of the century and threw it all up to become a pirate in the Red Sea. That would have been in about 1910. He went to Djibouti and actually worked for the same merchant who had employed Rimbaud back in the eighteen-eighties. He soon discovered that the world's biggest market for hashish was Egypt because it had recently been made illegal. In those days it came mainly from Greece, where it was a major export. De Monfreid devised a brilliant new smuggling route. He would buy the hash from villagers up in the Greek mountains, take it down to the port at Piraeus, load it as an innocent cargo on a steamer heading down through the Canal to the Indian Ocean, and offload it in Djibouti. Then he would smuggle it back up to Suez in a sailing craft of his own, a crude wooden *boutre* indistinguishable from a thousand other native vessels. Hugely risky. Bear in mind that this was during the First World War. Egypt and the Red Sea were even more than usually a hotbed of spies and informers living off the conflicting political designs of the great powers who intersected in the region. The British had the Canal; Lawrence of Arabia was in military intelligence and just about to get into gear to help the Arabs get rid of the Turks; the Ottoman Empire was fighting a rearguard action; the Germans were there; the French were there; the Italians were there. Plus the usual mixture of rogues, riff-raff and freebooters like de Monfreid himself, each looking for something to steal or someone to shop. It was an incredibly dangerous area and he had to run the gauntlet in his sailing boat all the way up the Red Sea and through the Gulf of Suez. The first time around he didn't even have a reliable contact in Suez whom he could trust. He eventually got rid of the stuff to Greeks with family links to the growers he'd bought it from, and for nothing like its true value. By the time I arrived in Suez de Monfreid had retired or gone back to France or maybe he was pearl-diving down in Djibouti. But there were still plenty of people in Suez who had known him and there were even a few left like this old Arab Milo introduced me to who had actually sailed with him. I think they had run guns together.

– By that time hash was heavily outlawed and the drugs trade which had once made Egypt famous had been much stamped on by Thomas Russell. Known as Russell Pasha, he was in charge of the Egyptian police until he retired after the Second World War. Do you know any Egyptian history? In de Monfreid's day Russell's predecessor, Harvey Pasha, had tried to do something about both drugs and prostitution. But not only was he an ass, he was hamstrung by laws called the Capitulations. These were a hangover from Ottoman days and had never been repealed. Effectively what they meant was that no foreigner in Egypt was subject to Egyptian taxes or law courts. Virtually every non-Egyptian in the country had a kind of diplomatic immunity. The year I arrived in Suez Capitulations were finally abolished, and although we foreigners were still immensely privileged we could no longer be quite so blithely lawless as in the past, especially with a man like Russell Pasha in charge of the police. So if the dangers of hash smuggling were increasing even as I landed in Suez, so were the rewards.

– And that was what the Second Mate of the *Otranto* was doing. I soon found out they'd come by a slightly different route from ours on the *Orontes* and had stopped off at Piraeus after Naples. Some of the Orient liners did that, plus any number of other companies' vessels. This red-haired fellow obviously had a contact in Piraeus who supplied him with hash. Presumably it came already moulded so it could be worn inside the shoes. Ah, those dear dead days before they'd thought of sniffer dogs! Then in Taufiq he'd simply hand it over to Milo for cash. Unfortunately for him the day I blundered in Milo had been unable to meet the ship and anyway it seems the Mate had never met him before: he normally turned the stuff over to an intermediary. As far as he was concerned anyone who came aboard in Taufiq knowing what was what and prepared to hand over twenty quid must be the right chap. It was a nice little sideline. What he didn't realise was that the usual fellow had been arrested since his previous trip and all he knew of Milo was a brief physical description he'd been given in Piraeus. The poor man was so convinced I was an informer I expect he broke up the hash and flushed it into the harbour before I was back on deck.

 ˙   – The whole thing made me pretty thoughtful, I can tell you. I mean to say, five-weeks' salary disguised as a pair of filthy old cork insoles. Five weeks' hideous tedium in Anderson & Green's pesky office with Simpkins moaning on about his innards: all of it could be compressed into one nerve-racking transaction. Sooner or later any intelligent person considers such things, of course. Quick profits versus possible disaster. *Would I dare? Do I have the nerve?* And there's seldom a clear-cut answer because everything depends on how desperate one is. The fact is, I wasn't desperate. I had a decent education, no debts, no dependents, a British passport and a job. I told myself I should err on the side of caution but what I really meant was that the temptation wasn't enticing enough. There was not much romance in petty smuggling. I felt I could do better, in the sense that each of us is suited to a particular kind of excitement and I already had some idea where mine might lie . . . Let me tell you a story.

– One morning when I was about fifteen my father made me an odd proposition. Out of the blue over breakfast during the school holidays he asked me if I fancied going to a funeral. Just like that. Some big cheese at Lloyds had died and my father had been deputised to attend, probably representing his department or the agency or something. I've no idea why he asked me along. For company, perhaps, or because he thought it might be interesting. In any case I put on my only suit and went. It was held in one of those City churches. Wren? Gibbs? Hawksmoor? Very full, anyway, and with proper printed order-of-service cards. Lots of glossy top hats and left-over Edwardians in wing collars and spats. Afterwards we went on to the wake: a stand-up buffet in a hall with black beams, that's all I can remember about the place. It was probably one of the livery halls.

– I tucked myself into a corner and was doing quite well on crab sandwiches when I became aware of a man next to me doing even better. I can't now remember his face but I can remember his *presence*, if you know what I mean. He was very easy, chatty, as if he'd singled me out as the only person in the room worth talking to. That certainly struck me at the time since I was easily the youngest and at an age when one hardly flatters oneself as being a fascinating conversationalist for an adult. I remember that and the speed with which he ate, which is the sort of thing that impresses schoolboys. I don't know where my father had got to; I suppose he was circulating among colleagues and saying the right things. In any case this stranger must have assumed I was a relative of the deceased and I was obliged to confess I'd never met the man and couldn't even recall his name from the service sheets in church. 'Oh,' said this chap, gobbling away at the sandwiches, 'that's shocking bad form. I didn't know the fellow from Adam, either, but I certainly know who he was and where he worked.' 'But if you didn't know him, why are you here?' I must have asked. 'I might ask you the same thing,' he said, and then, 'Can you keep a secret?' Well, has anyone aged fifteen in the history of the world ever replied 'No' to that question? Of course I said I could, whereupon he confessed that he had only come for the food. I was a bit slow so he explained that he had no job, or rather that this *was* his job, and the dark suit he was wearing represented his only working clothes. I still didn't understand. I expect I said I hadn't known there was such a job as just going to funerals. Was he a professional mourner or a mute, or perhaps in charge of the catering? He nipped off to refill his plate and then came back and told me how it worked. What he did was to scan the columns of *The Times*, the *Daily Telegraph* and the *Morning Post* each day, note who was being married or buried and where, and simply attach himself to the occasion in the hope that sooner or later it would lead to a square meal. He said it worked perfectly nine times out of ten, that he must have been to literally hundreds of weddings and funerals and had developed a pretty good nose for the ones that would be worth his while. What I liked about him was not just that he was so amazingly frank and confiding, which was flattering to a boy my age, but that he clearly assumed I would go into the same line of business in due course and needed some tips. 'My main advice to a youngster like yourself, clearly at the outset of his career, is "Avoid the Jews." Nice chaps and all that, and most generous with their nosh, but they're so damned clannish they know everyone. One has much less chance of gatecrashing. Actually, not just Jews but pretty much all foreigners, I find. They've got a far better idea than we have of who a second cousin once removed is.'

– Of course that brought me to my main question, which was how on earth did he get away with it? He was charmingly candid.

'Well, of course, now and then I don't, but that hasn't happened for some time. The amazing thing is that it should work at all, but it does, over and over again. Most people if they don't recognise you are far too embarrassed or polite to ask point-blank who you are. Especially at funerals. I once had to feign a weeping fit when that happened and I was most sympathetically escorted to somewhere quiet in order to compose myself. I was left alone in a drawing-room which happened to contain a decanter of the most glorious port I ever drank. You become accustomed to living a bit on the edge, just as you do to singing 'Praise my soul the King of Heaven' on a practically daily basis. You grow to like having to be alert all the time, carefully eavesdropping conversations for names, social nuances, atmosphere and suchlike. Of course, you need to have done your homework before coming. I've got *Debrett* and *Who's Who* at home, a few solid reference books like that, and I take the social magazines and read the gossip columns. You'd be amazed how much one can get away with. "Of course we've met before?" says some lady with a black veil gropingly. She doesn't care, anyway; this is just an ordeal she has to get through. All she wants to know is when she can slip away to be alone for five minutes with the gin in her handbag. "I doubt if you would remember me," I say in that soft earnest tone you use when the Grim Reaper has given them all a nasty turn. "I used to work with Geoffrey years ago. One of the kindest and wittiest men it was ever my fortune to meet." You can't go wrong, you see. Nobody's going to turn round and say that's funny because Geoffrey was nearly as cruel as his conversation was dull. If I've allowed myself to get a wee bit tiddly on the bubbly at a wedding reception I might even pretend to be a very distant relative. It's a bit risky, but so exciting I sometimes can't resist. Apart from the food the advantage of weddings is that you have two families, each with their own friends, relatives and satellites. It's perfect. Each side thinks you're part of the other lot. So you can shake hands with complete strangers and say, "If you know of me at all, I fear it will be as the black sheep. I've spent most of these last twenty years in South

Africa." Everyone racks their brains but it's a sure thing that every decent family will have some distant cousin who was banished to the Colonies. "Good God, you must be Roger's . . . now let's get this right, nephew? No, *godson*? Knew I'd get it. Well, good for you. Top up the old glass?" The most thrilling thing of all is to be invited back by the family after the reception. That's damned dangerous. Still, by that stage nobody will ever challenge you outright. Quite unthinkable for a complete fraud to have got into the house, equally impossible for anyone to risk calling your bluff as you all sit down to luncheon. "Cousin Desmond," you can hear yourself extemporising reminiscently in response to someone's overheard remark. "Now there's a name from the past. He was indeed in Jo'burg about then. Twenty-eight? Twenty-nine? Many's the hand of gin rummy I had with him." "Oh, *surely* you cannot mean that?" cries some sniffy old bird. "I'm quite certain the Canon would never have played those sorts of game. He was always a most serious young man at Lampeter." Crikey, this Desmond was a canon, was he? Better watch it. Still, now you have some delicious choices open. Either you say "Oh, *that* Desmond. I do beg your pardon, I was thinking of someone quite else" and everyone has a nervous laugh and you take lots more cold salmon to cover up the hiatus; or you can say in a worldly but regretful tone, "Well, you know how it is at that age, so far from home . . .", implying that gin rummy was followed in due course by strip poker. What I'm saying to you, young man, is that you must learn to observe people. Listen like a cat. Watch like a hawk. Miss nothing, and you can get away with anything. And on that note, and full to the brim with a complete stranger's funeral bakemeats, I will take my leave of you. I wish you a long and happy life.'

– I was pretty thrown by this, as you can imagine, and utterly fascinated at the same time. My father suddenly turned up and once outside he asked who that was I'd been talking to. It was a point of honour not to shop the man, and besides, he'd naturally never told me his name. I heard myself saying, 'Oh, that was

Rupert Barclay,' or 'Henry Vansittart,' just inventing a name, and my father said, 'Ah yes, I thought I recognised him.' I never forgot that. I never forgot the man at the funeral, either, but it was my father's little social lie that really stuck. It so perfectly confirmed what my charming fraudster had just been saying. One could always start at an advantage because people were so scared of being thought ignorant. People *want* to believe: that's the simple secret behind every scam, from the great religions down to free-loading crab sandwiches at a stranger's function. They really do *want* to believe.

– Well, there I was in Suez with all manner of tasty rackets going on around me, yet something told me they weren't for me. Not on moral grounds, nor even because they were risky. No, it was simply that they weren't my kind of racket. Even then I knew I would be more at home with misrepresentation of some kind. I wanted to be people other than myself. I'd been quite a good actor at school and very much taken by the whole idea of being able to project a different character if I chose. Maybe the fellow at the funeral had picked up on that: it takes one to know one, sort of thing. Have I mentioned that when I was a kid I used to pre-tend to be my own brother? Well, as you know, I haven't got a brother. But if I was sent down to Starr & Britt to buy a cabbage, say, I would buy it and go off with it and dawdle around looking at the fire engines in the fire station opposite for ten minutes. Then I'd leave the bag with the woman in the sweetshop and nip back to the greengrocer and ask Mrs Britt if my twin brother had just been in. And she'd say, yes, he's just bought a cabbage for your mum and honest to God, I can't tell you two boys apart. It used to give me a thrill. It made me feel scot-free in some way as if there was nothing I couldn't do because I could always pretend it had been my imaginary double. Even when I got into trouble and was caught and obviously the culprit, I still felt it wasn't really me it was happening to because the real me was undetectable. A bit like the Invisible Man. You could see his gin and tonic being raised and lowered but you never glimpsed the man himself.

Actually, I think that's me to a T, although a biographer might not agree.

– Now, the only one of Milo's rackets in Suez that piqued my curiosity was his line in pornography. As I'm sure you know, generations of travellers and especially servicemen came to associate Suez with 'feelthy postcards'. Most of them weren't at all filthy, not by today's standards. The enterprising were cashing in on that delightful piece of racist doublethink which made it possible to get away with pictures of girls with nothing on so long as they were not Europeans. Basically, the blacker and more 'native' they were the more you could have close-ups of their breasts and pretend that any interest they aroused was anthropological. The French always had a good line in these, especially from their North African colonies. In Egypt you could buy a lot of French stuff shot in Algeria. Girls with bare nipples would be subtitled something faintly educational like *Jeune Mauresque*. If the girls were decked out in finery or lying on a couch draped with saddle-rugs they would be given more provocative titles such as *Odalisque* or *Une Ouled Nail*, implying they were prostitutes and would willingly remove their clothes for you even if you weren't an anthropologist.

– This kind of 'meet-the-nations' photography had been going on since at least the eighteen-seventies and in 1936 it was still a staple part of the stuff Milo was turning out from pirated plates. He had a mass of material to choose from. Various Brits had been at it for decades in India and Malaya; Germans like von Gloeden and von Plüschow had been busy in Sicily; Vincenzo Galdi did it in southern Italy. You know, places with warm climates and low incomes. Mostly they were the pictures on cards you dropped into the post-box in Suez or Port Taufiq to *épater* the folks at home. Milo had other lines that were very much feelthier, and that was where the real money was. –

It is hot up under the Caramanli's roof. Milo is developing films in the dark room, Jayjay is next door pegging out fresh prints to dry on wires strung from wall to wall. Eyes, mouths, breasts and all manner of inflamed membranes are festooned across the room. The air smells of acetic acid. Unfortunately it is not possible to dry the prints on the hotel's flat roof overhead because that is the province of the laundrywomen who each morning hang out the Caramanli's yellowed sheets and threadbare towels. Jayjay has remarked that if these ladies are already steeled to the hotel's bed linen they probably won't be too shocked by pictures of Nubians mounting each other, but Milo is firm. He doesn't give a hoot about outraging their sensibilities, it's their gossip he doesn't wish to incite.

These, then, are the four-inch by six-inch prints Jayjay saw being hauled up the *Orontes'* side in a wicker basket by the passenger in the panama. He admits to himself that now the initial shock has worn off he is deeply excited by these damp images. Never in his eighteen and a half years has he seen anything so explicit. Regardless of gender or act, they have a cumulative effect. They reveal a hidden world which hitherto was of hazy and secretive outline, alluded to only in schoolboy gossip. The discovery is that the erotic need not be specific to achieve its effect. Enough that it be forbidden and to exist in such detail without requiring any imaginative effort, revealed by the dispassionate objectivity of the camera's lens. He notices that each print has a monogram in one corner followed by a letter and a serial number.

Milo appears with some strips of developed film which he hangs up with clothes pegs. 'Find anything you fancy?' he enquires.

'Not really.' Jayjay affects a man-of-the-world offhandedness. Inside, he is trembling. 'But I'm curious about how you get them.'

'I don't. I know very little about this racket. You remember Mansur, the fellow you met the other night in Al Ahilla? Fat fingers and moustache? He's the source of most of this stuff. Where he gets it I'm not sure. I know these ones with 'L&L' in the corner are French. The ones down here that look to me like local kids he arranges himself, I think. At a guess they're shot in Cairo. Those blackish lads and lasses over by the wall come from a German in Upper Egypt or northern Sudan. An anthropologist, I believe. Mansur knows him.'

'How on earth does he get them to do *that*?' asks Jayjay naively, indicating a print.

'Money, I should imagine. How else? Or perhaps down there they'll do anything at the drop of a lens cap.' Milo sounds indifferent. 'Anyway, we'll give these another hour and get them packed up. I've got Mansur's runner from Port Taufiq coming at six. He'll take care of them. The Egyptians aren't much good at the technical side but they're fine for distribution and anything that needs the personal touch because they know exactly who needs bribing, and how much, all the way through the Port. Show them a dark room, a tank of developer and a thermometer, though, and they give that baffled little nod and say *sa'b awi* as if you've asked them to split the atom.'

Jayjay thinks back to meeting Mansur and recollects a direct stare and an excellent command of English. A few days pass and then one evening when he knows Milo is out of town he finds his way back to the Al Ahilla or New Moons café. From the rubbish-strewn street outside it looks the dive it is: dim lighting, tiled walls, men in all manner of native robes sitting around low tables on which stand hookahs, their long tubes leading to drowsy bearded mouths. Not a European face is to be seen. At the doorway he picks out Mansur sitting where he had been on the previous occasion. He has just relinquished a hookah's amber mouthpiece and is gazing at Jayjay through a cloud of smoke. At once intimidated and excited, Jayjay finds himself edging towards him among the tables. Yellowish eyes follow him as he crosses the room but no sudden silence falls. Reaching Mansur, Jayjay bows slightly as he offers his hand which the Egyptian accepts mechanically.

'Please excuse my disturbing you but I'd like to talk.' To his relief Mansur nods, places a large hand on his neighbour's shoulder, levers himself to his feet and leads the way to a space at the

rear of the café. There they squat on stools as low as church kneel-
ers. At a command from Mansur a youth with a squint pours mint
tea from a long-spouted pot into two glasses half full of sugar.

'You were here the other night,' says Mansur. 'With Mr Milo.'

'Yes.'

Mansur inclines his head noncommittally and the customary
silence falls which is an integral part of Arab discourse and which
so nonplusses the anglophone races that they will essay even the
most mindless pleasantry in order to fill it. In due course Mansur
says: 'Mr Milo is a good man. He is your friend. But tonight you
have come alone. Is there trouble?'

'No, no. He simply went off this afternoon to Cairo for a week
on business. As a matter of fact I've been helping him recently
with some of this business of his. The photographs.'

'Ah, the pictures. You are interested?' Mansur's dark eyes,
together with the café's gloom, make his expression unreadable.

'Yes,' says Jayjay, surprised at himself. Another silence between
them in which the word goes echoing on.

'And what is your work?'

'At present I'm working in the Orient Line's offices here in
Suez.'

'You are a clerk?'

'I am the son of the company's true owner, who is neither Mr
Anderson nor Mr Green. Even Milo doesn't know this. You must
never tell him, Mr Mansur.'

'I understand. A spy. Your father has asked you to report
secretly on how his business is run here so you pretend to be a
clerk while you investigate?' The Egyptian smiles a little as he
drinks tea. 'We Arabs have a long tradition of such things. Our
history is full of stories of kings and princes who by day reign in
their palaces in silk robes and by night dress as beggars and walk
the streets. In this way they learn what their people really think of
them. They hear what their advisers and generals do not want
them to hear. So you do the same for your father with the Orient
Line? He must be a very wise man.'

'He is.'

'And you – are you a wise son?'

'I try to be.'

'Then,' says Mansur, setting down his empty glass, 'you are playing a dangerous game. You are spying both for your father and for Mr Milo. I tell you frankly, as someone who does business with Mr Milo, I don't like to hear of this.'

'You are mistaken. My father's shipping line has nothing to do with Milo. Neither knows of the other's existence. Nor do I care what Milo does. I am interested only in one of his business enterprises, the one he himself cares least about.'

'The pictures.'

Jayjay is aware of a racing sensation. Heart? Foolhardiness? He is trapped now by the lie he has just told. He cannot untell it, he cannot backtrack. He cannot recant and say that pretending to be a shipping tycoon's son was just a joke. He has passed a threshold and is tangling himself with racketeers whose violence towards rivals or traitors is quite as famous as is the brutality of the Egyptian police. A foreigner, he is blundering into a society of strangers, ignorant of their language and customs and oblivious of their networks and knife-edged alliances. He also knows he is banking on still being able to scuttle back to the safety of Anderson & Green or to some ill-defined British authority, spin them a yarn and be put straight on to a homebound ship. Yet it is pointless to pretend that he does not also recognise the promise with which the very walls of this café vibrate. He is overtaken by a certain reckless craving for the company of cut-throats even as he pins his hope on an escape route.

Once again Mansur is watching him through smoke, having called for a hookah. So far as Jayjay is concerned the air between them is filled with the outlines of unclear propositions, with hazy pleasures that make him fearful and the prospect of debts he may not wish to repay.

'You said you wanted to talk,' Mansur reminded him.

'I wanted to tell you that Milo is a man I like but he's not an old friend. I don't wish to compromise whatever you and he are doing together.'

'I see. And your offer?'

'There's nothing I can't get aboard an Orient Line ship, Mr Mansur. Or off it. I am the owner's son. Milo can't do that. Apart from anything else he hasn't got Port clearance. And if he had I could have it revoked.'

'I see. Yours is a position with valuable possibilities. In Suez Europeans, and especially you British, can do things we Egyptians cannot. I will not speak about the injustice of this state of affairs, nor about how long it will be allowed to continue. But yes, for the moment your situation could be highly advantageous to some-body with interests in overseas markets. And in return you want to take over Mr Milo's part in the manufacture of postcards?'

'No, I don't want that. I don't wish to take a single millieme from his pocket. I am interested in the business closer to its source. The camera end of things, if you like.'

'Ah, the camera. But I'm sure Mr Milo will have told you this does not take place here in Suez. This is a city of buyers and sell-ers, not of producers. The camera work happens far away.'

'I realise that. I'm prepared to travel.'

'What about your disguise as a clerk?'

'I've already done all I can. Anderson & Green have few secrets here. I've sent my father a report. Between you and me, he wants to send me to do the same thing somewhere else. Colombo, per-haps. For the moment I'm bored.'

'Bored. Excuse me if I observe how very young you are. But you have balls, I know that much. I don't believe Mr Milo knows you have come to see me tonight; and I don't believe you are an *agent provocateur* for either the British or *ash-shorta*, our police. I have known many spies and impostors but you are still too young to have been recruited and trained. Besides, no matter how good their cover the training always gives them a certain confidence which shows in the way they sit and stand. You have the politeness of the truly scared. Very well, Mr . . . Jayjay? Let us find out how

we are to establish this matter of good faith between us. If you are
to learn the secrets of my business I will be putting myself into
your hands. This is not in balance.'

'True. But I have thought how this balance might be restored.
I've heard there's an increasing taste for opium both here and in
Europe since it has been declared illegal. Don't they call it *rūh al-
afyūn* here? Or maybe that's the tincture we call laudanum. In any
case it comes from Siam and a lot finds its way to Ceylon. As I'm
sure you know, our steamers stop in Colombo on their way back
from Australia before they arrive here at Port Taufiq. These circumstances surely make it possible to restore the balance by one
means or another.'

Mansur takes the mouthpiece from between his teeth and
watches a worm of smoke crawl from its hole. 'It's good that you
know *rūh al-afyūn*. If you are learning our language I will gladly
help you. Your pronunciation is excellent, by the way. The
method you are suggesting to restore the balance between us is
interesting but it would take months to arrange safely. Even the
son of the shipping line's owner could hardly organise such a
thing tomorrow. The danger is extreme. And I have the idea you
are in a hurry,' and he shoots Jayjay a sidelong glance while
smoothing his glossy moustache.

Jayjay knows his own expression has given him away. He can't
conceal that he came tonight wanting immediate access to sensu-
ality. He has neither the character nor the patience to plot and
scheme for months on end, all the while earning his pittance as
office-fodder. Apart from anything else he is too young.

'However,' Mansur is saying, 'the process could be made much
quicker, this business of keeping the balance between what you
know about me and what I know about you. Let us call this *trust*.
Our trust is easier than you think to make certain. Tomorrow
night I will take you somewhere where you can see things and not
be seen. You will like it, this I swear. But tonight? Tonight you will
take me somewhere. And you will like that, too. You came here
looking for something, you cannot deny it.'

Jayjay is mildly in shock, realising he has just been propositioned for the first time in his life. This is not what I came for, he tells himself. It is not a price I'm prepared to pay, no matter what doors it might open. Or so he thinks until hot excitement wells painfully up beneath his apprehension as though already glimpsing the reward for paying the entrance fee. 'I'm not at all sure about that,' he temporises weakly.

Mansur watches him and keeps on smoothing his moustache which gleams as though oiled. 'Since you can't deny you came here as a hunter,' he says, folding his hands in a raconteur's gesture perhaps designed to conjure up an *Arabian Nights* atmosphere, 'I shall tell you a story about a hunter. It concerns a Turk in the high mountains of his country. He saves his money and buys a brand-new gun. He is very proud of the gun and eager to try it out. So off he goes to hunt bears in the forest. And his luck is good. His first day, he meets a little brown bear right in his path. He takes aim and fires, *pum!* Right between the eyes. It falls down dead. Suddenly he feels a tap on his shoulder and to his horror he finds a much bigger bear standing right behind him. Maybe it's the dead bear's father! But before he can lift his gun the bear says to him: "All right, Mr Turkish huntsman, you have two choices. Either I tear you to pieces or I give you one up the backside. It's up to you." Well, it's not much of a choice. Still, the hunter naturally takes the second alternative. It is extremely painful but at least he escapes with his life.

'He goes home full of shame and has to wait several weeks before the pain in his backside has gone. But at last his old passion returns and he takes his new gun and sets off again for the wilds to avenge himself. Obviously his luck is still holding because in only a matter of hours he comes on the very bear who caused him such pain. Without giving the animal a chance he brings up his gun and fires, *pum!*, and knocks it over stone dead. "Praise be to Allah!" he thinks. "I am avenged." But no sooner has he said this than he feels a heavy paw on his shoulder and turns to find a far bigger bear. This one is as tall as he is, three times as wide and ten times as strong. "All right, Mr Turkish huntsman," says this great bear. "Two choices. Either I rip your head off or you take it up the backside." Once more the hunter decides he has no alternative. But merciful Allah! At what cost in agony and shame! This time a whole year passes before he can even walk properly again. By the end of the year, though, some of the memory has faded and his old spirit returns. He has never in his life gone without hunting for so long and besides, he has a big score to settle.

'So off he sets again into the high mountains with his gun, full of determination. And there in the middle of a cedar forest he catches sight of the big bear which has just cost him a year of his hunting life. Since it is quite far away he takes careful aim and fires, *pum!* His beautiful gun is as accurate as ever and the beast drops in its tracks. This time when he feels a tap on his shoulder he is more resigned than surprised. He turns to find a real monster. This is a bear such as he has never dreamed of: a huge black creature straight down from the steppes of Russia, half as tall again as he is. The creature is looking at him thoughtfully as he stands there paralysed. At last it shakes its great head. "Tell me, Mr Turkish huntsman," it says. "Do you *still* believe you come up here just to hunt?"'

For some time, overcome by his tale, Mansur goes on shaking his own head and wiping his eyes while repeating the punchline. '"Do you still believe you come up here just to hunt?" That's such an Egyptian story, believe me.'

'Because it's anti-Turkish?'

'Well, that too. But because it's very wise. It has a meaning.'

This is just what Jayjay is afraid of, and something fails within him. It becomes pressing to sue for time. As though Mansur were a step ahead of him the Egyptian says equably, 'Not tonight, then. But soon. You can find me here or else in Al Kef in *tariq* al Baladiyya. You know it? By the *suq*. Never fear, my friend. You and I can do business. For the moment we have an agreement, right? I say nothing to Mr Milo, who isn't here, and you say nothing to your father, who isn't here either.'

They shake hands on this and Jayjay finds himself in the noisome back streets of Suez in a state between numbness and exhilaration. This persists until he reaches his hated billet in the Caramanli. It is a large room divided into two by a curtained doorway beyond which Simpkins is asleep and audible. It is porky Simpkins who, though unconscious, exposes the essential nature of their shared living space as no more than a bare cement cave. The loudest of tonight's awesome farts include sound frequencies that make the room briefly ring. Through the curtain drifts a disgusting and anomalous stench of burnt rubber and mutton. The intermittent blurts and squeaks and gassy blats are a wearisome reminder to Jayjay that he must tell Simpkins yet again that if he persists in eating chickpeas he may never survive to taste his mother's cooking. Suddenly, the squalor of such living conditions reveals itself as a world he has just decided to leave, which he realises he already has half left. After barely two months he is sick of apprenticeship with its magnanimous promise of more of the same for the next forty years. A further series of gruff barks from the other room drives him out on to the small gritty balcony from where he can see the street below with its thin cats and a donkey dozing between the shafts of a cart, one of its rear feet raised and resting on the tip of its hoof. Something has happened tonight, Jayjay thinks. I can't go back to being the person I was this morning. I won't go back to my father's world of ledgers and endeavour. I won't go back to Eltham.

The stars above the ill-lit town are brilliant, trembling in the unseen thermals as if the whole universe is in ferment. A tug hoots briefly in Port Taufiq. He suddenly feels adult. He has become someone who leans on a night balcony in Suez and thinks; leans on a balcony and inhales the pepper air.

7

A strange thing is how physically close to each other Jayjay and I have unwittingly been living these last fifteen years. Were it not for the jutting lump of forest below that prevents my seeing into the next valley, my house would have an excellent view of Il Ghibli. Our roofs could be joined by a beeline not much over a mile in length. Yet to reach his house by track and road requires twenty minutes of jolting down through the forest followed by detours around olive groves and vineyards on the lower slopes. Strictly speaking, I suppose it is not true that we were completely unaware of each other's existence. Over the years I had heard mention of an English 'lord' (pronounced *lorde*) living nearby and reputed to have a beautiful house. In turn, he had heard the odd conversational reference to an English writer living in eccentric seclusion somewhere up Sant' Egidio – and a hand would be waved vaguely towards the top of the mountain with its crowning metal nest of relay aerials and radio masts. Only when an article about me appeared in *La Nazione* was he able to put a name and out-of-focus face to this fellow countryman of his.

It might be supposed that two Englishmen living abroad and so close together would make an effort to meet, if only for the pleasure of deciding they despised one another. But the English are more complicated than that. It might next be thought that simple snobbery accounted for much of this exaggerated desire for privacy. But when it is so well disguised beneath self-effacing amiability it becomes anything but simple and contains equal measures of defensiveness and arrogance which foreigners generously persist in reading as a curious national reticence. Jayjay and I later acknowledged we were conscious of living on the 'unfashionable' side of Cortona – meaning there were so few other foreigners in our immediate area that we could claim still greater exclusivity for ourselves, this becoming a further reason for not socialising. In the earliest days of our joint project we adopted a particular tone of reminiscence for alluding to the distinguished minority status we shared. Now *Cortona* . . . (and one could detect the note of disdain creeping in) . . . We could remember a down-at-heel Etruscan hill town full of hunchbacks and slightly sinister tall, dark streets. In *those* days it had had about two hotels, one of them being the Garibaldi in Piazza Alfieri, run by those two ancient sisters now long dead. And do you remember *Il Sozzo*, Mr Filthy, who ran that minute restaurant up at Torreone? He looked like a Charles Addams character and had maybe three tables. You gave your order and if you were unlucky he left the kitchen door open and you could see into the black and cobwebby cavern where grimy children were set to work with bundles of kindling to light the grill. But when the food arrived, my God!, unbelievably fabulous, especially the grilled *porcini*: great thick meaty ceps drizzled with the greenest olive oil . . . *Il Sozzo* was dead too, of course; and anyway nowadays the place would be condemned and closed by the USL, 'the Oozly', the sanitary gauleiters of the new age. Really, Cortona had changed out of all recognition and was fast becoming a year-round rabble of foreigners, what with full-time American universities and German and Brit culture-groupies. And increasing numbers of them were not tourists at all but residents of one sort or another. They were either daubing in Mediterranean primary colours or developing crackpot theories about the Etruscans or writing heartwarming accounts of how they had restored their delicious Tuscan farmhouses. And as for the *yonder* side of Cortona, between the town and Lake Trasimene, well, places like Pergo and Montanare had practically become foreign ghettoes. What we could remember as slightly sordid village streets with a small grim branch of Despar selling flyblown salami and ammonia-laced floor cleaner were now aglitter with BMWs from Munich double-parked outside delicatessens selling *Sauerkraut* and *Bauernbrot* . . .

In fact, such an account of an imaginary ice-breaking conversation between Jayjay and me would be misleading precisely because the British are so complicated. Written down cold like that, it would make us sound like elderly grandees lamenting the arrival of the Johnny-come-latelys. It would also imply we were oblivious to the idea that in a stunning villa somewhere nearby might live an even older and grander foreigner who could remember mules and carbide lighting and could not distinguish between us and the latest interlopers. (And what, meanwhile, of the Italians whose land this is and who bear the whole damned lot of us with such fortitude?) But because we are more complicated, Jayjay and I had put inverted commas around such exchanges. They weren't about Cortona at all but concerned a mode of description – self-consciously snobby, deliberately overstated – that was parodic of the type of Englishman we *might* have been, but thank God weren't. And while this parody was going on we were sniffing each other out with antennae minutely attuned to the finest shades of accent and attitude. In fact, as it quickly turned out, we neither of us gave a damn about what went on over the next range of hills. So far as I was concerned I had been spending so much time either on my travels or writing them up that I had neither the spare energy nor the inclination to hobnob with people an hour's drive away. Besides, anything beyond the immediate neighbourhood was too unreal. These days when I glanced up from my writing table I hardly saw the chestnut forest below without it turning into a coco-palm plantation, even as the entire Tuscan backdrop shuffled itself chimerically into an equally familiar and fond coastline of the South China Sea. Where was I? Neither here nor there. The palimpsest of a lifetime.

Which left the puzzle of the *lorde*. The Italians, of course, are keen on titles. I don't mean they are interested in aristocrats, especially, but their useful system of social formalities leads them to bestow ranks on half the people one bumps into while out shopping. On any day one can hear the local mayor addressed in the street as *sindaco*, a time-server in the police as *maresciallo*, an accountant as *ragioniere* and virtually anyone who can distinguish a cog-wheel from a pair of compasses as *ingegnere*. Even I, to my very British humiliation, was addressed in the Co-op as *maestro* the day after that wretched newspaper article appeared. So it never occurred to me that this English *lorde* might actually be a bona fide member of the aristocracy until one afternoon when I was inspecting the vines on my terrace for scale insects and something caught my attention down by Hawkwood's castle at Montecchio. The castle had been restored quite recently and was lived in now and then by a Roman lady. For all its landmark position it attracted little attention so it was all the more surprising this afternoon to see the little road beneath its walls appear jammed with people, sunlight flashing off glass or chrome. Even binoculars revealed little detail beyond two glossy black limousines and some police motorcycles. A few days later gossip supplied an explanation.

'I'm surprised you weren't there,' said the barman as he tamped a fresh measure of coffee into the holder and locked it into the espresso machine. 'You being English and everything. That was your Queen Mother coming for an hour to visit our castle. The paper said she's as old as the century and likes a drink. Good for her, I say. *Corretto?*' He pushed my coffee across the bar and waved a bottle of spirits inquiringly over it. I shook my head and drank the coffee unlaced. 'The paper also said she stayed the night near here, but security was tight and they wouldn't say where. Around here we all know she stayed with that English *lorde*. Ghezzi was in next day and his sister cleans for someone in the Valle di Chio and she said it was obvious. How often do you see Rolls Royces and *Carabinieri* outriders in these parts?'

So I assumed the *lorde* was the genuine article after all and wondered vaguely who he was. But then time passed and all this fell rapidly out of my memory. (A little local excitement. Her of all people. Well, well.) By the time I met and began working with Jayjay I had forgotten about the Queen Mother, while the *lorde* existed in quite another dimension, fuzzily in the background somewhere beyond the circle of farmers I knew in the immediate vicinity. I began to be drawn into another and quite unexpected world, that of pre-war Suez and its pornography rackets. And then one morning, after a productive session in which he was in expansive mood, Jayjay offered me a lunch-time gin and tonic before we had a bite to eat.

'Only I can't offer you a decent gin, I'm afraid. I dropped the Gordon's yesterday and all I have in the house is some cheapo standby stuff I keep for impoverished hacks and scribblers such as yourself.' And he produced a bottle whose label said 'Lord Gin' and displayed bogus coats-of-arms and references to London. It was enough to jog my memory.

'Talking of fake lords, Jayjay, did you know there's one living around here? The Queen Mother is supposed to have stayed with him a year or two ago.'

'Really? Possibly there's some confusion here. She certainly stayed with me.'

'*You?*'

'Right here in this house. And luckily I had plenty of undropped Gordon's, not to mention Dubonnet. But there are always bodyguards and ladies-in-waiting to be considered. Reggie Wilcock, to name but one. Lord Gin's quite good enough for Reggie. He was here too, of course. Page of the Presence. The one thing about the House of Windsor the tabloids always miss, bless them, is that it's far and away the campest show in town. Did you never read that story in Woodrow Wyatt's diary where Reggie and Bill Tallon, the Page of the Backstairs, were a bit slow getting the Queen Mother's evening meal up to her? She phoned down and said, "I don't know about you two old queens, but *this* old Queen would like her dinner." They're a riot. Just like the Royal Yacht *Britannia* used to be in its heyday. Talk about cruising. It positively shrieked its way around the world.'

'In any case, Jayjay, *you're* not a lord.'

'Of course not, no more than you are. But you know what they're like around here. I've spent the last fifteen years trying to make it clear that I'm not a British aristocrat living *incognito*, so obviously that's exactly what they think I am. I've made it perfectly plain that I'm as common as muck and I thought most of my more savvy local friends had realised it was one of those self-perpetuating jokes, when I suddenly found myself doing a bed-and-breakfast number for the Queen Mum. My credibility at once dropped to zero and my social status rose accordingly. I am now a *lorde* and there's nothing I can do about it.'

'But how come you know her?'

'I've known her for years, on and off. We're hardly intimates and she has a wide circle of friends. She really did come to see Hawkwood's castle and I happened to be a handy bed. She is well over ninety, after all. We originally met through Anthony Blunt in the very early fifties when he was Surveyor of the King's Pictures. Or it might just have been the Queen's Pictures by then. I'll tell you some time. It's not very interesting.'

'So you're the *lorde*.'

'How we become our own myths. Look at Jeffrey Archer. Now there's a man for whom I have a sneaking regard.'

'Another of your acquaintances?'

'Oh no. No, all I meant is I recognise a fellow artist in the sense of someone who made himself up as he went along. Brilliantly, too. He has been everything: policeman, MP, novelist, baron . . . Call-girls and the Old Vicarage, Grantchester. All of it him, none of it him. I love it. People set far too much store by vulgar consistency. To maintain a consistent character from one end of your life to the other takes just as much energy and subterfuge and self-deception as it does to slip into interesting roles as they're offered. More, probably. One easily gets carried along by the sheer thrill of transgressing.'

And lo! the stews of Suez.

Three days went by before Jayjay ventured to look again for Mansur, three days of hesitation filled with premonitory whiffs as of bridges bursting into flame beneath him.

– Funny, isn't it, how one believes one is carrying on a stern inward debate about whether to do something when all the while the decision has long since been taken? It must have been obvious to everyone but me that I was withdrawing from the job at Anderson & Green. I would clock in on the dot each morning, race through the work and absent myself for the rest of the day. It was only a matter of time before 'Pusser' Hammond or somebody more senior gave me my marching orders. And then what? I didn't have a bean to my name other than the ridiculous salary they were paying me. Young, irresponsible and led by my hormones as I was, I nevertheless realised I had to live on something. I was just beginning to like Abroad very much indeed. I didn't want to go home a virgin, not in any sense, and for me Eltham reeked of virginity.

– So I went back to Mansur and yes, I paid his price and no, unlike his Turkish huntsman I felt no compulsion to repeat it. Still, sixty years after the event I can admit without a blush that it was far from traumatic. And to pre-empt your two foremost improper questions (ever the stickler for detail) the answers are 'On the Caramanli's roof' and 'Brylcreem borrowed from Simpkins'. In fact it was over almost before I knew it, in true Arab style, and had I been an 'Ouled Nail' I could have gone back to my tent thinking I was quids in after a good night's work. As soon as it was done I could see things were on a different footing between us. Mansur was now prepared to trust me because by the standards of his own culture I was compromised. As the passive partner I was in a position of shame, and anything I later decided to do or say that went counter to his interests could in theory be nullified by the threat of public exposure. Now it was up to him to keep his part of the bargain, and he was as good as his word. I think he knew that I had yielded for political reasons even if curiosity and an unfocused libido had played their part. So he wasn't obliged to despise me while claiming affection. –

Mansur leads the way through a butcher's shop lit by a Primus pressure lamp. In the white actinic glare the few remaining chunks of unsold camel meat glitter with bluebottles. The small boy in a robe and round white skullcap who is supposed to keep the flies off with a whisk has fallen asleep. A milky gleam of eyeball shows beneath a half-closed lid; his cap is skewed to reveal patches of ringworm on his scalp the size of shillings. The evening hubbub of back-street Suez is a pervasive surround. There are people at the rear of the shop, people in the passage leading inwards into the warren that lies unsuspected from the street. They recognise Mansur, exchange greetings with him, glance with only brief curiosity at his European companion. These are courtyard regions of naphtha flames and candles, of limp piles of fodder with tethered goats standing amid pellets of dung. Children squeal, a wireless plays, feeble lights reveal dim tiers of balconies rising on all sides on which glow charcoal braziers and cigarette tips. Above it all the unexpected night sky is a rectangle of stars. The air enclosed by these steep buildings is heavy with cooking smells, excremental, alive. Jayjay experiences a not disagreeable sensation of being led out of his depth.

Mansur has explained everything. Jayjay has an hour. He must swear to be silent. Not a movement, all right? They reach a doorway where an old woman is sitting, deeply shawled, in a heap of robes. A paraffin lantern stands on a splintered deal table. The floor beside her is strewn with empty cardamom pods. Mansur greets her and as she looks up to return the greet-

ing the shawl falls away from her face to reveal the dark blue tat-
tooes of tribal markings above her nose and beside each wrinkled
eye. With one thin hand she twitches the shawl back across her
chin in the token gesture of the Moslem woman who is touch-
ingly too old to bother, while she thrusts the other out
incongruously to reveal a watch with a foxed dial which she taps,
glancing at both Jayjay and Mansur. Everything is agreed. Time
is rationed. The woman gets to her feet and finds a stub of
candle which she lights from the oil lamp and hands to Jayjay
before leading the way over to one wall. Where the building's
front and side join, a hole eighteen inches wide and four feet
high is disclosed behind a sheet of sacking which the woman
holds aside for him. As he squeezes past her he smells the cardamom on her breath.

Having been briefed by Mansur he knows what to expect. The
black slot he is in is between two walls, although it is unclear
whether the outer one is completely false or merely that of the
adjoining building. Unpointed cement has oozed from between
the mud-coloured bricks on both sides and hardened into protruding tongues that catch at his clothes. After a few yards he
finds rough stairs cobbled together out of more bricks and carefully climbs. The flame he carries illuminates very little beyond its
own tiny dazzle. The cramped passage continues at the top of the
stairs and here he notices a small source of light around which
some bricks have been removed. Placing the candle on the floor
he looks through this chink into another world. It is a room in
bizarre contrast with his side of the wall, being furnished in a
style he thinks of as Louis Farouk. There is a vague Frenchness
about the lace curtains in the window, the chintzy wallpaper curling along its seams, the heavy carved wash-stand and the flounced
pillows on the bed. The Egypt of her new king, on the other
hand, is unmistakably represented by the two stiff chairs uphol-
stered in gold velveteen and a writing table with heraldic legs, its
surface protected by a rectangle of green American cloth. Clothes
are heaped carelessly on it. Above the head of the bed is a lighting

fitment: two shaded bulbs springing from a riot of acanthus leaves done into a gilt plaster-of-Paris plaque. From the way light is falling on the bed Jayjay deduces that his own viewpoint must be from behind the acanthus spray of a similar light fitment along the wall beside the bed. Only an aperture thus ingeniously disguised could remain undetected so close to the protagonists of this stolen spectacle.

In the next hour Jayjay watches the same girl with three different clients. She is about his own age, with large breasts and heavy dark hair – probably Greek, he thinks. He is rigid with embarrassment and excitement. Nothing in Eltham has prepared him for this, and neither have his most vivid imaginings accurately foreseen the effortless reality of what takes place beneath his fascinated gaze. In order to distract himself from his guilt at thieving these private scenes he splits into several observers. The first of these takes note of all sorts of peripheral detail about the room and its occupants: the way the light falls, the holes in socks. The same observer quite lucidly speculates about how he might never have guessed from their faces – had he glimpsed these entirely ordinary-looking people walking along Rue Colmar in plain daylight – that they lived another life after dark. Maybe everyone did, and it left no more discernible mark on their diurnal selves than eating dinner? A second observer is not speculative at all. He feels his entire being oozing through the aperture like ectoplasm in order to participate in the activities scarcely four feet away. Like an inflamed Tinkerbell he is everywhere, alighting briefly on this membrane and on that, flitting from breast to scrotum, from buttock to nape, committing everything to indelible memory. And above and behind these observers yet another presides who, despite Jayjay's neophyte ignorance, recognises the isolation in these encounters. These are closed people transacting brief and urgent business. They are in no sense lovers. They are more like electrified globes, sealed fates that bump into one another, discharge themselves and leave behind a certain residue of sadness. It does occur to this observer that sadness might always be attendant on the act, regardless of the absence or presence of love.

The peripheral observer, meanwhile, has noted that the first client – the one whose clothes were on the writing table – might have been a middle-ranking Lebanese banker with stained underwear; the second any of the twenty-ish clerks from the pool at Anderson & Green; while the third is a quite dashing young Egyptian wearing a spruce uniform he recognises as that of the harbour police at Port Taufiq. It is easy to imagine this tall youth with the neat moustache doing the rounds in his motorboat, visiting each of the scarlet-painted buoys in the roads and opening their inspection hatches to see whether they have been used as drop-boxes for contraband. 'Pusser' Hammond has told him that this is one of the favoured smuggling techniques. Only a Port policeman who isn't on the take would dream of opening the inspection hatches in full view out in the roads. Most take the buoys in tow and wait until they are safely inside the maintenance yards before opening them and stealing the loot. That is why the buoys in Port Taufiq are always freshly painted, 'Pusser' said. They are constantly in and out of the maintenance shop.

This clean young officer is unquestionably a fine specimen of manhood, with his lithe body and unexpected concern for the girl's pleasure. But Jayjay notices the girl always keeps her eyes averted, as she did for her first two clients, as though her thoughts are far away even as her body performs with intimate flexibility. Legs up, legs down, legs apart; up on knees and elbows, kneeling, spreading, tensing, relaxing. And always the eyes skewed off to one side. In between clients she had slipped on a blue peignoir and walked to the open window, looking out through the fake lace, down at the noisy street, up towards the stars, her hair falling back. Now her eyes seem blankly fixed on Jayjay's own across the policeman's glistening shoulder. Does she know he is watching? Is she aware of hollow walls and paying voyeurs? He jerks his head away from the crack, guilty and alarmed. What was the deal here? Was she knowingly performing for him as well as for her client?

He becomes aware of a tickling between his ankles and trouser-legs, an irritation that has gradually pushed itself forward into his consciousness. The candle at his feet has dwindled to a standing flame in a pool of wax but it is enough to reveal that this fetid slot between the walls is alive with cockroaches. Bending down to prise the flame off the floor he notices that the brickwork beneath the spyhole where he has been pressing his body is encrusted with what look like dried snail trails, though some are fresh. His fingers dripping with scalding wax he retreats to the top of the stairs before the flame goes out and fumbles his way down towards the faint glow that marks the sacking-covered entrance.

The old woman is still there. She points out through the door-way at a packing case with a lamp on it at which Mansur is drinking tea with several companions. 'Shukran ya 'aguz', he murmurs awkwardly to her. Only when he is outside does he realise how stiflingly hot it was between the walls of that brick oven. He can feel sweat beginning to dry all over his body. Were he not almost certain that Mansur does not drink Jayjay might think he was in his cups, for he greets Jayjay like a son who has come through an initiation with flying colours, proudly encircling his waist with a thick arm and apparently explaining this European to his companions in rapid Arabic. Jayjay thinks he catches the words for 'important' and 'ships'. He is numb with unfocused desire and accepts a glass of mint tea, then another, and finally a third.

'Hot in there,' says Mansur meaningly. 'Did you like it?'

'Pretty much,' Jayjay replies, inhibited by the presence of these robed strangers who doubtless know exactly where he has been and are expecting a roguish response.

'Well, drink up, because you haven't finished yet. What did I promise? That I will show you something you will like. If you are not yet sure, you must see something else. That girl, she's beautiful, isn't she?'

'Yes. Yes, she is. In her way.'

'Very hairy. She is Christian. She does everything.'

Time passes. The same quarter of town but a different spyhole. The same cockroaches, the same sweat, a newly awakened longing. Instead of a brick wall some rough wood panelling with a plank wrenched out and a narrow view between two cobbled-in sheets of eroded three-ply. This time a far less genteel room, more a skimped cubicle hollowed out of a much larger space, a plywood pocket in what surely was once a sizeable drawing-room whose lost grandeur probably survives in dust-shrouded cornices and dadoes and curved bell handles now hidden behind the partitioning. Seventy years earlier this might have been the house chosen by Ferdinand de Lesseps and this the very room to which he returned exhausted each evening from the Canal diggings, a roll of plans beneath one arm, his frock coat marked with a wandering white tideline of dried sweat.

This time no disenchanted girl condemned to her cell awaits the night's random visitors. The room is empty. A naked lightbulb like a teardrop sheds more of an ochre glow than actual light. It shows the iron bedstead's springs sagging beneath a blotched mattress as thin as a biscuit. A scant seven feet above the lino-covered floor the lank air retards the blades of the slowest ceiling fan he has ever seen. The room has nothing about it of either aftermath or anticipation. It is static and lost. Then the door opens unexpectedly and an Egyptian boy enters, dressed as for school in a grey shirt and white cotton trousers. He is maybe twelve, and there is a certain jauntiness about the way he walks in his thin-soled slippers. He is carrying a book. Into the room behind him comes a white man of about forty wearing gold-rimmed spectacles. He looks like a French provincial piano teacher. He has a resigned air and shoots a glance around the room which seems to confirm his mood.

Why does the boy remind Jayjay of one of his contemporaries at Eltham College? Why does the man seem to resemble one of the College's staff, and even the lino evoke that on the kitchen floor in Beechill Road, when none of them has any real similarity? Unbidden and without awkwardness the boy hops on to the bed and arranges himself primly on the iron hoop at its head, knees together, leaning back against the wall and opening the book on his lap as though following a script. He begins to read aloud in a husky boy's voice, slowly and with difficulty, as if in class. The slippers fall with soft plops from his feet sticking backwards through the bars. On his cheek nearest Jayjay, just beside the ear, is a shadow of dark down. The book's cover proclaims it as the *Collected Poems* of Dante Gabriel Rossetti.

> *The blessed damozel leaned out*
> *From the gold bar of Heaven;*
> *Her eyes were deeper than the depth*
> *Of waters stilled at even . . .*

(although these are only approximately the words the boy speaks in his thick accent). There is no nervousness in his voice, only a touching suggestion of formality. The man kneels on the mattress before him, gazing up at his pupil with bitter supplication. His hands reach out as though finally obliged to intervene. They gently part the boy's knees, caress his inner thighs, begin to unbutton the cotton trousers. The boy's voice never falters but he does glance down when what the man is looking for is springily disclosed. He stops reading as they both regard what has been brought to light with differing shades of devotion. In both faces there is a hint of amazement that, for this moment at least, the entire world should have honed itself down to this single fine point of concentration. The planet beyond the window has ceased to exist. Almost with reverence for so sublime a banality the man slowly bows his head and the boy resumes his reading. Shortly afterwards he stumbles badly over a word, tilting the page towards the weak light and frowning.

'Herseemed,' the man prompts; then, raising his head, more distinctly says: '"Hersheemed." It means, "It seemed to her."' He, too, has an un-English accent. Prickles of sweat glisten between the cropped grey hairs on his scalp.

Herseemed she scarce had been a day
One of God's choristers . . .

The scalp disappears as the boy rests the book on it as on a gently bobbing lectern. A few lines later he lets the volume fall to the bed. The blessed damozel has served her purpose; libido is ousting literature. He leans back against the wall as again the hands reach upwards to unbutton his shirt and stray across his taut brown stomach. The boy's arms are rigid at his sides, his hands grasping the iron bedstead as he slides his lower half a little forward. After a while he brings his thighs decisively together. Jayjay notices how closely he is watching, unlike the girl earlier with her averted eyes and apartness. He is intent. So clearly vigilant of his own sensations and their convergence, his downward gaze becomes almost contemplative as he reaches the moment for letting his hands fall to the back of his teacher's head and pressing. His nails whiten with the firmness of his fingers. The man's own eyes are closed. Jayjay, greedily tensed against quarter-inch plywood only inches away, is terrified the panel will act as a sounding-board and fill the room with the amplified pounding of his heart.

Within minutes the teacher is buttoning up his own trousers and the boy is on hands and knees under the bed, retrieving his fallen slippers. The man picks up the Rossetti and smooths a crushed page before briefly slipping an arm around the boy's shoulders as though this is the only part of their transaction that requires a rationed daring. The boy smiles at the man's shirtfront. They both seem to have reached some small, amicable plateau, and it dawns on Jayjay that this might be a regular event between them. The man bestows cash as if it were pocket money rather than payment. Seconds later the room is empty once again.

A timeless fifteen minutes pass for Jayjay. This is something he hadn't known about, except through dark allusions in popular newspapers. It comes as a complete revelation that it is so widespread and international an activity as to merit formal marketplace procedures. He has a vision of himself, seen from far overhead in the soft Egyptian night, as a mouse crouched in the world's wainscoting. He is trapped, as he has been throughout this revelatory evening, between self-contempt and absorption. The self-contempt remains empty, theoretical; the engrossment embodies thrilling aspects of discovery as though he were at last making his way towards a place he was always destined to reach. It is akin to the feeling he experienced in his first week in Suez when the taste of fresh coriander ambushed him as at once alarmingly strange and nearly familiar, so instantly did he recognise it as a missing flavour which now, being identified, would become part of the rest of his life.

The thin door opens again and into the room come two more Egyptian boys, this time rather older, both well-built student types of perhaps sixteen or seventeen. They have the faintly deracinated air of people whose conversation has just been interrupted. They sit on the bed, waiting. One yawns. And there, closing the door behind him and shooting the cheap bolt carefully into its socket, is Richards. Richards of the small moustache and the pale forearms he now exposes by removing his linen jacket as though shedding the burden of command and eager for time off. Old hand Richards, who hadn't minded announcing that he set great store by first impressions and was not much for cockiness, has taken off his shoes and is padding towards the bed in cotton socks. The same Richards who Milo thought deserved to be sold as a slave to Arabians, Jayjay's senior at Anderson & Green, takes from his pocket what looks like a small pot of face cream before allowing the youths to remove his trousers unceremoniously. The boys are displaying signs of a puppyish, self-centred enthusiasm that borders on contempt.

And once again Jayjay cannot *not* watch. There is something about Richards' body, something about the root-white torso with its brown extremities, that damps his own excitement; yet this is more than made up for by the rising of sheer glee. Oh, what hostages we unthinkingly hand over to fortune as we broadcast our pretensions! As we bray our little observations about manners and standards, what rods are being laid up in pickle for us – or, as in this case, in Pond's cold cream! One after another the youths, who have removed only their shoes, punish Richards deeply and forcefully for being Richards: for being English, for being in Egypt, for being white, for being *mibun*. They are as indifferent to his initial pain as they are ruthless toward his eventual pleasure. Jayjay, impersonating his trinity of observers barely three feet away behind the panel, is intent on seeing everything and forgetting nothing even as a part of his brain is able to make certain plans and calculations. How beautifully, how thoroughly is Richards exploded! How timely this manner of delivering himself, crushed into rat-coloured ticking in a stifling plywood bordello by contemptuous youths still wearing their trousers, their buttocks bunching spasmodically beneath the thin material!

– Oh, it was wonderful at the beginning, before it went sour. He summoned me to his office the very next morning and started straight in about how right his first impressions invariably were, about how he'd known the moment he clapped eyes on me coming off the *Orontes* that I was not Anderson & Green material. 'I have here' (Richards said) 'your time-sheet which shows you have consistently been absenting yourself from the office during work hours. It's obvious you are in no way suited to a clerk's job.' 'Absolutely correct, old man,' I told him. 'The moment I saw you on the quayside at Port Taufiq I thought, now *there's* a fellow with a head on his shoulders. A true judge of character, or I'm a Dutchman. And I was spot-on. As you so brilliantly divine, I am not one of nature's clerks. Since we're in complete agreement about that, I suggest you bump me upstairs here as soon as you can and I'll try my hand at a bit of directing. I rather fancy that quiet little office at the end of the corridor.'
    – I really did think for a moment his face would burst. Speech eventually found its way through the congestion. There was a good deal of stuff about insolent young puppies to be got rid of

but eventually he reached his punchline about how I had a week's salary due and a steerage berth back on the *Orford* at the end of the month and I would be well advised to stay out of his way until then. Oh, and a little bird had told him I had fraudulently acquired a Company badge to which I was most certainly not entitled as a raw apprentice, and he wanted it back right this instant.

– 'No, no,' I said, 'you're being hasty, old man, as I'll explain if you'd just listen for a moment.' 'Don't you dare "old man" me, you saucy little sod,' said Richards. 'Very well,' I said. 'Gloves off. No more old men. Let's talk about young men. Specifically, let's talk about Ibrahim and Samih' (for of course I'd identified them through Mansur). Bluster. Never heard of 'em. Nor of a pot of Pond's cold cream, such as only last night helped blaze a trail its manufacturers probably never considered . . .? It's true: shock really does make people change colour. I remember he walked to the window and stared out. He seemed about six inches shorter. 'You rotten, rotten bastard,' he said in pure Birmingham. It went right through me. In eighteen and a half years I had never felt so contaminated by something I'd done. 'Listen,' I said. 'I promise you it was sheer bad luck I found out. I truly don't give a fig about your private life, Richards. And what's more, I hereby give you my word I shall never mention this again to a living soul: not to anyone, anywhere, ever. As far as I'm concerned, nothing leaves this room.'

– Actually, I was beginning to be quite frightened of what I'd done. In those days if such a story got out a man could be utterly ruined. A provincial fellow like Richards might go to any lengths to avoid exposure. It probably crossed his mind that here in Suez and with his knowledge of Arabic he could arrange to have me found floating somewhere out in the Red Sea, half eaten by sharks. Yet all I could think of was that he might kill himself, which was still the proper thing to do. I certainly didn't want his blood on my conscience for the rest of my life. The odd thing was, now that by sheerest mischance I had him at my mercy I began to feel almost tender towards him. He looked so shrivelled. 'I suppose you want money, then,' he said dully. 'I haven't much, you know.' 'No, I don't,' I told him. 'All I want is something you can quite easily arrange, and that's merely for me to continue in this job for as long as it takes me to find something better. All you have to do is edit or tear up the time-sheets and give reasonably satisfied reports of my progress. I'm also going to hang on to that Company badge of mine. And that's it.'

– In the circumstances, of course, I was asking practically nothing, as Richards knew perfectly well. Terrible scenarios of blackmail had no doubt been parading across his mental retinas, hotly pursued by equally dire remedies he might need to resort to. He looked at me almost fearfully. 'Can I really believe that's all?' he asked, bitter as well as hopeful. 'I swear it,' I told him, and gave him my hand. In those days one still did that on solemn occasions. He took it as though it might bite and dropped it almost at once. 'Did you, did you, er, actually *watch* . . .?' he asked, and his eyes filled with tears. His vulnerability shocked me into a confession of my own. 'Only for a bit. If it will make you feel any better, a similar thing happened to me a few days ago.' 'To *you*? You mean, you were watched?' 'No,' I said, 'just . . . well, what happened to you. The same. But only one person instead of two.' I thought maybe I'd gone too far and it would prompt him to some tearful complicity which I really did not want. Richards and I had nothing whatsoever in common. '*I* didn't pay,' I said with a touch of scorn. 'It was more or less unavoidable. These things happen. Not something you will be mentioning to anyone, no doubt.'

– You know, anal intercourse is the most wonderful social catalyst: I really can't recommend it too highly. Judiciously employed it can achieve remarkable things, and will do so for as long as a little shame still attaches to it. I suddenly had carte blanche to carry on drawing a salary in return for very little work while also being enabled to slip quietly into a more congenial world. All sorts of doors might be opened now that the entrance fee had been paid, while everybody had their reasons for keeping their lips sealed. These forms of social bargain are why one likes living in a

Mediterranean country, wouldn't you agree? People in these parts understand them to a nicety. In fact they love them; and the subtler they are, the better. It gives even business relationships an intimacy and zing which I really miss in Anglo-Saxon climes with their desperate and ultimately futile insistence on having everything out in the open. In fact, I'm not sure Anglo-Saxons or Americans have any pride left these days. They're just litigiously watchful for insults, which is not the same thing at all. Nor do they have any shame. They think anything they do is sanctioned by some sacred notion of individual rights or self-expression. But here in the Mediterranean a sense of shame and personal honour still exists, just, and the unspoken deal is that with a bit of care everyone can stand to gain unless you've badly wronged somebody or gone back on your word, in which case you're dead meat and deservedly so. But as a way of parlaying all our little weaknesses up into bargaining chips the system works beautifully.

– So I went back to the Caramanli that afternoon feeling pretty satisfied even though residually caddish about having cut Richards down to size. He was a pompous toad who needed deflating, but the humiliation I had inflicted on him was unfortunately overkill. Anyway, I felt I now understood a few things about him: that perhaps he was pompous out of self-defence; that he had probably acquired his Arabic more for the pursuit of pleasure than as a career move; that it was doubtless no mystery why he'd elected to stay on in Suez when he could have moved up in A & G and gone back home. In short, one way and another I had learned quite a lot recently: at least enough to ensure that whatever happened now I would never be able to return to Eltham a virgin.

– Thereafter Richards fades. We kept each other's smutty little secret and within a few months he'd been posted elsewhere. But when I was in Cairo years later I discovered he'd served with distinction as a Desert Rat and was decorated for bravery not long before he was killed at Bir Hakeim. Summer 1942, that would have been. I expect he's buried at Tobruk. Poor Richards. He may have been dive-bombed by a Stuka but I think he died of shadows.

– Yet that still wasn't quite the end of that momentous evening's voyeurism. A week or two afterwards in Shari' Ataqa I idly noticed some schoolkids coming towards me along the pavement, all wearing English-style striped cotton blazers. And there in the middle was the boy I'd seen through a hole in a wall reading Rossetti. I was absolutely amazed. It was unmistakably him (how could I be mistaken?) but he looked so much smaller. Judging by the way his ankles showed below his trouser-cuffs he was just beginning his growth spurt, but even so he seemed to have shrunk. I must have been staring as they came level, their heads so much lower than my own, for he broke off from a lively conversation with his friends to glance a bit frowningly at me as they passed. Haughty? Not exactly; but I was sadly aware of being no part of his universe, shut out of his circle. I couldn't match the reality of what I'd seen in that room with what I was meeting on the street. I was left feeling slightly injured: that he ought at least to have greeted me with a blush or some other bashful acknowledgement of how well I knew him. Technically, of course, we were total strangers. Yet I would quite truthfully have been able to tell him: 'I know what your cock looks like. I know the expression on your face when you come: something even you don't know.' But how can one say that to a stranger, let alone to a child?

– Ah, intimate knowledge gained without the requisite intimacy. Is that what it feels like to be a spy? A doctor? A priest? Privacy invaded in the pursuit of knowledge. Part of a voyeur's armoury. Part of a poet's, too, as well as an impostor's. –

For some time now I had been aware of becoming drawn into Jayjay's history at a level which occasionally disturbed me: faint but clear evidence that someone else's narrative can set up tensions as it meshes with one's own. I suppose this is inevitable when engaging with a living subject. (The dead can generally be dealt with by means of a comfortable tone that treats them indulgently or humorously or with more or less admiration.) The living have all sorts of juts and barbs on which one's pride may snag and be wounded. Or else, as in Jayjay's case, they confront one too forcibly with the less satisfactory aspects of one's own character. Also, there are no coincidences. Biographers and their subjects sniff one another out as much subliminally as by conscious design. He had read my books, I was intrigued by him. Our psyches had caught wind of each other's pheromones, and knowing this was both piquant and a source of unease.

I now felt I knew exactly the sort of young man he had been. It was a type I myself would have found intimidating, even something of a reproach, had I met him then. No matter how sensitive and impressionable he might have been, with how good an eye and ear for childhood's scenery (if rather less so for Eltham's human inhabitants), I do not believe Jayjay was subtly reinventing his teenaged persona to make him sound maturer, more decisive, less insecure than he actually had been. I think he really was that self-confident at eighteen and a half, away for the first time in his life from family and friends, walking the streets of Suez with a worldly eye open to the main chance and greedy for details, precocious with a certain brisk beadiness. Some of us remain children longer than others. Compared to Jayjay I had been a baby at that age, drifting somnolently from one safe haven of hallowed walls, which was my public school, into another afforded by an Oxford college. There was no real break between these venerable institutions. They were simply stages in a seamless process claiming to bestow a manly independence of mind even as it infantilised us into conformity. At eighteen and a half I had never been to a public political meeting and flirted with socialism, still less had I ever watched a Greek prostitute turning tricks in a Suez flophouse. I would have found those tropical positionings and glum transactions threatening. And the difference between us extended beyond matters of passive experience into resourcefulness of behaviour. Even had I acquired the sort of hold over someone that Jayjay had over the luckless Richards, I would never have dared capitalise on it in a way that so adroitly served the interests of both parties, any more than I would have had the nerve to court the

company of brigands running illegal rackets in the Middle East.
And as for paying the price he claimed to have paid (and I'm quite
sure did pay) for entrance into their seamy world, I do not believe
I would have been capable of his unruffled mixture of abandon
and pragmatism. What for me would have been an ordeal seemed
to have been a transient event for Jayjay, one to which he alluded
almost casually. But there again, a gulf of sixty years might so
divorce a distant trauma from the present as to endow his remembered self with the urbane disguise of a lifelong sophisticate.

Yet for all the difference between us, I could not dismiss the
sense I had of something being not quite right in Jayjay's
account. I am often not very bright about people's motives which
others manage to see through with cynical ease, so maybe I was
missing an obvious inconsistency in his early life story that any
intelligent person might seize on. But so far was I from identi-
fying it that I did not even know where – if at all – it lay, or what
question to ask to elicit the illuminating reply. After all, two
people who have known each other only a matter of months
confront one another with two unspoken lifetimes and a good
deal of catching-up to do – or as much as will be allowed. There
are bound to be gaps and opacities. All the same, I did wonder
why he had waited until now to find a biographer, to regurgitate
the semblance of a life, an authorised version: *plop!*, a Life in
three hundred pages. This man of whom I was becoming both
wary and fond gave off an intermittent bleakness not at all that
of a mere blithe nihilist such as anyone might affect to be these
days, what with millennial scenarios of germ warfare and environmental catastrophe mustering over the horizon. His was no
empty cynicism reliably ringing its hollow note when struck by
an idea. Nor was he the retired diplomat I had initially taken
him for, comfortably recapitulating a felicitous career in genteel
surroundings. He felt to me unmistakably (and this was where I
might be mistaken) like a man who had been deeply enough
wounded not to bother with pretensions, whether of the material
kind or else through a picaresque re-jigging of his own history.

I kept noticing that soldierly habit of his of tucking his hand-kerchief into his cuff.

The palimpsest of the Tuscan/Far Eastern landscape at my feet acquired another layer: a vaguely Middle Eastern, thirties blur, lacking borders but full of individual details. In the afternoons up on my hillside I might be sawing up next winter's fuel or splitting baulks of scrub oak with an axe whose blows echoed from the woods. I could stop with the flashing blade arrested overhead like Excalibur, suddenly struck by the oddness of the stranger whose house lay so nearly visible below and whose unsimilar yet vaguely congruent life gave back something (but what?) of my own that threatened to be painful. How best to live that wisp of time . . . How best to live it so that it would least resemble a soap opera full of episodic whirlings of activity, metropolitan frenzies, relationships melding and falling apart with gusts of stagy emotion and the pervading lie – or perhaps the pervading truth – that this, *this* is social realism. This is reality as lived by the majority of the Western world.

– Do, do, do – said Jayjay once, disgustedly. – Only a juvenile wants to *do* all the time. The astute adult wants to *be*: to live his imagination instead of forcing it into abeyance under a top dressing of mere busyness. How to live one's life is a deeper matter than just stuffing available time with random doings. As has recently been forgotten, living is an art, and like all art requires talent and diligence. Stylishness and pleasure are both a part of it; but they, too, must be a little rationed if we are not to become poseurs or blunted. Remain sharp: that's the aim. Sharp sadness, sharp enjoyment, sharp hunger. Sharp attention or nothing. No slumping while the days scamper past in an undifferentiated blur. There'll be time enough for rotting: the only thing everyone makes an equally good job of. –

After the short silence due this gem I told him sadly that it was all too obvious he'd reached the age when intelligence is ousted by mere wisdom. Still (I said) you could probably scratch a geriatric living thinking up mottoes for Christmas crackers. He was impressively ribald in return, but Japanese technology does not lie. That was what he'd said, those the words Jayjay had actually spoken, shorn only of pauses and ers and laughs. Sharp sadness: that was how he'd chosen to head his list and it is up to the biographer not to smooth it out into something lesser like 'an accurate melancholy'. Sharp sadness, I now think as I bring the bright axe down into too green a chunk of wood where it buries itself immovably, sap welling around it. Meanwhile I see from the cassette's date Japanese technology also captured a remark he made at much the same time as he recounted the loss of so many of his virginities in Egypt.

– Sex is an economical fuel. A good tankful before the age of twenty enables a man to coast through the rest of his life, if he has to, with an occasional eking-out. As with food, a lean diet does wonders for pleasure and longevity. –

This is surprisingly stern, very far removed from the guzzling fleshpottery of present times. It hints at a later abstemiousness either chosen or forced upon him, although of course it may be pure blarney. From time to time I allude to his initiation, calling it 'Suez' as a shorthand and a euphemism. 'Suez' soon became buried beneath a growing heap of other experiences and elsewheres; but, as he more than once said: 'Whatever else, I never forgot the blessed damozel.'

In the meantime, though, this mountainside I had unknowingly been sharing with the impostor *lorde* Jayjay seems to be trying to expel him from my attention. As I said, the Far East of my other life keeps surfacing its coconut palms through the chestnut forests below my doorstep. The deciduous and cypress greens of Europe darken imperceptibly to the colour of jungle fatigues. In place of the flat agricultural expanse of the Val di Chiana at the foot of the hills I see the South China Sea lapping around the promontories of Cortona and Castiglion Fiorentino. The buzzards revolving in the thermals above my house take on the plumage of fish eagles and in the terraced slopes beneath Etruscan hill towns my inward eye sees the terraced paddies of eight thousand miles away with their narrow silver panes, their piled slivers of water and rice. Sonic ghosts lurk beyond these blurred horizons as the whop of rotor blades and the sputter of M-16s. Arcadia and munitions: Southeast Asia's Siamese twins, joined at the heart.

This other life will not let me go. Utterly familiar yet constantly surprising, it draws me back over and over again for business I now know will remain for ever unfinished. Business of the heart and head as much as business to live by, although that too is beginning to press. My projected book on dictators and assorted monsters is now demanding attention, which I imagine is why that distant landscape pushes up so insistently through Tuscany each time I look up from chopping wood, just as it increasingly surfaces in my thoughts to distract me from Jayjay and his doings. As I have made clear to him more than once, it is a prior commitment that at intervals will have to take precedence over his tale. It is a job of work requiring no less attention than his and for me has twenty years' longer history behind it.

It is a curious sensation to be tugged between two places although it must be a commonplace in these days of mobility and migration. The image of divided attention is wrong, though, because it implies attention halved. Instead, something expands to make a full world of each. Now I start drawing up lists, looking through address books and sending messages off to that other world, trying to fix the interviews I shall need to conduct with its former satraps. I am fascinated by the deposed. It is endlessly gripping to watch their deft manoeuvrings to tear off some choice little lumps of power from the now rotting carcase of the regime they formerly served. In the way they smoothly accommodate themselves to the new status quo, no less than the way they are in turn accommodated, one visualises the hydrodynamics of a shark. It is a nearly aesthetic pleasure to watch them in action. With luck I shall be able to do so in person in a few months' time. One needs patience to set up interviews in Asia. My quarries scoot about the globe. Letters take for ever.

8

The businesslike mornings spent down at Il Ghibli had now shed
their last suggestion of formal interviews. Our arrangement began
slipping imperceptibly towards the latter part of the day. It was
not long before Jayjay was suggesting I stayed for dinner, and I
wondered once more whether he might be lonely. And then,
having accepted, I had to consider whether I might be as well.

By having asserted on our first meeting that how one chose to
live one's paltry allotment of years was the only interesting question, Jayjay inevitably brought my inquisitive scrutiny down upon
himself. Maybe it was unfair to expect a man on the doorstep of
his eighties still to be narrowly watching each passing minute
the better to cram it with edification or pleasure. Yet from what
of his everyday domestic life I observed – and by the end I believe
I saw pretty much all there was to see – he certainly didn't waste
time. By this I mean he read a good deal and watched old films
from an extensive video library. He would occasionally glance at
the news on television, but never for more than a few minutes.
'That's enough of *that*,' he would say decisively, turning it off. 'An

inherently trashy medium, don't you think?' He enjoyed planning his garden and would think hard before having this or that planted, imagining how things would look four months or even years later. He would conduct detailed conversations with Claudio about aphids and copper sulphate solution. Claudio, who smelt agreeably of fresh garlic and leaf-mould, would stand there with a sickle worn thin by sharpening hanging from a thick hand, listening in a silence that was neither deferential nor blank. His forte was disease and bonfires. It was almost with pleasure that he surveyed the local landscape and noted how many of the cypresses were dying. 'C'è la malattia in giro,' he would announce. 'They'll all have to come down sooner or later.' Jayjay called him the Grim Reaper.

Sometimes I would catch Jayjay just sitting, though not with that puffy, absent expression of the truly sedentary. I never had the impression that his mind was idling in neutral but that he was considering or else watching inner clips from a long life. I now think I never met anyone who gave such clear evidence of a constantly active mind.

He would hardly ever allow me to take him out for dinner, preferring to cook it himself at home which he did skilfully and without fuss. I would occupy a corner of the kitchen table and keep him supplied with gin and tonic while being given the occasional task such as preparing Brussels sprouts or peeling potatoes. He was quite particular about food, in the sense that he hardly minded what he ate so long as it was cooked with care and imagination. He wouldn't eat anything in the nature of fast food. He had once eaten a hamburger, he said, leaving me waiting for an amusing anecdote that never came. That *was* the punchline: he had once eaten a hamburger. There was nothing else to add.

As he chopped and sliced and stirred he would tell me gleefully how everything he was doing was, in fact, *wrong*; that according to the sacred lore of Tuscan cuisine it was tantamount to blasphemy sautéing this or that in butter or adding capers to that particular sauce. Eventually I discovered he was really carrying on a jocular feud with the absent Marcella, taking as much pleasure in cooking against her as in cooking for us. The feud was obviously long-standing, a rivalry that must have grown over the years, giving equal pleasure to both parties.

'Dear Marcella, now, I think I've more or less got her tamed, but every so often she catches sight of something I'm cooking and gets that Tuscan know-all tone in her voice. You remember that *arista* we had the other evening? She caught me preparing to marinade it overnight in oil, wine and herbs. What was I thinking of? And anyway, didn't I know that one always put garlic slivers *into* the meat and never directly in the marinade? Then when I was cooking it she made a great fuss about its not having been salted. I told her I would do it after I'd sautéed it, just before I added the liquid, or else it would draw all the juices out of the meat. You could see she took it personally as well as considering it an offence against centuries of hallowed tradition. Quite. Centuries of hallowed but dry *arista*.'

A definite congeniality attached to these expostulatory conversations of ours in Jayjay's beamed kitchen. Italy might have been a country we both loved, but all foreigners everywhere enjoy an occasional grouse about their foster home. It reminds them that they belong to the planet and not just to a particular spot on it. In any case our exchanges reinforced something between us: a shared uprootedness, perhaps. Nor was it simply a matter of our nationality, either, since unlike many foreigners we never grumbled about perennial Italian targets such as bureaucracy or corruption. Both of us were widely travelled and had spent years of our adult lives in lands whose bureaucracies and corruption were worse than Italy's by a factor of ten. Besides, we had long since come to appreciate the convenience of being able to solve little legal contretemps at a civilised personal level. On a visit to London a few years ago I was stopped by a policeman in Knightsbridge traffic for making an illegal turn and came within an ace of handing him a fiver out of a lifetime's sheer habit before remembering that this was England and we British did things differently. In short, greasing the wheels of life was nothing to jib at, whereas not being able to cook something without a Tuscan housewife saying you were doing it all wrong was a serious issue for complaint.

I liked overhearing the running battle that Jayjay and Marcella kept up when she was in the house: it was so obviously based on deep affection on both sides. So far as I was able to judge his Italian was flawless, and when she became mischievously bossy over his cooking or other domestic habits he would lapse into local dialect to remonstrate with her. 'Ddio boia, o che fè?' he would ask, peering disdainfully into the saucepan into which she was stirring some ingredient. He perfectly produced the slight goatlike bleating of *Ddio*, that thick peasant sound which made her collapse with laughter to hear in the mouth of a foreigner even though it was the language her father Claudio, and therefore she herself, had spoken from birth. Or he would eye the huge bowl of salad she had prepared for lunch and exclaim in mock disgust 'Mmadonna sbudellèta, erba, erba! Un sò' mica un bòe! O un cunìgglio . . .!' Marcella would pretend to be shocked by the muscular Tuscan blasphemies but it was obvious she found them as reassuring as she found Jayjay precisely because he understood the old ways of which they had been part and which had only recently been thrust below the surface of received Italian life, down into abeyance beneath the flavourless lingua franca of television and demotic culture. One could see the flirtatiousness of this eighty-year-old man and forty-year-old woman as they worked on each other's sense of humour, and not for the first time I was struck by the sheer attractiveness of the man if he wished to charm.

It seemed he had inherited Claudio and Marcella, father and daughter, together with the house nearly a quarter of a century previously. They lived in an adjacent farmhouse a little further up the valley from Il Ghibli, surrounded by terraces of olives which effectively ran unbroken into Jayjay's own. The year before Jayjay had taken the house in 1978 Claudio had been almost the last small farmer in the region still to be tied to the ancient system of *mezzadria*, or *métayer*, whereby as tenant he gave his landlord half of everything he produced. When the landlord died in 1977 Claudio's house and land became entirely his own property and he was a free man ('Oggi siamo tutti signori', people took pleasure in saying as they bought their wives cheap furs and went off to Africa on safari). In those days Claudio still kept a flock of sheep that grazed the terraces. Now he bought his mutton in the Co-op and owned a tractor with which he ploughed meticulously around the olives to bring air and nutrients to their roots.

I soon learned that Marcella was in and out of Jayjay's house most days: that far from being the thrice-weekly charlady I had initially taken her for she filled a role in both their lives that combined something of a wife, something of a sister and something of a daughter, as well as a watchful family friend keeping an eye on an elderly relative. If she herself was not around, her father very likely was, foraging purposefully nearby, blue with Bordeaux mixture or looking for something to chop down. But Marcella generally contrived to be there each day for at least half an hour and it was a surprise to learn that she had three children of her own to look after as well. Her young husband Eugenio had been killed in a horrendous and unnecessary accident seven years ago when employed as an engineer by the state railway. One Sunday morning he and a maintenance crew had been working on a stretch of the overhead power line between Arezzo and Florence when somehow the current for that section had been switched back on without warning. Eugenio and three others on the wheeled gantry were killed instantly. I never formed any very clear idea about Eugenio's emotional legacy. I seldom heard him mentioned and the children, two teenaged girls and a ten-year-old boy, seemed not obviously fatherless. His financial legacy, though, was much better defined. Since the FS was a state industry the union had very properly extracted some decent sums by way of compensation and at forty Marcella was also drawing a widow's pension.

It became clear to me how wrong I had been – betraying, no doubt, the sentimental indulgence we impose on the elderly – to suppose Jayjay might be short of company. A less lonely person I never met, at least in the superficial sense of his apparently having as much affection and companionship as he wanted. (It was necessary to qualify this by saying that his desire for company had distinct limits and to observe that he was a man used to being a loner who had built up the strength of those who expect no help.) Marcella's children treated him like a grandfather, as one of the family; and it was obvious that the little boy Dario, in particular, adored him unreservedly. Equally plainly Jayjay adored him in return, and the two indulged in a sort of pre-erotic version of the flirtatiousness Jayjay and Marcella shared. One is reduced to calling it flirtatiousness because there seems no other adequate word. It was more piquant than teasing, though kinder, while never edging too close to suggestiveness. Dario would listen spellbound to Jayjay's stories of other times and distant places: of a haunted oasis south of El Kharga lived in by werewolves who went loping off across the desert after sunset; of the gold death-mask Jayjay had watched being made for a Greek shipping magnate of his lover who had fallen from a trapeze; of a maze designed by a stranger for the botanical gardens in Samarkand which had had to be ploughed up in the nineteenth century because nobody who entered it ever came out again. Jayjay, supreme ghoul himself, understood the essential ghoulishness of boys and delighted Dario with accounts of horrid recipes he had eaten around the world. The sheep's eyes and tenderised puppies led naturally to a description of General Idi Amin's famous fridge full of his enemies' body parts. Yet in more dangerous matters he was obviously quite scrupulous. I encountered an example of Jayjay's tastefulness towards Dario when the boy once showed me Lady Amelia's squashed dildo and gave me a version of the story Jayjay must have told him. In this slightly edited account the object was simply a model of her dead husband's cock which she had carried about with her as a sentimental keepsake, like a lock of his hair. Pretty weird, huh? said Dario. But listen: Lady Amelia was nothing compared to her sister, Agatha. *La Agata* had kept a plaster cast of every pet she ever owned and lived in a palace whose floors were strewn with plaster Pomeranians, whose sofas sagged beneath the weight of plaster pussy-cats and whose ceilings were hung with cages of plaster bullfinches. Even the bath was full of plaster gold-fish. And when she died . . .? No, said Dario, firmly shaking his head, 'they didn't make her into a plaster cast. But when they cut her open to see why she had died they discovered her heart was made of plaster . . . Hee-hee, got you there! Just for a minute you believed that, didn't you? (passing on with glee the very narrative prank with which Jayjay must have caught him).

The first time I had seen Jayjay and Dario together they were playing with a rocket kit that involved filling a plastic Schweppes tonic bottle with water and pumping it up with a bicycle pump. The bottle, poised on three red fins, suddenly took off with a great drench of water, flying to an extraordinary height before twirling down. It disappeared with a faint crash among Claudio's vegetables with Dario in hot pursuit, whooping with pleasure.

'The critical thing,' explained Jayjay when he caught sight of me, 'is the amount of water. You need the mass, of course, but too much water means not enough room for the compressed air. We think about a third full gives the best results, *giusto*?' He turned to Dario, switching back to Italian as the boy trotted up with the rocket, his blue T-shirt blotched with water. Suddenly shy in the presence of a stranger, Dario turned towards me with a smile, leaning confidently back against Jayjay. For a moment I had almost forgotten Jayjay was so much older than Dario, their easy intimacy being that of boys at play. But the old man's hands were gravemarked and shockingly large against Dario's chest as he stood with the child's fists clenched around his middle fingers. Thus might any boy face the world, a parent at his back, I thought with an unseemly pang of something like envy.

If after hearing a session of the tall tales with which Jayjay cap-tivated Dario I sometimes set the nose of my pickup truck almost grimly on the homeward track up to my empty house, calling Jayjay a pinchbeck Munchausen or Walter Mitty under my breath, it was nothing but private pain speaking. This merits a brief, parenthetical explanation simply because it has a bearing on my relationship with Jayjay. For reasons into which I will not go, it was not until I was forty that I met the only person with whom I have ever been capable of sharing a house. Frances, thirteen years my junior, was uncomplainingly bohemian, so we never much addressed (certainly not enough, as it turned out) questions of relative comfort or relative security but simply assumed an amicable permanence. Our daughter Emma was the result; and I could not have imagined that becoming a father in middle age would so ensnare me in pleasure. Emma's finding speech inside herself and rapidly building up a vocabulary – partly overheard, partly invented – was so enthralling to me that it was as though she might have been the human race's last child and I entrusted with the handing-on of the entire language, the whole culture, everything known and unknown. The egotism of unqualified love, you will say. I will allow 'self-importance'; it felt nothing to do with the ego and far more to do with some absurdly grandiose sacrament that at the very least required as great attention to the details of Emma's upbringing as to those of her bodily welfare. (The first time I properly examined her tiny fingernails a few hours after her birth I had found myself on the verge of tears.)

For the purposes of this book, at any rate, this is a story soon ended. Middle-aged men who have lived mostly as wanderers cannot easily re-invent themselves just because they become fathers. In theory the idea of 'settling down at last' ought to imply a degree of relief: no more returning to an empty house, no more roaming the cruddier parts of the globe with a frayed nylon bag and sour trousers. I'm afraid for me it has overtones of scuttling for refuge. I began to yearn to find the house empty, while the cruddier parts of the globe increasingly returned to me in dreams positively aglow with the ache of association. I adored Emma; but then I have adored quite a few people over the decades. Can one construct a life around adoration unless one is religious? The truth is I am no good at exclusive relationships. I never have been and never will be. Deep down I lack the interest as well as the requisite skill. It took me years to discover this plain fact and longer still before I could admit to it. So powerful is my native culture's propaganda I grew up accepting that to fail in one's relationships was to fail in life itself. Even in university days we would bandy about words like 'inadequate' and 'immature' with the confident earnestness that meant they applied only to others. The ready equation was drawn: unloving, unloved. But no, that was not me at all. I like easygoing, rather masculine friendships such as Victorian men favoured and many cultures still do. They have entirely sufficed and I have never wished for more. (Sex, of course, is an unrelated matter.) So for most of my adult life I have been content to leave 'relationships' to the majority of people who clearly think they're good at them. I know my limits. Or thought I did. How on earth, it will be wondered, could I ever have imagined I might enter a committed domestic relationship and become a father at the age of forty? How indeed. There probably is an answer; but teasing apart the various layers of self-delusion, contingency and the nearing rumble of the damned Chariot's wheels would be wearisome.

Enough to say that less than two years went by before Frances left to marry a dullard who owned a sound studio in Ladbroke Grove. I might have imagined for her a man from the shires nearer her own age and background, someone more solid, less verbal than me. What she chose was a decaying hipster of fifty who kept up an unwitty patter about the famous pop stars and voice-overs who had recently been in his studio, his voice made even louder by a lifetime's talking while wearing headphones. I hope he reads this, but I don't believe he's read a book in his life other than the odd technical manual: thus do the sublimely ignorant protect themselves from thought. In any case Frances took our daughter with her to join his own vague and extended family who apparently spent much of the time lying around in a haze of cannabis fumes or worse. So what *was* the missing ingredient? I would ask the walls of our empty house, still marked with odd streaks of crayon, and receive no satisfactory answer. Me, I presume. I also presumed money (of which this man had a good deal more than me) but without ever completely believing it. These things are opaque, mysterious. What was not mysterious was the sheer pain of missing Emma, who will be sixteen next April. I still cannot quite believe it was all snatched away through my own fault; but it was, and it can never be restored or caught again. Children slough off so many skins so fast, together with former fathers.

So now when I watch Jayjay playing doting grandfather to Dario's equally doting grandson and note with a pang the boy's own grubby little fingernails, it can mobilise something within me that comes perilously close to jealousy. For a while I bought myself off by imagining that by the time I was in my sixties Emma might have presented me with an honorary grandchild. This, I pretended, would sop up the love which had once begun to well but which was never permitted to flow for long enough to become part of the main stream of someone else's private history. These days, at the moment of arriving home when the pickup's headlights crest the last slope and cut the silent house out from the edge of black space on which it stands, I no longer rely on its ever happening. We make our own luck, and isolation often seems like a refuge from far worse.

Such, then, was Jayjay's domestic ménage, and such my own. And if I was secretly surprised at finding his so rich, I was correspondingly downcast by the unintended reminder that my own lacked by comparison. It seemed like another reason for feeling slightly inferior to the person whose life I was supposed to be writing, a very bad state of affairs indeed. Even if his subject is Wolfgang Amadeus Mozart a biographer still holds in reserve one final incontrovertible superiority: that he is not at this moment lying somewhere beneath the foundations of a launderette in Vienna but alive in living air, making himself cups of coffee, tripping over the cat and whistling about the house as if immortal. Shorn of such an advantage over Jayjay I resolved to discover in him either something I could openly admire or else something I could secretly despise, either of which may serve as the basis of a workable alliance.

– Suez was my nursery, and I wasn't ready to leave it until nearly six months were up. By then Richards had left and there was no-one to cover for me so I took a week's wages and walked out on Anderson & Green, a mutually unregretted move. I had also seen and heard the last of my involuntary room-mate Simpkins and his cavernous farts. I was whizzing, picking up the language, learning the rackets, discovering Mansur's limits as a fixer. His limits as a lover were quickly reached, thank goodness, although I did grow quite fond of him. At least, it seems to me I did; but then the whole of that era in my life when I was shaking out my new plumage in the Middle Eastern sun seems to glow. Nostalgia, you know. Lost youth, all that. No doubt things were a bit more equivocal at the time.

– It was now 1937 and I had already made a few useful contacts in Cairo and elsewhere. The time had come to say goodbye to Milo, whose rackets had afforded me some modest savings, and start travelling. I decided to go up the Nile, partly because I really needed to get out of Suez and partly because I very much wanted to see this mythical river. A further reason was that Milo had given me an introduction to a German anthropologist named August Moll-Ziemcke who was working in what in those days was the Anglo-Egyptian Sudan. I think his village was called Hamir, but maybe that was the name of the district. It's so long ago. It was somewhere past the Fifth Cataract, on the east bank of the Nile near Atbara. More Nubian than desert Arab. I knew he was planning to spend a couple of months in Khartoum, possibly to get the manuscript of a book* finished, so I arranged to meet him there. I took a train to Cairo and set off in a series of river steamers, allowing myself a leisurely eight weeks for the journey.

* *Hort- und Verleihverhalten eines halbnomadischen Niloti-Stammes* (Berlin, 1940).

– And what a journey! You must remember that with the exception of river steamers taking Cook's tourists up to Luxor that part of the world was still little touched by the twentieth century. Well before one reached Upper Egypt one could imagine that the view from the Nile was essentially unchanged from what it had been a thousand years ago, maybe even two or three thousand. And once one had passed Wadi Halfa it was like being lost in time. Both sides of the river were pretty much nomad territory, the tribes moving about seasonally with their flocks. It would in theory have been possible to set off due west across the Sahara and not to see a living soul until one reached the Atlantic ocean 2,500-odd miles later. The winter rains had only just ended and there were some lush savannahs still visible with great carpets of wildflowers and misty green acacia trees. Egrets, hornbills, kites, and those king-fisher-blue Abyssinian Rollers: it was unbelievably beautiful and *primordial*. One could easily believe in the Garden of Eden. I gather it's virtually gone now because the climate has changed and there have been ten-year droughts recently that have decimated the vegetation. The wretched nomads have mostly been driven south to fill the slums of places like Omdurman and Khartoum or else north to work in Libya. A millennia-old culture and way of life broken up and destroyed in only a few decades. The longer I live, the less I enjoy talking about those pre-war days of travel, of places and people which are either all changed beyond recognition or vanished entirely. It isn't the same planet today. It feels as though a different sun rolls from an exhausted sea to light up lands that bear little relation to those I knew. My exact roads are effaced for ever; they can't be wandered again. Nor should one try, of course. But it's not true that it was ever thus. The degree of change has never before been so huge or so swift, and it will never now be reversed.

– I got off a rusty little boat at a nowhere town called Abu Dom, all because I'd met a young Sudanese official on board who was connected with the NAO. That was the Native Administration Ordinance which the British had set up as a way of keeping the dozens of different tribes, with their conflicting migratory traditions and ancient rivalries, in some sort of harmony. In fact it was a scheme that worked quite well and depended on power being given back to local leaders such as *nazir*s and *omda*s. This fellow I met on the boat was some sort of policeman. He had been on an official mission downstream and was badly delayed in his home village by a wedding or a circumcision or other vital ceremony. So there he was, due back in Omdurman in ten days with getting on for seven hundred river miles to cover. At our rate of progress it would have taken him a month because the steamer's boilers kept leaking. He proposed we went overland from Abu Dom to Omdurman, which would have been about a hundred and eighty miles because it cut off a great loop of river. Since he was hoping to arrange for us to travel with a caravan, and since he said we ought to do it in little more than a week, I volunteered to join him. He explained it was a route that was fairly frequently travelled, unlike most other desert routes, and we might even strike lucky and get a lift on a Citroën half-track or something like that.

– Well, we didn't, and retrospectively I'm glad we didn't. We found ourselves with a group of Kababish – I forget now which tribe they were. Nurab? That rings a bell. They were taking camels to sell in Khartoum, about two hundred head. It was an astonishing journey and hellishly tough since I'd never sat on a camel before. Twelve hours' slogging by day, riding or else walking when the going was too soft. I'd fancied until then that I was getting on reasonably well in Arabic, but I was floored by the dialect they were speaking. Not only was their accent peculiar but half their words referred to parts of camels or species of bush or qualities of sand. It certainly resembled no language that would get you by in the back streets of Suez.

– The thirst was awful. Just when you thought you would die they stopped and brewed up scalding sweet tea and stuff called *kisri* that I've never forgotten. It was a kind of primitive polenta, but don't confuse it with our polenta here. Ours is either maize flour or chestnut flour and liberally covered with *ragù* sauce. Theirs was made of millet, and I think it was rotten millet at that: rancid and bitter. If you were lucky they put a dab of goat butter on it. At night you slept on skins in the lee of the camels which hunkered down on their knees in the sand. It was mortally cold, so cold you couldn't sleep properly. Besides, there were always people astir. They set watches and patrolled all the time because they were terrified of being caught asleep by camel rustlers from other tribes. I'm not sure the Kababish ever did go to sleep completely.

– I can't now remember exactly how many days it took us. It seemed to last for a period impossible to measure by ordinary means. I have always thought of it as being ten days and I expect that is about right. In all that time we passed one oasis with a village, if you could call it a village. Four or five cane huts with straw roofs. There was a well there and even an *umbasha*, a sort of police corporal, so it was practically a township. I saw into one of the huts and there was almost nothing in it. A carpet, a rope bed, some pots and hangings. Nothing that couldn't be rolled up and loaded on to a camel in a matter of minutes for the next migration to pastureland. They didn't want to settle, those people. Their whole culture was centred on nomadism and I had the impression they felt no sentimentality about places as such. All they cared for was wandering, and they paid the minutest attention to landscape and season and vegetation so as to know whether it was worth trekking a hundred miles to a particular pasture. Sometimes we met other travellers and the greetings seemed to go on for ever before they got down to the real gossip. Although to me the desert looked completely empty I gradually formed the idea that there were surprising numbers of people purposefully roaming it and swapping news so that the vast emptiness was to some extent knitted together by an efficient bush telegraph.

– Certainly I came to admire the people I was with. They weren't at all friendly, actually, especially towards a foreigner like me. I was too ignorant of all the things which to them made a man and was not even worthy of their contempt. I had no animals of my own, no wife, not even a single slave. I knew nothing about camels, couldn't make a hobble for one, didn't know how to make a gazelle trap, didn't know what to do if a *simun* blew up, couldn't navigate by the stars . . . You name it and I couldn't do it, apart from knowing how to use a typewriter and a wireless and find my way around the London underground system and all the other things that to them counted for nothing. Mine was a world so far beyond their universe it didn't exist at all. It literally meant nothing to them that I was English and therefore represented the ruling power in the Sudan. It meant something to my policeman, which is why he was so friendly, but not to the Kababish. To them Khartoum was the terrifying outer fringe of another world in which they had no part. 'Sudan' itself was just a name they'd heard in the mouths of travellers. I was nothing more than baggage on that journey. No, worse than baggage because neither was I useful nor could I be sold at the end. Really, being surrounded by hostility and contempt, especially in conjunction with the hardships of the trip, ought to have made it a miserable experience.

– Yet I loved it. It was like casting off an old skin and acquiring a flexible new guise. When you're just nineteen and on the loose in the world you notice everything and love most of it. You notice the way you can smell camels in the desert before you can see them. You notice the metallic centipedes that look as if they're made of chromium. You are astounded by a landscape that in certain lights and conditions can surround people with golden dust, so when they lead a goat or squat to relieve themselves they seem to move in their own private aureoles. Or else at dusk a plain of volcanic pebbles can take on surreal tints as if they were a broken pavement of emerald or malachite. And because these wastes demanded such specialised survival skills I could feel my own ignorance stretching to the tips of my fingers and the ends of my toes. The nomads' ability to read any tracks we encountered finally gave me proof of the belief I'd formulated at Eltham College: that it ought to be possible to negotiate the world via an entirely different set of senses and a completely alien body of knowledge. We would come upon a jumble of animal and human footprints in the sand and the Kababish would dismount and look at them and within seconds they could not only say exactly how many animals had made them but which tribe they belonged to and how long ago they had passed. My policeman acted as interpreter for me and said they were always right. What was more, they could recognise the tracks of individual beasts and people. Each camel had its own name and its owner could tell its tracks from a hundred others, often even years after he had sold it. Good trackers could tell a male from a female by its footprints and even say whether the female was pregnant and by how many months. One evening we caught up with another group and I saw with my own eyes that, as had been predicted hours earlier, there were indeed thirty-seven camels, three of them bulls in rut, belonging to the Awlad Fahal or whichever tribe it was, one of whom was old Ibrahim the brother of Whatsit with his bales of ostrich feathers. They could do it with people, too. They could tell so much from a person's tracks, down to essentials of his character, that I became ashamed of my own footprints because of what they might be revealing. You've no idea how vulnerable and inferior that can make you feel, knowing that your every step gives you away. I felt thoroughly transparent to those opaque people.

– We eventually reached Omdurman and the Kababish left us without a wave or a handshake. They were the toughest people I have ever met anywhere. By then I had experienced enough of the hardship of their lives to admire them immensely and I'd seen enough of the desert to have been bitten by the bug. It's obvious from your books, James, that with you it was more the sea that got into your bloodstream. But with me it was sand. If ever I yearn to undo my life and return to a time and a place it is to 1937 on the fringes of Northern Kordofan. As it happened it was only a few months before Wilfred Thesiger, who was then in the Sudan Political Service, visited almost exactly the same area to hunt Barbary sheep.

– Having said which, though, one needs to be a bit accurate about this famous desert bug. Ever since all those Doughtys and T. E. Lawrences the myth of the desert's lure for certain kinds of romantics grew to the point where there was practically a recognisable British Foreign Office sort who devoted his life to Arabic studies and rough journeys, to say nothing of some quite rough sex. I once heard them referred to as 'sitah' types, which stood for 'sand in the arse hole' as well as meaning 'buttocks' in Arabic. That, at any rate, was not the bug that bit me. As soon I reached Omdurman, in fact, it became clear that the Sudanese there looked down on the Kababish as feckless vagrants who would cut your throat as soon as look at you. As far as they were concerned nomads were unlettered barbarians rather than noble savages. And later on I noticed that Cairenes and Alexandrians felt pretty much the same way about the Bedouin who came into town to sell their sheep and whatnot. To city-dwellers these were shiftless swindlers who didn't wash enough. Someone once remarked on the way the writings of travellers like Doughty, Thomas, Lawrence and even Thesiger helped create a myth of the romance of desert folk and went on to draw a parallel with the way Sir Walter Scott's novels had created a similar romance about Scottish Highlanders, generally viewed by Lowlanders as a lot of unkempt barbarians who would be the better for a job of work instead of a life of drunken banditry.

– This was not the sort of mythmaking I was caught up in. I admired the Kababish, I was humbled by their survival techniques, but I can't pretend I *liked* them any more than they liked me. I neither wanted to be them nor to join them. I would have been happy to know that I should never again in my life have to sit on a camel or eat *kisri* at dawn with frozen fingers. No, all I meant was that I found the desert extraordinarily beautiful, a particular landscape that happened to become woven into the sappiest period of my life when my nerve-endings were buzzing with new sense-impressions and my bloodstream fizzing with hormones. It's a matter of simple association, really, rather than any deep affinity between me and deserts. –

Jayjay's passing mention of my books, hinting at the way the sea washes through me and my own nomadic past, suggested a contributory reason why he should have chosen me to write his life. Here and there I had written of my own youthful travels, which began as soon as I had broken out of my education's golden cage. He had no need to tell me how it had felt to roam the world at a time when the going was very much less convenient and a necessary hardiness was its own reward. (Those hot awnings beneath which one found oneself sharing food with incomprehensible strangers! The improvised bivouacs in high stony passes! The close, fronded nights where one understood nothing of political intentions and lay in sleepless dread of attack. The eggshell mornings when the sun levered itself above the sea's rim to reveal passionate scuff-marks in the sand next to where one had been lying. The huge, brawling diversity and strangeness of it all was intensely thrilling. Greedily one partook of as much as one could bear and then broke off for a while to walk monkishly alone, silent, sleeping beneath unfamiliar constellations and waking on beaches where all the footprints were one's own. Still, it does not do to overlook the longueurs: the listless weeks spent hanging around, bored and morose, detesting the people, their primitive stupidity, even the sun itself with its mindless habit of following one blinding day with another, each indistinguishable. *What am I doing here?* The traveller's inner cry spurts bitterly up, involuntary. And there is no clear answer; not until, maybe as much as thirty years later, it writes itself as a book.)

So I can see that Jayjay, with his stated concern for spending a life well and an awareness of how formative his own early travels had been, perhaps found something in my history that we held in common.

– This German anthropologist I had come to visit in the Sudan, old August, was a strange fellow. Very tanned and pale-eyed, thinnish beard with Struwwelpeter hair. We met as arranged in Khartoum where he gave me a vivid description of the village in which he'd been living for the last two years. He told me he had

a hut to himself made of stakes with a conical reed roof. I visu-
alised it as being at one end of a dismal village that sort of lay and
panted in the shade of some palms and acacias. I also had the
impression that everything there seemed to be composed of dust,
twigs or skin. I say 'old' August but he wasn't old at all – late
twenties, I should think. He only seemed slightly elderly to me
because he had very punctilious, old-fashioned manners. His
family was good Prussian military stock and I never did discover
how he'd made his getaway into academia. He told me how much
his parents disliked Hitler: 'Jumped-up little Austrian guttersnipe'
sort of thing. But this was 1937 and even the Prussians in the
Wehrmacht were willing to give Hitler a chance because he'd
pushed so many goodies their way in the shape of nice new uniforms, good pay, and first-rate new weapons and equipment. Plus,
of course, bags of swank.

– Old August was a million miles removed from all that. It
was the first time in my life I'd been obliged to wonder about
field anthropology, and I'm still not completely satisfied. I
mean, what is it really *doing*, one culture studying another?
Compared with anthropology, even a missionary's job is clear-
cut. That's just religious imperialism, still somehow hanging
on in an age that otherwise claims to have renounced imperialism and all its works. But field anthropologists are supposed to
be neutral observers. They're supposed to record intimate
details of customs and practices in a society not their own, and
all without participating, so as not to produce that famous
quantum effect of the observer changing the thing observed.
Tricky, that. And one does also wonder about their private
motives. Why *there*? I mean. Why *them*? In August's case one
did well to suspect some fairly intimate reasons. Since I don't
read German I never read the weighty tome he was just finish-
ing and in any case it sounded far too academic for me. But at
the same time as he was writing that, he was keeping a studio in
Cairo supplied with films and photographs which were by no
means academic. He also turned out to be writing an equally

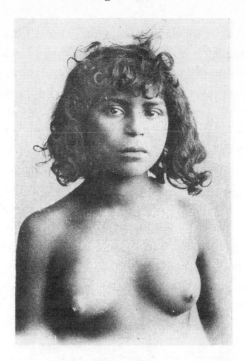

risqué memoir or possibly novel that eventually found its way
into print via some small German publisher before it was seized
and burned by the Nazis.* These days copies must be exceed-
ingly rare if they exist at all, but I gathered in Cairo during the
war that at least one had escaped and clandestinely done the
rounds there before the rest of the edition was destroyed in
Germany. It was rumoured to be very strange and interesting,
which of course meant obscene, and had to do with lenses, the
difference between being an observer and a voyeur and so on,
all mixed in with some pretty confessional stuff. I don't think
anyone was surprised that the Nazis burnt it, but we were all
shocked when we heard of poor August's death in Omdurman.
He had been interned by the British at the start of the war but
later allowed to go back to his village. None of us had the least
doubt that he'd been assassinated.

* *Der Liebe Objektiv und Ziel* (Weimar, 1941).

– But that's to jump ahead a few years. When I first met him in Khartoum, August proved to be most amiable. He was quite open about his photographs once I'd dropped a few names and revealed I was familiar with the business. He made no bones about it meaning more to him than just a hobby that paid for itself. It was a heart-and-soul matter for him, equally academic and erotic. He showed me a lot of his stuff. He did have some pretty horrid footage, like the films he'd shot of local circumcision rituals, both female and male. I couldn't watch those, not my sort of thing at all, but I had to admit they were expertly made. And here's a curious fact that maybe says something about the ambivalence of a certain kind of anthropology. Even as those films were treated by scholars as valuable archive material, pirated copies were selling briskly in Egypt as pornography and I'm told stills from them even crop up today in Scandinavian porn mags. Furthermore,

those very films were used by the CIA in the fifties and sixties for the induction of new recruits. Young potential agents were made to sit in a darkened theatre and watch August's circumcision footage. The ones who threw up or left in a hurry were simply thanked, given their fare home and scratched from the list. It was officially reckoned that if you fell at the Moll-Ziemcke hurdle you were probably too squeamish ever to make a good field agent. No hard feelings.

– But the bulk of August's photographs had scant pretensions to be considered as anthropology although after sixty years I expect they contain some valuable details. I have to say I think he was a first-rate photographer, especially given that he was working in the back of beyond, and this must have extended beyond mere technical ability. He must have had considerable charm or something because none of the people in his pictures ever looked terrorised or drugged or haunted. Quite the reverse. They seemed to me relaxed and reasonably intent on what they were doing – people screwing, kids tossing off, the usual sort of thing. Nothing gross, as the Americans would say. And to this day I don't know how he achieved that because I presume his subjects were mainly drawn from the people he was living amongst and I can't see how he could have done that without compromising himself and becoming notorious. Perhaps he became a sort of Kurtz figure, living in his Nubian fiefdom. But that doesn't seem likely in the Anglo-Egyptian Sudan, which was rather well administered. Even less does it accord with what August told me about the prevailing sexual mores of that region. On my journey with the Kababish I had occasionally wondered what they did for erotic fun and August was able to enlighten me. The answer was, precious little. Forget recreation: it was procreation or nothing. Men coupled with their wives in a matter of seconds. Not a stitch of clothing was removed and the woman was anyway circumcised. Anything in the way of foreplay was thought effeminate. It's true that August's people were Nubians of sorts rather than Kababish, but I shouldn't have thought sexual practice on one bank of the Nile would be vastly different from that on the other.

– I don't know. I can't remember the details of all his pictures. Maybe he'd shot most of them in the slums of Omdurman. He certainly had a good few pictures of non-Nubians with altogether lighter, Arab features. Heaven knows where he took those. He moved about, did old August. I do remember he had problems preserving film in the heat, getting it processed, keeping dust out of the camera. He had a friendly technician in the Siemens lab in Khartoum, which I believe was the only one of its kind in the country in those days. He had a Siemens cine camera before it was stolen. Then he bought a Kodak Cine Special with two lenses, which is the one I saw. Brand-new model, a beautiful camera for its day, actually. Quite compact and light. I remember it could even do tricksy things like fade-outs and dissolves. No doubt that was how August made his stuff look so professional.

– I must have spent about three weeks in Khartoum, quite a lot of it with him. The rest of the time I roamed about the area trying to work out what to do. (Always that question!) Khartoum was much hotter and dustier than Cairo, besides which it felt immensely provincial. None of that immemorial Egyptian decadence and sophistication that occasionally reeked of ancient Greece. It was definitely Africa we were in. I could see that August's life there was an end in itself for him. He was content to go on living at an imaginative point where certain things important to him converged: vision, voyeurism, lenses, black skin, sex, dust, twigs. But I knew I wasn't like that. Those all interested me, of course, but they were tangential. Some of us do indeed make better observers than participants, but I'm not one of them. I like to get my hands grubby. What I wanted, as I now perceived it, was *contacts*. I wanted to know the useful and meet the powerful: people who could walk through the grandest doors without noticing that I might be following them into the room. And I now thought I knew how to go about it.

– Every so often when he needed money August would pack up a fresh batch of pictures and send them off on an Imperial Airways flight to Cairo where a chap called Mehdi-something passed them on to a few contacts like Mansur and the Greeks in Suez. They relied entirely on street trash to hawk it around, especially in the Port Said and Suez docks. They also farmed some of it out to people like Milo for duplication in little dark rooms on top of hotels. But distribution was haphazard and amateurish. They were not getting the stuff efficiently and reliably into the hands of people who would pay real money: the Egyptian middle classes, the Pasha class, the diplomats in the foreign legations, all the people whom it was worth squeezing. Above all, there was a large British floating population in Cairo, with small branches in places like Alexandria and Port Said and even, in season, Luxor. Lots of grandee drones and litty, Lawrence Durrelly sorts. Well-born ladies who liked muscular Pyramid guides out at Gisa. Well-born gentlemen who had a liking for boat-boys on *dahabiya*s moored on the Nile. I could see distinct possibilities.

– So I sold my watch. It was a Benson, rather a nice one my father had given me as a travelling present. That afforded me several pangs, actually. But I'd met a fellow in a café who liked it and I think I let it go because it was a constant reminder of home and my father. I hadn't even written to him about leaving Anderson & Green, though no doubt by now they would have told him. As far as he was concerned I must have fallen off the map. Anyway, I sold his watch to buy pornography, which now looks to me a decisive act for any son. I bought a bundle of carefully selected films and negatives from August, told him I could put his pictures into the hands of paying connoisseurs rather than leering touts, embraced him like a brother and set off back down the Nile to seek my fortune. –

9

The Cairo in which Jayjay arrived on his Nile steamer in 1937 was the biggest, liveliest and most sophisticated city on the entire African continent, as well as the most cosmopolitan. It was also jumping with intrigue and skulduggery that represented the cross-currents of European politics in the run-up to war as they intersected with the various factions of Egyptian nationalism. The nationalists had mainly turned into amateur seers, desperately trying to predict which alliance with which great power might prove most advantageous to the cause of Egyptian independence and to their own elevation. The sizeable British community held itself considerably aloof and ignorant of these cryptic currents. In the way it managed this lay something fatally in tune with the end of Empire. Most British residents made no effort to mix with Egyptians and it was quite possible to spend years in the country without speaking to any other than one's house servants. The British had their own shops and clubs and hotels; there was an endless social whirl of parties and dances and entertaining visitors. As usual the military formed a special sub-species with its own barracks and cantonments, its own sports and dances and social life, its peculiar codes and traditions. None of this prevented there being many individual Britons in a wide range of professions scattered the length and breadth of the country who greatly loved Egypt and its people. They often worked tirelessly to demonstrate a fundamental benevolence in the British presence. But in Cairo, at any rate, most British civilians seemed devoted largely to the pleasures of their own bizarre exclusivity, which typically entailed a degree of scorn for those excluded. At the end of 1937 Jayjay was to be introduced to Dr Cecil Alport, a distinguished man who had recently arrived from London to take up his appointment as Professor of Clinical Medicine at Cairo's main teaching hospital. Years later Dr Alport was to publish the memoir I had found in Jayjay's lavatory in Il Ghibli which recorded his astonishment on discovering this aspect of the British presence. He wrote that

> 'the habit – common in the extreme – of referring indiscriminately to every Egyptian as a "Wog" is a form of cheap snobbery which gets us nowhere. It is said that the term "Wog" originated in Alexandria and Port Said during the war of 1914–18 and was first applied to dock labourers because of the armbands with the letters W.O.G.S. (working on Government service), which they wore. But today the word "Wog" is used indiscriminately, as a term of disparagement and contempt, to indicate Egyptians of every class from Cabinet Ministers to the humblest fellahin. Similar expressions are used to describe nationals of other countries, particularly the Mediterranean races, and I have heard them uttered sufficiently loudly for the persons indicated to hear what was being said. The studied rudeness, arrogance and lack of consideration with which the majority of Englishmen treat foreigners merely results in doing England a great deal of harm in the eyes of the world . . .'*

* Cecil Alport, *One Hour of Justice* (Dorothy Crisp, London, ?1947), p. 53.

It was as an ostensible member of this curious society that Jayjay arrived from the Sudan, very tanned and travel-stained and with a large and heavy wooden crate of pornographic images that smelt pungently of resin and acetic acid.

– You might think I would be glad to find myself among my fellow countrymen, but you would be wrong. I was still entranced with being on the loose in the world. I'd spent the first eighteen and a half years of my life among Britons and I could spare their company for some while yet, except as potential customers. I had very little money, no job and nowhere to stay; but my number-one priority, I remember, was to lose my virginity with a woman. In Suez I had taken to heart Milo's warnings about not risking it with girls one couldn't be sure of. We were all wary of venereal diseases then, you know. No penicillin in those days, and sulphonamides were still being developed. I'd heard horrendous tales about young men whose lives had effectively been ruined by a chance encounter. After all that voyeurism you can imagine I was pretty attuned to the idea, but so far I'd met nobody in Suez or the Sudan with whom I was prepared to risk it. August had certainly shown me some bedraggled whores in Khartoum who were a powerful argument for chastity. I now reasoned that Cairo could supply a good selection of nice English or other European girls who might welcome the odd carnal aside. This is exactly what preoccupies young men most of the time, of course, even as they pretend to be laying the foundations of a serious career. No doubt you can remember what it felt like. I had reached the stage when I could eroticise anything I looked at. Laundry on a roof, a ruined house, even a donkey cart passing in the street: they could all be turned instantly into props for fantasies. My damned penis dangled over any and every landscape like a rare and bursting fruit. There was no avoiding the thing, and nor did I wish to. It's a very powerful combination when youthful sexual energy is added to the egotism of childhood. It reduces the entire planet to a matter of sets and actors among whom one performs one's starring role over and over again in an infinite variety of costumes. Do you remember that?

– I used August's contacts as well as a couple I'd inherited from Mansur. They helped me find some cheap lodgings down towards Sayyida Zeinab. Very *baladi* but I didn't want to go to an obvious expat area like Zamalek. Too expensive, too European. It was an apartment above a row of shops owned by some Greeks. Just a couple of cockroachy rooms, but they were a pied-à-terre. Somewhere south of our street began the unmapped warren of Sayyida Zeinab proper. Crowded mud houses, no sanitation, filthy wells, left-over palm trees. In the middle was the mosque of the good Sayyida Zeinab herself, who is not only the patron saint of Cairo but the Prophet's grand-daughter. She has a big cult following, something like Padre Pio's here in Italy, and her mosque is a great centre of pilgrimage. At once I had a sense of there being at least two Cairos: the one of the grandees, many of them foreign, and the other of the ordinary Moslem people. Indeed, I hardly met a Briton who wasn't completely incredulous when he heard where I was living. It sounded both wilful and dangerous, even perverse. I was accused of slumming. Still, nobody down in Sayyida Zeinab seemed to mind. If they thought it odd they never said so. I don't think they gave a damn. Egyptians are very easy-going about things like that. There were already a few Greek and Italian traders in the area, plus some Lebanese who sold home-made sweetmeats that all seemed to be made of nougat or honey. In this ancient cosmopolitan city nobody cared about a boy from Eltham with shady contacts.

– In fact it was a most interesting place to live. It turned out that a group of nationalist students used to hold meetings in a nearby house to which army officers came wearing *galabeyas*, with turbans to disguise their haircuts. It was all quite political, though it took me a little time to discover it. I later found out they were members of Aziz el Masri's 'Ring of Iron' group. Meanwhile I'd found the man with the studio and started negotiations. I had met Petron once before in Suez when Mansur introduced us. He had a studio up in Mousky at the back of Ezbekiah Gardens. It was part of a small printing company he owned. There were quite a few presses in that area churning out calendars and cheap dictionaries and a mass of other stuff. A photographic studio meant you could make your own plates, and quite a lot of Petron's revenue came from advertisements: pictures of famous doctors in fezzes recommending their own ointments, or bonny Egyptian children who were growing up big and strong thanks to Virol or Radio Malt imported from the UK. So running a line of pornography on the side was pretty lucrative since he was merely using his own facilities out of hours. He did all that sort of work at night after his staff had gone home. The costs of contact paper and developer were simply passed on to his ordinary customers.

– I was quite firm with Petron. I told him that from now on August Moll-Ziemcke was dealing directly with me and with nobody else, and showed him a selection of 'teasers' from the films I'd brought with me from the Sudan. We did a deal on the spot. He admitted that as a non-Briton he'd found the upper echelons of Cairene society impossible to break into; but somebody like myself, well, that was a different cattle of fishes, wasn't it? So I had myself some trousers and a jacket made and started hanging around obvious places such as hotel foyers: Shepheard's, the Continental, the Metropolitan, working my way up to the Gezira Club, as it were, though that was far too grand and exclusive for the likes of me. Groppi's café was particularly good. Their so-called 'Garden' branch was just across Ezbekiah from the studio. I found exactly what I was looking for: limp and dusty memsahibs puce from the heat, fanning themselves at tables shaded by ferns. They were often accompanied by daughters who had come into town to buy stuff for a new fancy-dress costume or something and were doing the rounds of department stores such as Davies Bryan's, Robert Hughes and Cicurel's. I was fair-haired and quite comely and more than young enough to be part of their set. The freeloading mentor I'd met at that Lloyds funeral in my early teens came to my aid in spirit. These were not difficult people to pick a conversation with. Thereafter, with some adroit lying and worming, I was in and making friends of my own. I kept very quiet about having been an apprentice clerk with a shipping line, of course. Being an impostor seemed to come so naturally. I dissembled prettily and mysteriously, my tan and my desert reminiscences and snatches of Arabic hinted at Lawrence-of-Arabian derring-do. I sold more of August's footage to Petron and had some better clothes run up. I now could lounge in the foyer of the Metropolitan looking like one of those boy dandies in Saki's stories with names like Clovis and Reginald. I still had no regular income, and I still returned to cockroachy rooms off Sayyida Zeinab where I had to fold away my finery in dark paper with camphor or it would have been devoured. Most people's clothes smelt of mothballs then; nobody noticed such things in the tropics.

 – I put the word around that I would give lessons in conversational English and soon had several students. I remember some Egyptians and one or two Europeans, including a young diplomat from the Italian legation. I don't remember his name but he turned out to be a crucial contact. In the meantime I'd met Mrs Maunsell. Agnes Maunsell was the wife of an army officer who I think was based out Heliopolis way, probably at Abasiya barracks where they had married quarters. She was almost twice my age but that still only put her in her mid-thirties and she looked younger. I'd stopped off for a mid-morning coffee and a meringue at Zubi's on Shari'a Adly Pasha, between Groppi's Garden and the Turf Club. I was reading a newspaper on one of those wooden holders and trying to look coolly cosmopolitan, and now and again between pages I noticed her glance at me. Finally she came over to my table and excused herself before asking if I was Bobby Onslow's son Patrick whom she'd heard was down from Cambridge and in town on vacation. No, I said, unfortunately I wasn't. That's a pity, she said, because I was about to ask him to a party. I told her that was perfectly all right and that she could just as easily ask me to the party, especially since

Patrick Onslow was notorious for having halitosis and no conversation. I'm sure we were both ad-libbing furiously but she
played up and said, Oh dear, that doesn't sound very promising,
does it? Would I be disturbing you if I joined you for a moment?
You seem to be someone who could help me with my guest list.
By all means, said I, gallantly, and had the waiter fetch her coffee
over.

– An hour later we were in bed. I couldn't believe it. The phrase
'bored army wife' evokes the wrong image for Agnes, although
that is indeed what she was. It implies a leathery old campaigner
with a gin habit and there was nothing remotely leathery about
Agnes. She had very good skin and smelt of Fayyum roses. She
started off in Zubi's by telling me her cat had been run over by a
gharry earlier that morning and it had had a strange effect on
her. Yes, she was sad about the cat because she'd been fond of it.
But it had triggered one of those sudden perspectives when you
become quite bleak and see life grinding on to no particular purpose or pleasure, stuck in Cairo and bored out of your wits with a
husband who has malaria he can't shake. Trying for children hasn't
worked and is no longer much fun and I can't imagine why I'm
telling a youngster like you all this out of the blue, please forgive
me . . . A tear or two, quite genuine. Nobody noticed things like
that in Zubi's, anyway. It was full of men in fezzes with their
Lebanese mistresses and tears were all part of the ambience, as
were occasional slaps and furious arguments behind potted palms.
Agnes was sad, an obviously affectionate and sensitive person who
didn't greatly like her life and who had just glimpsed a long stretch
of identical years before the pay-off. And the pay-off would have
been bad enough on its own: a small rose-girt bungalow near
Camberley (or similar) which was supposed to be compensation
for all those years of service but which that morning must have
looked to her like the bitter end.

– So there we were, letting ourselves into an apartment on
Kasr el Nil which was owned by some girlfriend of hers who was
out at work all day and had given Agnes a key so that she could

have a place to escape to when Abasiya barracks became insuffer-
able. I was dreadfully excited and at the same time very nervous
because I was about to commit adultery. The flat was small and
hot and the *persiane* were all closed so the light was thrown on to
the ceiling in stripes. We were standing in this gloom with all our
clothes on and it was very *adult*. It felt less like a madcap exploit on
her part than a temporary remedy for the sort of problems one
only encountered by being married. It was such things that made
her seem older than I, rather than any physical signs; but it was
exactly that which made it exciting because she was doing it knowingly, deliberately. It was me she had chosen in Zubi's. It was me
she wanted.

– The thing I remember best from the whole encounter with
Agnes was her erotic silence. Until then she had been quite
chatty, but now she took her clothes off without a word. I found
myself doing the same; and it was as if she had drawn a curtain
around the bed enclosing us and excluding everything else so the
traffic noise and the hawkers' shouts filtering through the shutters
from the street below seemed to withdraw. I suppose no-one ever
forgets the first time he embraces someone completely naked.
The entire body turns to nerve-endings and becomes precarious
from head to foot. I remember thinking that this was it, this was
what I was meant to be, a lover. Not a shipping clerk, not a
pornographer, not an empire-builder. Just a lover, albeit a still
very inexperienced one. I was apprehensive about knowing what
to do and in what order, and in my nervousness made some face-
tious remarks; but she knew everything and spoke not a word.
Soon I became too distracted for speech. That sense of having
been invited into a private world was the thing which most
touched me about her: that she should have chosen me as company. Her silence was inclusive. We must have been on that bed
for three hours and in all that time I believe she spoke only one
word, though several times: *Again*. If ever I began some post-
coital pleasantry, such as wondering whether all Egyptian flats
smelt of Flit and paraffin, she laid a finger on my lips. It made the

whole experience serious, not at all casual. For long afterwards the memory of her small command *Again* was deeply erotic to me.

– We repeated this scene quite a lot in the following weeks. I must have asked her pointedly if she made a habit of doing this with every young man she met, since male vanity inevitably asks. Oddly enough I can't remember her answer, if indeed she ever bothered to reply. Was the key to her friend's apartment an answer? Not definitively, no, not even in Cairo in those days. I had the impression that the morning we first caught sight of each other in Zubi's was the day Agnes had decided to commit adultery, come what may. Not flattering to me, in some ways, but I did believe in her story of the squashed cat. For a month or two I walked tall until the novelty wore off and I grew to dislike the smell of the rosewater she used. That and a certain quality I could only think of as 'provincial'. She was . . . well, she *was* an army wife, and people don't become army wives by accident. It's a highly specialised social scene. Her mind was like that of so many Britons I met in Egypt, something of a closed loop. But Agnes had glimpsed something outside the loop to which she had partial access in a shuttered room on Kasr el Nil, and maybe that sufficed. Not for me, though. I was too young to appreciate what it might have meant to her as an older person, that the very precariousness of bodily contact is strangely consoling. It is not actuality that threatens to collapse, only the pretence and fantasy in which we clothe it. The immediate tactility, the electric curiosity that bodies have for each other: that is real. It is a fuel that keeps one benign and going, something to make the world expand no matter that one day the same world will abruptly contract to measure six feet by two. To say *Again* in a kerosene-scented room in Egypt is, at that moment, to have made no bad choices and not to have failed.

– But teenagers can't think like that, of course. Just then they want as much gratification as they can lay their hands on. They're too young to have failed yet. They're running on biochemistry.

The only certainty they have is that you can't add too many of your own drops to the human gene pool. There's nothing mellow about first-time sex.

– Looking back at that period now I'm amazed at my energy, all the more since it contrasted strongly with the lassitude that afflicted so many of my fellow countrymen. The heat, the flies, the prevailing culture of *maalesh* and *bukra* used to knock the stuffing out of them. Their summoned efforts, constantly met by the bland 'Never mind, my friend. Tomorrow, *insh'Allah*,' seldom induced a philosophical patience. Instead a peevish weariness overtook them until the most ordinary things seemed to require huge effort. But whatever it was in the air that drained them seemed to pump me full of fizz.

– I was living pretty dangerously, really. I had at last found some customers among the diplomatic community. At the same time, through one of my private pupils, I had acquired some student contacts up at Al Azhar, the great university which in those days, as later, was home to radical Islamic movements like the Moslem Brotherhood. Retrospectively I was able to re-interpret some of the things Mansur had said in Suez that had slightly puzzled me at the time. I remembered a remark about the British effectively holding the whip-hand in Egypt and his not being sure how long this state of affairs would be allowed to continue. *Would be allowed.* When I was newly arrived in Suez I naturally assumed that where their colonies were concerned the British would hold the whip-hand for exactly as long as it suited them. A bunch of natives were in no position to do anything about it that couldn't swiftly be settled by a gunboat or a detachment of Royal Marines. That was a pretty typical attitude at the time, especially for an untravelled kid a long way from home seeing chaps in pith helmets ordering Gyppos around. I don't think I even knew Egypt wasn't part of the Empire.

– But living in Cairo on the fringes of Sayyida Zeinab I soon gained a different perspective. This immense and ancient country was part of Islam, not an adjunct of the House of Windsor. As in any Islamic home we foreigners were welcome as guests, but we were not at all welcome as self-appointed rulers of the household. I began to take an interest in the students' nationalism, an interest that was cautiously, *very* cautiously, reciprocated. They were naturally wary that I was some kind of spy, a plant by the British Embassy's dirty tricks department to infiltrate the Moslem Brotherhood. My improving Arabic was seen as potentially dangerous as much as an earnest of good intentions. You can hardly blame them for being suspicious. El Banna was a deadly serious organisation that had secret training camps in the Mokattam Hills. Really, my interest was little more than an emotional response to what I saw as ordinary Egyptians' daily subservience to English men and women. I hadn't the maturity and experience to know that if one could remove the British presence overnight, the same Egyptians would simply go on being subservient to their own pasha class. Despite all that communism I'd heard from Michael at school I was politically juvenile. All I understood was that subservience and oppression had been part of life in Egypt for at least five thousand years and that people could deal with it so long as they were oppressed by their own kind. Being oppressed by foreigners, no matter how enlightened they claimed to be, was another matter. So bit by bit I found myself drawn towards the nationalist cause and increasingly opposed to the ruling presence of my own countrymen.

– Meanwhile, though, I was having a good deal of fun going to the oppressors' parties and selling them pornography. It's a waste of time looking for consistency or principle in someone on the lam in his early twenties, especially a born impostor. However, I was a good conspirator because I was discreet and could always remember my own lies. I never forgot who I was supposed to be with whom, just as I never allowed the various strands of my activities to touch. That was particularly true where sex was concerned. Since I was so keen on this fatuous idea of myself as a great lover I may as well give you a couple of illustrations.

– I had wormed my way into a party somewhere along the Giza

Road. It was at a big house painted yellow which for that reason was known as the *beyt dahabi* or Golden House. I really can't now remember whose the Golden House was but it was a focus for social events. The name of Lady Orpington comes to mind, or is she one of Saki's characters? That's exactly the problem: so many of the people one met in Egypt in those days were straight out of Saki. Anyhow, it doesn't matter. It was a party with a band, of course, with fairy lights rigged in the garden and elegant servants dressed in long white *galabeyas* with plum sashes around their waists. Somewhere between all the rumbas and tangos I found myself next to a girl called Joy, which is not a name one hears much nowadays. We were standing in the garden under a magnolia eating a fearful dessert out of glasses, very English, a ghastly compound of mangoes and condensed milk with green glacé cherries on top: I can remember those perfectly. Joy was a member of what was known as 'the fishing fleet', débutantes who had been presented at Court back home but who hadn't yet landed the right husband by the season's end. The fishing fleet sailed far and wide, quite a few girls going to India and even beyond. *Can* there have been aristocratic rubber planters? It seems very unlikely. Anyway, Joy was staying with cousins in Cairo although I never did find out who they were. She was my age, very 'fresh', as we would have said, something of a charming little vamp and therefore not quite fishing-fleet material. I also thought she had far too much sense of humour to be a good fisher-girl if she were hoping to hook some dashing young officer who played polo in a pipeclayed helmet. We were both rather drunk and in need of relief from the band and the condensed milk, so we found ourselves drifting towards the end of the garden well beyond the last fairy lights. By that time she was kissing with a degree of ardour one didn't at all associate with the fleet, most of whom were canny indeed with their favours until they were sure they'd netted the right bachelor. I now suspect that Joy was slumming with me in between more serious attempts on truly eligible young men, but that was fine by me. We found a promising-looking garden shed but no sooner had we groped our way inside than there was a guttural challenge from the darkness and an oil lamp was lit to reveal a gardener and what seemed to be his entire family. Of course this was Egypt, we told each other as we stumbled away helpless with laughter. What else would one expect to find in a garden shed but a gardener and his family asleep? We found a way out of the garden, nearly fell into a canal, and reached the road. Well, where to but the pyramids by moonlight? What could be more romantic? So we prodded a gharry driver awake and off we trotted to Giza.

– In those days the pyramids were still curious relics rather than nationally sacrosanct, and you could climb them if you had a head for heights and were reasonably fit. Indeed, there were native pyramid runners who specialised in racing up and down the Great Pyramid for visiting dignitaries who paid well for a good display. Winston Churchill signed a photograph for one champion and years later I saw it hanging behind the reception desk in a hotel in Cairo, the proprietor having made good on his youthful success as an athlete. And athletic you needed to be if you were going to make a race of it. As you know, most of the pyramids' casing was looted over the millennia since the dressed stones were ideal for building. Quite a few houses in the older parts of Cairo are built of blocks taken from the pyramids. The denuded slopes of the Great Pyramid are now a series of giant steps up the exposed courses of the big slabs used for the main construction. Believe me, it's hard work climbing a staircase four hundred and fifty feet high with steps that come halfway up your thigh.

– In the cool of the night, though, taking one's time and with the prospect of carnal pleasure at the summit, to say nothing of a bottle of tepid champagne one of us had thoughtfully liberated from the Golden House, it was a spree. The inevitable guides, guards and dragomans wrapped in their *galabeyas* at the bottom had woken up and needed pacifying with piastres. By now my Arabic was good enough for me to make a joke of it while warning them sternly that their job was to stay at the bottom and ensure we were not disturbed. I wasn't too confident about that. It was clearly impossible for them to guard all four faces of the Pyramid at once and like everyone else the Egyptians are keen voyeurs. I was also worried about parties from the nearby Mena House Hotel, which ran special excursions to view the pyramids by moonlight. Still, we were lucky because that night the moon wasn't quite full and we turned out to be the only couple sitting on top among the graffiti of tourists who stretched all the way back to Herodotus' day. The three-quarter yellow moon shed its radiance over an astounding view. Endless desert at one's back and the lights of Cairo ahead. The palms below glistened with a buttery sheen. In the distance the Nile's dark stain and, away beyond it, the Mokattam Hills with a few scattered points of light. It was magical and immensely sexy. I was never much affected by all that mystic hokum surrounding Egyptology, so I didn't feel that by having intercourse on top of the Great Pyramid I was somehow participating in an age-old fertility ritual. Nonetheless, the mere fact of having taken a girl away from a party and brought her to this highly pregnant place beneath an audacious moon was itself aphrodisiac. I couldn't resist playing up to Joy and pretending I felt the presence of the spirit of Osiris or some such. Hokum can be deployed to good effect. And I must admit it was a powerful experience, screwing on a little square plateau held aloft by the most massive and ancient building on earth, exposed to the eye of that yellow moon. It was remarkably like being on a sacrificial altar, which is what Joy said as she enthusiastically offered herself as a far from silent victim.

– This, too, was a revelation. In terms of lovemaking Joy was as distant from Agnes as it was possible to be. Rather than lapsing into silence she became voluble. She wanted to hear me say what I was going to do before I did it, she wanted gutter language, she yelped at the moon. I was distracted at first but then old Osiris came to my aid, bless him, and the whole thing turned into rather an animal affair. Definitely pre-Christian. I remember binding her hands with a chiffon scarf. One of the fishing fleet tied up in port for the night and unable to sail away before dawn at least. We drank the champagne and made curious use of the bottle. It was all a bit perverse and mad and we had a thoroughly enjoyable time until we made the mistake of falling asleep.

– I was woken by the first rays of the rising sun striking the tip of the Pyramid even as everything below lay still in shadow. I was stiff with cold but even so it was impossible not to gaze out across the Nile and the desert and think that this was living: to watch the Mokattam Hills outlined against a gold and salmon blaze while in the gulf between lay various shades of lavender and indigo pierced here and there by the pale fingers of minarets. And then the dawn chorus of muezzins rising out of the lavender mist like white shoots piercing soil, each out of phase with the others and giving the impression of spontaneity rather than ritual. For about five minutes it made me want to become a Moslem because it seemed such a perfect expression of a landscape. How else would a desert religion sound, and what more natural than to allow one's early prayers to ascend with dispersing mists even as the last stars are fading? Hugely exposed to the sky as I was up there, I suddenly perceived how important the heavens were in a landscape like a fatal ocean that men had to cross by faith and navigation. The crescent moon on top of every minaret was exquisite and correct. I understood why the Arabs had been such wonderful astro-nomers. I also understood why Christianity had always failed to move me. It was a misplaced religion, a transplant, a hybrid, fun-damentally out of tune with the English landscape.

– Then Joy woke and I was annoyed because I'd almost forgot-ten her, scrumpled and sandy, my reason for being here at this moment, watching this unrepeatable but daily-repeated drama. It was she who pointed out that during the hours of unconsciousness someone had climbed up and relieved her of her handbag and me of my wallet. We clambered back down in two separate silences of very different origins though at least neither had any connection with shame. –

Why are you telling me these things?
– I thought you'd be interested. They're part of my life. –

Just sexual exploits, surely. We've all had them, even those of us who haven't.

He is a little aggrieved and falls silent, gazing fiercely at a nearby lavender bush. But so am I aggrieved, feeling that his life is after all turning out to be nothing but a succession of conquests in ever more bizarre locations. I want to hear what has hurt him, what has made him weep in the night. I want to hear what he did when the magic of being young began to bore even him. I want to know if self-proclaimed impostors are like a fennel root, whose successive layers can be shucked off to leave nothing beyond a stunted green shoot at the centre. And why might a person claim to be an impostor, anyway? Isn't it like the Cretan in the famous paradox who says all Cretans are liars? There is no way in logic to know which of his claims is true and which false. So why do it? Offhand, I could think of three possible motives. One was to reassure himself that he had had an interesting life; another was to convince other people that he had; the third was in order to conceal something. In any of these cases it was dissembling, hence tedious. So why had I initially been seduced by it? I supposed because we actually do expect people to be honest about themselves. If their confessions seem not greatly to their credit, their degree of honesty intrigues us and we assume other revelations will follow. In Jayjay's case I was right.

– They're part of my life. –

So you said. Of course they are, Jayjay. I had no business interrupting you. I'm sorry.

– You've put me off my stroke now. Though to be honest I no longer know what to talk about where my years in Egypt are concerned. It all seems so much of a piece I can't separate out some of the vividest memories or much of the chronology. Everything from this period seems to be sliding gradually towards the war. But I did say I would give you another example of myself in the guise of a lover, and it's a bit disgraceful so I'd better tell you or else you will think I'm presenting you with too rosy a view of my former self. –

No I shan't, Jayjay. You're an impostor, remember?

– Ah, but I'm a *truthful* impostor, you must never forget that. You'll hear no lies from me. Just versions and the occasional omission. Anyway, looking back to that period now, the sheer weirdness of the life I was leading does strike me. For some of the time I was social climbing and being taken to parties or dinners or on excursions. Another part of the time I was successfully peddling very high-class pornography to a rather different set, although there was some overlapping. Then there were the English lessons I was still giving, very conscientiously, even down to setting and correcting homework. And finally there was me at home, living pretty frugally, quite content with *baladi* food from corner stalls in Sayyida Zeinab. I used to love that, especially at night when the stalls were lit by hurricane lamps or candles. Bread filled with *ful*, dark boiled beans dressed with olive oil and chillies, maybe a duck egg or two. Plus pickled turnips on the side: mauvy-pinkish lumps fished dripping from earthenware jars. Onions. Roots. Tubers. Garlic. It was peasant food, basically unchanged since the Pharaohs. The bread, especially, was wonderful. There were baker's ovens every few streets and they never seemed to cool. Like brick or mud igloos they kept churning out a stream of round, greyish, flat loaves along the lines of Greek pitta bread but coarser and altogether more muscular. When eaten hot, filled with beans or tuna, they were all one wanted to eat for ever. It was a pleasure just watching the ovens being raked out and replenished with bundles of firewood and the sweating boys with flour smudges up their brown arms balancing cloth-covered trays of fresh *khubs* on their heads as they set off through the streets to hawk it. Then back to the oven for more.

– I came to love everything about Cairo street life, even the stenches and filth, the shit and the noise and the cockroaches, the donkey-stale and the beggars and the children with glistening sores . . . Perhaps that sounds too much like scene-setting?

No, Jayjay, just corny. *La boue*, you know. *La* photogenic *boue*.

– Well, all right; but I really did want to immerse myself in it, no matter how corny it may be that I should have felt a need to scour off Eltham with a bit of Egyptian harshness. I spent hours squatting with people, drinking endless glasses of syrupy tea, listening, sniffing, practising my street Arabic. I came to understand the economy of giving: the cigarette here, the box of matches there, the lump of cheese I'd bought which I didn't really need, a candle or a medicine bottle of paraffin. In return I received some lessons I never forgot, especially regarding the sanctity of food. Bread was a gift of God, and as such was sacred. If one ever saw a crust on the ground, no matter how dried and gritty and filthy, one picked it up and put it on a ledge somewhere, on a window sill or a wall. Anywhere so that the gift of God would not be trampled underfoot. All over Cairo, even in the centre, one saw pieces of practically fossilised bread tucked up on ledges beneath a drift of soot and dust. Eventually I actually *felt* what that meant, rather than noting it as an interesting social detail. Most of the denizens of Sayyida Zeinab had nothing. They were living pretty much on the daily edge of destitution. Yet the good humour and generosity were something I had never encountered before, least of all in Eltham. Mine was a very different angle, but I did begin to understand why old August was content to go on living down in the Sudanese back of beyond. Somewhere beneath us both lay a revulsion. At inherited gentility, perhaps? At being too out of touch with first and last things, the roots and tubers of it all?

– Anyway, 'genteel' is not quite the word to describe an episode that occurred on a houseboat owned by a French aristocrat. I shan't name him because he had an inelegant death and there seems no point in further distressing whatever descendants he has. Enough to say he was well known in certain Cairene circles, and far beyond. I shall call him Etienne. I'd reached him quite early on as a discerning buyer of August's best films, though through an intermediary. But he obviously wanted to meet me in person because I now received a summons to his houseboat with a request to bring 'anything new' from August. Etienne's houseboat was as famous as he was. It looked like a set Cecil B. DeMille might have dreamed up for Cleopatra's barge. Not effeminate, mind you, just freakishly decadent. It was moored on the Imbaba side of the cut, almost level with the Gezira Club. It was blue and white and gold outside with lots of teak and brass and a sort of Saracen pavilion on deck that was taken down when the *khamseen* was blowing. Inside it was rigged as a thoroughgoing sin palace, all rugs and divans and muslin drapery. It smelt of patchouli and hashish. There was even a small marble pool that could be filled with wine or milk or rose-water, depending on the occasion. The night I was there it was full of brown youths.

– In case you're wondering, there was a strong vein of tolerant sophistication about such things. Most of the older British residents in Cairo prided themselves on being unshockable, which is unsurprising seeing that Cairo offered things unavailable in Surrey and Hampshire that were largely the reason why they were residents in the first place. The very oldest could remember the series of scandals that had shocked Germany at the beginning of the century when the Kaiser's own friend and adviser, Prince zu Eulenburg-Hertefeld, as well as several other high-ranking individuals like Count von Moltke, were accused of being homosexual and charged under Article 175 of the German penal code. This would be about ten years after the Wilde case in England. When the news reached Cairo it was treated with shouts of mirth. 'My God, if they had 175 here they'd have to prosecute half this city,' the old boys said. 'The streets would be empty. The Government and the Court would practically vanish overnight.' In the Automobile Club a motion was proposed that only applicants who could be charged under Article 175 should be deemed fit for election to its exclusive membership. Thirty years on, nothing much had changed where Cairo's tolerant habits were concerned. The city's highly visible police chief, Russell Pasha, had more important things to worry about than endemic buggery. There was the drugs trade, for one. He was making excellent headway there but it was uphill work and needed constant vigilance, as I myself knew from Suez. Then there were always the nationalists and their student supporters like the Moslem Brotherhood and Ahmed Hussein's Young Egypt. They would take to the streets and riot at the least provocation. I well remember seeing Russell Pasha on his massive white horse at one of those riots, completely unprotected and quite cool in his red fez and black uniform, marshalling his police with the stock of a riding whip, pointing here, pointing there. No, he had enough on his plate without worrying about the erotic follies of his fellow-Europeans. Besides, there were always the widespread rumours that his own private life was pretty well stocked with mistresses. Cairo was not a city in which pots bothered to call kettles black.

– One way and another the spirit of live and let live was broad and buoyant, and on it floated many a *dahabiya*, including Etienne's sin palace. Some houseboats were owned by successful belly dancers and some by King Faroukh's courtiers and they all had in common the more or less elegant pursuit of pleasure. That night Etienne's pleasure was audible from dry land. I turned out to be the youngest of his guests but nowhere near the youngest person aboard. Even as the *bawab* saluted me across the gangplank I could hear children's giggles from the stern. Etienne was tall, thin, thirty-fiveish, with a neat moustache. He had a good deal of charm, certainly enough to make you think his slight divergent squint must be part of it. He looked me over appraisingly, plucked eyebrows indicating surprise. 'If I may say so, you don't fit the conventional picture of a man in your line of business. But then, of course, had you done so I would scarcely have invited you here. The dear Raffalovitches did say you were presentable, but I hadn't expected someone who would fit quite so well into my preferred ambience.'

– And with that graceful compliment the revels began. It was a highly peculiar evening. Just keep Eltham firmly fixed in your mind because only then will you appreciate quite how baroque it was to be served dinner by naked boys with wreaths in their hair. Imagine Eltham Congregational Church on a wet Sunday when I tell you that light was provided by nude children upside down on the floor, each with a candle plunged in his rectum. I think this was in imitation of one of the Marquis de Sade's more harmless fantasies and to be honest it wasn't a great success. Every so often one of the boys would cough or shift his very uncomfortable position and the effort would expel the candle with a plop, the light would go out and the child squawk as hot wax spilled across his bottom. I think there were five of us dining: Etienne and I and three others? Something like that. I remember everyone laughing a good deal as each child was coaxed into becoming a candlestick again. Now and again I would glance down and see a little convulsed face peering stoically up from the depths of a cushion. I don't think they were unduly put upon, and eventually they were all given a piece of fruit before scampering off somewhere towards the stern to peel the wax off their scrotums. In fact they looked considerably better fed and incomparably cleaner than their coevals in Sayyida Zeinab. I presumed it was them I'd heard giggling when I arrived. They were probably rehearsing being candlesticks.

– After dinner there was a film show. We lay around on cushions while Etienne showed us reels from his extensive library of films, including several of August's. Meanwhile some rather older boys, early to mid teens, had crept in like shadows and sprawled among us. Under the influence of the films a good deal of fondling and caressing went on, leading quickly to rather more. By the light of the projector one could catch all sorts of gleams in the darkness, anatomical details with glistening highlights. At first I found it difficult to get into the spirit of the occasion because all the while a very distinguished-looking old retainer in a white robe was doing the rounds with a brass tray, serving us cardamom-flavoured coffee. He would bend over each guest and wait respectfully until the man had a free hand, then gravely serve him a little cup. Afterwards he did the same with Turkish delight and hashish rolled into little balls the size of peas. I was disconcerted for him, quite pointlessly as it turned out because I gathered later that although he might have looked venerable he had behind him a good half-century of seamless wickedness of his own.

  – The rest of the evening was pure orgy, with Etienne as an attentive host in between being pleasured by a very young Delta peasant kid who was already hung like a mule. The boy was from Tanta, I remember, and had barely turned twelve, but he put us adults to shame. I was excited by the whole thing, it being the first orgy I'd ever been to. I suppose that helped; but there was something else that appealed to me in all that tense brown flesh with cardamom on its breath, in the thick rugs and cushions, in the semi-darkness glowing with an occasional cigarette end and the silent images pouring on to the screen. Voluptuousness was the part of me Eltham had denied, having conspired to pretend it was not an item of luggage needed by my immortal soul on its one-way journey. Strictly 'Not wanted on voyage.' Yet even as a child I'd glimpsed a quite different voyage for myself through quite other landscapes. Once, I'd wormed my way into a privet hedge full of poisonous dark-green light, an erotic cathedral of difficult traceries which expanded so I could live in it, unknown to passers-by, not a boy in a hedge but the pilot of a celestial vehicle on his own trajectory. Then there was a cut in the narrative, a fadeup like one of August's, and suddenly there I was at an orgy floating on the Nile, feeding a dusty cushion of Turkish delight to a naked boy with a face straight off a temple frieze at Karnak. Yet it was unmistakably a section of the same dreamed journey. The child in the Eltham hedge was the very man on a Cairo houseboat, unseen by passers-by. But alone, that's what I'm saying. Alone and trying to catch up. Alone and needing details as a defence against the future. We splashed in the marble pool into which the old servant had sprinkled jasmine oil. I think I was drunk or drugged by then, although everything was so clear I can smell the jasmine to this day. And by the light of a poolside lantern I could see we'd been joined by one or two of the older candlestick boys. Seal-like rompings ensued. I remember noting that small boys' orgasms are briefer in duration than adults', though immediately repeatable. Also, that before they fully reach puberty boys' ejaculate tends at first to be grey rather than white, hardly slimy and not at all flocculent. Droplets lay on a maroon rug like three or four seed pearls. –

Did they really, Jayjay? I wonder what Captain W. E. Johns would have to say about that. Do you think your boyhood hero would have approved of this writer's eye of yours?

I find myself torn between exasperation and a need to record these details in a scientific spirit. As well be accurate about juvenile sperm as about bees, I suppose. Still, this particular snippet, even though culled from the rarefied world of a pre-war orgy, can hardly be arcane knowledge given that half the world's population has either passed, or will be passing, through boyhood. So what is all this selective blurt? He must know I can't be shocked. I want to pick him up, I *will* pick him up, on that word 'alone'.

'Alone and trying to catch up', you said.

– Did I? –

Yes. What did you mean by 'trying to catch up'? With what? With whom?

– Oh. You know . . . Something like making up for lost time? That's it. Eltham again, naturally. I felt I'd fallen behind. I was in pursuit of the *unwrapped*. Anyway, the only point of my telling you all this scurrilous stuff is merely to illustrate how at that time I kept my various pursuits quite separate. That must surely be an impostor's gift, to live on several tacks at once, each of them interesting to me. But I was also open to anything else that might come along, and what came along was the Second World War. Before that happened, though, I went to Alexandria. And *that* is the beginning of the roundabout answer to the question of how it is I come to be living here at 'Il Ghibli'. –

But I still can't guess the weight of 'alone'. He's concealing something here. Yet if he can be frank about paederastic orgies it's indeed hard to imagine what he might jib at revealing.

Suddenly such matters (as well as Jayjay and his entire story) will have to wait for a while. A phone call arrives from a distant capital, from another precinct of my life. Although I answer it on a bright Tuscan afternoon it comes from the dead of night. 'The General has agreed to see you, but his son is trying to dissuade him. Now is the time to jump in, James.'

So jump I must, thousands of miles, on the off chance that a retired multi-millionaire will keep his word. Just before my friend hangs up I distinctly hear a dog bark in the background eight thousand miles away and at once that landscape rushes in at me from over the planet's curve. Jayjay and his Egypt drop from sight and in their place I see Southeast Asia. I am in a familiar book-lined room with windows opened on the tropic night beyond the mosquito screens, the dogs loping in the compound beyond, the whirling haloes of insects around the security lamps. On my last visit I probably passed a remark to the very hound I have just overheard. Why should the chance barking of a dog be more potent than the voice of a friend in summoning a distant land into being? Suddenly the place is here again like a phantom limb that aches with the memory of its former life, insistent in its solidity. From nowhere comes the thought of how James Ellroy summarised the philosophy of the Kennedy era: Look Good, Kick Ass, Get Laid. I reflect how equally well that could apply to the despised and defunct regime of the country to which I have been recalled. Kennedy, though, is revered, his own nation being major-league ass-kickers with the power to do a Kremlin job on history. My damned beloved useless country whose dogs can be heard down phone lines eight thousand miles away lacks the power to whitewash history. On the other hand it will remain forever forgiven. I have to think my life is strange.

'The General has agreed to see you', but the dog is the clincher. Later, I throw things into a bag then fail to sleep. After all, Jayjay pretty much fell on me like an overripe mango, whereas I have been hoping and scheming for the last three years to get this ex-general, ex-minister, to talk. Yes, jump.

The next day Jayjay affects not to be put out in any way when I explain the urgency of my departure. He essays graciousness, fails. 'It'll all be the same in a hundred years,' he says lugubriously.

10

Sunset. A familiar strand of coral chips. The sun has just sunk between clouds like torn-off wings, down through parakeet colours into blood. A few fishing boats drawn up beyond the high tide mark. One or two being painted or overhauled are rolled up on palm boles, leaning on an outrigger, keel clear of the ground. Their interiors are heaped with crisped fronds to protect them from the daytime glare. Others, readied for a night's fishing, are being carried down to where the flaccid water barely lolls against the shore. Several are already out in the bay, low dark splinters with an oar rising and dipping against the crimson lightfall, each bow tipped with the spark of an oil lamp.

A great advantage in being a jobbing writer is the variety offered by having more than one job on hand. This evening Italy, Jayjay and his ongoing Egyptian saga occupy a space unrelated to distance, far away on the yonder side of tonight's chromatic horizon. The planet rolling over in its sleep will soon disclose this same cinnabar doorstep behind which a new day is even now preparing to yawn open on Tuscan hills and light up a small row of beehives overlooking a broad valley. My bees: checked and given a reluctant farewell dusting of oxytetracycline powder mixed with icing sugar against Foul Brood. They are already in another universe. Jayjay is elsewhere still, frozen on the brink of the Second World War where his narrative has been abruptly snapped off to enable me to fly away and talk to the carefully assembled monsters and heroes of a more modern age. This is contract work; Jayjay's is still a gentleman's agreement. So I have abandoned him in 1938 and returned to the world's other side, to the little village I know best where I greet old friends and acclimatise myself before going to the capital to begin fact-gathering.

And there was my hut in the forest beneath the mango tree, its grass thatch lank, its crafty shoulders hunched. Amazing that it should still have been standing; that the rusted hinges should have creaked and the split-bamboo door opened on an earth floor sadly unswept and marked with the tracks of land crabs. On the sagging basketwork walls I found still pinned, limp with damp: (1) last year's calendar, given away by a Chinese dry-goods store in town; (2) a crayon-coloured invitation to speak at the Elementary School's Christmas party and help judge the competitions; (3) another invitation, this one to a godchild's high-school graduation ceremony; (4) a mildewed matchbox (empty) on a string; (5) the blade of a knife I broke when trying to repair the trigger of a speargun shortly before leaving the last time. How odd it was that in a climate of typhoon and termite and rot this mouldy, wormy structure should still have been here with its freight of habitation and memories! How odd it was that I, too, was here after six months' absence, still alive and suddenly having to think where to hang things, pausing to remember which key fitted the padlocked inner room. Evidence of too many strands to a life, perhaps; the way it takes a day or two for the right words to come back, for the right ordering of time, for old patterns of living to resurface and take charge. Strange how one body can house so many lives at once, including a European self and a tropical self, each appearing so different while really being no more than apartments in the same block. Or maybe wings of the same palace, since it feels an expansive, palatial sort of life, with bunk-holes in cultures and continents.

The single inner room was the hut's central box, raised a metre above ground on four legs. The rest was walled-in lean-to. I climbed the wood steps and let myself into the interior of a grandiose lobster pot with spicules of daylight sifting through the walls and down from gaps in the thatch. Coco-lumber frame-work, bamboo slat floor through which at night one could watch the big hermit crabs crawling about and listen to the hollow knock of their borrowed shells. On a shelf heaped with worm dust was a plastic bag with half-forgotten clothes inside: mouldy T-shirts, shorts. Nothing else needed. Bat shit, gecko shit and fragments of thatch covered the floor. Pyramids of pink, ginger or saffron dust dotted every horizontal surface, depending on the kind of timber being eaten away. Even while I was absent for half a year and the house stood empty it was being gnawed busily from within. As I stood there in the hot gloom, sweating in long trousers, a gecko in the thatch began its quacking call and I knew I was home, just as in Italy I know I'm back when I can smell the bees before I can even see their hives, and in London the characteristic clatter of a black cab idling places me at a familiar point on the earth's surface.

So on to the beach this first evening, seated around a driftwood fire with friends. Some I knew when they were small children, and several of them now have small children of their own. So it goes on, on this beach, which itself is nothing but the cycle of life made for sitting on with friends: fish bones, chicken bones, cuttlebones, goat horn, mixed into fathomless tons of coral chips. And proba-bly, if one knew it, quite a few human bones too; for fishermen regularly disappear out there in the strait and in time parts of them must find their way home by stealth as skeletal fragments unnoticed among the charnel multitude. This sense of sitting on the heaped-up past (which is equally the heaped-up future) is greatly consoling. It gives significance to our gestures, to every component of this well-loved scene. Larbo and Iyan are, as usual, in charge of the cooking. They have improvised a hearth of coral chunks and raked out a corner of the fire on to it. Fish spitted on green palm ribs are already curling and emitting gasps of steam. The glowing coals light up faces and the insides of forearms as one by one the fish are scrutinised and turned. A large pot of rice has already been brought from a nearby house. Children chase about in the background, their hard little feet sending up clatters of coral. More people emerge from the darkness with broad smiles, bearing bottles. They join the group. 'Welcome back,' shyly. 'You were away too long, James.' 'Have you heard about Bado? He was electrocuted. What will happen to his two little children and his poor wife?' 'There was trouble here during the election, did you know?' 'You remember Larry's dog, Boyong? It was a great shame. He went with Larry when he went to see the Governor and you know how frisky he used to be? The Governor's bodyguards thought Boyong was attacking their man so they just shot him. Right there on the spot. Larry couldn't believe it. A pity. Boyong was a good dog. No compensation from the Governor, of course.'

Overhead are the shifted constellations, several of which cannot be seen from Italy. And behind everything, invisible beyond the circle of firelight but breathing through our very marrow, is the sea. One needs to walk down to the shore to view clearly that star-lit sheet, pooling and seething its blacks and silvers to the middle distance and lit at its furthest edge by silent electric flashes. These lightnings outline cloudbanks like pink and pearl mountain ranges. At one's feet the rising beach trips up the small waves so they constantly topple and fall on their faces, drawing back to try once more, over and over again, endlessly driven but always caught by the same simple trick of physics. One more of the help-less cycles which we share (thinks the traveller, having himself just returned) as the roast fish turn, the stars heel silently over-head, the faces around the fire show new lines and the newly dead are solemnly toasted. And this is the consolation of being wel-comed on a distant shore and pulled into a fire's circle by yesteryear's balding children: that I should wish one day for my own bones to be trundled here in the tireless surf, to be raced on by the unborn, to be gossiped over by people saying nothing different from what is said tonight. The same banalities, the same ancient jokes.

Because my godchildren approach shyly from the darkness or squat beside me with the firelight lively in their eyes, because this cycle of greeting and catching-up is such a regular event, and because the sea's steady pulse underwrites these contracts of affection, my own daughter Emma now feels greatly distant to me, like a dream child whose physical existence is in doubt. I once derived conventional comfort from thinking that through her I might at least pass on some genetic inheritance, that a coded drop of me could diffuse into the great leaky river as it meanders aimlessly onward. But then at a certain age one is overtaken by a resigned modesty that becomes impatient with notions of personal survival, above all with the idea of a self that could be perpetuated by the random couplings of one's descendants. In fact, if we were looking for tokens of individual survival we would do better to open a handful of the very beach on which we are sitting. It is precisely the relic of an individual that is digging so painfully into our left buttock: one that can be groped for, removed, and identified by firelight as a large Textile Cone, a seashell faded and abraded but nevertheless the self-built house of a creature that once on nights like this went grazing across the seabed with its eyes on stalks.

The glasses of drink circulate, the women leave carrying plates and pots to be washed up, the children straggle off to hut floors spread with sleeping mats. We are left, the men, the elders, the bottle philosophers, feeding the fire and swapping stories while idly watching the lights of fishing boats out in the strait. From that far darkness drifts the intermittent putter of small engines as the boats move from one favoured ground to another. Nearby, a scrunching and coughing marks where a dog has found the discarded spine of a grouper. 'We don't want to talk politics, James, but we think you ought to know . . .' 'As you know, I'm not a gossip, James, but had you heard . . .?' The village captain was suspended from his duties a month ago for trying to cheat a neighbour out of some land and then attempting to induce a crony in the local Land Registry Office to falsify documents.

And so to bed, walking back up the forest track with the usual half-hearted torch, the stream gurgling off to the right and the fruit bats flapping in the crowns of coconut palms. The mechanical chorus of frogs in the paddies, the overlapping sounds of geckos, the night creatures' hoots and screams: these annihilate time for me, carrying on exactly where I left them last. And lying on my back on the floor of the hut, gazing up to where a late rising moon cuts slits in the thatch with a silver blade, I think that nothing has changed since I was last here. I am not a day older. I shall mourn the electrocuted Bado (whom I knew since he was twelve) and even the shot dog Boyong, who had a sense of humour greater than that of the Governor's goons. Yet these latest deaths are also part of the cycle, and the level at which I grieve for them is itself an offshoot that in time will wither. The scandals are the same. Maybe the only new thing in the interim has been Jayjay. His life story so far has made me consider to what extent his experiences are at all consonant with my own. When I first came to this village by the sea I was exactly twice the age he was when he first arrived in Suez. Yet the last twenty years have given me a pungency of experience I associate with having been much younger than I actually was. It was like a second beginning. Unlike Jayjay I know that important and interesting things have happened to me after the age of thirty, though they include dreaming. Perhaps because of the unchanging nature of life here the feeling still persists of this place being able to stop time, something it shares with my hillside fastness in Italy.

And thus I tilt towards sleep on the floor of the hut, mulling over the routine I will pick up again tomorrow. By night I shall go fishing with comrades and by day discreetly plot to have the day-care centre re-roofed without putting the village elders' backs up. This will not be easy since by hallowed tradition all funding for such projects passes through their hands, on the way undergoing severe erosion. After the drinking and cock-fighting and paying-off of old grocery debts there would normally be enough left to thatch half the roof. Subtlety is needed and ingenious double binds thought up in order to shame the elders into aiding their own community rather than helping themselves out of precedent responsibility to their own families. What, then, will be the effect of this latest piece of news about the captain's suspension . . .? (The tilt becomes a headlong slide into unconsciousness.)

A week later I am in the capital, having forsaken the roots and tubers of the provinces for urban living. My ex-General, who had turned out to be in Hong Kong on business when I arrived, finally agrees to a preliminary meeting in a few days' time. In the interim I seek interviews with family members and minions of the ex-dictator, with various demi-saints of the resistance, with racked priests and student leaders who now carry briefcases in place of banners, with men who bring their bodyguards into the room while carrying guns of their own. Having acclimatised myself to the provinces I must now do the same for the city. In place of forest tracks are the hot and roaring concrete caverns of Asia. Through them I move between appointments in sumptuous apartments, palatial private villas, vile private palaces.

   At last the evening with the ex-General arrives, my reason for having flown half around the world. He has a suite in one of those residential condominiums lined from ground floor to penthouse in rare hardwoods. Their entrance halls are scarcely to be distinguished from the foyers of exclusive hotels. Behind marble desks and sprays of flowers sit handsome girls and impeccably suited men with soft manners and stone eyes. You cannot even approach a lift without first having been identified and invited to ascend by your unseen host far overhead. Even then another lithe, respectful killer accompanies you in the lift and steps out with you into an airlock, an antechamber containing a plush-and-gilt sofa that has never been sat on, a sage green carpet and an antique ormolu mirror set with one-way glass from behind which you and your escort are scanned by cameras. Eventually one half of the great double doors (taken from a twelfth-century baptistry in Provence, you will shortly learn) opens and a beaming minder bows you in while running his eyes over your jacket for wrong bulges. Behind you the bulletproof lift doors close with the noise of a safe swinging shut. And there, rising politely to his feet with a little cry of welcome from a deep chair beside a blazing fire of gas logs, is that famous face, the wily survivor, the ex-President's right-hand man, the very one whom the racked priests swore before God had taken personal charge of their racking at an interrogation centre back during the Emergency. It is a good face, much better than the press photographs suggest: Asian-patrician but without the obsidian glance. Thick greying hair kept short (the military legacy), beautifully cut Italian suit, the graceful way in which he takes your sweaty paw in his cool dry hand.

One of the true measures of that kind of wealth and prestige has to do with temperature. In his presence you are awkwardly hot at first until you adjust to the cool of the air-conditioned room, which will allow you eventually to sit beside the gas log fire even as you know the tropical night outside is pressing up against the picture window like a hot poultice. For the moment, standing at the window beside your host (for he has followed you with the courteous affectation of having never before noticed the incredible view), you can feel on your face the heat conducted from the outside even through double glazing. The glass is hot to the touch. And beyond it lies the jewelled city as though seen from an aircraft: those exact sweltering canyons through which your taxi was crawling only ten minutes ago, earthbound and choking. Height and silence render the hectic seethe of ground-level activity remote. Lights and lights and lights of all colours; some winking, some moving, some revolving, all of them pouring up their throbbing activity in glacial silence. An ailing moon bandaged in yellow hangs overhead. Of the firmament visible from a coral-chip beach in the provinces there is no trace. The neons of this single city occlude whole galaxies.

You talk a bit about the ex-dictator, your host's friend since university days, his fraternity brother connected by marriage as well as by shared political deeds. Just a comment or two to touch base, nothing as vulgar as direct questions yet. This is a preliminary sounding-out. I have to convince him that I am worth his while to talk to and maybe worthy of a careful admission here and there. He has to convince me that he has something worth my listening to which I haven't already read in a hundred newspaper articles. The charm offensive begins over dinner, for which we are joined by his wife Luz and the younger of his two sons, Henry, who has just finished at Harvard Law School and is supposed to have a mind like a rat trap. It is Henry who was opposed to my interviewing his father. I wonder what deal they have made. The dining-table is circular, Chinese-style, with a raised section in the middle that revolves on bearings to the touch, allowing the diners to choose dishes from the selection laid out.

'When I was a kid,' says Henry, 'I always had a secret desire to spin this thing really fast so all the food and sauce would shoot off into everybody's lap. I can't think why I never did it. Lack of nerve, I guess.'

'If only you had lacked the nerve for some of your other, equally antisocial escapades,' says his father with an indulgent smile. 'One thinks of the lizards in your sister's bed, the firecrackers at Choo-Choo's wedding, the antlers in the graduation picture, the –'

'Dad!' protests his son. 'Unfair. Tales out of school. I'm sure your guest doesn't want to listen while you air the family's dirty laundry.'

Think again, Henry, I say to myself (as we all laugh at this just-us-folks-at-home way of putting a potentially awkward guest at ease). Though I want to examine much dirtier linen than that and it belongs to Dad, not Junior.

Luz then puts her oar in. She is a petite lady whom I know to be nearly sixty while looking fifteen years younger. Despite her size she can undoubtedly do the matriarch role but tonight she has decided to be down-home while flying a little flag for the arts (out of deference to me in this otherwise too masculine, too material-ist household). She asks about the province I have just left which none of her family has ever set foot in. 'Sadly. It's scandalous how untravelled we are in our own country,' she says, and her son nods like the American citizen he now practically is. 'I've heard such good things about your writing. It's a real honour for us that you're here. I'm ashamed to say that my boys aren't very bookish where literature's concerned, although I do my best to keep up. Tell me, how do you rate Dean Koontz?'

It goes on affably. They are pleasant, civilised company in their way. The food, unobtrusively replenished by two neat girls, is excellent. At the end of the meal, slightly to my surprise, Luz retires with some excuse about having to supervise domestic arrangements. We have obviously reached nut-cutting time when things will turn a bit political. Still, this lady is herself no political virgin, having been mayor of a notoriously tough city until three years ago. Maybe she's just sick of it all and wishes to retreat into the image of herself she has been projecting all evening, that of a housewife and mother who reads a bit and is on the board of sev-eral leading charities. More likely, though, she knows her husband and her newly qualified lawyer son can more than take care of this pipsqueak British writer. The range of sanctions at their disposal is so huge it's a joke. The disgrace of a dozen years ago hardly matters now. The networks built up during the previous regime are still there, just less visible. Old loyalties still operate, now fur-ther cemented by intermarriage and business alliances, to say nothing of the tacit mutual blackmail posited on knowledge of dark deeds and skeletons, always with the assumed threat of incriminating documents stashed away in a Swiss vault (the Far Eastern version of Jayjay's pact with Mansur). Add to this prodi-gious wealth, and the degree of potential overkill is truly absurd.

(The pipsqueak British writer, wearing his only decent pair of trousers, has gone to the window for another brief glance out before accepting a cup of coffee and regrets that he doesn't even have the option of putting on the armour of God. Not that the armour of God is a patch on Kevlar. Game, set and match to earthly powers, as always.)

My host and his son welcome me to the fireside and we sit in our three easy chairs before the unconsumable blazing logs as though we had been invited back to the Senior Tutor's rooms for a nightcap. 'So tell us a bit about this book of yours' seems consistent with the illusion.

'Well,' I say, 'I'm starting from the premise that the previous regime, and particularly your man, have been seriously misrepresented by the Western media in several important ways, and I'd like to see if it's possible to redress the balance. It probably isn't.'

'Apologetics?' Henry asks acutely. 'Or just plain revisionism?'

'Certainly not apologetics. Revisionism in the strictly non-Marxist sense, and then only to the extent of re-interpreting facts rather than denying they occurred.'

'They lied a lot about us,' says my host with unexpected vehemence. For the first time he sounds ex-military. It may just be the gas flames, but his eyes seem to flicker with the bafflement shared by his angry fellow officers when they had begun to sense the tide of global public opinion turn against them. The mess-hall expostulations . . . Had they not always been on the side of the angels? Had they not been patriots, pro-democracy and anti-Communist? The trouble with the American public – civilians, of course – was that they were so lulled and insulated by their wealth and general pig-ignorance of the world they didn't realise that saying they were committed to the crushing of global Communism was all fine and dandy, but at some level someone had to get their hands dirty in order to do the electorate's bidding. And that meant the military. God knows, hadn't we taken enough casualties of our own? Good men were *dying* in this crusade . . .

All this dead rhetoric I can read in my host's eyes. It is not difficult because I've read the same grievance in the eyes of so many
other ex-officers over the years, betrayed by a sudden lurch in
public opinion. It's that lurch they can't get their minds around.
The obvious thing is to blame it on well-intentioned liberals who
hadn't realised their strings were being pulled by the international
Communist conspiracy, that diabolically scheming dark power.
The more intelligent officers saw at once that this explanation
wouldn't do because it quickly spiralled into a paranoia which
accepted that Washington and the media were already in
Communist hands (though what *about* I. F. Stone, huh?). Still,
the grievance is real that one moment they were blue-eyed boys
winning freedom's war and the next they'd become murderers
and torturers with potential atrocity charges hanging over them at
The Hague.

'What exactly do you mean by "re-interpreting facts"?' Henry
asks me.

'I mean a re-interpretation using the notion of cultural difference. We are not in Europe or America here. We are in Asia. But
the world's media are dominated by Western technology and
Western cultural assumptions, and largely Anglophone ones at
that. To interpret highly complex historical, social and political
upheavals in an Asian country using the yardsticks of distant
nations with completely different histories and attitudes is pointless. Anthropology knows better than that; why shouldn't the
media?'

'Sounds reasonable. So what are you going to write about my
father?'

'I can't say yet. It depends on what he wants to tell me.' We
both look at the handsome man sipping seventy-year-old malt
whisky.

'Well,' says the old fellow, who is barely eighteen months my
senior and approximately eleven thousand times as rich. 'I don't
think it will make any difference what I say, will it? Sure I'll talk to
you, James. I'll be happy to. Partly because I think you're a fair

person and I think your project also sounds fair, and partly because I believed in my friend, my President, and I still do and I'm damned if I'm going to be ashamed of it. I took an oath of loyalty and that means something to me. He has been seriously misunderstood and vilified, and if you're giving me the chance to set the record a little straighter then I'll take it. About my own reputation there's probably nothing to be done.'

'As Lord of the Tongs, you mean?'

Henry glares at me sharply.

'Exactly,' his father says imperturbably.

The pun on 'tongs' in this journalist's phrase hints at his Chinese ancestry, at an allegation of corruption, and at the electric curling tongs which were said to have been the instrument of choice of a close brotherhood of officer-interrogators whose existence was widely rumoured but never proved. The only small weapon I have in my otherwise empty armoury, too puny to deploy unless he backs up heavy denial with legal menaces, is a notarised deposition from a US army major. My host had been seconded to Operation Phoenix in 1970, had gone to the States for counter-insurgency training, then on to Vietnam. He had been a first-rate pupil. The ex-major I interviewed outside Baltimore gave chapter and verse for a series of interrogations conducted in a hangar on the perimeter of his base near the Cambodian border. The screams from that isolated building had been audible half a mile away to mechanics working on O-1E Bird Dog spotter planes. They had glanced at each other and turned up the country & western music on their transistor radios. Shades of Edward II. By the time my host's curling tongs were cool enough to pack away in his jungle green canvas grip, the hangar's big doors had been opened to let out the stink of burnt hair and roast meat.

'I'll talk,' he says again. 'But I won't whine, you understand? I naturally won't incriminate myself but I shan't necessarily conceal everything we did. It was dog eat dog, never forget that. We were fighting a war out there and the same was happening to us guys when we fell into their hands. And that war was linked to what was going on in the Emergency over here. I'm not going to cry crocodile tears over the past or massage my conscience in public. No, sir. What's done is done. Certain things I regret, though not all, not by a long way. I shan't pretend I lose sleep over it just to please your readers. I don't.'

And this, too, requires an act of revisionism, though less cultural than temporal. One has to think one's way back to those years when all parties to a grim war waged it with the age-old command ringing in their ears, Win At All Costs: the edict the Nuremburg trials had turned into Catch-22. Torture was like litter and pollution: one of the inseparable consequences of the hegemonic attitude. Dominant cultures did not attain or retain dominance for long without a constant level of dirty work well away from the public eye. The Oliver Norths and John Poindexters were simply the unlucky ones who made it to the witness stand, the iceberg's tip.

We talked of other things, drank superb whisky, assessed the current President's lamentable performance, swapped reminiscences, decided we could work with each other. When it was time for me to go my host said:

'I hope you don't mind if young Henry here sits in on our sessions? I have nothing to hide from my son and he's a first-rate legal adviser. It might save you a lot of trouble later. I mean if he can spot potential libel right there, you and your publisher won't have to worry about it at a later stage when things could get expensive.' He smiles his easy smile. The deal.

He's flinty at that moment but not sinister. I like and am surprised by his plain speaking. I had expected fudging and evasiveness. I had expected to be headed off by family gossip or long monologues about regional delicacies I ought to try. But no. He was more to the point than I had dared hope. The truth is I like that plain, military integrity when I meet it. It's quite aware of all the counter-arguments but refuses to get bogged down in liberal muddiness just for the sake of sounding repentant. Actually, I'm sick of people wanting to look good. I warm to those who don't mind looking themselves. Best of all are the ones who refuse to disavow the past.

I go back to my lodgings in his bulletproof Land Cruiser, driven by an ex-sergeant who left the army to go on driving for him. It turns out the girls who waited at the dinner table are the sergeant's own family. They come from the same provincial town as my host, so the household is cemented together by regional, military and blood loyalties. 'He likes you,' the ex-sergeant confides to me as we shoot a set of red lights in the thin traffic. 'I can tell. He's very suspicious of journalists. But he likes you.'

I turn things over as I try to sleep. Have I been seduced? Down here at nearly ground level the night outside is filled with ambient light and the muffled roaring of air conditioners. At two a.m. horns sound in the street, echoing off concrete walls. From somewhere at the bottom of this canyon comes the amateur wailing of karaoke bars. Exhausts blare, sweat runs into the pillow. How familiar these urban tropic nights are, unsleeping with coffee and dilemmas. Have I been talked around, softened up, compromised? Are Henry and his father still sitting in front of the gas logs, laughing at how easily they tamed the pipsqueak British writer? And should I care if they are? But they won't be. There is no need for duplicity. My charming host is who he is and who he was, just as he admits. Someone who is straightforwardly a patriot, a paterfamilias and an interrogator, as well as many things besides. I am dramatising myself with these squeamish reflections about supping with a long spoon, about Nietzsche's cautionary bon mot that when you look into the abyss, the abyss also looks into you. But of course. We *are* the abyss. I and Jayjay and everybody else.

In the semi-dark I find myself wondering about Jayjay. I am more than ever certain he is concealing something from me. In the aftermath of an evening's talk about military events and the unblinking necessities of battle it crosses my mind that he, too, might well have been caught up in some specific horror during the Second World War. Indeed, the more I think of this urbane man as an ex-officer, the more probable it seems that he may have been party to something squalid and unheroic that the times had made obligatory. He is very much of a generation that knew how to keep quiet, that had the strength to live daily with past deeds and old loyalties without the public confessions, self-flagellations, claims of post-traumatic stress disorder and similar modern modes of bleating. As soon as this idea comes to me a new Jayjay takes convincing shape. Not necessarily a torturer, but maybe a man who took some painful decisions wherever it was he served. (And it shows how little I really know of him that I can see him equally in flying gear bombing a Gestapo HQ in France in which there were known to be Allied prisoners, or in naval uniform ordering a surfaced U-boat to be rammed despite survivors in the water, or doing nasty things 'out East' with Orde Wingate's Chindits.)

Trying to skirt a private abyss of my own, I sense a strange congruence that links together tonight's interrogator, Jayjay and myself. The interrogator's national identity must surely be muddled from so many years training with Americans and abetting their policies, while his son Henry is himself virtually an American. And both Jayjay and I have lived almost everywhere but in the land of our birth. This compromising of our respective roots maybe gives us all a more panoramic moral view, or at least one in which being condemnatory is no longer an option. Maybe it was the abolition of Judgement Day that led the internationally righteous to set up their war crimes tribunals as though the crimes of peace were already well accounted for. I have long lost all interest in issues of public guilt, with the whole fake-dignified panoply of robes and editorials. These days I am only ever gripped by the skewed inheritance of our common lot, by private pacts and secret expediencies, by the unassuaged greeds and griefs that precede court and clinic.

The karaokes wail, the sweat trickles down. My own past keeps me from sleep. In turning and turning on this vile bed I sense the hooks off which I am trying to wriggle. Only one hook, really, when it comes down to it. Lucky the man who is not haunted by a vignette from a far-off war in this selfsame part of the world, an episode burned into the brain. The main protagonists are all dead. But the journalist–adventurer–witness tosses and sweats and is forever condemned to re-live the scene. He was young then, but so were the dead who might yet be alive (the tireless conscience insists) had it not been for his crucial failure of nerve at the one moment when they might still have stood a chance. Unlikely, it's true, but there's never any telling. And now there is nothing *but* telling, the private nag of blame. Over and over again his courage fails, ducking for cover, and over and over again they die. It is all far in the past, one lost incident among uncounted such, and no-one else cares or even knows any more. But it concerns memory as much as it does conscience. Jayjay was right when he alluded disparagingly to that Buddhist amnesia necessary in order to live eternally in the present. By disenfranchising the past it involves damage to the moral self. Besides, I think, why privilege the ever-skidding moment when *now* is no more real than *then*, and certainly not to Jayjay and myself? Our pasts float ever before our eyes like retinal debris or the hair in the gate of an old cine projector, fluttering to betray as film the scene one is thinking so real.

Well, whatever old Jayjay may eventually confess to he is safe from my judgement. Not only do I have a secret of my own from time of war but he did much of his best living before I was even born, when the world was another place. The past really *is* a different country, with its own language and customs. One blunders about in it with fading maps and dog-eared phrasebooks, baffled by dialect and rates of exchange, all censure suspended . . .

The sky outside seems lighter. I wonder how my bees are getting on.

Two months went by. Every so often I would quit the roaring Asian capital for the provinces with the urgency of an underwater swimmer coming up for air and bursting into sunlight. Being down among the denizens unquestionably had its fascination. Being made privy to things about which most people remain

mercifully ignorant was gripping, but you held your breath. At
such depths you were among essentials. You cleared your mind of
cultural baggage and moral outrage. You acknowledged the muscles and teeth of survival. Sharks, too, were beautiful. But it was
still airless down there, a place for quick visits, not for lingering
in. When I could stand it no longer I would surface and take the
familiar series of buses and ferries until once again I was pushing
open my creaking bamboo door and dumping my bag on the
unswept earth floor. Within minutes a row of eyes would show
above the powdery windowsill and on the sill itself a row of little
white fingernails. Had I brought presents back with me? Candy?
(for this was a culture where returning travellers are expected to
bring gifts for unfortunate stay-at-homes). The sheer relief of
innocent normality was itself a kind of gift.

Here beneath the mango tree I worked up my notes, savouring
the ambient smells that drifted through the hut's glassless window
and permeable walls. Cooking fires, tropical rot; the smoke of a
fire for roasting piles of halved coconuts so that the meat shrinks
away from the shell like curls of brown oily leather to be further
dried as copra. The smell of the muddy track drying in the midday
sun; the scent of afternoon rains remoistening dried earth. The
world of air-conditioned condominiums and gas log fires was centuries away. Cultural baggage and moral outrage remained clutter.
The day-care-centre roof stayed unrepaired. The yielding obdu-
racy, the social complexity, the ripple effects of any action taken in
a community this small led to a familiar resigned inertia. I went
fishing instead, split and salted the catch, laid it on the edge of the
thatched roof to dry in the sun.

I used to wonder how I knew when my time was up in my various bunk-holes. Was it because I suddenly felt apprehensive
about my bees? Was it because I worried that my house in Italy
might have fallen victim to storm damage or thieves, all alone up
there among the forests? Not really. Things *that* far away can
take care of themselves. No, the moment for leaving was determined quite arbitrarily by the return flight stipulated as part of a

cut-price ticket. In a corner of the hut I found my shoes, now a pretty blue-green with mould. I shook bulbous spiders out of my trouserlegs and brushed worm dust from a shirt. The very casual-ness of farewells to friends and neighbours, as though we were saying goodbye before going to town for the day, were earnests of return. The bamboo door (through which a determined child could force an entry, let alone a determined adult) was padlocked, the backward glance resisted. The hut, the mango tree, the village itself dwindled to a dot beside the sea, which became ocean, which in due course turned into the Mediterranean and after a while led to my standing on another of my doorsteps fumbling with a key that felt strange.

It was nearly a fortnight before I had the time and inclination to contact Jayjay once more. There was the usual alp of mail to deal with, the normal week's adjustment to a different daily regime and sundry chores. Above all there were the bees to see to. It was a bad time to have been away because some of them would have swarmed in late April and I was resigned to finding a diminished community. After so many weeks wearing my investigative writer's disguise it was a great relief to slip on a beekeeper's mask. I stuffed some smouldering sacking into the smoker and went into each of the hives, softly removing the roof and crown board and slowly peeling back the polythene quilt, puffing a little smoke under the corner and giving an additional small puff here and there as more of the bee-laden frames were exposed. As usual I had the quick image of a brain surgeon lifting off a portion of skull. One by one I raised, inspected and gently replaced the frames, revelling in their smell, their orderly packed cells, the bees moving across the surface. Then back went the quilt and the crown board with great care lest any bees be crushed beneath its edge. This was not just because I felt tenderly towards my bees but also for reasons of self-interest. Squashing a bee breaks its venom sac and the smell of venom stimulates attack, which is why it is a mistake to kill an annoying bee. And once you do get stung, other bees will home in on exactly the same place to plant their stings. So your movements are slow and deliberate and bees that settle on your hands can simply be shaken off into the hive before you put the lid back on.

In this way I worked through the hives, finding nothing amiss. The piece of sacking in the smoker lasted just long enough, a reward for sparingness. Smoke is a blessing and one could hardly work without it, but it should be used minimally. Until I began keeping bees I had assumed it was used as an anaesthetic to stun and subdue the wretched animals, but that is not the principle at all. A whiff of smoke acts as an alarm to which the bees respond instinctively by staying on the comb to fill themselves with a three-day emergency supply of honey. What one is aiming for is placid, gorged bees too good-tempered to go flying around looking for an intruder to sting. It is panicky and inelegant beekeeping to use too much smoke. It does the bees no good and can even taint the honey.

I stripped off the mask and walked up to the house thinking how odd it was to be back here, so far from the sound of the sea and from those air-conditioned apartments where one tiptoed forever warily across the eggshells of past crimes. It struck me that the sort of writing I had been doing over there had something in common with beekeeping. Both were delicate, faintly dangerous operations, exposing secret workings that went on in the dark and were capable of defending themselves to the death. Neither activity felt accidental, each was a solace. A little smoke was essential. Certainly bees and their fastidious rhythms were a marvellous antidote to the messiness of shifting around pieces of paper and ideas. On the other hand tough and worldly affairs could in their turn be a profound relief after a surfeit of loony apiarism. Anyway, for now the bucolics were taken care of. The next job was to go down and see Jayjay.

Il Ghibli looks astonishingly beautiful in its early summer setting. Were it not in order to see friends, why would I ever swap Tuscany's graceful, crafted pastoral for the monotony of coconut palms and the undifferentiated landscape of Southeast Asia?

Claudio, who is standing on the lawn, raises a billhook over his head in salutation like an executioner gravely acknowledging the crowd's praise for a clean cut. Jayjay greets me at the door. I think he looks a little thinner.

'Welcome back, stranger,' he says, and I wonder if there is not a slight edge to the familiar jocular tone. 'How goes the Empah? Come in and tell us homebodies wondrous tales of foreign parts. Did you see the Yxtiloi, whose faces are in their hinder parts? And what of the famed Ligno bird that hatches from pods on a tree and has been hunted almost to extinction by the cuckoo-clock industry?' There *is* a slight edge.

'Your garden looks stupendous,' I say emolliently.

'Doesn't it? We must thank Claudio's rough genius. Also, of course, the Great Landscaper, who disposed these hills so artistically. Come, we shall admire his handiwork from the terrace as usual, our receptiveness further enhanced by strong coffee.'

'You've not been well, Jayjay?' I ask with concern as the light falls on him sitting at the table with its familiar tiles. There seems to be a faintly yellowed look to him, although perhaps it is the early stages of a seasonal tan.

'A passing malaise,' he says. 'Like life itself. You, on the other hand, have that tropicalised look. Bronzed and fit, as the cliché has it. Well, tell me how it went.'

I oblige as he listens with his head cocked, gazing up at the top of Sant' Egidio outlined against summer's blue. At length he says:

'How invigorating difference is, isn't it? How stale to remain all the time in one place. Never having to negotiate with another set of moral rules makes one flabby. I can't help suspecting people who shy away. I always thought that phrase of Hannah Arendt's about the banality of evil oddly unsatisfactory. To me there was always something defensive in it, something evasive. *Banal*. It reminds me of the way middle-class Brits dismiss anything that disturbs them, like pornography or modern art, by calling it "boring". Monsters are us, only a bit more so. They're often a good deal more interesting than the virtuous. Thank goodness we'll both be safely dead before the entire planet is brought to heel beneath some hideous Judaeo-Christian concept of order and rectitude. I'm thankful to have been born in time to have pranced in pagan sunlight as an unfettered being.'

'Enter Pan, left, cavorting wickedly on a heap of ravished wood sprites. Do I now have to view you as the goatfoot god of Arcady, Jayjay? A cross between Norman Douglas and the Piper at the Gates of Dawn?'

'Damn you . . .' He puts his dripping cup down abruptly and dabs at his mouth with a handkerchief. 'If I laugh, it's chiefly because I'm so glad to see you back, James. There haven't been many laughs here of late. Is it too impetuous of me to hope that we can sooner rather than later take up where we left off all those months ago?'

'I'm ready to start when you are. Are you in a hurry?'

'I'm not, but my body may be.'

On my way to the downstairs lavatory I manage to corner Marcella. 'How ill is he?'

'They won't say. He was in Arezzo hospital last month for four days of tests. He's not a young man any longer, is he?' This was said with faint surprise, as if she had never considered it before. 'Have you seen any difference in him?'

'Not really,' I say reassuringly. 'A bit thinner, perhaps.'

In the lavatory I notice Henry Kissinger is missing from his place behind the guest towels. The Vietnam era floats up irresistibly to remind me of my sleepless speculations one night a few weeks ago and my plausible fantasy that Jayjay might be hiding something from his own war a quarter-century before Vietnam.

11

Some time in 1938 Jayjay moved to Alexandria. He couldn't now remember exactly why, beyond saying he needed a change from Cairo and wanted to live by the sea. If his life in Cairo was anything like as complex and compartmentalised as he implied, it may be that something had gone wrong and he made a judicious departure. Perhaps a couple of his casual, oddly affectless affairs with women had tangled, involving him in threats and recriminations? Once again he said he couldn't recall, but that he wouldn't be surprised if it had been something like that.

If Cairo was part of the Islamic world, Alexandria was essentially a Mediterranean city. Greeks, Jews, Italians, French, Lebanese, Turks, Syrians: there were substantial communities of these and many other nationalities, including British. It was a city to which wealthy Cairenes moved to avoid the heat although in the hottest months they generally left Egypt altogether, heading for Paris and London. Their boys went to Victoria College in Alexandria and there was always the family's villa, complete with retainers, otherwise standing empty until one or other member of the family chose to visit. Despite the British-style education French was still widely spoken among the older Egyptian élite. This was not without significance in a country so heavily under British control. The British had bombarded Alexandria during their takeover in 1882, an event unlikely to have endeared them to the Alexandrians, whereas the days under Napoleon at the beginning of that century had left an enduring cultural legacy.

When he was fifteen Egypt's new young King, Faroukh, had spent less than a year in England while supposedly studying at the Royal Military Academy in Woolwich. He had thus been practically in sight of Eltham College even as Jayjay was completing his own final year at school. Faroukh was abruptly summoned back to Cairo in April 1936 when his father, Fuad, died. He had only just turned sixteen, an inconvenient age at which to inherit a kingdom, especially one effectively commanded by foreigners with whom he had never felt any personal empathy. The British Ambassador in Cairo, the mountainous Sir Miles Lampson, had already sent the boy a telegram of condolence whose official tone was unlikely to touch the bereaved Faroukh's heart. Had the youth been privy to the penny-pinching bureaucratic niceties that in fact surrounded the telegram's dispatch he might have felt that the British Government's expression of grief was grudging, to say the least. The draft of Sir Miles's telegram from the Cairo Embassy, in his Napoleonic scrawl, read:

'I beg your Majesty to accept my deepest sympathy and most sincere condolences on the death of your August father His Majesty King Fuad and to accept my most fervent wishes for the continued prosperity of Egypt under your Majesty's reign. Miles Lampson.'

Beside this draft another hand had scribbled querulously, 'Mr Monypenny: Who will pay for this? F.O. ruling is that telegrams of condolences cannot be charged to them. Can No. 3 account help?'*

* Public Record Office, FO141/538.

Maybe it wouldn't have mattered anyway; King Faroukh's emotional alliances would never have been with the British. As a young man his father Fuad had spent happy years at the Military Academy in Turin and had kept with him a core of Italian servants. These in turn became warm, racy company for his son Faroukh as he was growing up in Abdin Palace. King Faroukh's Italian sympathies impinged fortuitously on Jayjay's life because one of his Cairo contacts with an intense interest in Moll-Ziemcke's Sudanese photographs was an Italian who worked at the Palace. Renzo was perhaps a fixer rather than a full-blown courtier, in the sense that he acted as a liaison between the Palace and the Italian legation for such things as washbasins in Carrara marble and the medallions Mussolini was minting, which the King wanted for his Palace collection. Faroukh was an obsessive and spendthrift collector of just about anything, especially gold objects and pornography. Here Renzo was soon acting as middleman in a private trade route that stretched via Jayjay all the way down to August Moll-Ziemcke in the Sudan. This ensured that Renzo's relations with the Palace were excellent, as also with Jayjay himself. One of the things Jayjay had acquired from him, other than a useful smattering of Italian and a good deal of money, was the name and address of Renzo's sister Mirella who was living in Alexandria. She was connected with the Italian legation there and according to Renzo was a fund of information. If ever Jayjay were in that city he should be sure to look her up.

Once arrived in Alexandria, Jayjay betrayed a consistent pattern of behaviour by finding a place to live outside the European community. He rented rooms on the wrong side of the tracks, literally, on the Lake Maryut side of the main station. He had come with a list of contacts both social and professional (for he now thought of himself as a professional English tutor when he wasn't being a professional pornographer). At some stage he presented his compliments to Mirella Boschetti, Renzo's sister, and told her he had brought a letter from her brother in Cairo. She turned out to be a vivacious lady in her early thirties whose position at the legation was broadly described as Cultural Liaison Officer. To some extent she was a counterpart of her brother at Faroukh's palace in that her duties included a certain amount of fixing, although ostensibly only in the field of the arts. Among other things she was responsible for ensuring that Italian cultural concerns were as well represented in Alexandria as those of the French. This was a challenge, seeing that the works of Anatole France and Saint-Exupéry commanded a far wider readership than did the poems of d'Annunzio and the speeches of *Il Duce*.

Mirella Boschetti has invited Jayjay to lunch in her apartment on Saad Zaghlul, explaining that as a mother she likes to be home when her children come back for the midday meal. Mirella reads her brother's letter of introduction as the servants haphazardly lay the table, glimpsed through the open door of the dining-room. Over the meal she suggests in a mixture of Italian and shaky English that Jayjay comes with the reputation of being disreputable and dashing. Does she know about her brother's tastes? he wonders.

Also at table are Adelio and Anna, rising twelve and eight respectively. They strike the Jayjay of 1938 as 'very Italian', meaning they are chatty and constantly interrupt their mother's halting attempts to make conversation with her English guest in order to tell her about their morning at school. Adelio has a few simple English phrases, Anna none. Both know the sort of kitchen Arabic they would have picked up from nurses and maids and servants. Jayjay notices they use the Alexandrian word for 'table', *tarabeza*, instead of the more classical *towla*, *tarabeza* being simply the Arabised Greek word *trapeza*. He muses on such Mediterranean linguistic trivia while waiting for the children to eat up and go. Over half a century later he will record his early conversations with Mirella as though they both had an easy language in common, whereas in those days when his Italian was sparse communication was too slow and difficult to be worth reproducing.

When the children at last scamper off she says 'My brother tells me everything, of course. We have no secrets from each other.'

'Oh, really?' Jayjay says. He has no idea whether she is being devious, maybe fishing for indiscreet confidences from a position of ignorance. 'Such as what?'

'I know what he does at the Palace, of course. The King relies on him a good deal for private matters. Renzo says you are very helpful in satisfying certain of the royal interests. Don't we live in an interesting country and at interesting times?' She laughs sarcastically. 'Had I been told when I was Adelio's age that one day Renzo and I would be earning our living in such strange ways, and in Egypt into the bargain, I would never have believed it. We're from Tuscany; we naturally assumed we would be spending our lives in Tuscany.'

'And your husband? Is he here in Alexandria?'

'No. He and I are incompatible in all sorts of ways these days. He's in Tripolitania, a military man. One can't possibly live there. Inconceivable. It's just desert and barbarians. They hold motor races in Tripoli and the coast is full of Sicilians trying to grow oranges. I married young, you see, when I was not yet nineteen. At once I was pregnant with Adelio. I was so naïve, so ignorant. I never took politics into account. I never thought we were going to build an empire in places like Tripolitania and Abyssinia, or that it would have anything to do with my own family. But military men go where they are sent. Tripoli! Oh God, you should see it. A provincial town where the natives eat live locusts. Can you imagine that? They strip off the wings and legs and burst the bodies between their teeth. Really, it's more like living in the Old Testament than the twentieth century.'

Once again Jayjay is unclear about Mirella's intentions. On the face of it her remarks about Libya amount practically to treason, especially when aired to a foreigner. He knows, of course, that plenty of metropolitan Italians are less than keen on Mussolini's empire-building, while most would do anything rather than find themselves in Libya in the company of a lot of Sicilian peasants.

Her brother, for instance, dramatically claimed he would take his own life before being banished to either Libya or Abyssinia. Renzo couldn't imagine life without King Faroukh, to say nothing of Groppi's and houseboats. Jayjay decides to be gently provocative and see if Mirella can be drawn further.

'But I thought Italians were proud of having colonised Libya and cultivated so much of the coastal strip? I thought it provided jobs for landless Italian peasants who are busy turning it into the Garden of Italy? I always imagined it as one of Fascism's showcases.'

'It is, of course. Certainly when I'm in public it is. But here in my own apartment, having lunch with a disreputable and dashing young English friend of my brother's, Libya is a boring hell-hole of ungrateful Bedouin who are good for nothing. But really! Well, perhaps they're good for hanging. You should see the things we've done for that country. We've put in roads and hospitals and schools even when Italy herself goes without. But it's still not enough to make the place civilised and nor is it enough to stop the migrants grumbling. Half of them are indolent Sicilians who aren't proper Italians anyway, not as we Tuscans are Italian. They're practically Arabs themselves. Certainly first cousins. Alexandria's much better than Tripoli, believe me. Even so, if it weren't for my job here and the children with their schoolfriends I would go home tomorrow. I know Adelio doesn't really like it here. He was nearly seven when we came and he still remembers our house in Pieve di Rigutino, the cypresses and the olives and the vines. And look at this.' She waves a hand to indicate the apartment, the dusty city outside, the vast hopelessness of Egypt.

Over the next month it seemed that Signora Boschetti had plans for Jayjay, for she regularly invited him to lunch or to cultural functions she had helped arrange. To his disappointment it transpired she already had a lover, a Hungarian count named Bathory-Sopron who used to call for her in a flamboyant Delahaye with three spare tyres strapped behind as though he were about to set off for a distant oasis rather than the beach at Sidi Bishr. He looked exactly as one would expect a Hungarian count in his forties to look: like a character in an operetta by Franz Lehár, complete with mustachios and ramrod gallantry. Surely, thought Jayjay, this dinosaur was too farcical to be anything other than an alibi for Mirella, or maybe a gesture; at any rate something more for public than for private consumption? By then Jayjay knew many of the town's more accomplished gossips and fully expected to learn that Count Bathory-Sopron was better known to his intimates as 'Daisy' and liked being thrashed by policemen in his villa on the Bourg-el-Arab road. But no-one could discover anything more detrimental to his reputation than the mustachios, so they simply assumed he was one of the many spies in town who were the life and soul of beach parties with their capacious cars, silver picnic sets and wind-up gramophones.

Mirella's plan for Jayjay was that he should become something like a private tutor for Adelio. She was nursing a dream that her son might one day become a diplomat and knew that fluent English would give him an advantage when applying for the Italian foreign service. Her idea was that Jayjay should spend at least three afternoons a week with him, speaking only English and taking him around. At first Jayjay didn't know whether to feel sorrier for Adelio or for himself. By this time he had become better acquainted with the boy, who seemed not quite as lively as he had first appeared at the lunch table. He was moody, not in the usual pettish manner of children when thwarted but more with a kind of melancholy. With his pointed chin and prominent ears he was by no means a handsome child, although his eyes demanded one reserve final judgement. They were large and dark with curved lashes so long they seemed to cast a shadow. Without actually being any different in colour from the rest of his face the skin around his eyes appeared a shade darker, even sunken. Really, they were romantic eyes in a tubercular sort of way. Sometimes the boy let his face slip into an expression so wistful Jayjay wanted to comfort him, to extract whatever dark secret lay behind his look and erase it with an adult's power. But he was reluctant to devote three afternoons a week to the company of a child.

On the other hand he did want the money, he did want to learn Italian and he did want to go to bed with Mirella Boschetti. And when Mirella leaned with him out of her drawing-room window to show him a battered Fiat tourer parked outside and told him it was his, his mind was made up. Not that the car didn't present certain problems, the main one being that he couldn't drive. She explained it wasn't hers, that someone at the legation had left it when he was posted back to Rome. It was a tenth-hand runabout, a flivver, but it ran and would enable Jayjay to get around. He and Adelio, she suggested, could now visit any of Alexandria's beaches without being dependent on trams. The thought of having his own car was suddenly a distinct thrill, and not being able to drive repositioned itself as a minor inconvenience. Still, it did cross his mind that Mirella seemed keen to get her children out of the apartment on a regular basis. Little Anna could doubtless be parked with friends rather more easily than could her much older brother.

Jayjay learned to drive in an afternoon on the acres of scrub behind town. There was no driving test as far as he could discover. He had been advised simply to take a bottle of Metaxa brandy and three Egyptian pounds to the department that issued licences. Within minutes he had been officially classed as 'one hundred percent driver' and waved on his way. Driving in Alexandria proved not as threatening as he had feared, partly because such traffic as there was moved slowly, often being obliged to keep pace with donkey-carts and gharries. It was also much simplified by there being no pressing obligation to keep to a particular side of the road or to give the slightest indication of one's intentions. Furthermore, in the case of a collision a European driving a car was presumed by policemen to be always in the right, no matter what the crowd said, provided he survived the impact.

Then began a series of strange outings with Adelio. He could feel the boy's great hollow eyes on him as he fumbled with the

Fiat's gear lever, as if Adelio were comparing Jayjay's driving with
his mother's. It was as if there was some kind of complicity
between them, an alliance perhaps based on their youth (since
there were only seven or eight years between them, whereas
Signora Boschetti was a parent). It was also based on a tacit understanding that they had both been banished for several hours.
('Don't bring him back before five-thirty at the earliest,' Mirella
would tell Jayjay. 'He needs all the English practice you can give
him. He's so lazy.') They went swimming, they ate ice creams.
They drove this way up the coast, then that. They made reed
boats on Lake Maryut and observed the shipping in the harbour.
They sat in Mirella's beach hut in Stanley Bay and watched the
gully-gully men wander the sands performing conjuring tricks.
Very occasionally they would have a rather grand tea in Pastroudis,
when Jayjay felt expansively as though he were taking his own son
out for a treat. Bit by bit he came to understand Adelio's moodi-
ness as that of a highly intelligent person who withdraws and is
guarded rather than of one who feels slighted or unappeased. His
melancholy, too, was merely a part of his character, strange only if
one expected all children to be unremittingly light-hearted and
easily bought off. Both he and Jayjay were quick students and after
some months were conversing with considerable fluency in both
English and Italian. Still, Jayjay often found it a strain being
responsible for chaperoning and entertaining a child thrice weekly,
and the ever-present questions of 'Where can we go? What shall
we do?' weighed heavily on him most mornings.

One day when they had driven along the coast past Montazah
to swim they sat on the rotted verandah of a wrecked beach hut
that had apparently been swept out to sea in a winter gale and
then stranded. It lay skewed on the otherwise deserted shore, and
while a good deal of its back was missing it still afforded welcome
patches of shade. Adelio had fallen silent after asking Jayjay careful questions about his family in England. Suddenly he burst out:
'Promise me you won't! Just promise me you won't!' And then,
fiercely anxious, 'You haven't, have you?'

Jayjay understood at once that Adelio was talking about his mother. Suddenly obliged to relinquish the small fantasy he had been nurturing, he said: 'I haven't and I never will, Adelio, I promise.' And that was it. One of the futures he had been looking forward to, now sealed off. It was a novel sensation having to be responsible in a sexual matter, and by no means agreeable. Eyeing Adelio sideways he saw the boy staring seaward, clasping his thin knees as though they might tremble violently, a tear crawling down beside his nose. 'I never will,' Jayjay promised again, soberly meaning it and putting an arm around the bony shoulders. Fine hairs ran from the nape of Adelio's neck between his shoulder blades, marked now as a whitish line where salt had dried. A deep shivering of unbearable tension like a small motor was transmitted through his arm. Jayjay was suddenly overwhelmed by the child's vulnerability. It was the first time it had occurred to him that the social life these enclaves led might entail casualties. It was all very well for the gossips to meet in Alexandria's clubs and cafés and regale each other with tales of who-whom, but it was a very different matter seeing one's own mother gliding about town in a Delahaye driven by a mustachioed count.

'I hate this country,' Adelio said, hurling a mussel shell at an empty bottle. 'It was all right at home. Everything was all right.'

'And your father?'

'He was always with his regiment. Pordenone, Ustica, now Tripoli. I don't think he cares about us. I just wish we could go home. Mamma, Anna and me.'

'I know your mother would like to go home, too.'

'Oh, yes. But she just *says*, she doesn't *do*. It's not good for us, this place. It's dull and ugly and we don't like the natives. You look up and they're always there, like bundles of rags with their hands stuck out for *baksheesh*. I hate them.'

Following the boy's contemptuous gaze Jayjay glanced behind and saw through the missing back wall of the hut a distant figure in a *galabeya* sitting under a stunted mimosa tree not far from the car.

'He's just trying to earn a living by guarding our car for us.'

'Protection racket, more like. If you don't pay him he'll smash your windows with his stick.'

When it was time to go the sun had started to set and the Arab was still there beneath the mimosa, a Biblical figure somehow incomplete without a flock of sheep. As they passed Jayjay greeted him in Arabic and received a grave acknowledgement. The Egyptian had a grizzled beard and a cloth turban with a plum-coloured crown. It was safe to assume that he had done the pilgrimage to Mecca, so Jayjay addressed him as '*Ya hagg*' and passed a remark or two. The man removed thick brown peasant hands from the folds of his robe, entwined with a string of worn beads. Staring out to sea he said that he came to this place every evening when the weather was fine just to look at the ocean and to watch the setting sun. 'For,' he said, 'only Allah knows how many more sunsets he will permit me to see. So while I still can, I come.'

After a few exchanges of this sort Jayjay took his leave with various pious wishes and they started the car. On the way back into town Adelio said in amazement: 'You can actually speak Arabic, can't you? And you were very polite.'

'Why not? He's an old man who has been all the way to Mecca and back. He said he goes to that beach most days just to think and watch the sunset. He would have been deeply insulted to have been offered money. He would have been extremely angry if he could have heard you saying he was running a protection racket.'

'All right, he's the exception. But most of them aren't like that.'

'But Adelio, how would you know? You never speak to Egyptians except to give them orders, do you? And they're always towns-people who expect a strange cold relationship with us haughty foreigners. That old man wasn't from the city. Don't forget it's his country. We're just foreigners. All our attitudes are wrong.'

But Adelio only looked at him queerly with his shadowed gaze, as at a newcomer some years his junior.

– I don't quite know what I thought I was doing. I had no plans. Time seems endless at that age. You drift as though becalmed in a great ocean of it. Provided you're enjoying yourself you may as well do one thing as another. I still had my ambition to walk through important doors, though. I think by then we all knew there was going to be another war, but it was difficult to sense the implications. Hitler's preliminary skirmishings in Europe were remote indeed from the perspective of a young person having the time of his life in Egypt. What did the *Anschluß* with Austria mean to me? What did it matter to a twenty-one-year-old eating ice cream in Pastroudis that the Germans had invaded the Czech Sudetenland or seized Bohemia and Moravia? Where *was* Moravia, come to that? I had just been on a quick visit to Cairo where I agreed a deal with Renzo whereby we would start exporting August's photographs and films direct to Rome, using the Italian diplomatic bag which Renzo could arrange. He said that expanding our operations to metropolitan Italy would be lucrative. Well, it would; but I was thinking much more about how useful this little industry was proving to be in terms of names. I was compiling quite a list of people in high places with much to lose if their interest in Moll-Ziemcke's private version of anthropology became public, and it certainly wouldn't hurt to add some Fascist grandees in Rome to this dossier. I have no wish to appear virtuous but it's nonetheless true that I never intended blackmail in the ordinary sense of extracting money with threats of exposure. All I ever wanted was to establish a mutual understanding as I had with the luckless Richards in Suez, at the most being able to lean on people who could open doors for me. The very last thing I wanted was to expose any of my clients, who would simply drag me down with them. As yet I had no clear idea of which doors I might need to open but meanwhile I considered it would do no harm to discover what I could about the vulnerabilities of a wide selection of people of various nationalities. I just love that situation of two people having mutual dirt, when instead of trying to ruin each other they agree to make it work to their advantage. We've had this conversation before, but it's one of the things I like best about Mediterranean sophistication. It's not about morals. It's all to do with the art, with knowing *how* to live.

– Renzo, though, was not a schemer in that sense. He was in it for lucre. He loved the pictures too, of course, but what really interested him was the King's money. I would give a lot to know what happened to the royal pornography collection when Neguib sent Faroukh into exile in 1952. It was presumably burnt by all those zealous young officers like Nasser who were so eager to purge Egypt of the decadence of a puppet monarchy and its corrupt foreign influences. If so, and a lot of soldiers full of Islamic ardour simply ransacked Faroukh's palaces, it's a great shame because I understood from Renzo that the collection was truly fabulous. In fact he compared it with the ancient Library of Alexandria which the Arabs burned in 696 AD. Very keen on burning things they disapprove of, the Moslems. Just like Christians. So one presumes a good deal of Moll-Ziemcke's stuff went up in flames together with what Renzo said was pornography from all over the world, including priceless Persian miniatures as well as Greek pottery and Egyptian papyri. There was also reputed to be a set of Caracci's original *Lascivie* and even some of Raimondi's *Sixteen Positions*, the engravings of Giulio Romano's drawings that were seized and destroyed by order of the Papal censor. I know he had a complete set of prints of Lemoine's *A Thousand Cocks* of 1908 because Faroukh showed them to Renzo. They cost the King a fortune because Lemoine had only printed five sets before the Brussels police arrested him and destroyed all the plates or negatives or whatever they were. It was the first time anyone had done a comprehensive photographic study of the erect penis. It was Lemoine himself who called it *Mille Queues* or *Duizend Pikken*: a thousand different cocks in all shapes and sizes, from toddlers to greybeards. So who knows what happened to them? I can't believe Faroukh managed to take the entire collection with him to Monaco. I still nurture a small hope based on my knowledge of human nature that there were some token burnings to satisfy the nationalist zealots while the bulk of the collection was spirited away into private hands.

– Up in Alexandria I began living most comfortably on our pornography enterprise, and that was even after Moll-Ziemcke had been well paid for each of his instalments from Khartoum. In fact I was able to drop some of my private teaching, although I kept on with the Boschetti family. Maybe at the back of my mind I was still hoping that despite my solemn promise to poor Adelio I would be able to bed his mother. On the other hand maybe it was because I enjoyed being part of a family, no matter how tangentially. They were nice people, not snobby like so many of the British but warm and inclusive, and there had never been much of a family atmosphere in my own life. Since I had so much responsibility for Adelio I was actually drawn more and more into their circle, often fetching and carrying the children in my dented Fiat. The very fact that Mirella had found me the car was an indication of how much a part of the family I was invited to become. I even began to worry about what would happen if *Tenente* Boschetti should suddenly return from Tripoli, jingling his sword and spurs, although I would have been a lot more worried had I been Mirella. I never did discover what she did on those three afternoons a week when she had the apartment to herself, but I always assumed she entertained the real lover for whom Count Bathory-Sopron was surely a smokescreen.

– Still, when I look back at Alexandria of that period it is Adelio I remember best, and not simply because it was him I saw most of. He increasingly came to feel like the younger brother I'd never had. His vulnerability touched me very much. I thought he had the sensibility of a young poet. One day when we were sitting on the same deserted beach at Montazah where we'd met the pious old Arab he told me that looking at the sea sometimes made him want to cry. He glanced sidelong at me to make sure I wasn't laughing and explained that not only did it fill him with strange yearnings he couldn't name, he could also feel it dissolving everything and everyone he knew. There was nothing the sea couldn't swallow, including God himself. A very proper thought for an adolescent, and I told him so. It emerged that he was mocked at school by teachers and pupils alike for being odd and felt increasingly excluded from the company of boys his own age. It didn't help that he was not fond of games and sports, either. You must remember that he was attending the Italian School in Alexandria at a time when Mussolini's Fascism was at its most triumphalist. There was great pressure to conform, and boys like Adelio tried only at the cost of inner torment that was anyway wasted because it was an act the other children easily saw through. It was some time before he allowed me to learn that he was also teased on account of his ears, being called *Il padellino*, or Little Frying Pan.

– Bit by bit I understood that he was mainly being scorned for having a mother who drove about town with an extravagantly absurd foreigner and a father who was an absentee cuckold, although everyone at school wanted a go in the Delahaye which was one of the most glamorous vehicles in Alexandria. I find it hard to explain why I was so affected by Adelio's being made to feel humiliated by his own mother's behaviour, but I did. To a Briton of that period it was also sympathetic that an Italian kid should be so indifferent to the propaganda they were being fed daily at school: all that stuff about Africa being their natural empire. He knew the songs, of course, and the slogans. But he said he just associated it all with the military and his father. And that was yet a further reason for his unpopularity at school: that he had no real interest in joining the armed forces and fighting for *Il Duce*. His idea of being an Italian patriot was becoming a diplomat, as Mirella hoped he would. He liked making cases and was a good debater. But the notion of having to live in a barracks with more of the same sort of people he knew at school held no attraction for him. He certainly didn't want to have to fight and possibly kill people, although he admitted he would cheerfully shoot his mother's Hungarian Count given the opportunity. Now and then we would plot the Count's assassination just for fun, idle flights of fancy while eating ice creams. We both knew it was a game and

Bathory-Sopron was neither here nor there. The Count's demise wouldn't change anything for the Boschetti family since there was a rich supply of varyingly glamorous or preposterous representatives of European aristocracy in Egypt. But although it was a game, it was one founded on knowledge we shared of how distressed he actually was by Mirella's behaviour and how deeply he hated the Count. It was then I realised that if I ever did break my promise to him and contrive to bed his mother it would smash him up utterly because I had become the one adult in his life he trusted and could talk to.

– It might seem odd now that the most serious conversations I ever had about matters of personal loyalty and patriotism and fighting for one's country should have been with a twelve-year-old Italian. Yet regardless of our difference in age it was a topic that was obviously going to have considerable significance for us both in the near future. If England went to war with Germany again, what was I planning to do? I didn't feel the sort of patriotism that makes a warrior, but neither did quite a few Britons in Egypt who had no connection with the military. We just wanted to get on with living our lives, especially those of us who were enjoying ourselves. On the other hand we weren't blind. We knew we were living in a country that had uneasy relations with its ruling foreign power and there was no plausible war scenario that wasn't going to embroil Egypt in one way or another. Sooner or later I was going to have to take a decision and it probably wasn't going to be easy, regardless of whether I came down on the side of duty, tactical disappearance, enlightened cowardice or whatever. Also, you have to remember that I had listened respectfully to Michael's rhetoric at Eltham College about not fighting to save International Capitalism and Imperialism. I had found it easy to sympathise with the basic notions of Egyptian nationalism that were shared by all the young Egyptians I ever met. Why would I want to fight for my country when my country's presence in Egypt was so transparently one of self-interest? Really, the sort of patriotism needed to fight a war is possible only if your country is invaded or when you have a captive and biddable population that hasn't travelled much. Once your citizens have globe-trotted and intermarried and formed friendships with all manner of foreigners their loyalties are no longer so clear, and the primitive rhetoric of politicians and the gutter press is ineffective at best and contemptible at worst. –

Here you are, Jayjay, domiciled in Italy over half a century later. A somewhat compromised Englishman, but an Englishman for all that. We've heard a good deal about the boy from Eltham, but is there anything of the patriot left in you?

– Oh . . . What an awkward question. You sound just like a journalist. How can I put it? I would be patriotic at the drop of a hat if I thought for a moment the loyalty would be reciprocated. –

The exile's cry. Once again, I don't think Captain W. E. Johns would have approved. Or John F. Kennedy, for that matter. Ask not what your country, etcetera.

– Exactly. Primitive rhetoric. And within a year or two of Kennedy's speech thousands of young Americans were asking how it was helping their country to give their lives in an immoral war halfway around the globe. Let's not go into that. All I can say is that when the news reached Alexandria that England was at war with Germany I was a very long way from experiencing a simple patriotic urge to join up and start killing the enemy.

– The first thing that happened was that the Egyptian Prime Minister, Ali Maher, declared martial law. Under this the terms of the 1936 Anglo-Egyptian Treaty were implemented and the country's ports, roads, airfields and railways placed at Britain's disposal. The few Germans in Egypt were rounded up. Those who were members of the Nazi Party were sent up to Alexandria and interned in Adelio's school, which meant that he and the other students had to be farmed out elsewhere around town. We still didn't know which way the Italians were going to jump, but from the British point of view a glance at the map of Africa gave one a pretty good idea of what was likely. To the west there were about a quarter of a million Italian troops in Tripolitania and Cyrenaica, and to the south the Duke of Aosta had much the same number stationed in Italian Somaliland and Ethiopia. It would surely have made sense to Mussolini to take Egypt and the Sudan, thereby joining up his territories into one massive African empire. By now General Wavell, our Commander-in-Chief Middle East, had arrived, and he looked at the map and made the same calculation. It didn't look good. The Italians outnumbered us five to one. You could hear teachers from Adelio's school, Fascists to a man, calling cheerfully to each other across Saad Zaghlul 'L'Egitto sarà a noi!' Mirella herself was becoming a little infected by the enthusiasm of her colleagues at the Italian legation but she still gave me luncheon three times a week and encouraged me to take Adelio off for the afternoon. Indeed, she was impressed by the progress he was making in English and wanted our arrangement to continue.

– It was a very odd period. For an unattached, self-employed Briton like myself there was very little pressure to be warlike. A good few Britons of military age had already left Egypt on roundabout routes to return to England and join up. But the complete uncertainty of what was going to happen to Egypt made for a kind of hiatus for the rest of us. Basically, we just went on enjoying ourselves even as more and more men in khaki flooded in from places like Australia and New Zealand and India to reinforce Wavell's scant division or two. This was excellent from the point of view of my business, of course, since selling troops pornography is about as challenging as selling rat poison in Hamelin. Then the disquieting news reached me that August had been interned in Khartoum as an enemy alien, poor fellow. Still, I had enough of his negatives to be able to supply the market for the indefinite future and I was not about to enlist in the army unless forced to. It was here that all my party-going in Cairo began to pay off. I had some excellent British contacts who knew I spoke Arabic and had Egyptian student friends. These party contacts had just been chaps a few years older than myself whom I'd last seen dancing with girls from the fishing fleet. Now suddenly these same fellows were popping up in uniform with quite impressive ranks, or else in civvies but attached to mysterious intelligence units that looked most unlikely ever to have to fire a Lee-Enfield rifle. For the moment I skulked and considered my options while the Italian Fascists in the streets went on assuring everybody that Egypt would shortly be theirs. As I said, a very odd time.

Meanwhile, Hitler's military machine was doing impressively well in Europe and the Egyptian Government was becoming increasingly pro-German. Most of my nationalist friends as well as the Wafd Party were arguing that Britain's being involved in a European war and stretched throughout her global empire was a golden opportunity for the cause of Egyptian independence. They, too, began openly supporting the Germans. Then in June 1940 Mussolini finally made up his mind whose side he was on and Italy was suddenly at war with the Allies as an Axis power. By late September the so-called Italian Army of Liberation had crossed the Libya–Egypt border and had occupied Sollum and Sidi Barrani, sixty miles inside Egyptian territory. The following month the Italian Air Force bombed Maadi, a suburb of Cairo. The majority of British women and children in Egypt had already been evacuated to South Africa, and you can imagine that the atmosphere was pretty panicky. We were all expecting to be over-run by Marshal Graziani's 10th army at any moment. The real thing was happening at last and we were about to become prisoners of war. Alexandria, which was where they would arrive first, was very tense but subdued, except for the Italian Fascists going around loudly counting the days until they could throw garlands around the necks of their victorious compatriots. But there were quite a few Italians in Alexandria who were not at all sure they wanted to be conquered by Fascism. It was obvious Mirella herself had her doubts. She told me it would give her no pleasure to see the city reduced to a military garrison like an overgrown Tripoli. What then of cosmopolitan lotos-eating? But suddenly the British launched a counter-offensive and Wavell's commander of the Western Desert Force, O'Connor, re-took Sidi Barrani, carried straight on westwards and by Christmas had taken well over twenty thousand Italian prisoners.

– This was a great boost for British morale, of course, but it hotted up the problems between the British Embassy in Cairo and King Faroukh. It was widely believed that Faroukh, already well known as an Italianophile, had a secret radio transmitter in one of his palaces and was in constant touch with the Italian High Command in Rome, presumably passing on the gist of Sir Miles Lampson's conversations with him as well as any information he could glean of British military intentions. Lampson put the King under a lot of pressure to 'get rid of his Italians', meaning all those Palace electricians and cronies and including poor old Renzo. Faroukh's brilliant answer was 'Just as soon as you get rid of yours,' referring to Lampson's second wife who was half Italian. It was a famous riposte and gave a pretty good idea of how strained relations between the Embassy and Abdin Palace were. Meanwhile the Egyptian press was saying that the British could never have done so well against Graziani without the help Egypt was giving them under the terms of the 1936 Treaty, and this alone ought to have earned Egypt its complete independence. The British replied that the Egyptians ought to be damned grateful to them for having saved their country from an Italian conquest.

– It all helped to make up my mind. Eighteen months into the war I had reached the point where I couldn't go on skulking, especially not with fellow Brits in tattered uniforms limping around Cairo on crutches. My private feelings were still quite clear that I wanted nothing to do with this war, but it's easy to be shamed into doing things against your better judgement. Do you remember all those studies about bravery some years ago? They found that in nine cases out of ten, acts of heroic wartime bravery are committed not out of hatred of the enemy but out of fear of being thought cowardly by one's own comrades. It's all about not looking bad in front of one's friends, and that was pretty much exactly what drove me to enlist. Maybe if I had been back in Eltham I might have tried to fail the call-up medical with the old gas-and-milk dodge, but there again I'm not sure. To this day I have no idea whether I'm a coward or not. I'm not even certain what it means. The fact is I was brought up to fight. We all were, of that generation. It was in the air. Most men over forty that one met had served. The First World War had been over a scant twenty years and ever since then there had been constant rumours of another war to come. In every Briton's unconscious was the knowledge that we had a huge Empire to defend. I don't think any of us seriously believed we would live our lives out without at some point having to fight. Anyway, brave or not, shamed or not, I enlisted.

– Well, I say 'enlisted', but this contact I had in the SOE Cairo office told me I wouldn't be doing England any favours by becoming cannon-fodder in the Western Desert. I would be much more use otherwise deployed since by now I spoke excellent street Arabic, quite passable Italian, and knew my way around Cairo and Alexandria. I also had some potentially valuable Egyptian contacts. SOE, of course, was Special Operations Executive whose chief remit (apart from denying its own existence) was to build up and co-ordinate the underground resistance to the Axis in Europe. It had offices in various neutral cities like Bern and Istanbul and Cairo. Each office had two sections, one of which handled special operations and the other propaganda. I was assigned to propaganda, which pleased me since I had always fancied myself as anyone's advocate. But the first job I was given was to stay in Alexandria and help look after a warehouse of SOE equipment that was being stockpiled in secret for eventual use in the Balkans. It was a large garage at the back of Sidi Gaber station and funnily enough it had once belonged to the Italian legation until being commandeered quite early on. I liked to think my old Fiat had once been housed there, but I don't suppose it had. There were a lot of submachine guns in crates, also stacks of walkie-talkie radio sets with those great chunky batteries that looked as though they'd been dipped in butterscotch: some kind of greased paper they were wrapped in. I took it in turns with a fellow named Sid Dix to keep an eye on all this equipment. The windows of the garage had already been whitewashed and barred and special locks put on the doors, so guarding it wasn't too difficult. In fact we didn't have much to do for several months. I had less spare time now but was still taking Adelio to the beach whenever I could. It was also one of my duties to report what I could about the Italian community in Alexandria, its morale and so forth. Effectively, I was expected to spy on close friends like the Boschettis. Needless to say I passed on nothing about them, but neither did I mention to them that I was now officially employed in their legation's former garage. Funny how easily an impostor slips into game-playing . . . Am I boring you? –

Absolutely not, Jayjay.

Liar! Hypocrite! But how to explain? How can I tell him that these days his biographer is prey to a sound like that of surf on a far-distant shore. It has made him impatient with narratives where nothing seems to weigh much more than anything else, all scurrying along with the sole purpose of getting a tale told, of moving someone from Eltham to Suez to Cairo to Alexandria to (eventually, if I have the patience) aged eighty at the foot of a hill in Tuscany. It is true: I lack the patience to hear out the full 'And then . . .' of his life, its long-ago busyness and its rehearsal of scenes whose exact sequence no longer matters. My own life shoulders it aside (and what greater failing could a biographer admit to?) It is a part of having passed an arbitrary age – maybe forty-five, maybe fifty – that no matter how languorously the sun sprawls on to a Tuscan hillside, no matter how glitteringly the bees burst from their hives to swerve into immediate invisibility, there lies behind it all that familiar mortal shore in far-off Asia. Here in Italy it is sheer chance that I happen never to have followed a friend's coffin to Montecchio cemetery. For all the winters endured here, for all the memories of mud and snow and gales, this place has managed to retain something about it of a perpetual summer holiday, certainly with shafts of melancholy but miraculously preserved from the grind of a normal reduced existence. The two kilometres of forest that separate my house from its nearest neighbour represent more than mere distance; in some way they form a *cordon sanitaire*. But none of it is proof against the sound I can always hear at the back of my mind as if borne on the wind from far over the planet's haunch: that Asian beach of coral chips being washed by the constant sea, the unresting chafe of pebbles. There, I have indeed walked behind a coffin. I have helped whitewash graves for All Souls' Day, tearing mats of greenery off inscriptions in the cement, watching how the wiry roots pull away clots of mortar rotted by the sea wind. Year by year the names blur and fade even as memories of their once living owners remain sharp, as though photographed in the intense glare of tropic light, walking and laughing in my own past, forever handing me a glass, hauling in a fish or laying a hand on my arm, brown on white.

However, for a biographer to tell his subject that his life story is becoming a bore is not easy. Apart from the likelihood of giving offence it leaves the writer still more isolated in his peculiar fastidiousness, apparently unsatisfied by ingredients that the majority would find interesting, even gripping. I mean to say, here is Jayjay being swallowed up by the Second World War in a theatre full of misfits and weird political cross-currents. The divided loyalties, the remoteness from Europe and Hitler's blitz, the unwarlike aspect of Cairo and Alexandria with their well-stocked shops and frenetic night-life: surely all these would constitute a raconteur's dream of endless episodes and reminiscence? (That time the Brigadier was left standing in only his underwear to greet King Peter of Yugoslavia . . . The consignment of London Rubber Industries' condoms, Other Ranks, For the Use Of, that was inadvertently dispatched to SOE's typing pool as carbons . . .) Plus, of course, the flashlit derring-do of Stuka attacks and desert warfare. The biographer acknowledges the appeal of all this, adding only that he seems to have seen or read it all before somewhere. It is only feasible to repeat it if we know something about the narrator that damages his account, or undercuts it, or sets it at one remove from the filmic. Otherwise we run the risk of writing the sort of book that wins literary prizes and later gets given the middle-brow Hollywood treatment. With some temerity I put this to Jayjay, not bluntly but more as a suggestion that might bear think-ing about before he embarks on the next episode of his saga. He is less offended than surprised. Like most people he thinks uncon-strued events are enough in themselves. He has never encountered anyone so hard to please. Surely his job is to relate the facts and mine to give them a writerly gloss, the literary depth and so on? I reply that out of a silk purse one could no doubt cobble together a silken sow, but I am not in the stuffed toy busi-ness. Real depth requires real information.

The fact is I can't wait for him to get serious, to spill some beans, *any* beans. I am now more than ever certain that at some time during his war there was an episode that took him by the scruff and gave him the sort of shaking from which there is never a complete recovery. His airily putting himself down as an impos-tor is surely a legacy of this. Did he not just say he was brought up to fight? And did he not immediately add some reflections on cowardice? Perhaps like me he failed in some awful fashion. I do hope so. I yearn for him to get into uniform, to hurry through these preliminaries for battle. However, it is unfortunately not a biographer's task to hustle him but to pounce the moment I think he is becoming slippery. So after delivering a stern reminder that his narrative stands in urgent need of complication I shut up.

On that note we part for a while, quite amicably and with no suggestion of finality, though with the feeling of an impasse that somehow needs to be overcome. There is too much eggy youth about his tale so far, and the sound of that distant coral-chip strand too insistent in my own ears. I find myself thinking about curling tongs. Often these days I walk out of the house in the early morning to stand as on the rim of a vast bowl of landscape at whose bottom lie dark pools of mist. I watch as the overtaking light leans around the mountain's shoulder to spill across the forest tops below. Sometimes a sense of quite unearned fortune grows in pace with this light that has rolled all the way from Japan to pour into a Tuscan valley. At the end of a rotten sad century there is the apprehension of having unjustly escaped. Surely such fortune must be paid for? Maybe a bitter band is even now making its way silently up the track towards the house, intent on its bitterness. Shortly I shall find myself incredulously digging a shallow pit as the men lounge around smoking. Without warning the first *roncola* blade will thud into my back and a gout of blood hit the spade handle. The methodical thudding will go on, accompanied by grunts of effort. Then my eyes are put out with a pocket-knife still greasy from cutting salami for yesterday's lunch. Sudden darkness will turn on its head and become still blacker, heavier, suffocating as they refill the pit and stamp down the soil. The same sun will go rolling blithely onward to the Americas and beyond to greet Japan again. This fantasy comes less from guilt than from incomprehension. So many hundreds of millions have made far grimmer ends this century, why not I? In the banal lottery of earthly existence atrocity is visited on some and fortune on others, irrespective of virtue or deserts. Both are reprisals for having drawn breath.

I stand on the particular grass beneath which I shall probably never lie (or else may soon be lying as the billhooks are wiped, the knife folded, an eyeball kicked with disgust into the irises that fringe the terrace edge). At this moment it so happens there are no bodies between my footsoles and the tilted slab of rock that underlies the shallow soil like muscle. There is probably nothing of flesh and blood beyond the odd mole. But there so easily could be: more nourishment for this landscape whose bucolic tenderness, now revealed by a risen sun, is testament to millennia of spilt blood. On certain days it is all too plain that Tuscany's rich patina was achieved by force, by whips and priests and landowners. It is merely the casual irony of a later age that we itinerant leisured folk can praise the scenery from our terraces and feel that in some way we can possess it or consume it, and all without reflecting that today it is our own elbows at which Death stands. We need only turn our heads a little to glimpse him; so we go on staring rigidly ahead, busily admiring ourselves for being able to admire the painterly effects of olive and cypress and the lavender light that slants across these aromatic hills.

12

I can't fault him for being less edgy than his biographer, after all. Nor can I blame him if now and again I tire of a certain prosaic quality in his narrative. It is only the thought that he is being evasive that exasperates me, but I can't think what would change that now. He is ill, I am in no doubt about it. For the first time I wonder if we can ever make a book out of this. I have gained a friend, but I may yet have to file our relationship ignominiously as 'Bits of a Biog.'.

There is still much in Jayjay that I envy. He is thoughtful, although I'm not sure he ever drifts very far from the world, being satisfyingly tied to it by sensualities of all sorts as well as taking an easy pleasure in being who he is. That is how I should like to be, too (I think as I stare out of the window over the Val di Chiana's panorama). That is how I should like to be if I were a stronger personality. I have this fatal weakness for floating away, even as I sound brisk and occasionally forceful. I can imagine people who have met me over a dinner table reflecting later that although the words I spoke came over as individual enough at the time, the person who spoke them now seems smoky, insubstantial. Whereas anyone meeting Jayjay over dinner would carry away the clear impression of a solid and ever-present persona, not one that would slink off, leaving its owner vacantly crumbling bread until jerked to his senses to blurt 'I'm so sorry – I must have missed that.'

Yes, I am a little jealous of the man whose life I have stupidly trapped myself into writing. He came well disguised but I can now see he is another incarnation of that figure whom I have been meeting throughout my life, the person who knows what he is doing. In my days of youthful travel I would run into people of my own age waiting in an Indian bus terminal at midnight or urging me in the small hours to do a bunk with them from a fleapit hotel in Recife because expected funds hadn't arrived. These characters always seemed to have a next step to take and to know why they were taking it. I lacked this inner plan. Adrift in a continent, I could never see why any particular destination might be preferable to any other even though I generally liked it well enough once I had got there. And the same uncertainty or rootless docility has dogged me through the years to the point where I can acknowledge it as mine. When one has passed fifty one can disown *nothing*.

But I do regret it. Much of the time, if not most, I regret it. Apart from anything else, who but a weak and indecisive person would have allowed himself to drift into a late cohabitation and then let both that and his only child drift away like one of those small clumps of thistledown that float in through an open window, eddy around a few inches above the kitchen floor for a while and float out again? Inconceivable that Jayjay would have let such a thing happen. And nor is it because I don't care enough. I do. *Amo et fleo* (or I should say: I believe I have loved, I have watched myself weep). It is mainly that I have so little conviction of the weight of love and tears. The moments in my life when I have been most content are those when I was not in love and still less shedding tears. If I have to visualise them, an image comes to me that originated perhaps on that distant Asian coast, or maybe in this very house until four or five years ago when I finally put electricity in. It is of sitting at a table before an open window. Outside it is night, and an oil lamp on the table lights up the page of a book or a half-scribbled letter. What I can hear is the soft buzzing of the lamp: a hollow sigh of hot gases rushing up the chimney, together with the faint hiss of oil burning on the broad wick. It is the sound that defines silence. Beyond the lamp, out in the night's velvety warmth, there may also come the spongy lolling of wavelets on a level beach or else the machine-like chirr of crickets. Yet the lamp, while not making these in any way inaudible, somehow enfolds them in its hush. From its hot little heart it radiates silence, and out and out that silence spreads until it pervades the universe. At that moment my lamp is both at the centre of the universe and filling it. The very sky asprawl with starfields has something to do with that flame, as if the constellations were rustling up through the glass tube to spread out and set in an instant in deep interstellar cold. Thus my little lamp creates the firmament around it even as it shrinks it, and all in this clear, resonating silence. Time dissolves, and love and tears shrivel to join the seared midges and insect detritus falling slowly on to the golden page. They fall and fall in company with *Why me? Why here?*, and only that vast speck of resounding flame is steady. This happens, and brings balm. But I don't think it happens to Jayjay, and why should it? He has too much else. Well. Even these days I still light my oil lamp from time to time. I may tell myself I'm economising on electricity but the truth is I like its smell and sound. Also, I think better by lamplight.

The dinner table I mentioned earlier was quite real. It was no mere figure for my inability to fill a seat as memorably as Jayjay always would his at any festive gathering. It was one night last winter when I went down the hill to supper with friends I have known for twenty years, all of them locals: a farmer and his wife, the farmer's two old parents, an engineer at a pasta factory down the road together with his wife and daughter, a nursery gardener, a self-employed builder. The quantities of food were extravagant:

cuisine not haute but sturdy, and produced with a lot of care. Jayjay was not there but it was just the sort of commonplace gathering in someone's beamed kitchen at which he would have been in his element. Everyone lapsed into dialect with the first plate of *crostini*. Blasphemies peppered the air. The wood-fired oven threw out a cheery warmth, the cat dozed atop the extinguished television set. On the sooty walls were cheap framed pictures from Castiglion Fiorentino's Friday market: Padre Pio with his celebrated stigmata, an all-purpose snow-and-pines scene that looked like Canada, a basket of puppies with roses bound over the handle. There was also a yellowed newspaper cutting with a barely discernible photograph of Fausto Coppi, the champion cyclist between the late thirties and early fifties, a boyhood hero of the farmer's father.

The conversation rambled reassuringly to cover completely predictable topics. Local gossip; politics; sugarbeet; vines and olives; somebody's operation; a boy who (*pig-Madonna!*) needed to stop wanking, get off his backside and do a decent day's work (*Madonna ugly-wolf!*); a recipe for *baldino*; a woman who dyed her hair; amiable obscene jokes; much laughter; compliments to the chef . . . And without warning I saw heads. I saw how all our heads around the table were in some truthful way *exactly* the same heads that had talked around a similar table on this spot two hundred and fifty years ago or two thousand five hundred – Etruscans, whatever. Different names, different language, fairly similar food, but not different thoughts. The same heads having the same thoughts passed through them. Not for the first time I saw how our much prized individualities are a fiction. There is only this succession of heads in which the same thoughts take up residence, roost for a while and then pass on through the next generation in their long, aimless, repetitive narration. There will always be heads to host the same thoughts as ours long after our own are full of roots, just as there were before this current batch of 'us' was born. Who is this dim storyteller who exists outside us and goes on putting ancient jokes into generation after generation of skulls, filling them with the same banalities?

Once again I suspect Jayjay is untroubled by such moments. He would assuredly not have been the one sitting in silence, fiddling abstractedly with a chunk of bread. Had he been silent at all it would have been because he was trying to work out why *baldino* should look like a sort of chocolate flan, given that it is basically just chestnut flour, water and fried rosemary baked together. Far more likely he would have been in the middle of one of his tales of foreign parts and other times, so marvellous to people who have scarcely ever left this valley and one of the reasons why he is a perennially popular host. To the end of my life I shall be able to hear his voice: never loud, but the sort for which others fall silent on account of a certain charm and urbanity that contrasts in a piquant manner with the often risqué things he says. That odd mixture of travelled grandee and earthy Chianino is somehow irresistible. 'So this Major Sansom fellow, who was in the Cairo Military Police in those war years, ordered an investigation and they discovered that the household was an efficient nest of spies because every single member of it, regardless of age or sex, was on the game. *Ddio lupino!*, even the cat's *culo* looked like a zucchino flower . . .'

And yes, for this too I am jealous of the man, even though a sour and aloof little voice tells me that it's all a bit *easy*, somehow.

Then one day everything changes. There are no premonitions as I bump down the track through basking Red Admirals. It is one of those hot summer mornings when lavender bushes are still being pummelled by clouds of Blues and Skippers, among which scarce Swallowtails float loftily in their blond finery. The richness of summer is coming to a head. Within a week or two the nectar flow will dry up and the remaining wild flowers turn to hay. The bees will be obliged to make the long aerial trudge down to the irrigated rape fields far below. On this morning, though, Jayjay's garden is almost blowsy with the freight of summer sap. Maybe something in this sheer fecundity is enough to make my host aware of a thinness in the account of his life so far. Maybe my dissatisfaction has had its effect. Maybe, too, the state of his health has at last prompted him to gather his nerve. For what he is about to tell me contains elements of both confession and explanation without fully being either. He is also divulging a secret he has been keeping for so long that deciding to keep it no longer amounts to recklessness. Over sixty years a secret must surely transcend itself to become as much a part of its keeper as a pair of spectacles that brings the world into private focus; or else a habit one cannot shake, like always giving a little cough before one speaks.

Whatever the reason, the scene that confronts me (outwardly the same as ever, with us sitting on his terrace with my notebook and the remains of mid-morning coffee on the table) is profoundly different today as Jayjay gazes into the blue air over Sant' Egidio as if into a lens through which he might see his whole life refracted.

– Empty. It's empty, isn't it? There's something missing from my life as I've narrated it. –

Not much about the heart, perhaps? Plus the odd inconsistency. Little skatings. Is this where you confess to Rosicrucianism, Jayjay? A previous life in Babylon or on one of the planets of Aldebaran? (But I'm thinking *At last! Here it comes!* and ready myself for a tale of military disaster, of treason, cowardice, massacre or interrogation. That's the real reason why he chose me to write him: he sniffed out my own lapse through hints I've let fall in my books. We are uneasy comrades-in-arms, he and I.)

– *Et in Babylonē ego* . . . Not quite that, no. I thought I could slide around having to mention this, as I've done for so many years, but I find I can't. The longer I go on talking about my life while omitting its centre of gravity the more hollow it feels, the more like a direct lie. Well, I can't bear that. Did you ever read Berlioz's memoirs? –

(*Berlioz* . . .?? And yet after all I must have had some unconscious inkling for after a moment's double take it hits me with an inner thud like a long-awaited letter dropping on to the doormat.

Visions of war thin away as my thesis crumbles. For Jayjay, ignominy had taken an entirely different shape.)

Not *Estelle*?

– Exactly. The boyhood passion that lasted him a lifetime, outliving mockery, two marriages and countless lovers. Only in my case not Estelle, but Philip. You remember Michael, the boy at school whose politics I admired? His younger brother. He was two years younger than me. It was the beginning of the autumn term and I was looking at the new timetables on the school notice board and there he was, just arrived, although I didn't know then that he was Michael's brother. It felt exactly like an electric shock, one severe enough to cause radical damage to the heart. Have you ever had that? Have you ever been, as the French say, *foudroyé*? It's as if you had suddenly caught sight of a huge object moving across the sky which nobody else has noticed. You alone are thunderstruck, the rest of the world just goes blithely on with business as usual. And how could I have known, there in the middle of a mob of my schoolfellows all pushing and shoving around a notice board, that at barely sixteen I had just received the equivalent of a death sentence?

– At once, such *love*. As though gold dust were seeping through my blood. Everything I was or ever could become handed over on the spot to a perfect stranger, unconditionally. It depended on nothing, neither on recognition nor reciprocation. It was beyond all logic. It was even beyond rebuff, though I never risked that. Just a passion that could only grow and not diminish, fed by a casual word here and there whenever we bumped into each other by chance, although never is chance so painstakingly engineered as by a desperate lover. That was the secret of the whole Michael business. I know I told you I was fascinated by him but I wasn't really, although he did impress me. Nor was I ever very interested in his politics, certainly not to the extent I made out and half believed myself. Michael was just an excuse. I cultivated him as a way of cementing a link with Philip. I'm not sure either of them ever guessed. –

What was their name?

A strange, closed look comes over Jayjay's face, like that of a man who stands on a shore watching the ocean that has recently drowned his entire family.

– I can't tell you. You'll laugh at this old fool keeping a last school secret from over sixty years ago when most of the boys are long dead and the rest beyond all caring. Yet I told nobody then and cannot say the name now. I never shall. I shall die without saying it to anyone. It will fall out of my brain into the earth and dissolve. –

It's true you never mentioned Michael's surname. I noticed it at the time because you're generally punctilious about names. It was a small thing, but it stuck.

– Maybe I wanted you to notice. That's the worst of clandestine love: it's the one secret bursting to be told. The surname doesn't matter but Philip himself matters dreadfully. Now you know, and you're the only person I've told in over sixty years. You've not yet dismissed it with one of your jocular remarks and I'm aware it leaves me with some explaining to do. I know it's absurd, but although Philip has in some sense been my life I hardly knew him at all. A two-year age gap in adolescence is anyway quite a gulf, and most boys have no inclination to mix with their juniors, who simply strike them as childish. Also, in a formally streamed school one had one's own contemporaries and classes and games teams and it was quite possible to go for days without bumping into someone from a different niche in the school. Apart from anything else he was a boarder and I a day-boy. Still, I befriended a couple of his classmates enough to discover he was an avid reader of *Popular Flying*, in which the earliest Biggles stories were being published at the time. When Johns himself visited the school I had him sign an autograph for Philip as well as for myself. I hoped it would buy me into my idol's favours but all it did was slightly increase his stock among his contemporaries. So how, you're going to ask, could a junior with whom I had almost no contact (and that only over a scant eighteen months more than half a century ago) have become my life?

– Dear James, I wish I knew. It might have made sense had we been physical lovers, but we never were. Largely innocent I may have been, as we all were, I was still aware of those sorts of erotic possibility. One never did that with real friends, only with people one didn't necessarily like at all. It was part of the code, I suppose: a protection against love which was so important for the maintenance of a good school or even of British society. No, it wasn't sex I wanted with Philip but everything. I wanted to spend the rest of my life with him. I wanted his soul. I wanted to *be* him, seamlessly. To inhabit his bones.

– I was partly *foudroyé* because of his looks, obviously. Michael was handsome but Philip was downright beautiful, there is no other word. Not at all effeminate, just beautiful, flawless. It was like being confronted with a masterpiece. Even his contemporaries seemed slightly respectful, which is hardly something that comes naturally to a bunch of ink-stained fourteen-year-olds. Of course this was the eye of love, and I could always hear that little sceptical voice inside saying he was just another scruffy kid though admittedly a lot less plain than some. But it made no difference and anyway his looks are not the whole story. He had about him an intriguingly foreign air. I think I mentioned they were a missionary family in Tanganyika Territory? When I first saw Philip he'd just arrived back from a summer spent in Africa and he was a study in brown and blond. I remember being fascinated by the colour of his neck against his shirt collar, by his hands against his cuffs. Among us pallid English children he was an exotic, and it was that which did for me. It was as though my entire sixteen years had unwittingly been lived in a world slightly out of focus and in that instant's glimpse a synapse closed or a critical molecule shifted and a new universe sprang into being with pin-sharp clarity. And all might still have been well if it hadn't done something to my heart at the same time. How was I to know that at that moment, which not even an onlooker could have detected, my life's entire course would be set? I went on believing what we were constantly told: that our futures depended on studying hard and passing the right exams, that qualifications were the key to everything. Yet as it turned out I need not have bothered to sit a single damned exam. The lightning-stroke of Philip had bleached away everything else and pointed me in a direction neither his nor mine, a direction I willy-nilly took up and have gone ploughing along ever since, further and further away as though I were intent on leaving the solar system. And it has led me here, for apparently the Val di Chiana mysteriously intersects with the outer reaches of the solar system. I'm sitting here on this terrace in Italy, talking to you on this astonishing summer's day, all because one morning in Eltham in 1934 for maybe thirty seconds I saw a boy looking at a notice board. And *that* is the story of my life, so maybe you can stop writing and I can stop talking.

– An odd case indeed, you're thinking. It doesn't make sense. Well, nor to me. But it may at least make sense of things in my story which must otherwise have struck you as anomalous. I could see you were not altogether won over by the explanation I gave for going to Suez, for instance. You thought it strange that my father would have banished me to bring me to my senses and get me away from Michael's dangerous political influence, and you were right. The truth was almost the reverse. I badgered him to find me a job in Suez. Philip had told me he was going out to Dar-es-Salaam to see his family for the first time in two years. He said he'd always liked Suez, for some reason, and I came to associate the place with him as a name in a fantasy world I was creating for us both. As I mentioned, there were quite a few boys at Eltham whose families were overseas, either Bible-thumping or doctoring or running the Empire, and they were the ones I tended to befriend. Some fascination attached to them because they felt different, they knew different things, odd languages and weird customs. I imagined they were familiar with stifling markets in Mombasa or Madras or had drunk cows' blood with the

Masai and knew the smell of opium in the back streets of Shanghai. My adolescent obsession with Docklands warehouses and cargo vessels was all part of the same thing. I think I described it as being a kind of poetry for me. And everything met in Philip. He became an icon. He personified Overseas for me, he embodied the landscape for which I yearned. So I imagined that by getting a job in Suez I might gain a foothold in his enviable world as well as being physically closer to Tanganyika. Pathetic! Of course. But that's how children are when in the grip of love. Maybe we all are. Perhaps that's the whole point of icons: to annihilate the rational.

– So because I went on at him my father reluctantly found me the job with Anderson & Green in order that I could at least survive in Suez. Why Suez? he wanted to know, and I spun him some tale. Actually, it must have been a relief to get me out of the house because I'd become intolerably moody and mooning and cross. I used to be driven into inner frenzies of jealous despair each time I saw Philip laughing with his friends, other boys his own age. Even glimpsing their names on a games list gave me a miserable shot of adrenaline. Once I overheard him talking to another colonial kid in some African dialect and my jealousy ran wild. What secrets were they sharing under cover of a language understood by no-one else in the school? Oh paranoia, envy . . .! Was Philip telling his friend how embarrassing and repulsive my attentions were? Worse, were they lovers? But the very worst of all was that nothing excludes like a foreign language and I realised I should never get close to him. Always and always I would be shut out. Even now, at practically eighty, I can catch sight of two kids with their arms around each other and still feel a distant pang of exclusion, like the memory of an ache for something that probably doesn't even exist for them any more than it did for Philip. So at the time, eaten alive by adolescent dissatisfaction, I must have been a horrid creature to have around the house which probably made it a little easier for my father to arrange to put a lot of miles between us at my request.

– I found out Michael wasn't going home to Africa that summer: he had long since left the school. Philip would be travelling alone and I was able to meet him in Suez on the British India's *Kenya*. That, incidentally, was the occasion when I first got hold of the company pass from 'Pusser' Hammond, not when we went to meet the *Otranto*. It was very strange seeing Philip in Port Taufiq. I went aboard on some invented pretext and found him up on deck taking pictures of the harbour with his Kodak. 'Good Lord!' I said, elaborately amazed. 'What an incredible thing! Fancy you being here!' and so on. 'Oh, gosh, *Jebb*,' he said, blushing a bit with surprise. You must remember that orders of seniority were significant then and to him I not only counted as a senior in terms of school but now, having left the College, I was an adult with a job. For one awful moment I thought he might 'Sir' me. Fatuous chit-chat for five minutes, at the end of which we shook hands and wished each other goodbye. It was one of the few times I had ever physically touched him, and it was the last. It was also the last time I ever saw him, spoke to him or heard his voice. Like Lot's wife I risked a backward glance but he'd gone back to his Kodak. –

And from that moment you became pure salt.

– For all the hopeless tears I shed over that boy you might well say so. –

Did he know?

– I've always wondered. He must have noticed something. We're all quick to sense other people's interest in us, adolescents doubly so. At some level he undoubtedly knew, but I wouldn't think the knowledge ever became fully conscious. Too difficult. Too threatening, even. Anyway, there it is. And I've no idea what you call it. You could hardly describe it as an affair since that implies the active involvement of at least two people. How is it possible to love somebody you don't know? Infatuation? Calf love? Phrases like that have all the wrong connotations, with their overtones of a temporary madness that's soon outgrown. The whole notion of 'first love' contains a suggestion of child's play;

but what if first love turns out to be last love, too? What if it energises a lifetime? Berlioz was twelve when he was *foudroyé* by the eighteen-year-old Estelle. He was a famous man of forty-five and she an unknown widow of fifty-one when he tracked her down, wrote her a respectful letter and finally met her again briefly. And he, too, could never write her full name. I don't think this rare and inexplicable kind of passion can be patronised as 'calf love'. Whatever else it is, it is neither trivial nor something out of which one grows. It is more like a miraculous sustaining wound that never heals. Philip is my phantom limb, cut off in adolescence but still occasionally paining me and giving me the exquisite illusion of being there. –

(This image jolts me. It is the very one I sometimes use to myself when describing the absent country in my life.)

– Do you know, to this day I catch myself speaking to him, so much a part of me has he become? On a morning like this I might get out of bed and stand at the bedroom window and watch the olives emerge from the early shadows like a secret and say quietly to them, 'Oh, Philip . . .' Something between a sigh and a prayer and a fond remonstration. I know it's ridiculous. And times without number over the years when I've suddenly found two minutes' respite in an aircraft washroom or some horrid lavatory in a bar in a ramshackle tropical town I've stared at the wall while peeing and said, 'What *am* I doing here, Philip? It's you who did this to me. It's all because of you I roam and roam. Guiltless you may be, but I blame you all the same, and love you all the same. And shall do always because it's too late to change now, too late to break out of this fond servitude even if I knew how, which I never did discover. Well, damn you, my dear.' –

Jayjay is still staring up at Sant' Egidio (which is Italian for St Giles), but that is not what he sees. At last he blows his nose and tucks his handkerchief back into its customary place in his cuff.

– Well. There is little we can do to protect ourselves from our own tenderness. Mine has been a blighted life, wouldn't you say? A wasted span? How *NOT* to spend fourscore years? But the truth is I've flourished, in my fashion. Having your heart irreparably broken would require your long-term connivance. It's far more painless simply to give the thing away, as I did. Expect no returns and you'll not be disappointed. –

Yet this is said without bitterness and indeed almost tenderly, as though he recognises that with so strong a thread running through it his life cannot have been altogether thrown away; that no matter how heretical and inconvenient the thread, it draws a whole together. This constant inventing and re-inventing of someone who scarcely was, this living a life for a figure who is omnipresent yet never there strikes me as containing the essential pathos of religious faith. Yet by being a solo effort Jayjay's is surely a more pure act of the imagination and, in its way, quite grand.

No others, then?

– Oh, lots of affairs. All those women in Egypt, and I nearly married at least twice. But . . . there was always the *but*. In the last resort they never felt like the real thing. Imagine, lying around in some tumbled pit of sheets with a girl I was sure I loved, yet always with that inner conviction that this wasn't it. Not the genuine article. Can you explain it? Arrested development, whatever that might mean? Some perverse urge to remain true to a former version of myself, no matter how much it might blight me? –

And what became of Philip?

– For a long time I didn't want to know. I was sure he'd been killed in the war. But many years ago I had some discreet snooping done because by then I wanted proof that this mythical creature who ruled my life really did have an objective existence. And he had. Royal Navy during the war, convoy protection; sunk outside Murmansk but by a miracle plucked out of the water in under a minute and thawed out. Survived war; became a farmer in South Africa; married an English girl from Devon out there; two kids; etcetera. I learned all that twenty years ago. He may be dead now for all I know. But I was glad to have found out about him. I could say that because of him my own life has been eccentric, adventurous, interesting and so on. And I could say that despite me his has probably been quite a bit less so once the war was over. I was pleased his life appeared to be so normal. It's all very well but most people don't actually want adventure and eccentricity: they want an ordinary family life and a secure living. So I'm happy for him. I suppose he may have turned into a bald, leathery old *Kaffir*-beater but for me he will always be the boy I first knew with fine blond hair and those still unshaven sideburns that come to silky wicks.

– So what was it? What is it? I've read a lot but the books don't know. With the modern passion for medical categories into which everything must be squeezed it would doubtless be referred to as a sexual dysfunction. I think by now you'll have to agree that I'm neither bashful nor inhibited about sex, so I can at least give the point due consideration and say truthfully that it doesn't feel like a sexual matter so much as, well, a poetic one. Besides, I'm not sexually dysfunctional. I've never had any problems on that score with either gender. No, it isn't a dysfunction in the sense that a fetish would be, without which one might be impotent. I'll certainly allow that it involves the erotic; but the erotic is another category that has been debased and shrunk to become a shorthand for genital sex, whereas genital sex is only a single aspect of the erotic. The erotic thrives on subtleties, on matters of poetry and the imagination, but we're living at the wrong time for those to be understood. A tabloid stupidity has overtaken our culture and we no longer understand anything about human behaviour that can't be compressed into a headline. I don't believe the twentieth century, and still less the twenty-first, ever will understand such things. The more they use quasi-medical notions of pathology to pry into the way we function, the more closed to them does the human heart become. Meanwhile we do our real living in entirely other directions. –

And all this time there has been a bee flying around us, settling on the edges of saucers and cups, pulsing her abdomen in the sun. It is odd because there is no sugar on the table. It is as though she alone has misread the dance of a returning worker up in one

of the hives (with a proprietorial silliness bordering on the super-
stitious I automatically take her for one of my own bees). Here she
is, the dunce of the hive, expecting to find a rich source of nectar
and finding instead an old man breaking a lifetime's silence to tell
a rather less old man about a love as powerful and insubstantial as
a sunbeam.

Would you ever think now of meeting him?

– Of course I've *thought* about it. Thousands of times. But it's
too late. It always was. What can be said on the brink of annihila-
tion? Could I stand there and say to this old farmer, having first
taken him out of his wife's earshot, 'I have loved you more than
my life for most of my life'? He would think I was mad, and so I
should be. Or else we would lapse into an updated version of that
ghastly farewell on the *Kenya*, every detail of which is burnt into
me by the glare of an Egyptian sun. No. I have only one thing to
say to Philip, and it cannot be said now any more than it could
then. These useless loves must go in silence to the grave. It's the
only proper place for them. –

The bee has finally left, but I notice she first bequeathed us a
tiny dab of clear golden excrement on the rim of a cup. This pin-
prick glints in the sun like one of those flakes of jewel set in the
mechanism of an old-fashioned watch. I find myself troubled by
what Jayjay has told me, touched, distressed on more than just his
behalf, as though what he has exposed is a part of the hidden
works of any human soul. So it comes as a shock suddenly to hear
my own voice. I am as appalled by its hard-nosed tone as I am by
the actual words it speaks.

I'm sorry, Jayjay: I still can't quite buy that account of your
father's role in your Suez caper. I don't know why, but it isn't
right yet. I can't make the dynamics of your blasted family jell at
all (and then, with one of those leaps when the voice crashes on
even as the lagging brain cringes to hear it): it was to do with your
mother, wasn't it? Your mother, Jayjay. Exhibit B?

There is a long, long silence. I am horrified at my ill-mannered
temerity. When I dare glance at him he is weeping, silently, very

dignified, staring up at the mountain and letting the tears run down ignored. Eventually he gives a brisk dab.

'This'll never do,' he says in a way that makes it clear he is no longer in narrative mode. Automatically I put down my note-book. 'Come on, I think we need some more coffee. I'm not running away, James,' he smiles a little abstractedly. 'I'll come back to it. But just at this moment coffee is what I need most.'

– It would be too absurd for a man of my age to weep for some-thing that happened in his teens, don't you think? I admit I was dreadfully upset and messed about at the time but that's all long in the past. When I started on this curious project with you I really had no intention of getting into any of the story about Philip, so I also hoped I might slip by without mentioning my mother except as a bland childhood presence. You can pick me up for disingenuity, certainly, as well as for being a lousy tactician. I rea-soned that in telling my life story with, shall we say, enough picaresque detail I should not find myself obliged to trespass into areas I have never mentioned to another soul, living or dead. I'm still unsure whether doing so is down to some secret desire on my part to unburden myself or to your technique for interrogation that shocks one into confidences.

– My stupid tears just now were not brought on by what my mother did sixty years ago, although my reluctance to talk about her at all is a measure of the antipathy I once felt. It's an antipathy that has long become fossilised, so that not speaking about her is purely a matter of habit rather than of ever-present trauma. No, I was startled into tears by hearing myself disclose secrets, which suddenly meant having to acknowledge a lifetime moulded by those secrets. I feel as though I've committed treason and deserve to be shot. It's an uncanny thing hearing myself explain to a per-fect summer's day how I come to have lived the life I have, and why it has led so inexorably here to this terrace in Italy with you and a coffeepot. One rarely has to account for such things out loud. Still, it's curious it should be so affecting because I'm sure most people do have moments when they look at their lives objectively, as though they were actually a third party, and are incredulous at what they see. But I suppose making it public is another matter.

– Well, my mother. It was that filthy religion of hers that did for her. We went through all sorts of hell the more she became fixated on heaven. I suppose these days it would be labelled a mania or something, and never mind what I said earlier about pseudo-clinical categories. To be blunt, the poor woman went quite off her head. When it's a matter of mental illness the phrase 'she suffered from' is significantly inaccurate because it involves her family and friends, too. We all suffered, believe me. The worst of being a child when your mother goes off her chump is that there is never a moment when you can tell yourself, 'It's all right, she's mad. She didn't mean that. She doesn't know what she's saying.' Quite the reverse: children will accept all manner of extraordinary behaviour as the norm simply because it happens at home. It takes a long time to come out from under the ether, to acquire distance and realise that none of your friends' mothers quote the Bible from memory at mealtimes for half an hour at a stretch. Nor do they accost complete strangers in the Co-op and inform them that God is watching their every move and has big plans for Eltham. Perhaps we were more tolerant of eccentricity in those days. Or it may be that people tended not to interfere if someone was a pillar of the community, a nicely spoken lady who could still zip through the daily crossword and add up bills in her head at lightning speed. It was years before they finally saw fit to cart her off to Colney Hatch, which I think is now called Friern Barnet or something. And that was because she tried to drown a baby at its christening. Yes, I agree it's funny, and the incident did rather excite attention. It happened during the war, when thankfully I was in Egypt. There were newspaper stories that she'd torn the baby from the vicar's arms and held it face down in the font, screaming about how it was a child of Satan. They saved the baby but my mother took a good deal of subduing, possibly because people seem generally reluctant to rough-house in church. They carted her off to the bin where she died in 1949, wholly demented. Or dementedly holy, depending on one's viewpoint. Perhaps the saddest aspect of it all was that her beliefs never even gave her the happiness they promised and to which she was surely entitled. My lasting memory of our household is that it was not one which had been made privy to Good News. Indeed, poor Dad never recovered.

– Well, you can imagine the scandal in a place like Eltham. It even got into some of the Fleet Street papers. If you're sufficiently zealous I'm sure you could dig it out of the archives and check it: I may have the odd detail wrong. Possibly, seeing how low-church my mother had sunk by then, it wasn't a font christening at all but one of those baptisms with total immersion. I suppose that would provide a better opportunity for drowning babies. But when I read the accounts the thing that leaped off the page at me, other than the fact that my own mother had star billing in a humiliating story, was that the baby's name was the same as mine. It was about to be christened Raymond. It took me straight back to the events that had led to my hurried departure for Suez.

– To put it briefly, my mother had found out about me and Philip, and by the most improper means. Foolishly, I was keeping a diary in which I was confiding my adolescent anguish. I'm afraid I'd even called it 'Liber Amoris' in imitation of Hazlitt's equally frantic and vulnerable account. You can imagine the sort of things I wrote in it. Awful poems, declarations, blacknesses, with occasional ecstatic triumphs: 'Spoke to him today! When I gave him TS's notice about the Junior Colts XV our hands met . . .!' The whole thing was ridiculous and extravagant and gusty. Of course it was. I was a teenager, after all, and besotted beyond reason. My mother must have been snooping in my room one day when I was at school and found the diary. It was inexcusable that she read it, but then I was stupid to have associated religious people with moral scruple. She went quite cuckoo. She tore straight down to

Mottingham and confronted me at the school gates, waving it and shouting Leviticus in my face. I managed to get her away before she could storm in to demand that the headmaster uncover the identity of the boy with whom her son was having this filthy alliance, this bestial coupling, this . . . and so on and so forth, most of it at the top of her voice, to the edification of my schoolmates and the local citizens. Thank goodness I had never named Philip in the diary: I referred to him only as 'IB', after Beethoven's Immortal Beloved. A childish but effective code.

– Life at home became impossible. Dad tried to act as a mediator but you could tell he just wanted to run off to the office where nobody shouted passages from the Old Testament and everything happened quietly and purposefully. He did make an awkward attempt at father-and-son intimacy, trying to convey that he'd heard these things, *harrumph!*, happened, and, er, they didn't strike him as all that terrible since they mostly blew over as soon as a chap got out into the world, you know, girlfriends, decent job, plenty to do. I'm afraid we've got to face it, old man, your mother's a bit, er, hah, unwell at present. I'm wondering . . . I'm wondering if it really *mightn't* be better, all things considered, and seeing that you've got the School Cert. to worry about, if . . .? 'You mean, Dad, you'd like me to move out? To go? Leave home?'

– He blustered, but that was indeed what he meant. Talk about injustice. *I* wasn't the one rampaging around shouting imprecations. It obviously never occurred to him that it was his wife who ought to be removed for a while. It's true I could see he was miserable about sending me away but he evidently felt that once I was out of the house my mother would calm down and could eventually be talked around, enough at least so that I could come home again. You've got to remember that in those days psychiatric help was pretty crude. It was mainly straitjackets or great draughts of that horrible-tasting stuff that used to stink the house out, paraldehyde. My father wanted peace at all costs, and the price of peace was having his son leave the house. I don't think I ever quite forgave him. At the same time my mother informed me in a conversational aside that a seraph she knew had told her I was a child of Satan. So I went and stayed a couple of months with some cousins over in Hither Green. I could easily commute to school from there, it was only two stations away. But it was the beginning of the end of Eltham for me. –

A child of Satan?

– That's what she said. She also called me the Devil's Officer, I remember. I think she was confused to the point where extreme religiosity and her work in the Censorship in the First World War had become entwined. I believe she thought I had been recruited by the Devil and that my wretched diary contained his coded instructions for infiltrating the Earth with his shock troops. Sort of fifth-columnists. And since this 'IB' was clearly someone I knew at school, she would occasionally show up there even after I'd been exiled to Hither Green, earnestly warning anyone who would listen that Eltham College was the lair of the Great Beast. I'm glad to say this tended to make people laugh uncontrollably but the police were sometimes called to have her removed. If it made my position at school pretty vile so it did for a wretch named Irwin Bretton on account of his initials. The ribbing he got was doubly unjust since he was a famously dim piggy boy whose only known interest was in making cranes out of Meccano. He had quite a bad time of it without, I suspect, ever fully twigging the nature of the accusations. Just as well, probably. The teachers were sympathetic enough and so were my friends, but some of the other boys . . . Well, you know how children are.

– But why *me*? Why would my mother take against her own son unless she already had some long-standing grievance or dislike of me? Surely even the violent antipathies of the insane generally have particular roots, whether imaginary or real? It's true we'd never been close, she and I. I was certainly more so to my father, though as must be clear to you by now we were in no sense a close family. I sometimes wonder if it didn't date right back to my infancy when her brother was killed in the war. Apparently that

was when she started becoming fiercely religious. I tried to think
of a specific heinous act I had committed but could only come up
with the usual childhood misdemeanours that had caused a bit of
a scene at the time. I even wondered whether I was perhaps not
my father's child at all, and 'Satan' just a lunatic's pseudonym for
someone she'd met at a bus stop. Had she enjoyed a hasty dal-
liance even as she was engaged to my father, for which she later
experienced guilt? And was that why she never really showed me
much maternal affection? I shan't ever know and it hardly matters
now. The poor woman simply got barmier and barmier. Thanks
to paraldehyde she flew off the handle a bit less and instead would
hold long, earnest conversations with people like Elijah while she
did the crossword. In fact I believe Elijah told her the answers. It
sounds funny here on a summer's day but at the time it was mis-
erably frightening and upsetting. I felt I'd been betrayed by both
parents while my love for Philip had been exposed and defiled.
When I realised Philip's identity was still a secret that aspect of the
thing seemed less melodramatically bad; and as for defilement, I
converted that adroitly into a soothing feeling of private martyr-
dom. This was a love for which I'd been publicly mocked, reviled,
made to suffer, yet with Christlike fortitude I'd borne it all . . . You
can imagine. The net effect, of course, was to add still further to
the sacred status Philip held for me. I must say it became nearly
impossible to resist telling him what I was going through on his
account and that the least he could do was take me in his arms and
let me cry on his shirtfront. But resist it I did, thank goodness. As
for the *trahison des parents*, by the time I read the reports of my
mother and the christening it was nearly ten years since I had
seen either of them and that whole overwrought era had receded
and become a good deal blunted. By then what I actually felt was
sorrow. For my mother, for my father, for us as a not very successful family unit. From time to time I can feel it even now.

– But in the meantime I had been banished to Hither Green.
My mother wrote to tell me how sorry she was that I was a child
of Satan and would need to be burned in everlasting flame. My

father wrote to Anderson & Green. I reclaimed and burned my incriminating diary. The *liber* if not the *amor* perished in flames. And at the end of all these writings and inveighings and burnings there was I, silent on a dock in Tilbury with a brand-new trunk and mixed feelings, as well as a Benson watch and fifty pounds from my father who tried not to cry as he tucked the envelope into my top pocket. So yes, by the time I arrived in Suez I was pretty glad to be out of it. That description I gave of my excitement at being abroad was accurate enough, even if it said nothing about the various traumas that had obliged me to be there. But since I was looking forward to seeing Philip imminently on his way through Suez I suppose I had all the motive I needed to stick it out. –

I took what I had heard back up the hill. This shocking revelatory morning had been capped by Jayjay informing me that he was dying. It was official, he said, and swore me to secrecy. He would tell Claudio and Marcella in his own good time. 'Nobody's indispensable,' he said with a smile of remarkable sweetness. 'They are when you haven't yet finished their biography,' I retorted. Oh Jayjay . . . No wonder you threw caution to the winds this morning and broke your silence. And there I was until only a matter of hours ago still complaining that you weren't coming clean, that your life was boring me, that my own was more insistent.

Sometimes I have this pressing desire to visit the bees and watch them on their sorties. Their unreflecting industry is an antidote to human messiness and travail, the love and tears of it all that billows up like cannon-smoke at Waterloo to obscure friend and foe and even the sun that might otherwise guide us home. At their busiest period in summer the worker bees live only a matter of weeks before they are worn out and their sisters (for they are all females) on corpse duty tug the bodies out of the hive and dump them on the entrance sill. Nobody's indispensable. Most mornings there are two or three dead bees lying on the threshold of their home as evidence of brisk housework. The whole community

gives off an intense healthy smell hard to describe because it has such a wide range of associations. Of honey and sweetness, naturally, but equally of good housekeeping. There is a piercing cleanliness about it. Being obsessively clean, bees much dislike the smell of human sweat. To wear stale clothes while beekeeping is a solecism that greatly increases the chance of being stung. Even in the cool of dawn, summer hives diffuse their scent into the still air so powerfully they can be smelt fifty yards away. If work itself has a smell it is surely one of the components of this hive-scent and carries with it a faint hint of reproof, even of menace. These are creatures doing their living at a hectic pace and in their own arcane way. Our factory is our home, says the smell: you disturb us at your peril. Only those as clean and hard-working as ourselves have any right to the fruits of a labour that costs us our lives.

I often stand by the hives, sniffing this industrious incense that in some way slows the heartbeat. In fact, so restorative are bees that I invariably regain the one thing they conspicuously lack, a sense of humour. I know I am back in kilter when I can say to them: 'I'm sorry, girls, but it has to be said. When all your many virtues and talents have been duly listed and praised, we're still left with one unignorable drawback: you're dumb. Dumb, dumb, dumb. There's so little flexibility programmed into you. I have only to move this hive two yards to one side and most of you will be unable to find your way back home again. Even a single yard would be enough to confuse you and, if it were winter, a good few of you would freeze to death inches from your own front door. That, I'm afraid, is *dumb*. You're going to have to do better than that if you ever want to take a step up the evolutionary ladder.'

To stand beside a beehive and laugh at its occupants for being easily disorientated may at best look like a small consolation. At worst one would sooner not speculate.

13

The sense of shortening time was confirmed by an almost imperceptible change in our arrangement. The sessions Jayjay and I had together were as frequent as ever but now less open-ended. After a couple of hours he would begin to tire. Six months was the span his doctors were predicting, the last part of which could hardly be expected to yield much in terms of work, and I had already inescapably committed two months of this precious allowance to my other book. With much difficulty I had arranged a further series of vital interviews in places as far apart as Hawaii, Canada and Australia where judiciously retired members of the old regime were living high off the hog. These were men, and in two cases women, who had reluctantly agreed to talk to me only after mutual friends had leaned quite heavily on them. The least appearance of casualness or date-breaking on my part would be as fatal as if I were to hint that my real mission was to write some sort of journalistic exposé. Now I would have to leave in a week's time. I explained this apologetically to Jayjay.

'I quite understand,' he said. 'The tug of the exotic, the light of tropic suns. Mind you, I feel it's a little unseemly going on with this beachcomber act of yours when you're easily old enough to be a grandfather. One only hopes you don't do a Crusoe in cut-off jeans.'

'Would that I could. This is a trip for well-cleaned shoes and a polite smile. Something you need never again affect.'

'Only you, James, would have the appalling taste to turn a death sentence into a stroke of fortune. Still, thank you so much for pointing out the silver lining I might otherwise have missed. However, and joking apart, I'm perfectly aware you have your other work to do and must go. Don't worry about it. Besides, there's not so very much more I can tell you about myself now. I feel as though I've said it all, for what little it's worth.'

'But the great and the good? The Henry Kissingers?'

'Oh, they're easily dealt with. Still, you may remember that even before you agreed to take on this chore I did tell you that my first thirty years were the ones that counted. Probably true for most people, in any case. When I look back now the things of my life that seem most valuable and formative are all from that period and the recent half-century is a blur by comparison. That, I'm afraid, was the era of the great and the good. Not that I haven't enjoyed much of it immensely. But it's an odd irony that one should recall more fondly the process of learning how to live than doing the actual living. True of sex, too, I'm afraid. It was a revelation to start with but degenerated into a mere pleasure.' Jayjay looked reflective for a moment then suddenly waved an elegant hand to indicate the beamy sitting-room, the terrace beyond the open French windows, the famous garden. 'What am I going to do with all this *stuff*?'

'It depends on your spirit of malice, Jayjay. You can always leave this place to someone with the proviso that it is converted for *agriturismo*. That way you can ensure the Valle di Chio will be made privy to the bayings of pink foreigners on holiday losing their tempers with their kids. It will be highly instructive for the locals about cultural difference, especially if the foreigners are British. You know, the whole rigmarole that begins with always getting up too late to go anywhere or shop properly. There's the mother who vaguely feels she wants to see Fine Art and the father who's grumpy at having to pretend he does, too, although he'd far rather sit in the shade and get pissed because it's so damned hot. Those excursions with the children in the back of the car, surly with computer games, barely appeased by promises of ice creams and swimming pools . . . Yes, I think you could do worse than leave that as your legacy to the neighbourhood.'

'Heavens, James, what an unspeakable father you would have made.'

'It's true.' I have never told Jayjay about Emma. I am indeed an unspeakable father.

'But I don't feel at all vindictive, and least of all towards the Valle di Chio which has given me generous shelter these last twenty-odd years. Well, these are my problems, not yours. A week, you said? We'd best return to Egypt at once and finish up there.'

'Before we do, Jayjay, could I just get something straight about Adelio? In the light of your recent revelations, that is.'

'Were we lovers, you mean?' he pre-empted me with slight impatience. 'No. Not exactly. I shall explain all, while at the same time glumly registering how depressing it is that from now on you will inevitably suspect my motives if I betray the least interest or concern for any male below the age of sixteen. You don't have to protest,' he added, raising a conciliatory hand. 'It's a sign of the times we live in. Once those stupid categories have been imposed no-one is allowed to fall between them. Pseudo-science has spoken. If you're not this you're that. One can never again be something quite other.'

A further sign of the times was that Marcella came in to ask if I wanted coffee. Hitherto she had let us fend for ourselves but I could see she was now keeping a firm eye on Jayjay. I had no doubt that if she thought I was over-tiring him she would ask me to leave. Nor was he any longer allowed coffee on his previous awesome scale. Apparently the doctors had told him that at his age the body's metabolic rate is quite slow, which is why they were able to talk in terms of six months rather than three. They alleged that gingering things up with large doses of caffeine was quite the wrong thing to do in the circumstances. These days Jayjay had to make do with tisanes, and he would stare sadly at the bloated sachet as it floated at the rim of his cup like a corpse in a pond, diffusing a thin ichor. The world divides itself into coffee- and tea-drinkers and the two seldom overlap.

– By the end of May 1941 Crete and the Balkans were in German hands and Axis forces were again massing on the Egyptian border. Once more things looked bad for us up in Alexandria and they suddenly looked worse still when the Germans began bombing the city. Churchill had already warned Mussolini that if he bombed Cairo the RAF would bomb Rome but Alexandria was obviously considered fair game.

– That first raid was chaos. We were told to stay put while they tried to evacuate civilians. But the more the sirens went and the Germans tried to hit the harbour and the main station, the more I realised nobody knew what to do. There were no real contingency plans. Or if there were, the right people hadn't stayed to implement them. My only thought was for the Boschettis. I left SOE's warehouse in Sid Dix's charge and went straight to their flat. There, parked right outside, was the Hungarian Count's Delahaye. I roared inside brandishing the Webley revolver I'd been issued and which I'd never loaded. I found everyone huddled on the kitchen floor, including Bathory-Sopron who had an anti-macassar wrapped around his head. I was amazed to find anybody there. I assumed that the Italian legation would have taken care of its own but to be fair no-one really knew what the hell was going on, the wretched Italians least of all, given that they were now being blitzed by their own allies. The Count, meanwhile, turned out not to be injured, merely petrified. I got the family out of the house and into the Delahaye, grabbing a spare tin of petrol I had in the back of the Fiat. At the last moment the Count tried to get in. He still had the antimacassar wrapped around his head. I was suddenly infected with Adelio's loathing of the man. I shoved the muzzle of the revolver into the area of his moustaches and told him to start walking. I then hopped behind the wheel of his car and tried to head out of town, hoping to reach the Damanhur road.

– Bombs were going off in the distance, the roads were a mass of refugees, carts, panicked horses and so on. It was a bit of a nightmare, really. And yet in the middle of it all I remember seeing a lemonade seller calmly sitting under a tree with his brass urn, offering refreshment to the people as they stampeded past him. Then there was a massive explosion right behind us and the car was kicked forward by the blast. There was a shriek from Adelio in the back to say that their house had been hit *and* the Morettis' *and* the Lebanese restaurant *and* Mr Abbas's laundry was on fire. Eventually we did get on to the Delta road and joined the general stream of traffic. At this point I had no idea what I was doing or where I was going. I wasn't a proper combatant but oughtn't I to stay in Alexandria and look after the warehouse? So powerful is the urge to join refugees streaming away from a sky-line marked with boiling black clouds of smoke that I just glanced in the mirror and kept going. '*Madonna santissima*,' Mirella kept on saying fatalistically. '*Madonna cara*. We're as good as dead.' 'I don't suppose you have any *documenti* on you?' I asked. 'No pass-port or anything?' But of course none of them had a thing and presumably all their private belongings were now entombed in the inferno of their apartment block. I had no idea how I could explain myself and this carload if we ran into a military check-point, as we surely would outside Cairo if not in Damanhur or Tanta. By now I was assuming that the raid was a softening-up operation as a prelude to Rommel's full-scale invasion, and there seemed no future in going back to Alexandria, not even for Mirella and her family. I told her I was heading all the way to

Cairo where she and the children would just have to throw themselves on brother Renzo's mercy.

– And a strange drive we had of it, too. Mirella climbed into the back to comfort Anna, who was petrified. Adelio seemed not to need comforting and took her place in the front seat on my right. As a matter of fact he appeared to be enjoying himself, as I suppose you can when you're fourteen, have just seen your mother's detested lover left at gun-point in the middle of an air raid and are now speeding along in the man's coveted roadster. He had always said he wanted to leave Alexandria and now he was. To my surprise we made it through Damanhur and Tanta without being stopped. I think the car impressed the Egyptian army. But we were stopped outside Cairo where we were diverted on to the Heliopolis road to make way for a stream of British army lorries heading for Alexandria. The road block was manned by the Egyptian army but staffed by British officers who couldn't recognise any of the codes on my ID card and were downright difficult about the poor Boschettis. In my case SOE was supposed to be so secret that not even the military knew about it, and anyway at that time Egypt was full of irregular units of varying degrees of secrecy and known by a bewildering variety of codes and nicknames. I remember my warrant card meant nothing to these fellows, unfortunately. Much telephoning went on before I was put through to someone who could vouch for me. Actually he was the chap who had fixed my temporary secondment to Alexandria. I told him I was bringing in an Italian diplomatic family who had current knowledge vital to our interests or some such nonsense.

– Finally they let us through and I took them straight to Renzo's flat. He was in, and unfortunately for him so was his Greek boyfriend Kostas in a speedily donned Charvet dressing-gown. Renzo explained away this gorgeous apparition none too convincingly as a business associate who had been taken ill. I think only little Anna believed it but there were more important things to worry about. At least the Boschettis were reunited with Renzo and for the moment safe, if badly hampered by having no papers.

I was anxious to get back to Alexandria and save what little I possessed, including a trunkful of pornography, before marauding
Axis troops could loot the contents of my flat. But I didn't succeed
in leaving Renzo's without hearing the beginning of fulsome
accounts by Mirella and Adelio of how I had saved their lives. It's
funny, until then it hadn't occurred to me that there was maybe
some truth in this. Had I not gone to their apartment and virtually
bundled them down the stairs at pistol-point they would no doubt
still have been crouched in the kitchen when the flat was hit five
minutes later. That part was sheer chance; yet it was a sheer
chance that was to lead all the way to this very house in Tuscany.
And in turn that was due to Adelio, who in some ways was the
strangest child I ever met. At the time I was still trying to fathom
his behaviour of the previous week, just before the raid on
Alexandria. –

It is the last time they would drive together to a beach, although
neither of them knows it. The tension in Alexandria is worth
escaping if only for the afternoon. The powerful Italo-German
forces are halted only fifty miles to the west. In the kitchens of
Pastroudis and other fashionable patisseries pastry chefs with
icing bags are writing *Viva l'Italia* and *W Il Duce* on the new
batch of cakes in order to display them in time for the invaders'
arrival. They also spell out *Sieg Heil!* and, as though greeting
tourists rather than troops, *Willkommen in Ägypten* in flowing
blue and pink icing. Jayjay has wangled a free afternoon and he
and Adelio are heading eastwards along the coast in the dented
Fiat, away as if by instinct from the advancing front. This time,
by the sort of mutual consent that is unspoken, they drive well
past Faroukh's palace at Montazah and out along Abu Qir bay.
The road is deserted. Soon it shrinks to barely more than a dust
track, a causeway between the sea on the left and Lake Idku on
the right. On a small rocky promontory they come upon the
remains of a tower. As he parks the car in its shade Jayjay
explains this was a lighthouse that was struck by a stray salvo

from one of Nelson's ships in the battle of 1798. There is evidently something in the place and the moment that diverts Adelio's attention away from the thermos flasks of ice cream wrapped in towels. The utter stillness, the empty churning of the sea, the singing heat and a jewelled lizard moving with jerky prehistoric tread over the scarred stonework: all conspire to produce a reflective melancholy. There is no need to mention the great army at present camped over the horizon. Instead Jayjay observes how often this piece of apparently deserted terrain has been the scene of battles; that only a year after Nelson defeated the French fleet in this very bay Napoleon won a land battle at Abu Qir when in turn he defeated an Ottoman Turkish force that outnumbered his men by more than two to one. Adelio gazes around at the empty landscape as it simmers and trembles in the heat.

'But there's nothing here.'

'I know. Plenty of battles have been fought on territory nobody particularly wants.'

'A bit silly, don't you think?'

At the foot of this lone promontory the sea has sculpted a series of hollows in the low sandstone bank, less caves than niches as though for a series of statues that have never been placed there. In one of these Jayjay and Adelio dump their clothes. They swim, and then hop back across the scalding beach. The sand in the shade of the little cliff feels deliciously cool to their feet. Adelio anoints his soles with chocolate ice cream and rolls his eyes in bliss in a gesture copied from the cinema. Half a mile offshore a twin-engined aircraft suddenly appears flying very low, heading westwards. It is just too far away for the markings to be visible. Adelio thinks it is a Caproni, Jayjay a Bristol Beaufort. It drones away towards Alexandria.

'What's going to happen?' Adelio asks.

'I've no idea. Nobody knows. If the Italians and Germans invade Egypt I expect I shall be taken prisoner and interned in a camp.'

'Won't you fight?'

'I don't know. What with? I'm not a soldier.'

'You've got a pistol in the car. I've seen it.'

'It isn't loaded.'

'Don't you care?'

'About what? Egypt isn't my country, after all. It's not my war, either. I was just caught in it here, like everyone else.'

'Yes, but you're British, and the British sort of run Egypt, don't they? But don't you care?' he asks again.

'Only about what happens to the people I know. My friends.'

'Including us?'

'Of course including you, *caro*. What do you think? Especially you. Your family has been wonderfully kind to me.'

'But things happen in wartime, don't they? I mean people get stuck, you know, on the wrong side and everything. You're English, for instance, and I'm Italian.'

'I know, it's crazy. Wars are like that. But as I said, nobody knows what will happen. Just remember that whatever does, you and I are friends and we shall remain friends. When it's all over in a few months' time, or next year or whenever, we'll simply go back to seeing each other. Back to normal again.'

'I suppose. You make it sound easy.'

Jayjay has to admit the truth of this. He *is* making it sound easy, as though he were the child trying to comfort himself and Adelio the adult obliged to be realistic. Not for the first time he feels Adelio to be much older than he actually is, maybe even older than Jayjay is himself. Absurd; yet the boy's brand of melancholy, already so characteristic and defined, is quite grown-up, almost elderly. It is as if he felt it necessary to voice his gloomiest fears and challenge Jayjay to put up a convincing argument against them. Maybe playing this game, Jayjay hears himself say foolishly:

'Why should I tell you lies, Adelio? Haven't I been keeping my promise to you?' Suddenly to his own ears he sounds like a wheedling child. Can he really be expecting this fourteen-year-old's praise for not having screwed his mother? Hopelessly he tries to think of a way of retracting or re-casting this gauche ingot of rhetoric that thuds between them.

'Oh, I know that,' says Adelio loftily, in a tone that plainly says, 'And I should think so too', which also suggests he might have had a frank conversation with Mirella. 'It's all right, I do trust you. Honestly.'

They go swimming again, largely to wash off the sticky patches of dripped ice cream to which the reddish sand adheres. When they are dry once more Adelio asks suddenly: 'Can I take your picture?'

'Oh. Yes, all right. Why not?' Surprised, Jayjay hands him the second-hand Leica he has bought with the proceeds from selling August's work to the crowned head of Egypt.

Adelio snaps him twice. 'Promise to give me them when you've developed them,' he says. 'It'll prove what you've been saying. About us being friends, I mean.'

'Then I shall do likewise and take your picture, too.'

As Jayjay fiddles with the camera, re-setting the aperture stop, he is aware of surreptitious movement. When he glances up Adelio is egg-naked, looking vulnerable and slightly red.

'Go on, then,' he says with a touch of defiance.

Jayjay is too surprised even to raise the camera; shocked, actually, by this unexpected provocation, this baring of more than flesh. His first thought is that Adelio must have found out about his commercial activity and is swept by acute embarrassment. That the boy should imagine this is the sort of picture he might want is humiliating. Yet the way Adelio now sits with his knees drawn up, meekly staring out to sea, suggests something quite different. There is nothing whatever salacious in his manner or pose; no knowingness, no trace of teasing. What there is, Jayjay decides as he lines up the picture, is an astonishing generosity. This is not pornography but a family snap. Adelio is letting him record his side of a friendship which Jayjay has so far only verbally and tritely asserted. It is a gesture of trust, all the more so since he is at an age when adolescents are usually modest about nudity, especially with adults.

Is this, then, what August has felt in the early days of his camera-work down in that lonely village in the Sudan? The excitement at finding in sharp focus what was so long sought? A thudding of the heart and a breathlessness that make the camera hard to hold steady while the viewfinder blurs and swims? All in a rush Jayjay is ambushed by love. The vertical glare on the beach exposes the moment: the two of them alone in North Africa, nobody for miles, Jayjay's own shadow puddled around his feet like clothes out of which he has just stepped. Did he have some idea that this picnic snatched from the world's last moments of peace might end erotically? Not really. He has never mistaken Adelio for another of the flirty children he has so often dallied with at houseboat parties. Rather, he is more like the younger brother he never had, or something between a stepson and a ward, with potential lover hovering only indistinctly in the gaps. Certainly Jayjay has sometimes fantasised a moment when the boy might offer himself with an adolescent's polymorphous guilelessness. Yet now the moment has arrived it is quite different, altogether more serious and fraught with consequence. In one leap Adelio has gone too far and in doing so has revealed himself as defenceless. His awkward bravery in demanding the right kind of love fills Jayjay with a hopeless tenderness.

Adelio allows him to shoot an entire roll even as Jayjay begins to wonder whether after all there mightn't also be a small component of exhibitionism in the boy's demure willingness to be shot sitting, standing, lying, and finally knee-deep in the sea. Yet there is still no real hint of flaunting and nothing in the way he holds himself to suggest anything more than disclosure. As best he knows, he is giving himself. When the film is finished Jayjay slips an arm around his thin waist and hugs the hot body to him protectively, feeling the child subside against him and watching heartbeats flutter beneath the skin of his throat.

'I'll make you another promise, *caro*. I'll never show these to anybody else. They're just for us. Hey, you're awfully hot. Hurry up and put some clothes on otherwise you'll get sunburned. Besides, that Beaufort might come back.'

'Caproni.'

The moment has not quite passed. Standing there on the shore together Jayjay finds he still cannot tell Adelio he loves him as he wants to and as the boy clearly means him to. He is inhibited by the sundry chasms that divide families from outsiders, children from adolescents, adolescents from adults, males from males and Britons from Italians. Their mutual confusion depresses him by the way it aborts every useful impulse and kills the moment even as he feels oblivion's endless ocean lapping just beyond the tips of their toes. It always would be too difficult, too late. Yet in this startling fashion an afternoon that had seemed foregone has now acquired new intimacy. If so, Jayjay thinks sadly as he starts the car, it is entirely because of Adelio's initiative and not through anything I have said or done. He is moved to an intense feeling of protectiveness towards this peculiar boy, the 'Little Frying Pan' who made no effort to conceal his mocked ears from the camera's lens. Indeed, as Jayjay soon discovers when he develops the pictures, no detail is hidden of the narrow, bony body with its tendons and kneecaps and elbows, the pointed chin and sticking-out ears. 'This is who I am,' the attitudes say uncompromisingly. 'This is me.' Only the eyes maintain their strange veiled gaze. Not even the brilliant sunlight can completely eradicate the faint shadows around them. Adelio looks out of the photographs with a glance that is bruised, already hopeless of finding a sight he can entirely trust, even one that will surprise or ravish him. His whole expression suggests an inwardness, an early friendship with desolation: a pact with the sound of a door closing, a school bell, the sigh of wind in tussocks. A week later when the first Ju 88s begin dropping bombs on the city it is the instant thought of Adelio that makes Jayjay desert his post and tear across Alexandria in the Fiat. As he goes pelting up the stairs to the apartment it is not Mirella's name that he shouts. He is not looking for the woman he once planned to take to bed, but for her son.

– The Axis forces never did take Alexandria, as it turned out. We held them at bay although the air raids continued that summer and about seven hundred civilians were killed. I was suddenly kept busy and the Boschettis unfortunately had to be left to fend for themselves. I did lean on someone to ensure they received new diplomatic IDs that at least kept them from being interned.

– It was a very interesting time politically and as 1941 went on relations became steadily worse between the Egyptian Palace, our embassy and the Egyptian nationalists. I was still stuck in Alexandria when Colonel Robert Laycock's so-called 'Layforce' was plotting fantastic behind-the-lines operations that either fizzled out or turned into downright farce. Evelyn Waugh was one of his subalterns stationed in Sidi Bishr. He grew an appalling beard and became known as 'the Ginger Runt' or something, I forget what it was exactly, so he shaved it off. He once asked to see some of August's pictures and I showed him a selection. He examined them half greedily, half disdainfully, as if he had seen a good deal of that sort of thing from an early age, and then pronounced them 'rancid and doggy', a phrase I've never forgotten. He and Randolph Churchill came to borrow radio sets from our warehouse as part of their doomed attempt to drive the Germans out of Crete. They lost the lot on that little caper and did well to get back to Egypt alive, full of quite justified rage about the crass incompetence of the military brass-hats.

– Much of 1941 was purely chaotic as far as our war effort in Egypt was concerned. We didn't get a really good field commander until Montgomery was appointed in the summer of Forty-two. People were incredibly slack and disordered. It was as if all our brisk Anglo-Saxon purposefulness was too easily undermined by the prevailing outlook of a host nation whose roots went back so many times longer than our own. We seemed to become infected with a kind of Pharaonic inertia broken by intense panics over trivia. Strange military units proliferated, often working at cross-purposes. I suppose Cairo's being so far removed from Europe and even from the battlefields of Cyrenaica, plus the ready availability in the shops of all the things that were most rationed or unavailable in Britain, produced an unreal atmosphere. Personally, I've always thought that was the year we British lost Egypt for good, if indeed we had ever had it. It culminated in early 1942 with Sir Miles Lampson, our Ambassador, surrounding Abdin Palace with military vehicles and marching in to demand that King Faroukh sign his own abdication. Unbelievable when you think about it, especially in view of the Treaty we had signed in 1936. But well before then relations had decayed to the extent that there were graffiti all over Cairo saying 'Long Live Rommel!' while drunken Allied soldiers were carousing through the streets singing parodies of the Egyptian National Anthem with words like 'King Faroukh, King Faroukh/Hang your bollocks on a hook!' and 'Queen Farida, Queen Farida/Of all wogs you are the leader!'

– Meanwhile I had been approached by the publicity section of the British embassy who wanted me to ditch SOE and come and work on a counter-offensive against what was called the 'Whispering Gallery' of pro-Axis sentiment in Egypt. So I did. My job was to run a group of a couple of dozen Egyptians who could go around spreading anti-Axis sentiment. I'm afraid wars, like politics, really are conducted at this level of banality. Still, there was undoubtedly a lot of leeway to make up where our public image was concerned. Apart from the ubiquitous slogans extolling Rommel there was much café debate as to whether the estimable Mohammed 'Ider, as they called Hitler, mightn't be just the man to help Egypt obtain its independence, given that both the French and the English had become the manifest enemies of Islam by infamously reneging on their words of honour in the Arab countries they occupied.

– I must say I enjoyed the work. Besides being something of a challenge it enabled me to get back on the street and use my

Arabic, even though the line I was supposed to promote was not the one I would have chosen. But there were plenty of other advantages, including living in Cairo and not having to shoot anyone. I knew perfectly well I should be wasting my time trying to convert any of the hard-line nationalists but most ordinary Egyptians were quite easily swayed. I had no doubt that if ever the military tide turned and we looked like winning, the Rommel notices would be torn down overnight and replaced by posters welcoming the Allied effort. Not many months previously I had seen the pastry chefs of Alexandria hastily re-icing their cakes so they now smirked up from the patisserie windows saying 'Well played, Tommy!' and 'Rule, Britannia!' to passing British and Anzac troops. Suddenly I was free to use all sorts of old contacts even as I established relations with interesting and potentially useful people passing through the embassy. Good parties in the evening, too. And being assigned to a strange section that was neither military nor quite diplomatic also had its uses. Technically, I was listed as a Services Officer, which conveyed absolutely nothing to anyone.

– Perhaps because this was Egypt, war or no war, we none of us worked very hard and I was even able to push along the pornography sideline in my spare time. I had whole batches printed up from the trunkload of negatives I'd retrieved from my flat in Alexandria. It seemed like too good an opportunity to miss because Cairo was crawling with servicemen on leave or stationed in dusty camps on the outskirts. In the evenings they would roar into town, heading for the red-light district. As luck would have it one of the main zones, known popularly as 'the Berka', was quite close to Petron's printing house in Mousky which I was still using and where so much of August's pre-war stuff had already been processed. 'The Berka' was really a street named Wagh el Birket, and the area enclosed by it and another called Shari' Clot Bey was surrounded with signs put up by the military warning that it was out of bounds to all ranks. That didn't stop a lot of sex-starved soldiers fresh from the deserts of Cyrenaica invading the Berka en masse, gazing up at the whores on the lines of balconies overhead and shouting their offers. Or else they went to the nude cabarets in Darling Street where the famous 'donkey trick' was a must for those who hoped to see a slice of life before they died in the desert. From a commercial point of view all I needed was to keep Petron churning out the prints and have them run over to the Berka by kids with handcarts. The one thing I will say is that we maintained our quality. This wasn't the normal over-exposed, blurry, off-centre rubbish that passed for 'feelthy pictures'. Ours was well printed and sharp and priced accordingly. Both Petron and I did very well out of it and I even opened an account for August and deposited quite decent sums that I was looking forward to presenting him with when the war was over. Alas, in late 1942 I learned he'd been murdered. Poor August. He was a talented fellow and I'm sure he'd be tickled pink to know how his stuff goes on turning up even today. As always, it's quality that tells.

– These boozy, brawling troops did absolutely nothing to make our propaganda job any easier. They crashed and smashed around town, horrifying the locals and offending every conceivable Islamic decorum while singing outrageous songs about the Egyptian royal family. Not that you could blame them much. These were lads who only days before had probably watched their friends burn to death in the desert as their tanks were hit and brewed up. What was Egypt to them but beer, whores and time off from a murderous campaign? The Embassy and the brass-hats and all the Oxbridge intelligence types winced and moaned and demanded that officers hold their men more in check, but it only further served to point up the great division in Cairo between the real soldiers who were actually doing the fighting and the rump of high-ranking layabouts who pushed paper and had mysterious jobs with long luncheons. I have to include myself in this group, I'm afraid, at least from the perspective of those shattered and bandaged men in dust-stained battledress. There were a lot of pointed epithets in circulation to

describe us: 'The Gabardene Swine' and 'Groppi's Light Horse'
being two of the least offensive.

– So it dragged on until Montgomery arrived and the Battle of
El Alamein was won in October 1942 and it was clear to everyone
that the tide had turned for good. We felt it at once in Cairo and
in exactly the way I had predicted. Street opinion changed virtually overnight. Rommel's name vanished from the fly-posters and
'Mohammed 'Ider' was no longer bandied about in Groppi's and
the Arabic-language press as Egypt's potential saviour. The Eighth
Army pushed on westwards to Tripoli with the retreating Italians
hastily mining and ploughing up their airfields before they abandoned them. I remember some RAF pilots singing a song they'd
made up about half a dozen wretches they'd caught making con-
centric whorls with their ploughs on Castel Benito airfield just
outside Tripoli ('Benito' after Mussolini, of course). Some wag
had fitted new words to 'One Man Went to Mow', and the song
went:

Six men came to plough, to plough Castel Benito;
Six men, five men, four men, three men, two men, one man,
No man with no plough,
Work now finito.

Of course one needs to hear this yelled in chorus with beer mugs
banging on the top of a mess piano to get the full flavour of the
times. I'm afraid my heart went out to those poor Italian devils
who'd been stuck on their bulldozers in the middle of that expanse
of sand as the patrol overhead peeled off in leisurely fashion to
strafe them and turn them into a comic song. In any case by May
the following year there were no more German or Italian forces
left in North Africa except as PoWs. The war gradually with-
drew from Egypt, receding to Europe and the Pacific. A year after
El Alamein almost to the day, Italy had surrendered to the Allies
and declared war on Germany, a move that may indeed have been
pragmatic but which looked to us like abject turncoatism. But at

least the pastry-cooks of Alexandria could stand down and give their nerves a rest and for most of us it was pretty much over, too.

– You could hardly say I'd had a distinguished war. The only thing I'm proud of in those years was keeping an eye on Mirella's family. They soon left Renzo's flat. Pleased as he'd been to see his sister and her two children safe and sound, the fact was that Uncle Renzo was not cut out for family life. He was particularly irritated by his little niece wandering around the flat asking, 'Why isn't Kostas better yet?' He was more than happy to help them out financially just so long as they went away and allowed him to go on with his bachelor existence. I'm sure his Italian contacts in the Palace and the diplomatic service made it possible to find them temporary accommodation and my recollection is that they moved around quite a bit in Cairo for the next eighteen months or so. They were in an anomalous position, poor dears. Mirella's status in the Italian diplomatic service was hardly senior, anyway. Until Mussolini was strung up and the Italians changed sides the Boschettis really existed in a kind of limbo. Mirella had applied for repatriation when they arrived in Cairo but in 1942 most of North Africa was a war theatre and we had neither the time nor the transportation to spare for enemy non-combatants. The entire Mediterranean was equally in the grip of war, and not even hospital ships were guaranteed safe. So the Boschettis stayed. They were hardly alone. Cairo was full of people of various nationalities whose lives were temporarily stranded. The Boschettis simply became part of this floating population although they did have to report each week to an office in Garden City and were not allowed to leave Cairo. Nonetheless, these involuntary detainees did contrive to have a surprising amount of social life. Even their children's education went on after a fashion. Ad hoc schools were formed and people gave lessons as and when they could.

– It felt as though something had happened between Mirella and myself. Well, after all I was officially the enemy. On the surface, at least, she was still full of my praises for having saved their lives, as she kept putting it. For a while I wondered if in the course of her party-going she might not have heard some gossip about me, about some of my shadier contacts and activities. By then I suppose I had acquired a small reputation in Cairo as a mystery figure. Not an *éminence grise*, exactly, since I was hardly eminent. But a certain *gris* quality unquestionably hung about some of the company I kept, particularly people like Etienne, the French aristo who was still living aboard his Cleopatrine *dahabiya* on the Nile. He, incidentally, had proved his anti-Vichy credentials by keeping open house for such members of the Free French as shared his tastes. In fact it was later revealed that he had a secret transmitter on his houseboat which was used to pass messages to Free French troops in the field. Etienne was the first man in Cairo to learn of the fall of Bir Hakeim in mid-1942 when Rommel took it from the Free French after a vicious engagement. That was the battle, by the way, in which Richards was killed: the unfortunate fellow I'd spied on in that Suez brothel years earlier. The rest of the time Etienne spent as he always had, his pleasures unaffected by the war, at least so far as I could observe as an occasional guest. 'Monsieur Python', his favourite from Tanta, had long since been retired, a geriatric at nearly seventeen. He had been replaced by another child of only slightly less awesome endowment. It was on Etienne's houseboat that I regretfully concluded that I am at best a failed voluptuary. I am not by nature an orgiast although, being an impostor, I can impersonate one fairly convincingly for an evening.

– Maybe after all it wasn't my reputation that was influencing Mirella's attitude towards me. Certainly she was happy for Adelio to go on seeing me, although opportunities were not that frequent. I think she might have nursed a grudge about my treatment of her friend the Hungarian Count. We had no news of him for a while and I wondered if he had still been standing outside Mirella's house when a stick of bombs blew the building apart, in which case he was now surely numbered among the saints. Then I learned he had been arrested as a spy and interned with his fellow Nazis in Adelio's old school, which numbered him firmly among the sinners. So Alexandria's pre-war gossip, which had always languidly assumed that foreign gentlemen of leisure were spies, had been spot-on after all. I mentioned his arrest to Mirella in case she hadn't heard on her own grapevine, and although she evinced relief at his safety I'm quite certain the news of his profession came as no surprise to her. I have no doubt they used to feed each other information. Towards the end of the war we heard officially that Count Bathory-Sopron had been killed in a brawl in the prison. Germany was collapsing in on itself and it was a time of bitter recriminations. As for his flashy car with its weird-looking double front wings, that was stolen from outside my flat after I'd brought back my stuff from Alexandria so I spent the rest of the war without a car like everybody else. Presumably the Delahaye spent the duration hidden in one of the many garages tucked away that the RAF didn't convert into workshops and has probably been through a succession of salerooms ever since.

– Then the Boschettis heard that *Tenente* Giulio Boschetti had been killed early in November 1942 while serving in the 102nd Italian Motorised Division. A week later news came that he hadn't been killed after all but merely taken prisoner by New Zealanders. But a month after that the original news of his death was confirmed. 'I wish he'd make his mind up,' said Adelio with an apparent callousness I found slightly shocking. Yet he was now nearly sixteen and it was obvious that all sorts of resentment and anger lay behind the remark so I said nothing. I think it's fair to say that Adelio never quite recovered from his father's absences and his mother's infidelities and whatever teasing he had had to suffer for them at school; but there were other things I knew much less about. Anyway, it was from him I learned that invaluable lesson never to pass judgement on what members of a family do or say to each other.

As Jayjay falls silent and slowly levers himself to his feet I can see how ill he is. It is not just that he is visibly tired after talking for a couple of hours. He has suddenly acquired a slight detachment of manner very hard to describe exactly. Maybe towards our end the very familiarity of our own history wearies us. Surely we have recounted it too many times, if to nobody else then to ourselves, endlessly reworking and editing until it is a coherent narrative that fits more or less comfortably with the rueful self-honesty we acquire (how late!) in the run-up to eternal silence.

'Like a dream,' Jayjay says, not for the first time, laying a much rubbed envelope on the table before me.

I open the brittle paper carefully and shake out the batch of black-and-white photographs. Considering they were taken over half a century ago they are in excellent condition and were obviously skilfully printed. The outdoor setting in that vertical desert light normally makes for dull pictures, the sky a cloudless blank, the sea a featureless ledge halfway up the frame, the shadows too black. From them Adelio stares back at the lens or off into the distance with various tones of grey carefully preserved in the shadows cast by his hair and the angles of his body which has the undernourished, birdlike look of certain children beginning puberty. Despite all that Jayjay has said about him I am unprepared for the intensity of Adelio's haunted expression in one or two of the photos and the effect is not dispelled by a couple in which he is obviously laughing at something Jayjay has said. In one, the sun flares off the windscreen of the tiny far-off Fiat parked in the shade of a ruined wall that might once perhaps have been a lighthouse. In another, there are the thermos flasks and beach towels of fifty years ago. Adelio's touching, slightly ragamuffin face is frozen on the far side of that crevasse of time.

'Another first,' says Jayjay. 'The first time I've broken my promise to him. Until now, no-one else has seen them.'

'They're very affecting,' I concede, slipping them back in the envelope. 'I only wish we could use one of them.* Don't you have

---

* Until quite recently it would have been possible to illustrate the book with one of these photographs. But a new Victorianism has once more rendered certain human bodies taboo and we must await a more enlightened age.

any more photos of this period, Jayjay? It might help if we could illustrate this story of yours.'

'I have hardly any that you can use,' he says sadly. 'Almost everything was lost in one of my many moves when I had a good deal of stuff in store and the warehouse burned down. That was in England, incidentally, in the fifties. I also had some pictures from the Eltham days which turned up in the attic of Beechill Road when Dad died in 1949. Most of those went in the same fire. It's a shame, but it can't be helped. We will just have to rely on your graphic prose. But here's an odd thing. I shipped a couple of tin trunks of belongings back from Egypt after the war but they failed to arrive. Things were chaotic at the time, of course, and I assumed they were gone for ever. But several years later they were found in the steamship company's office in Naples, of all places, unharmed and still with the original lading bills. They sent them on and when they finally came I must say I opened them with a fair amount of curiosity since I couldn't for the life of me remember what was in them. Well, most of it was junk, although quite reminiscent junk. You know, clothes that looked like someone else's. All the linen was yellowed from the constant dust in Egypt. One only noticed it back in Europe where white comes up such a different shade. In addition to that, and right at the bottom of both trunks, I found these pictures of Adelio and the remains of my pornography archive dating from 1936, including a lot of August's work. I'll show you them sometime if you remind me but I fear if you can't use Adelio you certainly won't be able to use much of that stuff, not unless you want your book to become the first biography to be impounded by Interpol. Incidentally, James, I want you to promise there will be no photographs of me in your book.'

'What, none? A funny kind of biography that can't illustrate its subject.'

'If you can't do it in prose it's useless relying on pictures. I'm sick to death of my face.'

I narrowly avoid saying that he will never have to see it. 'Well, if you insist. Though I might accept with better grace if we could substitute some prints from your *feelthy* archive.' A shadowy thought at last takes on a clear outline. 'You made real money during the war, didn't you, Jayjay?'

'Oh yes,' he says, hitting me straight in the eye with that old Jayjay look, part mischief and part challenge. 'Heaps of it. I never mentioned I wound up as the owner of three clubs in the Berka, did I? Including a donkey-trick one. We had a notice outside ours to score off the other joints which advertised theirs as being 'The Original'. Ours said: 'The Trick Is Original But Our Donkey Is Changed Every Week For Reasons Of Fatigue.' Packed to the rafters each night. I'd even nobbled the district police commander so that rival clubs were frequently raided and closed. That's a story in itself because it was tangled up with the conflicting jurisdiction of our own military police. But yes, I think on balance you can describe mine as having been a profitable war, all things considered, even if it was one that Captain W. E. Johns and Major James Bigglesworth would heartily have disapproved of. Still, I played my part in the war effort. I successfully spread a canard that Rommel was homosexual, backing it up with a staged photograph using a South African lookalike being rogered by an Egyptian bricklayer from Helwan. We ran off twenty thousand of those and distributed them all over Cairo. Another idea of mine was to put about the story that truly dedicated Nazis all consented to have one of their testicles surgically removed out of solidarity with Hitler. It was well known to Egyptians that Allied troops sang a song about Hitler's having only one ball and this rumour of our enemies' partial emasculation, whether or not it was completely believed, made for a lot of jokes in Cairo. There was even an article about it in a popular Arabic newspaper. Every little helped; and though I admit I took good care that my war service should be as inactive as possible, I did what I was asked to do quite conscientiously. But yes, I made a lot of money on the side. Yes, too, I made some invaluable door-opening contacts which I shall tell you about if there's enough time. And finally, of course, I got to know Adelio and his family.'

'So what happened to him? He's the obvious loose end in the story so far. Where is he now?'

Jayjay made a vague gesture towards the view beyond the terrace.

'He's in the *camposanto*. He died in 1977. This is his house we're sitting in. He left it to me.'

14

See how the wicked prosper and the ways of the evildoers triumph!

Such are the thoughts of a modern Jonah as he unwillingly makes his way from country to country, from appointment to appointment, whisked by private helicopter to a five-thousand square-mile ranch or by limo to a tower block owned by the inter-viewee's corporation. Butlers usher Jonah into a series of drawing-rooms with exclusive views over a forest of blue gums, a panorama of ocean, the Chrysler Building or Hyde Park. Those are the Alps on the skyline. Your Princess Margaret has been to this little island resort of ours. If you like water we also have a place on a lake near Tashkent which I think you would enjoy: it's still a bit rough but we're slowly licking it into shape . . . Not only do the drawing-rooms have views of all the kingdoms of the world and the glory thereof but views of a good few of their rulers too, in the shape of photographs artlessly scattered about on book-shelves and unplayed Steinway grands. Jonah is pretty amused to see how many of the wicked appear to be close personal friends of kings and presidents and prime ministers. Here are beaming Saudi princes, African kings, American presidents; heads of states whose chief exports are inhaled or injected; the Pope himself and even in one case the late unimpeachable Mother Teresa.

Jonah is amused because they are a tribute to sanitising skills. What one normally hears about is the laundering of money, even though *pecunia non olet* and one might think it could hardly be deodorised further. But that is only the first step. The real challenge is the laundering of reputation. This is mainly a matter of waiting for Time the great healer to do his stuff, aided by astute donations to political campaigns and charities and the setting up of foundations for worthy causes. The days of crisis in distant hot countries, the firing squads and the curling tongs and the body parts in refrigerators: these are merely the malicious rumours of elsewhere and long ago, allegations much too dubious and far-fetched to be worth bringing before any august bar. The very fantasy of Judgement Day betrays the vanity of dead millions longing for redress. Forget it, says Jonah. You lose. Cherish all the fond hopes you may of earthly powers getting their comeuppance or of the spiritual superiority of the meek: they are merely analgesic. (Which of the billionaire oilmen was it – Hunt? Getty? – who made that quip? '*Let* the meek inherit the earth. We'll still have the mineral rights.') After all, these are the great and the good who set the world's agenda, and the world is all that is the case.

Still, there is a wry interest in going from one interview to the next, asking carefully prepared questions that hover on the edge of propriety. One does not expect these people to incriminate themselves, thinks Jonah. Yet when their answers are compared certain striking discrepancies do often emerge and new lines of thought suggest themselves. Cast your mind back to the time of the Emergency. You will recall that plans for building the nuclear power station were never put out to proper tender and the deal was sewn up with General Electric and its lead banker, Citibank. Great sums of money were squirreled away in Swiss accounts. But then the regime had second thoughts about the need to keep up appearances because this was such a major project. They realised it would be advisable at least to go through the motions of canvassing another bid, even if retrospectively. American Express duly appeared, flexing its young muscles in the field of international finance, suggesting that a much better deal for the nuclear plant might be struck with Westinghouse while the US Government's Ex-Im Bank provided long-term credit. At that time the President of Ex-Im Bank was William Casey, the ex-Director of the CIA. Suddenly the regime thought that Westinghouse plus the CIA plus the US Government looked a far more attractive alliance than General Electric and Citibank. However, the earlier deal had already been signed on the regime's behalf by the Chairman of the national power company, and the same man could hardly now turn around and put his signature to a contract with a different company for the same project. So he had to be dumped, and quickly, because the US presidential election was due in November and if the Democrats won Casey would be out on his ear and lose his presidency of Ex-Im Bank. So a new chairman was swiftly appointed to the national power corporation who duly signed the new contract, and General Electric and Citibank were out of a job. Just in time, too, because the Democrats did win the election and Casey retired from Ex-Im Bank. But then, Westinghouse was represented in the new deal by Asia Industries, who were paying a large retainer to, well, William Casey, so the good fellow lost nothing and remained a close Washington ally of the regime's.

Ah, but whatever happened to the gigantic sweeteners paid to the regime by *both* bidding corporations as well as by everyone else who wanted in on this lucrative nuclear power plant? And how come the plant itself was eventually built, at a vast overrun on budget and with more sweeteners at every turn, but never commissioned? It was mothballed as soon as it was completed and there it stands to this day, quaintly sited in a province of notorious seismic instability: a geological fact equally well known to local peasants and Westinghouse. If proof were needed that the chosen site was less than ideal it turned out to be not far from where a volcano erupted famously in 1991, temporarily altering the earth's climate and reddening its sunsets.

Whatever happened to all that money? *Si monumentum requiris, circumspice*, thinks Jonah as he is lunched beneath an awning on the island resort; as he hangs stuttering in the helicopter above an immense herd of prize cattle; as he is lofted to the top of the corporation's executive skyscraper in Manhattan. Or is this Hong Kong? One needs to go to the boardroom window in order to check. No matter that the foundations of this business empire are grounded on a forgotten bedrock of graft as well as of solidified blood and tears, the people who live in the penthouse suite are charm itself. They betray only occasional microlapses from their habitual high standards of warmth and generosity, as though victim to one of those tiny strokes or 'cerebral events' that leave people blinking for two seconds in a high street or getting into their car, aware only that something has happened which they cannot name and then cannot remember. These tiny asides (a sudden steely look, a ruthless remark, the abrupt closing of a conversational topic like a book being slammed shut) are easily dismissed as quirks and idiosyncracies. That apart, the prevailing décor is wall-to-wall geniality, the children especially with their beautiful ponies and excellent reading grades and scaled-down off-road vehicles capable of forty miles per hour, handbuilt for them by the Sumibashi Corporation somewhere east of Eden.

I miss my friend Jayjay, Jonah thinks as he lies in a grace-and-favour hotel suite (the hotel chain is a wholly-owned subsidiary of his host's). I miss him and I fear I may never see him again because he is dying. And this very morning I am going to cut short my trip and junk the last two hard-won interviews in order to hurry home before it's too late. I also long to return to more threadbare circles, to life stories of normal peccadillos where people sell pornography for a living and live out their lives inefficiently in the grip of futile loves for other people rather than for powers and dominions. But then, Jonah tells himself, that is a foolish sentimentalism because the super-rich also have nightmares and inconvenient libidos; they too have a Rosebud stashed in an outhouse, hidden behind the broken Sumibashi toys. And anyway, most of the poor would cheerfully settle for an empire with foundations of blood provided the underpinnings were well enough buried and their corporate offices soared high enough into the blue sky, flashing with stainless steel cladding and an equally stainless reputation. Who wouldn't opt for that change in fortune? Who wouldn't want the sort of power that can get into bed with Westinghouse and cuddle up to the CIA and yield heaps of untraceable money? And if it means that a few no-hopers out in the sticks with their buffaloes have to be kept in line with petrol enemas and curling tongs, and occasionally their children need their eyes putting out by men wearing jungle fatigues – well, that sort of thing has always gone on at the lower end of the scale. They breed like flies, anyway, and in five years' time even their own folks won't remember their names. *Redress?* The very word has overtones of loser.

Jonah decides to curtail his interviews and fly back to Italy not just because he wants to see his friend Jayjay, although that is the chief and most pressing reason. It is also because he already knows too much to print, while nobody gives a damn about this sort of stuff anyway. It is a weary wisdom that behind every great fortune lies a great crime. Who cares? And who wants to bring grief, lawsuits and possibly worse down upon themselves in a quixotic crusade that will benefit no-one? The dead are dead, and we are all earmarked for slaughter.

As he flies eastward across the Atlantic Jonah finds his interest in malefactors and their deeds dissipating like contrails in the thin stratospheric gale. By the time he lands in Rome Jonah is no more. He has been replaced by the pipsqueak British writer in sour trousers who booked the flight two months ago: the failed father and unworthy friend who deserted the dying subject of a biography he has yet to complete. He is also an inept beekeeper who leaves his charges to fend for themselves for six weeks in the swarming season. He may or may not try to do better in future – probably not, actually, as he is quite addicted to his wandering life.

I am shocked by the change in Jayjay in a scant six weeks. He has shrunk alarmingly and what I once pretended might be an incipient tan is now unmistakably jaundice. He is up and about, still contriving to be dapper even though his trouserlegs are emptier and in some odd fashion appear to move independently of the limbs within.

'Riddled,' he affirms cheerfully, catching my momentarily uncensored gaze. 'What you see before you, dear James, is a goner. Mercifully it doesn't hurt at all. Isn't that odd? The quacks reluctantly admit that I'm festooned with tumours the size of grapefruit from uvula to arsehole, but damned if I can feel a thing other than *weak*. Pathetically weak. The good news is that I've ignored the quacks and gone back to proper coffee. I couldn't be doing any longer with all those dead leaves and hot water. Tea just tastes wet to me. I've been feeling better ever since.'

'You're looking terrific, Jayjay. Years younger. A walking tribute to Lavazza's *Qualità Oro*. A veritable elixir of life, that stuff must be.'

'Ah, excellent. I can see that the high life of these last six weeks has done little to blunt our fundamentally sardonic nature. And I *am* looking terrific, it's true. I caught sight of myself by mistake in the bathroom mirror this morning and thought, "There's someone who has lived too long." Evidently after a certain number of years we're all condemned to look more and more like Somerset Maugham.'

'As painted by Graham Sutherland.'

'Exactly. *You* don't think I should be taking all these frightful drugs the quacks want me to take, do you?'

'I've no idea, Jayjay. Not unless you want to. What frightful drugs are they?'

'Those things that kill practically every cell in your body and make your hair fall out. I told Dr Farulli they might suppress my libido and I couldn't stick that at any price, not at my age. His face was a picture, as they used to say. I had a bit of a fight with Marcella over them but I won. Can't see the point in buying myself a horrid extra month, can you?'

I am impressed by his spirit. Gallows cheerfulness takes effort and courage. We know it's an act, but we also know that nearly everything about the face we turn to the world for eighty years is an act. We are all impostors. These things matter. We cannot allow standards to fall just because something as trivial as eternity is about to roll over and squash us.

'I'll tell you what is a bit lowering,' he concedes. 'You might think that as someone nears his end with all his faculties intact he would suddenly be able to dispense with all the blocks and inhibitions that had previously held him back. You might expect him to become as brilliant as he was capable of being, able to distil the experience of having been a unique individual who made his one passage through the world with a good deal of wry amusement. But no. If ever you were going to be brilliant it would have happened long ago. You just feel slack and grey and oppressed. Everything becomes the past, and the past becomes more dreamlike and inconsequential. You become mentally inert, which must be what the goofy mistake for other-worldliness. The entire process is disagreeable to a fault, so let's change the subject. Tell me about the great and the good in your recent life.'

I give him a brief outline after observing that I doubt whether they are much different from the great and the good in his own life, about whom he has yet to tell me.

'We must bring this tale to some sort of conclusion,' he agrees, and makes a valiant effort to make it seem as though things have not changed since the expansive days of a couple of years ago when he would hold forth for hours at a stretch on the terrace. It is now the first half of April and although the sun is bright its warmth is thin. Nevertheless Jayjay muffles himself up and insists that we sit outside at the table with its inlaid ceramic tiles, the percolator fresh from the kitchen still sighing and spluttering to itself between us.

It is an astonishingly beautiful morning. The increasingly freakish climate of the last ten years is resulting in minor heatwaves in February followed by premature spring. The crocuses and violets and grape hyacinths have long since bloomed and gone; the apricots, peaches and almonds have likewise already flowered and are now in leaf. The wisteria that winds its tendons across the front and side of Il Ghibli and over the pergola is about to blossom. It is one of those mornings when one can imagine the ground almost trembling with the pressures in the soil driving sap along roots and up tall trees to burst in green flame from every twig. On all sides this force is squeezing fresh colour out of what only days before must have seemed dead sticks. Jayjay raises his increasingly hawklike face to the summit of Sant' Egidio which today is leaning back and flying through small puffs of very white cloud. From somewhere down beyond the olives comes the intermittent muffled howl of a chainsaw as Claudio indulges his passion for lopping and felling.

Why here? I ask. Why this house?

– As soon as they could Mirella and the children shook the dust of Egypt off their feet and came back here to Italy. Their home was actually just the other side of Castiglion Fiorentino, in the hills overlooking Rigutino. What, about five miles from here? Hardly more. I tried to keep in touch with them but it wasn't easy. The war was over but everything was chaotic and in a state of flux. It was obvious to me that the British had at best a limited future in Egypt so I decided to go back to England. Really, though, it seemed to me that I had come to the end of a phase in my life and it was time for a change. In one sense I was right: those nine years since 1936 had indeed been a formative experience. But I was wrong if I thought that a change would necessarily mean something radically different. I couldn't see it at the time but from then on my life was essentially going to be permutations of things

I had already experienced and thoughts I'd already had. I don't know if that made me a case of arrested development. No more so than anybody else, probably. I was twenty-seven, twenty-eight: already past my prime had I been an Egyptian *fellah* or *bedou*, who were often old at forty and dead at forty-five. By sheer good fortune I had been spared disaster or an arbitrary death at a time when such things were commonplace. It was a miracle that I had escaped being blown to bits in Alexandria by only a couple of minutes. I remember getting back to Eltham all tanned and fit and excellently nourished and being obliged to wonder 'Why me?' London was a changed place. Eltham was a changed place. It was bleak and scrawny and full of bomb sites. People were pale and drawn and shivering: coal was well-nigh unobtainable. They certainly didn't look like citizens of a victorious nation. Hardly a family hadn't lost somebody. There were gaps in streets where the Luftwaffe had missed the Docks or else a V1 or V2 had landed. People were constantly finding incendiaries in their gardens. The poorer East End kids wore dresses run up from black-out material. And everywhere you went in central London there were little groups of young servicemen missing an arm or a leg or else blind, playing accordions or the spoons for pennies. They merely swelled the ranks of all the First World War veterans already shining shoes outside Charing Cross station or playing banjos or being commissionaires, taxi-hailers and door-openers for hotels. And I kept thinking, 'Why me?'

– It was the first time in nine years that I had seen my father. He looked a lot older and smaller than I remembered. He embraced me and wept when I came through the front door and he couldn't speak for about fifteen minutes. We just stood there in the hallway of Beechill Road, he rocking me as though we were late-night dancers down at the Palais. Over his balding head I stared at our front door's sunbursts and fanlight that had once been such potent images when I was homesick in Suez. I could see where he had stuck up the black-out material with drawing pins and sticking plaster. And there was the hatstand with both his bowler hats, his ration book on the seat next to it. Eventually he found his voice. He said he was full of remorse at having sent me away. He could only have meant to Hither Green but he sounded as if he felt responsible for my nine-year absence in Egypt. That made me very sad. He said it was wrong of him; he'd known it was wrong at the time but my mother, well, poor old girl, we'd none of us known how ill she was. We had, of course, but I happily connived at this harmless fiction. He said he still tried to see Olive at least once a month even though the journey across London out to Finchley had become increasingly difficult what with wartime disruptions to public transport, and sometimes it hardly seemed worth it as she either refused to see him at all or else appeared not even to recognise him. Thanks to being hit over the head every few hours with pharmacological blackjacks she was silent, biddable, inert, although she still liked to do the crossword every day in the company of Elijah, who knew all the answers.

– The worst thing of all for me was that although I could perceive the pathos of my homecoming I wasn't really moved. Not really. I was touched by this small old man named Harold who was my father, but little more. Too much had happened to me in the interim. I was no longer the moody lovelorn schoolboy who had left this house with a ticket to Suez in his pocket, although there was still enough of him to make me associate the place with the great unhappiness and resentment that had surrounded my leaving. I slept in my old room with the remembered wallpaper that now looked dowdy and faintly hideous. I paid my respects to the neighbours who, while welcoming, could not disguise the fact that the boy next door's returning was no substitute for their own son who now never would come home. The winter fogs closing in, while awakening all sorts of old memories and associations, seemed mainly miserable after years of hard sun. I was constantly cold. I kept warm by borrowing an enormous pram and fetching firewood from Well Hall Road where a stray bomb had badly damaged the tramlines. They were now digging up the road in order to re-lay the tracks. It was an example of an ill wind blowing someone a bit of good because it turned out that the original lines had been laid between tarred oak blocks the size of cobblestones that burned beautifully. I made as many trips as I could, carting back the booty, and by the end people were coming from far and wide and practically tearing up the roadway with their fingernails just to get something to burn. My father was so pleased. I suppose it was the first time his son had ever brought back something into the house that the family needed. We stockpiled the blocks in the empty coal cellar. Meanwhile the new Labour Government was busily laying out plots for pre-fabs on the parkland along the edge of Glenesk Road to ease the acute housing shortage. It was the very place where as a boy I used to gather horse mushrooms near the elm trees they'd just felled.

– As I said, I did try to remain in touch with the Boschettis. Adelio wrote me strange emotional letters I couldn't quite fathom. By now he was nineteen, rising twenty. The new post-war Italian state was carrying on with the old system of military service for boys of eighteen, but since his father was dead Adelio was now technically the head of the family, being the only son, so he was exempt. With hindsight it's clear that he was already in the grip of a lifelong melancholia which eventually was his ruin. Nowadays with its customary inaccuracy the medical profession can no longer distinguish melancholia. It thinks it's the same as depression but of course it isn't. In my experience depression nearly always involves some degree of physical inertia. By his own account Adelio's heaviness of spirit went with an increasing lightness of body and the energy to walk everywhere. He even described himself as 'getting thinner', so he must have become positively gaunt. He was weeping a lot, he said, without knowing why, and going on long excursions to these very slopes. He must surely have derived some pleasure from this since these were the half-remembered hills of childhood, his primal landscape. I believe he walked almost daily from above Rigutino across the Valle di Chio and up into the hills over Ristonchia, passing

Spinabbio and Campo Gelato, on up to the summit of Sant'
Egidio. I think you and I would hardly recognise these same hills
he walked then. They had been seriously over-grazed since well
before the war; but when the front passed in the summer of 1944
with the Allies pushing northwards and the Germans falling back
only slowly, most of the people down here in the valley took to the
hills to avoid the fighting. They crowded into the scattered farmhouses like your own up there and ate practically anything that
moved, even leaves and crickets by the end. So when Adelio was
doing his daily walk in the late forties this mountain would have
been practically a desert. No more hares and rabbits, hardly a
songbird, the foxes all gone. The provincial government then did
something unusually sensible. Faced with tens of thousands of
PoWs being repatriated from all over the world, most of whom
urgently needed work, Tuscany gave them the job of replanting
the forests that had been decimated for firewood or grazed to
extinction. As I'm sure you know, most of the conifers on this
mountain were planted after the war. The old chestnuts and oaks
are original, of course. Because chestnuts yielded the staple *farina
dolce* people took care of them, and scrub oaks grow like weeds
here in any case. But all the pines and most of the mixed deciduous trees were planted by returning prisoners of war, and because
nobody has any livestock today these hills are entirely ungrazed
except by wild boar and porcupines. I shouldn't think they've been
so thickly wooded since the time of the Etruscans.

– Anyway, Adelio volunteered to help with this replanting.
Mirella tried to make him go to university but he wouldn't. She
was even driven to write to me occasionally, mainly because she
was at her wits' end about her son. He seemed to lack all drive, all
ambition. He had given up the idea of a diplomatic career, he
said. He was quite disillusioned about politics and world affairs.
He just roamed the hills with a book in his pocket or dabbled at
planting seedlings with returned prisoners. Personally I wouldn't
have said he had the physique for that sort of work but he claimed
it was a solace. Time went by.

– I, meanwhile, was busy trying to capitalise on the contacts I'd made in Egypt. I decided that playing the impostor and inducing people to open some doors for me might compensate a little for the grimness of London. Compared with Cairo it seemed a place entirely devoid of fleshpots or pleasures. Everything was still rationed, restaurant food was abominable, there was a flourishing black market if you didn't mind dealing with spivs. Thanks to having worked for the embassy in Cairo I had a few friends in the Foreign Office as well as among ex-military types who were mostly demobbed and back in civvy street by now and trying to pick up what remained of their careers or family business. Julian Amery was an example of the latter. He had had a distinguished war in SOE specialising in the Balkans. It was for people like him that we'd stockpiled weapons in our warehouse in Alexandria. He kept volunteering to be parachuted into occupied Yugoslavia. I hadn't seen him since the summer of 1942 when he was posted home from Cairo. I hadn't even known he had survived the war. When I bumped into him in Whitehall at the end of 1945 he was most amiable. He remembered me as an Arabist and gave me some good introductions to friends of his in merchant banking. It was generous of him, especially since he must have been pretty preoccupied at that moment because his brother John was about to be hanged as a traitor. Awful scandal, really. John had run guns for Franco in the thirties and then made pro-Nazi broadcasts from Berlin for Hitler. His defence counsel tried to get him off by claiming that he was a Spanish citizen, but there was scant patience for that kind of technicality at the time and they hanged him regardless, just as they did Joyce who was claiming to be an American. You know, Lord Haw-Haw. Strange that the Amery brothers should have wound up on opposite sides of the same war, one decorated for bravery and the other executed for high treason.

– Merchant banking? Well may you wonder. It was more to do with my languages and contacts than it was with any interest in banking as such. I had surprised myself by discovering that I wasn't bad at business, at least at street level. It takes a certain insouciance, I suppose, to live off the pornography trade in a foreign country, and I had gained a good deal of confidence in my ability to busk my way along and know whose palm to grease. Given that the world of money, like that of politics, functions mainly on bluff and bullshit plus a degree of raw instinct, it was natural that an impostor like myself should have drifted into the sort of circles that needed *consultants*. That, really, has been my living since the war. Not only am I by nature a lover, albeit a failed one; I am also by nature a consultant. I know lots of people and I like picking their brains. I also like putting people in touch with one another, and the more disparate they are the more I enjoy it. And that was what I was doing in the late forties with Julian Amery's banking friends. Did Barclays DCO need to convince the new Egyptian minister of foreign trade and finance that it was in Egypt's interest for the bank to keep its offices and branches there, despite the growing unpopularity of all signs of British presence? Send for old Jayjay, who not only speaks the lingo but who knew the minister personally when he was a leading light in the Wafd Party. Barclays were not aware that old Jayjay had once sold the minister a film of a British girl from Kenya, one of the fishing fleet who had become stranded in Cairo, being pleasured by an athletic Egyptian postman and a springer spaniel. Had they known they would no doubt have been horrified, suspecting blackmail, for back in those days the ethical code of the City of London was still deplorably rigid. But there was no blackmail involved. I flew out to see the minister and we reminisced about the war years in that expansive, tea-sipping Egyptian fashion. Neither of us alluded to the film; we both knew we remembered the episode perfectly. If anything it was a bond between us and nothing to do with vulgar threats. Over a leisurely lunch he agreed it was vital for Barclays to go on being represented in Egypt and I promised him that an account would be opened for him in London should he ever need, for whatever unforeseeable reason, to send surplus personal funds out of Egypt at a time when small-minded Egyptian politicians might make such transactions illegal. A year or two later I was sent on a similar mission to Tripoli where in those days of King Idris practically everyone who counted in government or the professions spoke Italian and only a minority spoke Arabic. Send for Jayjay again.

– It was on the way back from Tripoli that I flew to Rome, caught a train and went to visit the Boschettis. I found Mirella and Anna at home in Pieve di Rigutino but it seemed that Adelio had moved out and had gone to live with an aunt a few miles away. Anna was now in her late teens and had become rather a beautiful girl. It was curious seeing them again, now on home territory at last. We spent the evening reminiscing; and such is the power of reminiscence that wartime Alexandria began to take on an aura of the good old days, whereas at the time the political undercurrents of Fascism and the warfare that was about to engulf us had been anything but good. Either Mirella was being highly selective or she had an extraordinary ability to forget. She had after all worked in Mussolini's foreign service, yet to hear her talk one would think she had been just an ordinary housewife and mother who had never driven around town in the company of a Nazi spy but had simply been swept up in the war like anyone else. To some extent I suppose there was some truth in it: she had indeed been caught in Alexandria because she had a husband in the military. But there was much that was disingenuous about her version of the past. She invited some friends and neighbours over to the house and introduced me too fulsomely as the gallant Englishman who had saved her family's lives.

– The next morning she took me into Castiglion Fiorentino to meet the local grandees where she made the same introduction. Despite people politely telling me how honoured they were as they shook my hand I soon detected a certain ambivalence in the town towards the English. I learned that this was entirely due to a horrendous accident in December 1943 when an RAF aircraft trying to attack the railway station had released its bombs a couple of seconds too early or too late and had scored a direct hit on a school, killing great numbers of children. In point of fact the pilot had returned to the town some time after the war ended and had apologised in person, which was a decent thing to have done. Everyone had been impressed by his gesture and had accepted that these sorts of accidents happen in war when aircraft are under ground fire and travelling at God knows how many miles per hour. Nonetheless it had happened; the children were dead and the noun 'Englishman' would have inescapable connotations for this little Etruscan town until enough time had elapsed.

– I understood all this perfectly as I chatted away. But while by association I had to share some of the blame for what my wretched countryman had done, nobody I met was offering to take the least responsibility for what their countrymen had done in North Africa or anywhere else. People referred delicately to the 'mass insanity' of the Fascist years, but even that made it sound like a nasty disease to which they had fallen victim rather than a political ideology that millions of Italians had enthusiastically supported. Here were people who had thrown in their lot with Hitler, lost their war, switched allegiance and emerged on the side of the victors as if that was where their hearts had been all along. I considered this required some admission at least. Maybe I'm too harsh. All this was half a century ago and in those days Castiglion Fiorentino was an impoverished agricultural backwater. The *contadini* were illiterate as well as deeply oppressed by the Church, which of course had supported Mussolini. Still, the people I met acted as if the Blackshirts had always been elsewhere, as if nobody in Castiglion Fiorentino had ever sung 'La Giovinezza', as if the *manganelli ed olio di ricino* had been a bit of bad behaviour on the part of a handful of zealots down in Rome . . . You know, clubs and castor oil? If the Fascists caught someone they thought was not enthusiastic enough about their cause they administered a good beating and forced them to drink quantities of castor oil . . . Add to that what everybody in Europe knew about General Graziani's atrocious campaign against the Senussi in Libya in the twenties and thirties, not to mention bombing tribespeople in Abyssinia, and I began to get quite cross with Mirella and her pals and their collective amnesia. Obviously one didn't want apologies. Wars are not the fault of citizens. On the other hand there is such a thing as collective responsibility. I did think some acknowledgement of their part in what we had all been through would have been, well, *gracious*. No doubt I met the wrong people. Anyway, I suddenly realised that I had never quite liked her. Certainly I had once found her erotically attractive, but underneath there was something slippery in her character that I mistrusted.

– The day after that I went to find Adelio, who was after all the person I had really come to Italy to see. Our first meeting in four years took place in this very house, although in those days it was not called Il Ghibli. It was still a working farm then and all these ground-floor rooms were byres and stables with living quarters upstairs. His aunt and uncle had been as badly hit by the war as most and even then were still building their livestock back up to pre-war levels. I remember a lot of sheep milling about at milking time where this terrace now is. Adelio was in his early twenties and dressed like a farmer: heavy boots, muddy corduroys, collarless shirt with sleeves rolled up. But his physique was not that of a farmer. His forearms were thin and hairless, his clothes hung on him. He really hadn't changed much except for looking a little older. His great hollow eyes filled with tears as we embraced and I don't believe I was dry-eyed myself. I spent several days here with him. He wanted to talk but spoke with a slight effort as though he were out of practice. He was clearly overjoyed to see me, but behind that I sensed a troubled presence which felt all of a piece with the boy I remembered in Alexandria. He had fallen out with his mother and sister, I never knew exactly why, but it may have been at least partly to do with the war because he took a very different line from Mirella's. He said he was ashamed for his country and told me how much he had always hated Fascism. This I'm sure was true. I remembered all too clearly the tearful child whose schooldays had been made hellish with his classmates' bullying and militaristic braggadocio. It was an infection of the times that had permeated institutions from top to bottom and one would need to have been a much more physically robust and confident child than Adelio to have held out against it. Also, as he saw it, it was Fascism that had broken up his family by posting his father off to Libya.

– He took me on walks up the mountain here. In fact we passed your house several times, which is why I know it even though I have still never visited you up there and now never shall. In those days the land around it was cultivated terraces rather than the semi-jungle it now is. They grew a lot of maize for both animal and human fodder. Ah, polenta! Imagine – they were still plough-ing that thin rocky soil with great white *chianino* oxen. Atrocious labour. No wonder all those houses were abandoned in the sixties. It's funny to think I knew your house so many years before you did. I presume you've heard that an RAF pilot spent some months there in 1944 after his Spitfire was shot down? He had broken his leg and the partisans brought him there for safety. There were several families crammed into your house then, not just the farmer's own but various relatives and friends too, refugees from the fighting down below. They put the pilot in one of the mangers so they could throw hay over him if ever the Germans came look-ing for him, but in the event no Germans ever went up Sant' Egidio. They were too harried down at the bottom and in a few months the front had passed and there were no more Germans in the Val di Chiana until they began buying property thirty years later. –

I suddenly sensed how much more Jayjay knew about me and my life than I'd ever given him credit for. He had never before told me in as many words that he had known my house and its recent history years before I bought it and moved to this area. And on top of that there were those books of mine he'd read. How very much less of a stranger I must have felt to him than he had to me when we first met in the Co-op that afternoon, and how very unfortuitous that meeting now appeared! I wondered how much else he knew. With a strange shock I realised that he most probably had heard about Frances and Emma, whom after all my local friends had known for nearly two years. My failure as a father was hardly a secret even though nobody alluded to it in my presence, and Jayjay's own discretion meant that he would hardly be likely to broach the subject himself. I had surely been right when I remarked on the way biographers and their subjects sniff each other out. With sublime egotism the writer assumes this is entirely a one-way process, that he alone is stripping the meat off the bones in front of him. It would certainly be all of a piece with Jayjay's admiration for Mediterranean *savoir-vivre* that he could have acquired a little leverage over me as well, some knowledge of a squashy and tender area which I would prefer remained unprobed. Achilles was only known for one of his heels but both mine are vulnerable, as well as much else. I am glad this is not an autobiography.

– So Adelio and I walked and walked, and all the time we were walking I thought how companionable he was, except for an odd tension every so often. Then one day we were sitting eating bread and cheese for lunch and he suddenly produced this little celluloid case from which he took a photograph of me. I recognised it at once, of course: it was one of those he'd taken of me that day on the beach when we thought Alexandria would be invaded within days. –

'I still have the ones I took of you, too,' Jayjay tells him. 'And what's more, I've never shown them to a soul.'

Adelio is blushing, paring rind off a piece of cheese with a grimy pocketknife.

'I've never forgotten that day,' he says at last.

'Nor I. I fully expected we would drive back to Alexandria and find fighting in the streets. I didn't know what I would do. I felt so responsible for you.'

'I didn't mean the damned war.'

'What, then?'

'Can't you see? Didn't you realise? I wanted you to, I don't know, comfort me or something. I was laughed at in school, my mother was busy with that mustachioed ape of hers, I was scared of all the talk about war. You were about the only person in my life who seemed to care whether I lived or died.'

'Stupid, isn't it? Oh, Adelio, if only you had known how much I wanted to hug you.'

He slants a look from those bruised and haunted eyes. 'You really did?'

'Of course. I longed to. But I was too shy.'

'*Per l'amor di Dio!*'

'*Eh, lo so.* I'm sorry now. It's miserable. But listen, you were stark naked. Be reasonable. There's a limit to how much one can chastely embrace a naked teenager. It was . . . I didn't want to scare or disgust you.'

'*Porc . . .!* Disgust? If you want to know about disgust you should have tried being cornered by that man Bathory-Sopron.'

There is a short silence while Jayjay adjusts his view of this dead spy.

'He didn't?'

'He most certainly did. Several times. I had to fight him off. The last time I told my mother and she refused to believe me. She just laughed and said I was being malicious because I disliked her friend. That's why I think the greatest moment in my life was when you stuck a gun in his face and stole his car and drove us to Cairo. Disliked? I've never hated anyone as much as that man. From then on you were definitely my hero. But you were before, anyway. I would have done anything for you on that beach.'

Far below in the fields behind Montecchio castle on its little knoll the rows of mulberry trees are coming into leaf. Some way beyond them is the great expanse that was used not long ago as an Allied airfield when supplies were ferried in for the troops. Jayjay wonders if the mulberry groves will eventually expand to cover the airfield too, or whether the local silk industry will fall victim to the new passion for nylon and rayon. These days silk stockings sound unbelievably dated and no longer even luxurious. All one ever hears about now are nylons, which have become a prime black-market commodity in Britain.

He reaches over and covers Adelio's hand on the grass with his own. He can be quite clear-headed about things. That occasion out at Abu Qir, as well as many a similar afternoon, can now be viewed remorsefully as a lost opportunity. Yet he can't bring himself to regret it as much as Adelio clearly does. Had Jayjay been as physically demonstrative as Adelio now claims he wanted him to be it is likely that they would indeed have become lovers on that hot, deserted beach as occasional warplanes patrolled out to sea. Maybe Adelio is imposing his twenty-three-year-old's libido on that of his former fourteen-year-old self, but Jayjay is prepared to let that go and assume that he really had hoped for what he is hinting at. Not impossible. But it is not what Jayjay wanted, which had surprised him at the time seeing that by then he had come to regard himself as a polymorphous-perverse opportunist. It is true he has often been exactly that, and he has never had moral scruples about making love to a boy of fourteen if it is on offer, as it quite often has been. But in this instance it was Philip who got in the way. Jayjay's absurd commitment to that beautiful figment had inhibited him from having an affair with this flesh-and-blood boy, as it still does. Apart from that, the blunt fact is that he had never found Adelio physically attractive enough. This was partly by corrosive comparison with Philip but mostly because he had spent so much time with Adelio over the previous three years that the boy had come to feel very like a surrogate son, and the incest taboo had fatally compromised most potential for erotic possibility. There is a limit to how often one can console a crying child, or stop the car to let him sick up an overdose of ice cream, or make sure he's not going to get sunburned on the beach, without turning slightly into a parent. Jayjay is more than a little surprised that Adelio hadn't felt the same way about him, actually. Now he suddenly realises that something erotic is still what Adelio wants: that in fact he is in love with Jayjay and always has been and only this can explain those peculiar letters of his swerving between confession and concealment. Jayjay is astonished at his own denseness in not having perceived this years ago.

'But I do love you, Adelio,' he tells him, not untruthfully, and sees that mournful face light up all too briefly.

– I left Italy and drifted hither and yon, earning a good living as a consultant, an impostor, as much else besides. This went on for years. Adelio and I still wrote to one another and now and then I came to visit him in this house, which eventually his aunt and uncle left him. He promptly re-named it Il Ghibli. The *ghibli*, of course, is the harsh Saharan wind that blows up from the south in Libya. Adelio explained this choice of name by saying he remembered his father talking about it when on leave from Tripolitania. He said the wind was feared and hated by Europeans because it produced oven-hot, overcast and dust-laden conditions that often lasted several days. Evidently Adelio wanted a name for his house that would remind him of the force of nature that had made life hell for his father and others like him who had finally been driven out of North Africa altogether. He also liked the sound of the word and the way it looked when written as well as the touch of the exotic which it brought to a traditional farmhouse in the Valle di Chio's provincial seclusion.

– As for Adelio himself, he became more and more reclusive and bookish. I don't know that he ever earned what you would call a living, but in those days you could just about survive if you were a *signore*. Thanks to Claudio's managing the farm, as well as to the system of *mezzadria*, Adelio could subsist quite nicely on half the produce. He had a local reputation for being abstemious and bone-thin but it never extended to his being considered mean. People around here still speak of him as having been very polite and vague and sad, saying little but gazing long and earnestly at things with those wounded, shadowed eyes. The inspector of schools for the region, a Castiglionese who knew him well, once told me Adelio reminded him of the poet Leopardi. Not a hunchback, of course, but having a mind sunk in melancholia that verged on anguish. He read as he walked, which in these parts is guaranteed to get you noticed as both eccentric and intellectual. Nobody who met him, said the inspector, came away without speculating on the origins of such pain and what it might take to alleviate it. The gossip went that Adelio showed no particular inclination towards women or men, so anything in the line of domestic contentment seemed unlikely. He seldom saw his mother and appeared to rely on her for nothing, not even money. I can admit now that I used to give him money whenever I came here and would send it if ever he asked for it, which happened only two or three times.

– And then one day in 1977 the news came that he was dead. Not suicide, which I think everybody had half expected, but a heart attack. He was fifty-one. Claudio found him sitting in a cane chair in a little summerhouse that fell down years ago, stone dead. Strangely enough he was reading Leopardi's *Zibaldone*, which was open on his lap. I would love to know which of the poet's jottings accompanied him out of this world but of course the book got closed and Claudio has no idea. It was a great shock but an even greater one to discover that Adelio had left Il Ghibli to me. And that is how I came to inherit this house, together with Claudio and Marcella. It had never occurred to me that Adelio had anything to leave, let alone that he might leave it to me. I had even forgotten he owned the house. There was no explanation, no letter. His death was too sudden.

– I'm afraid Mirella never forgave me. She outlived him and died only about ten years ago having made it quite clear that I really had every moral obligation to pass the house straight on to her. By then I wasn't badly off and since I hadn't budgeted on getting Il Ghibli I could easily have afforded to do without it, especially at the time when the entire place probably wouldn't have fetched fifteen thousand pounds. Had Adelio's sister Anna been on her beam ends I might well have given it to her, but she had long since married a Florentine industrialist and had absolutely no need for yet another house. And if Renzo had still been around I might even have considered passing it on to him.

But he had followed his beloved King Faroukh into exile in 1952 and had completely vanished. So I admit it was with a certain malicious pleasure that I left Mirella stewing in Rigutino and moved into Il Ghibli myself. She, incidentally, clung to her old allegiances to the end. In the sixties and seventies she used to meet Giorgio Almirante, the boss of MSI, the Fascist party, whenever he came to Montecchio for reunions with the local faithful. I suppose they brought out the party regalia and sang all the old songs together. But as I think I told you, her politics were not why I disliked Mirella.

– And now there's only Anna left, and I haven't seen her in years. Poor Adelio! I've found myself dwelling on him a lot recently, what with having to tell you about him. I used to think his was a tragic, wasted life, but on the threshold of my own death I no longer think in such terms. I am sorry for his unhappiness but I don't believe I could have done much to lighten it even had I moved in with him. Not that those days were the ideal time, nor the Valle di Chio the ideal place for a ménage of that sort, though doubtless we would have got by. There are much odder domestic arrangements around here hidden away behind tall fields of sunflowers. But I think by then he was beyond being assuaged like that and it wasn't what I wanted anyway so it could never have succeeded. And there you have it. –

You were happy to move here?

– Yes. I'd reached the stage of having travelled enough and began to hanker for somewhere fairly permanent. –

Somewhere to hang your hat and display Lady Amelia's dildo?

– Exactly. I knew I couldn't live in England. I was living in Morocco at the time and suddenly Il Ghibli was presented to me on a plate, as it were. Since I already spoke Italian and knew the house it seemed the natural thing to do. –

This was the last coherent session I ever had with Jayjay. His condition worsened rapidly within a matter of days and with it came a degree of weakness that from then on confined him to bed.

There remained the notes I made after visiting him at Il Ghibli and thereafter in Arezzo hospital on his last morning. I am particularly glad I took them; for although by then he had lost interest in his biography as such, several of his observations and phrases were vintage Jayjay and showed that he was never less than his old sharp self right up to the instant of dissolution. He only once made any further reference to Margaret Thatcher, for example: a throwaway observation that she, like many politicians who acquired convictions, had committed intellectual suicide by lying down directly in the path of a train of thought that was travelling on a branch line.

Certain other questions remained glaringly unanswered, such as the circumstances surrounding his apparent familiarity with various protagonists of the Vietnam peace talks in the late 1960s, notably Henry Kissinger. It turned out that Kissinger's framed portrait had vanished from Il Ghibli's downstairs washroom for no more sinister reason than that Marcella had smashed it while dusting and not for any Soviet-style editing by Jayjay of his own past. Henry had not fallen from favour, merely from a lavatory shelf, and was waiting to have his glass replaced. Piecing together assorted references from several of our previous sessions, it seems to me likeliest that Jayjay's connection would have come via an old friend of his from SOE days in Cairo. By then this man was a member of the British Advisory Commission to Vietnam whose head, the counter-insurgency expert Sir Robert Thompson, was adviser to Presidents Diem, Thieu, Johnson and Nixon. Thompson's advice was sought and heeded since he had been credited with much of the British success in handling the Communist insurgency in Malaya in the late forties and early fifties. It now seems clear that the Far East had become one of Jayjay's stamping-grounds in the sixties although he never got around to talking about it – and this despite knowing of my own researches there. Crafty old thing. Or just discreet. However, he did once give a very funny description of crashing some high-level talks in South America, and he may well have employed a similar technique to get into the Manila Summit in October 1966. (It may be recalled that it was Jayjay's early account of that Summit which had bored me into accusing him of name-dropping).

In the case of the Rio Accords his participation seems to have involved nothing more calculated than his happening to walk past the British Embassy just as a diplomat chum was driving out in the second-best Rolls. The friend automatically assumed that Jayjay was on his way to the same talks in some advisory capacity or other and offered him a lift. Quick-thinking as usual, Jayjay promptly ditched his meeting with the Bank of London and South America and simply strolled into the talks with his diplomat friend on the grounds that it would be more interesting than a bunch of bankers. To an impostor of his brass face it would have been a simple matter to have dropped a few names, deftly fudged his exact capacity and eased himself into the proceedings. Like his boyhood mentor at the Lloyds funeral wake he knew that at certain functions nobody is asked for their invitation, nobody knows absolutely everybody else, and everyone assumes those they don't recognise must be there for bona fide reasons. Besides, he had a distinguished air of exactly the right kind. No security guard was ever going to stop and question a man looking like Jayjay who emerged from a Rolls-Royce with CD plates in amiable conversation with a delegate, certainly not in those days.

The plausibility (as well as absurdity) of this was further strengthened for me by a memory of my own of having once seen a newspaper report of just such an impostor who was a regular attender at diplomatic functions and parties without having the remotest business to be there. Like Jayjay he had neatly brushed greying hair and impeccable clothes and manners and had already gatecrashed so many of these affairs around the world that several presidents knew him by sight and greeted him, although they seemed a little hazy about his name and exact status. It now occurs to me that this person may very well have been Jayjay himself. It was precisely these activities that Jayjay never enlarged on, having instead accorded undue attention to his life up to the age of thirty.

It is too late now to remedy this lack but not at all too late for regrets. Personally, I would have preferred a vignette of Jayjay being introduced to Henry Kissinger to one of an orgy on a houseboat in Cairo, but there we are. An account of Jayjay hurriedly improvising theories of counter-insurgency would surely have been entertaining, while the picture of the boy from Eltham telling Lyndon Johnson or Harold Holt or Ferdinand Marcos that the Strategic Hamlets Program was just what South Vietnam needed is irresistible. Alas, he chose not to tell the story, put off no doubt by my assumption that he was trying to impress me: another black mark for the biographer. On the other hand I will admit that a description of any one such incident would suffice for us to get the general picture. A lengthy series of stories of how he had bamboozled his way around the diplomatic world for thirty years would soon become wearisome, its only interest lying in the names he dropped. Maybe after all he did well to stick to what he thought was important and leave us to fill in the blanks imaginatively. And maybe after all his biographer can be excused this particular blot. Many a famous portrait painter has painted only his subject's most suggestive and revealing features while leaving the rest sketchy or entirely blank.

My remaining visits to Il Ghibli before he was finally hospitalised were marked with that haunted fortitude that Jayjay, with his loathing of the mawkish, managed to infuse into the terminal scene. I can see him now, lying in his bed, very gaunt and with his eyes closed, listening to a matronly friend of Marcella's urging him that he had only to say the word and she would send a priest straight round: 'not the usual *tronnecone* but a good man with no cant to him. It's never too early for the sacraments.' Jayjay elected not to betray by the flicker of an eyelid that he had heard but as soon as the door had closed behind her he snapped both eyes open and said 'There are no sacraments, there are only contracts. And I've never signed. Perhaps you'd better tell her that, James.' It was reassuring that even when he was waning fast the secular was still dancing doggedly within him.

The last memory I have of him in that house is of coming into his bedroom and finding Marcella's boy Dario sitting on his bed, laughing. Heaven knows what remains of strength it required for Jayjay to be propped up on his pillows, talking animatedly to him while wearing Dario's bright orange baseball cap. It was many sizes too small for him and its bill jutted up at the raftered ceiling with jaunty defiance while in its shadow the dinosaur-chick eyes sparkled with flirtatious energy. Perhaps death in its camouflage of children's clothing was not wholly disagreeable.

15

I suppose I don't regret the tone with which this book opens quite enough to modify it. After all, it duly reflects the change in a relationship that had begun with a polite conversation in a Co-op and developed into that invasive intimacy which takes the place of friendship between biographer and subject. By the end the brittle, even harsh, jocularity between us had become a game: a defence against too obvious a display of affection and concern, as well as for me a way of defusing Jayjay's undoubted ability to irritate me. How often had he pounced at an unguarded moment of mine when I let slip an unwonted sentimentality, and I had bided my time before being able to retaliate! And then at the end: how was I to have guessed the instant his mortal darkening had had its onset? Unknowing that this was to be the deathbed scene, we took our last leave of each other in Arezzo hospital through the tears of a coughing fit, my stupid bouquet of glandular great blooms no longer a sharp little jab at his snobbishness but the blunt instrument of his demise. Maybe.

Seven months passed. Something about today's January scud

past the window (crinkled brown oak leaves driven horizontally by a freezing *tramontana*) makes it easier to admit to having gone back to Jayjay's grave a scant fortnight after his funeral last year. Is how we visit a friend's grave the only permissible way nowadays of visualising ourselves buried? Of allowing that this last tableau of a one and only existence ought to express something of private weight? I suspect this ancient urge is becoming a matter for stealth, almost for shame, in Protestant England.

There had been a surprising attendance at the funeral service in Montecchio, given that it was a May morning of such aching beauty that to waste it on church and death seemed downright perverse. Yet the turnout showed that although Jayjay had been a foreigner with no family of his own he was well loved in the locality. According to everyone I spoke to he had been a *gentiluomo* in a world where the type is an increasing rarity. Most remarked on his warmth and sunniness, and maybe it was this quality that made the weather less inappropriate after all. Claudio and Marcella were there, of course, together with Dario and his two sisters. I would have thought that at not quite twelve the boy could easily have begged off, but according to his mother he had insisted on going. Of us all it was Dario who showed the most signs of grief, and he was now and then overcome with fits of the weeping that nearly exhausts itself for a minute's respite until it discovers with a fresh shock the permanent reality of loss. I knew very well that out of the mourners that day it was Dario's presence that would most have touched Jayjay, the one he would have valued above all.

I am not quite sure what made me visit his grave a couple of weeks afterwards. For all that the funeral service was decently conducted there had been a certain perfunctoriness about the proceedings, as so often these days when basically secular people find themselves obliged to attend a religious rite. They are at once impatient, over-solemn and lost; and sensing their restiveness the priest becomes anxious to hurry things along. And so it went with Jayjay. No grand Latin cadences with their two thousand years of echoes, of course – not since Vatican II and Roncalli's policy of *aggiornamento*, of being up-to-date. My friend was hustled into the earth with a brisk rattle of Italian, the priest on autopilot.

What did it matter, you ask, seeing that Jayjay and I were both godless? But it had less to do with God than with the having-been-human, with the shortly-to-cease. Something was left unsatisfied. The peculiar dignity he had possessed, sitting at the table on Il Ghibli's terrace and talking to the smoke pouring up from Claudio's prunings or else addressing the summit of Sant' Egidio – this demanded better acknowledgement now he was himself less than smoke. No doubt it would have been even worse had we lived in Britain. He once remarked that the land that had given both of us birth and which until so recently had prided itself on the restrained gravity of its great public obsequies could no longer understand or bear the idea of dignity, mistaking it for pompousness or else for depression, something to be either mocked or counselled away. So I duly found myself there on a blue May afternoon, an atheist foreigner in the cemetery at Montecchio standing by the grave of another atheist foreigner. I had chosen the moment with some thought. At two o'clock in the afternoon the Montecchese would still be chatting in their kitchens or dozing. I would have the place to myself. No-one would come to replace flowers or votive candles for at least another two hours.

Jayjay's new stone was glaring brash and nude. At that moment a Red Admiral alighted on it, hooked its feet into the incised 'Jebb', let the hot sunshine fall on its enamelled wings and began stropping its antennae. Jayjay would have liked that, too. There were several early butterflies around, attracted by the sprays of fresh flowers tucked into the rows of marble niches. From behind these flowers peered oval photographs of the dear departed, smiling as though still claiming the right to be undead. To my intense surprise I began hearing in my head passages from the Order for the Burial of the Dead from the 1662 English Prayer Book. Stuff heard and learned in childhood, of course, back in the days before well-meaning philistines had bowdlerised the Church's central texts: part of my generation's cultural heritage, a generation that was probably the last to have grown up with it and its robust cadences as part of their basic education. (I recalled Jayjay lamenting this once. 'Never mind the bloody meaning,' he had said. 'It's the *sound* that matters. If you can make something sound weighty and beautiful, it becomes so.' At that moment I'd felt close to him.) And now here I was beside his grave, hearing phrases I had scarcely thought about in thirty years as if reading them from tablets. The preening butterfly glowed and sopped up the sun. The words took on a magnificence divorced from mere meaning. It was the measured sonorousness of spells, where the careful sequence of sound and cadence conjures solemnity until the day stands still and the voice becomes small and the awesome strangeness of living and dying bulks huge in the air all around. Nothing else exists. It eclipses castles and cypresses and blue horizons. It freezes the snake of dusty road on the distant valley floor with its trembling flare of sunlight off a car's chrome or windscreen. It silences the doves in their spring rut. Gradually meaning distils back out of sounds. This meaning has no connection with modern reassurance. It brushes aside sympathy and counselling. There is no truck with the consolations of ghosts or cryogenics. The meaning is flinty, uncomfortable. The sonorities are not after all a gorgeous diversion. They are a stern seventeenth-century confrontation with the irreducible. You are scarcely more alive than him you mourn, they say. He is now permanent, you are still temporary. You are here by the skin of your teeth, by the grace of God. You have no rights, you have only your wrongs. Prepare *now* to follow, because if you can stop your silly capering for a moment you will perceive there is no alternative and certainly nothing of greater importance. (Bury your head in your hands. Feel the skull, how it yearns to emerge.)

Beware, I tell myself with a start. Don't become too carried away by all this eschatology, these solemnities. You should heed Jayjay's own warning which he once expressed in his usual forceful manner:

'Just remember, behind all dignity something ignominious is forever capering, flashing its balls.' Very well, then, I will think more
about my friend than about his being dead. I will ponder certain
aspects of his character that I still need to clarify, in particular the
two words he so often used to describe himself: impostor and lover.
In his case they are intricately connected. At one level, of course,
there was nothing of the impostor about Jayjay, who was at all times
every inch himself. He knew very well who he was. Even when
mischievously affecting a role he was still the same person using the
same old wit and charm to try on the part for size. I admit his
repeated assertion of being an impostor used to irritate me if only
(as I said earlier) because it had the same effect as the Cretan assert-
ing that all Cretans were liars. Finally, though, he was not claiming
to be an impostor in order to deceive other people. It was not to do
with deception but with *concealment*. He did it to hide himself, to
dissemble, and it had congealed into a lifetime's habit. What he had
concealed almost until the end, even from his own biographer, was
of course the true nature of his love. (Neither pathetic nor preda-
tory, he had cheerfully observed of himself not long before he died:
'Instead of being a raving sociopath I am merely a harmless pervert
with charming manners. *That's* the advantage of a decent upbringing.') Oh how I miss that sardonic accuracy!

And suddenly, standing there in the little *camposanto*, I am
struck belatedly with one of those insights whose sheer force guar-
antees their correctness. I had just been writing up the account of
Jayjay's death in Arezzo hospital and had duly noted down the last
words I ever heard him speak. In the midst of racking coughs he
had seemed to gesture weakly at his nurse with an empty beaker,
croaking 'Fill it. Oh, *fill it!*' Yet he had spoken in English, a language the bilingual Jayjay would never have used to an Italian
nurse, especially one from whom he urgently needed something.
I now had no doubt that my friend's last thought and cry had
been for Philip, for the real but imaginary lover who had looked
at a notice board one long-lost autumn day and who in some
sense had been living with him ever since.

The beloveds who elude us; the beloveds who were, and are not; the beloveds who never were. What are these else but great works of the imagination, a lifetime's solid stonework? We build them like lighthouses on our eroding headlands: solid, reassuring, futile, sending out the same message over and over in all weathers to which no answer comes or is any longer expected. Sometimes they even coexist with flesh-and-blood partners, standing behind and occasionally outshining them until the ordinarily loved are reduced to mere silhouettes. That secret love of Jayjay's which endured for almost seventy years and went unknown to all but him: what was it? A possible answer came to me one afternoon while idly watching the bees fly back from the fields of sunflowers far below. They were labouring up from a storm zone into bright sunlight. Behind them in the distance the fields they had left were being thrashed by dark-grey columns of rain under a purple sky and a dilute rainbow was struggling to emerge. It reminded me banally of how Wordsworth's heart had famously leapt up when as a child he beheld a rainbow, and he had trusted it would still leap when he was old. At once I wondered if that was not exactly what Jayjay had meant when he spoke of Philip's bolt of lightning and the 'poetry' of his enduring presence it had sparked in him. Once the rainbow had done its work Wordsworth need never have seen another. Thereafter it suffused every landscape he surveyed. Likewise, once Jayjay had bidden farewell to Philip on a ship's deck in Suez the boy might as well have died. Whatever had flashed so marvellously in him had gone on shining for Jayjay with the lingering voltage of the original *coup de foudre*.

What was this if not a case of the commonplace transfigured? We have entered the terrain of burning bushes. Those who have never known a similar angel alight and scald a lifetime's sensibility should hold their tongue. In their easy philistinism they cry, 'A *rainbow*? How limp! How conventional!' or 'A *boy*? How creepy!', seeing only the outward guise in which an arrested instant chooses to robe itself. Rainbows and boys are simply items on the endless list of agents which for somebody somewhere have been for a heart-stopping moment inhabited by a power not their own. The transcendence blazed briefly and was gone without ever leaving the mind, and thereafter everything appeared differently lit, fractionally duller of shade. And those who suffer this can do nothing but look back as Wordsworth and Jayjay did with the sad certainty that it will never again happen with such intensity. Angels come but once in a single guise. Their residues are ruin and devotion and sometimes poetry of varying merit. Nothing for it but to make do.

Maybe poets can cope with it better. Maybe they can use their skill to spread scented fragments of that original vision throughout a lifetime's work as sparingly as a cook shaves a truffle. But when it happens to the life of the affections it leaves behind the ashes of dissatisfaction. The ghost can never be completely exorcised. Surely this was why Berlioz had to track down Estelle, his *stella montis*, when she was fifty-one, and also why Jayjay put private detectives on to tracing Philip when he, too, was in his mid-fifties. It was as if by forcibly dressing their obsessions in the ageing flesh of physical reality they might finally relegate them to the past. But in Jayjay's case, at least, it didn't work. Maybe for those struck young there never can be complete recovery, and a life grows around its wound like an oak around a lightning-sear. In that sense it was not an old man they had screwed up in Jayjay's Italian coffin but an adolescent who had lately been roaming the streets of the pre-war Eltham he so vividly recalled. It must have been this that made it seem as though Jayjay, no matter his wanderings, had always been concentrated on his sixteenth year. By contrast I felt my own lifetime spread thinly and ineffectually over the entire planet.

Yet to describe him as scarred but stoical is too sentimental. Jayjay's was, after all, only one more of the countless ways of being briefly alive, and my memories are overwhelmingly of a man who turned things to advantage and contrived to live with energy and gusto. He may never have loved certain people as they would have wished, and the one person may never have returned his devotion, but these are commonplaces of human existence. Other pleasures still extend on all sides like branches heavy with summer fruit, and these Jayjay had abundantly plucked.

From time to time I still kick myself for not having guessed the true nature of the man's secret, for having been so beguiled by my own ghosts. Not failed derring-do, then, but *love*. He had as good as told me when he recounted the story of Captain W. E. Johns's 'secret love' (Jayjay's own words) for the lifelong partner to whom he was not married. At the time, of course, I was naively thinking in terms of a woman: a failed marriage about which Jayjay would tell me in due course. Yet with hindsight his inclinations had been obvious from the beginning. The only physical presences he ever described with any sort of precision or tenderness were those of boys. This was true even of the sex scenes he voyeuristically watched or took part in. Yet I had missed these things and tell myself most others would as well. Too straight? Too stupid? As Jayjay astutely knew, it was enough to scatter women with erotic promise about the narrative and no-one would look any further. I am sure he took a malicious pleasure in watching me painstakingly throwing myself off the scent time and time again. Nor can I take much reassurance from a further reflection. If it was not on account of my war experience that he had felt kinship with me, what exactly was it that made him say I was the only possible writer he could have worked with? *Frère* or *semblable*?

Well. Maybe a biographer's summing-up, no matter how inept, acts for him like some form of exorcism. I have begun to feel freer of my former subject. At least now I can return to my own life. I can go back to my Asian shore and pursue my investigations there without the sense of having left a project unfinished, of time running out. But it is a scant consolation that it took the death of my friend to make this possible. I was (and am) surprised that writing Jayjay's life, a literary chore that had started so casually in Castiglion Fiorentino's Co-op, should have turned out to be no chore at all but an experience that constantly made me stop in the middle of everyday tasks and reflect. Such moments occurred while brushing my teeth or as I watched my bees at the end of their gallant flight paths wearily batting the air currents, laden with nectar, coming home. Our true affections, inscrutably hidden away, work and work, moved by an ordering and conventions not ours, responding as though to smells and sounds and light which arrive at an oblique angle to those of common day. It is no use hoping these uncommon loves will obey proprieties, still less the law. Outside, all sorts of miserable weathers may prevail. Inside, there is the slow build-up of a kind of sweetness. This, according to Jayjay, is part of the art. It is vital to say little and to know how little there is to say. Explanations are for those who think it matters to explain things. The only recourse is to live the one life, scrupulously dissembled, to which greater freedom accrues the more constrained it becomes. I realised that failed fathers, too, may live by this maxim.

I laid a hand on his warm headstone as I stood up and the Red Admiral that was still hanging from the letters of his name clapped its wings noiselessly and was gone in a flash of crimson and velvet. An old rogue, I heard myself think affectionately before at once correcting the thought. No, old rogues are a purely literary trope: colourful sinners we indulgently forgive in order to avoid the difficult commitment of actual love. And actual love was what I felt for Jayjay.

Since that afternoon I have twice been back to the cemetery. Perhaps after all he was right about my having been overcharged for the stone, and the quality was indeed slightly shoddy. Already I think I can detect a softening of the letters, a blunting of incised edges.

The weather has changed once more, the bitter wind has dropped and a general dampness rises as from the ghost of the huge marsh that in the days of the Renaissance still extended across the plain. Seen from above the whole valley is done up in creamy billows of mist. Alas, there is no longer need for me to go down. I still miss the morning sessions at Il Ghibli although I do visit Marcella and Claudio fairly regularly. In his will Jayjay behaved impeccably, leaving the house to Marcella. She and her family are considering moving into it and letting their old farm for *agriturismo*, a nice potential source of income. La Valle may yet echo to the fractious sounds of foreigners on holiday. He also left decent sums of money in trust for Dario and his sisters. Everyone speaks of Jayjay with affection and respect, although when I concur I do so with a certain tinge of irony I have no doubt he fully intended. For what did he leave me but the remains of his old pornographic archive: two hundred and seventeen photographs ranging in subject from Nubian toddlers to the donkey trick ('Our Donkey Is Changed Every Week For Reasons Of Fatigue!') They are all of them quite unprintable. In addition there are seven brittle-looking reels of what I take to be August Moll-Ziemcke's silent films. Two of them are 16 mm and the rest seem to be 9.5 mm. God knows how one could find a projector to take that size of stock these days but I have little incentive to view them anyway. I am in the awkward position that Jayjay undoubtedly calculated to a malicious nicety: the inheritor of a trove of material which is of historical, anthropological and erotic interest whose very ownership makes me liable to criminal proceedings of the most embarrassing kind. By the time this book is published I trust I shall have found a safe home for his dubious legacy.